HIT HARD

HIT HARD

AMY J. FETZER

KENSINGTON PUBLISHING CORP.
http://www.kensingtonbooks.com

BRAVA BOOKS are published by

Kensington Publishing Corp.
850 Third Avenue
New York, NY 10022

All Kensington titles, imprints and distributed lines are available at special quantity discounts for bulk purchases for sales promotion, premiums, fund-raising, educational or institutional use.

Special book excerpts or customized printings can also be created to fit specific needs. For details, write or phone the office of the Kensington Special Sales Manager: Kensington Publishing Corp., 850 Third Avenue, New York, NY 10022. Attn. Special Sales Department. Phone: 1-800-221-2647.

ISBN 0-7582-1107-4

First Kensington Trade Paperback Printing: July 2006
10 9 8 7 6 5 4 3 2 1

Printed in the United States of America

For my Castellana nieces:

Catherine Castellana-Mentillo
Cara Castellana
Alison Castellana
Mia Grace Wilson
And the newest, Emme Sophia Henkel

Beautiful, smart, and independent, true heroines.

I love you all,
Auntie Amy

One

Kalawana, Sri Lanka
2000 hours

He looked like Genghis Khan in a Corona T-shirt and khaki shorts.

Dark hair tied back and a stringy gray Manchu beard, Tashfin Rohki was as ugly as he was lethal.

But then, you couldn't tell the black hats from the white, anyway.

The fact that Sam Wyatt held a stolen Israeli Galil and smoked a thin Cuban cigar was just for openers. In the small clearing near the river basin about twenty yards ahead of him, Riley and Max were the ones in the hot seat, working a deal to retrieve rough-cut conflict diamonds that had found their way into the hands of the Tigers.

The feline kind would have been easier to deal with, Sam thought, but the Liberation Tigers of Tamil Eelam had been waging a terrorist campaign in Sri Lanka. The bastards wanted to create a separate state.

Damn selfish of them.

And downriver, Sri Lankan Army troops waited for some payback. But not till Dragon One commandeered the stones.

From under his cowboy hat, Sam squinted through the soft curl of smoke as Riley bartered like a vender in a souk.

He had to hand it to the man, his Irish blarney was in full throttle tonight. The moonlit, prehistoric look of the jungle and a half dozen grungy men surrounded by torches were a stark contrast to Riley and Max, the well-dressed diamond smugglers.

Sam swatted at a mosquito buzzing at his head. The motion drew the attention of the men circling the group. Weapons lifted a little higher, eyes narrowed. Sam smirked and gave his back-the-fuck-off stare. Paranoid pigs. Anyone who'd kill innocent farmers to make a point that no one got wasn't worth spit to him. A bullet, sure. He had a full clip. Hot and ready.

He didn't mind being the hired muscle tonight, well aware of his short fuse, mostly galvanized by stupid people. Ground level made Sam nervous. It took away control. In a jet, a chopper, he steered, attacked. Laid down cover fire. The enemy was a blip on radar, a target to take out.

Now the targets surrounded his buddies dealing diamonds in the dark.

He listened, tried to translate, but his Hindi sucked and the distance distorted the rapid chatter. All Sam got out of the bits and pieces was that there was a better price to be had somewhere else. Someone always had deeper pockets than the last guy, and the Tigers' intentions were simple: sell the stones, get cash, buy some nasty-ass weapons, and hurt their own people.

Riley poured the stones back into the leather pouch and doubled his offer. Client wasn't going to like that. Their assignment was twofold: get back the stones before they were faceted cut and flooded the diamond market, and second, find out what those rough diamonds were going to buy and stop it. Considering the company they were keeping, weapons were a definite. The proceeds could buy anything from explosives to shoulder-mounted rocket launchers.

It'd taken weeks to track this cache of stones from the Congo. They'd changed hands so many times it was hard to keep up with this new crop of black hats. Sam's idea of shoot first, ask questions later was nixed by the team, but then, they still hadn't gotten a lead on the weapons and who had them to sell.

Insects hummed beneath the brim of his hat, annoying him. I must need a shower, he thought, sick of the jungle. All he'd done in the past weeks was inhale the little critters with every breath. He adjusted the shoulder strap of the assault rifle, less for comfort and more for checking his aim.

The conversation grew suddenly animated, and Sam could tell Riley was pissed. He and Rohki were in each other's face. Not good. Yet Sam kept a watch on the men behind their leader. Specifically, when a short fellow with an old AK-47 took a step back. His expression didn't change, that's what alerted Sam. When you went backwards, you looked where you were going. This guy didn't.

Sam eased back, then rolled around the tree to his right, intent on canvassing the area and coming up behind the guy. Something was up. He cleared his throat, the sound, he knew, vibrating in Max's earpiece. Max touched his shirt collar, indicating he'd heard. Riley caught the gesture and mimicked it.

No one paid attention to him, all focus on Riley, the rebel leader, and how much money they'd get for the rocks. Sam didn't give a crap. It wasn't his cash, but letting this whole thing go belly-up because of one chicken shit wasn't in the cards.

"Outlaw," came through his earpiece. "What the hell are you doing?" said Logan.

Sam touched the throat mike under the bandana. "Hunting."

Logan was downwind near the river with a Sri Lankan Army commander who was no more than twenty-two. The Tigers kept killing the more experienced officers, hoping to create havoc in the ranks for a coup. Bad move. Loyal and righteous, it just made them all the more determined.

Sam continued through the Sinharaja rain forest, the air

so heavy it soddened his shirt, producing rivulets of sweat down his spine. His boots sunk into the decaying underbrush, the musty odor rising up like fog. It was an island, for crissake, where was the breeze?

He paused, and through the trees and vines, barely made out the little man. He wouldn't be so interested if this wasn't the guy they'd used to set up this meeting. Where are you going, little traitor, he thought, taking several more steps, his gaze flicking to keep a bead on his buddies, then to catch movement, progression. The little guy was almost out of sight.

The diamond discussion grew heated and Sam turned sharply, taking aim. It faltered when beneath his feet, the ground vibrated, a humming that climbed through his body and shook his teeth. Earthquake? The ground wasn't rolling, but the vibration grew with intensity, like a pot about to boil over. His gaze jerked to the little guy, then back to his team. They felt it too. The runt was moving faster. Sam made a decision and followed.

He'd taken three steps when the explosion ripped through the darkness. Men shouted accusations, scattered. Muzzle flash lit up the darkness with weapons fire. Sam turned back to his teammates, offering cover fire and heading to the chopper, their only escape.

"Cutter? What the hell is going on?"

"Bug out! We gotta bug out! Holy shit. Get this thing in the air!"

Sam flung his weapon over his shoulder, batting away the underbrush as he ran full out. Fifty yards ahead, his newly souped chopper sat on a stone slab near the river like a bird perched on the edge of a cliff. "What's the deal? Turn the engine over." Logan was a field surgeon and an ex-Navy Seal. He had skills aplenty, but flying wasn't one of them.

Sam burst out into the open, and froze, his eyes going wide. A wall of water thirty feet high rolled toward him, toward the chopper. Sam bolted, trying to outdistance the rush.

The Kukule Ganga Dam. Shitty timing.

Logan was tossing in gear, and trying to raise a warning to

Riley and Max. Sam threw himself into the seat, flipped switches, and turned over the engine. The rotor blades were slow to move.

The water wasn't.

"Come on, sweetheart, wake up, wake up." He gave it some juice, risking stalling the engines. The blades gained speed. Out of the corner of his vision, the water swiped the land, taking resort homes, docks, and Jesus, people. Soldiers not caught in the dam break ran to the hills. Water rushed over the riverbanks, covering the chopper's landing gear and sliding in over Sam's boots.

"Christ, Sam, get it up!"

"She's female, she needs foreplay."

"She's gonna get us killed! Riley, Max!" Logan shouted into his mike.

Then the blades hit the sweet spot and Sam glanced to his left in time to see the brunt of the water coming right at him. He pulled the stick, lifting the chopper off the stone in a sharp vertical climb. "Maybe you should hold on."

The water rushed beneath them, splashing the windscreen, and he banked left, speeding toward Riley and Max's last location.

Sam worked on his helmet with one hand, looking at the ground. The water was moving fast, nothing to stop it.

"That was too close," Logan said, and Sam glanced down. The spot where they'd stood was engulfed in water, trees torn out of the earth and shooting like rockets downriver toward the basin.

"You see them?"

"Not yet."

Floodlights on, Sam went lower, skimming the water, reducing speed, but the wind shears in the valley rocked and bumped the chopper. But the cockpit was his comfort zone and he wore the chopper like his favorite shirt. He glanced at the small GPS screen marking Max and Riley with a yellow dot. "Should be coming up on Max any second."

"Riley, Max, come in! Answer me, Godammit!" Logan pressed the headphones tighter, then shook his head.

Then the GPS area came into view. Rapids of fast-moving water, wood, even concrete from the shattered dam.

Logan rushed to put on a harness, hook up. "Where the hell are they?"

"Got Max, nine o'clock." Sam steered toward the area.

"I see him." Logan already had the yoke snapped to the cable.

"Wait till I get over him. Can't chance debris hooking that yoke and taking us for a ride."

"Hurry, man, he's hanging onto the top of a tree and it's not going to be there much longer."

Sam couldn't look. He had to use the GPS marker as a judging point.

"Riley?"

Sam's gaze searched the green grid. "His marker's gone." Oh, man. He swooped low and daring, over the waves of water breaking down the valley like strip mining. Land broke away, trees tumbled into the current, twisting up, spinning, nearly colliding into the underbelly of the chopper. Sam jerked the stick and the chopper rose short and fast like a bucking bronco.

Logan let off a string of curses, gripped the straps, then poised at the door of the chopper, his feet braced wide. "Thirty yards, there he is. He looks okay."

Sam flipped the switch and the cable whined, lowering the yoke toward the water.

"Get lower!"

"Negative, the trees are spiking! They'll take us out." He heard the rush of the water all around him as it battered anything stationary. Keeping his attention on the terrain, Sam couldn't see anything in the dark except the glare of his searchlights.

Logan directed him. Below, Max clung to what was left of a tree, the charge of water rushing past in a hard flow of jungle debris, old farm equipment, and corpses. Sam couldn't save them all, but he wasn't letting his buddies die.

Max hooked his knee over a broken tree limb, his body twisted to reach out to the yoke. The chopper jolted and Sam cursed, the hot wind shear driving it upward. He struggled to get back in position and could hear Logan's voice inside his helmet.

"Godamn wind. Okay, okay, right there. Shit, that's it for the cable!"

Sam had to get lower. The water splashed in thick, foaming waves. One clip by debris and they were toast.

"Good, good. That's it. Come on, Sam."

"This thing isn't amphibious, dammit."

Below, Max strained to reach, but the yoke swung like a pendulum, weighted and heavy.

"Shit, missed him, too far to the right."

"I'm coming in again, get ready." Sam made another pass and dipped the chopper as low as he could, hovering. "Logan, get him the fuck up, it's coming!" He could see it, another roll of water and matchstick trees.

"We got him. Up, up! Go! Go!"

Sam hit the cable switch, then pulled the stick back, lifting the chopper out of the water's path. A huge wave crested, sped past as the cable whined at the swinging strain, rolling in and bringing Max to the edge of the chopper.

Feet braced on the door ledge, Logan grabbed what was left of Max's shirt and yanked hard, pulling him inside. "He's in, he's in."

Sam glanced back. Max's face was shredded with cuts on one side, and his finger looked dislocated. "Where's Riley?"

"Downriver," Max gasped. "We got separated at the first blast of water." The dismal look on his face said he didn't think he'd survived.

Sam was having none of that shit. He hit the thruster and the redesigned chopper shot over the water like a first-strike launch.

Logan unhooked the harness, shoved a cloth at Max, then took the night vision binoculars to search for Riley.

Sam swooped low and slow, hovering, leaning for a visual, passing the search lamp back and forth. *Looks like bubbling stew.* All they saw was what the moon reflected. He couldn't be this far out, he thought. Debris slid weightlessly, roofs, tractors, entire walls off buildings bobbed on the surface. Then he saw him. "There, two o'clock!"

Riley rolled with the flow of mud and water. His dark clothing and the mud hid him, only the flesh of his face and hands were visible and popped through the surface. Like a leaf, nothing stopped him, nothing held him above water.

Logan directed Sam into position over Riley, Max on his knees at the door of the helicopter. "He stopped!"

Sam shined the spotlight. Riley was like a rag caught on a rooftop, his body flung back, water rushing over him. *Hold on buddy, posse's coming.* Sam dipped the chopper nose down, the wind making it rock. Logan put on the helmet and clipped the harness. At a thumbs up, Sam hit the cable switch. Logan lowered it over the side.

"Christ," Max said. "He doesn't look good."

A chill tightened his skin.

"Hold it steady."

But the control stick jumped in his grip, the wind trying to push them out of the sky. Sam knew if he didn't get some altitude under them, they'd go down.

"Lower, Sam, lower."

"Christ."

Max gripped the edge, gave him a play-by-play. "He needs to get some footing to strap him in."

Jesus, they weren't going to make it, Sam thought, ears tuned to the engines, the beat of the blades like it was a part of his body. He lowered another foot, his gaze flicking to the surface he could see through the clear nose windows, the mirrors showing the flow behind them. The water just kept coming.

"Logan's down, keep it steady."

Sam's muscles strained on the stick, the chopper like a living being wanting to rest. He made it land on the water, gear up, knowing that was his only choice to get close enough.

"He's got him! They're locked. Man, he's bleeding!"

Sam's stomach clenched. He couldn't think of Riley dead. He refused to let it sink into his brain. He smacked the button and the cable rolled in. Instantly he lifted higher, fighting the hot air meeting cold water beneath the chopper in the valley. The weight of the two men made the small craft unstable. The wench groaned under the stress.

Max reached for Riley, pulling him in before Logan. The pair fell on the floor of the chopper and Sam went turbo, speeding toward land.

"Is he breathing?" Sam said.

They said nothing.

"Is he breathing!"

"I don't know!" Logan yanked off the helmet and grabbed his medical gear strapped to the hull. Max rolled Riley over and water spurted out of his mouth. But he didn't choke, didn't stir.

Sam radioed Sebastian at Dragon Six. "Coonass, all aboard. We need an ambulance. We have wounded."

Logan pressed a stethoscope to Riley's chest. "He's alive, barely." Then he put a mask over Riley's face, turned on the small oxygen tank, moving it into his lungs and brain as Max ripped open his shirt. "He's been shot—those bastards!"

Sam almost looked, yet kept his attention on getting them beyond the broken dam and to land. The force of the water from the country's major water source was still ripping trees out by the roots and tossing them like kindling.

Logan slapped a pad over the wound, and Max held the pressure while Logan fought to keep Riley alive. The chopper shot over the land like a bullet in the sky, sleek and black. She was state of the art and all new, since some piece of shit a year ago loaded his last chopper down with C-4 and blew his baby to hell. He hadn't worked the kinks out yet. Now was the time.

"Hold on, we're coming in hot and fast." Sam banked hard to the left, and quickly set the helicopter on the flight deck near Dragon Six. The giant black cargo plane was the only craft out this far.

Sebastian was waiting with a body board, and rushed forward. Behind him, an ambulance barreled down the narrow landing strip toward the jet. Sam unhooked his helmet mics and rolled from the cockpit to the rear, helping them lift Riley onto the board.

"He looks bad," Sam said.

"He's unconscious," Logan said. "Dislocated shoulder, cracked ribs, a bullet hole, but I think he's slipped into a coma."

For a second, they all went still. Logan checked his vitals as the ambulance halted just beyond the rotors. Sam worked off his helmet, spitting mad and helpless as they put Riley and Max in the ambulance and along with Logan, sped off.

The blades were still moving as he dropped onto the edge at the open door and cradled his head. My fault, he thought.

Thirteen hours later

Rohki breathed slowly, the pain jolting up his chest as he limped along the walkway outside the airport. People jolted him and he clenched his teeth and smothered the urge to retaliate. Attention was not what he wanted. He felt the strong fingers circle his arm an instant before the gun at his back. The jerk of his body drove a surge of pain up his spine again as he looked up, staring into strange black eyes surrounded by swarthy skin. Zidane. Around them, taxis took on fares, airport guards chatted instead of watching their posts, tourists loaded with baggage rushed to catch flights out of the flood-torn area. No one paid them any attention as the tall man ushered him away from the crowd.

He jerked his arm free, then regretted the move.

Zidane only gestured to the small jet on the runway, guarded, engines running. "Quickly."

Together they descended the short ramp and walked toward the plane. Heat rose in waves, blistering his scalp. As he mounted the first step, he felt underdressed for such a luxurious jet. Then he was grabbed back, a curved knife suddenly near his eye.

"The stones."

"Of course, but they aren't cut."

That didn't seem to concern Zidane and he warned, "You have already tried to sell them once."

Rohki paled. How had he known?

"There's no turning back. Betray him and I will see your eyes in a jar." He released him, pushed him up the steps.

Rohki gave up on fighting his bruised body. A short man with Slavic features stood at the top of the gangway.

"Search him, thoroughly," Zidane said.

The Slav inclined his head and he stepped inside. He wasn't underdressed. While the outside of the craft was pristine, the inside was a dark hole, with only a few seats. A heavy curtain separated the rear section. He started to sit when two more men approached him, and without speaking, yanked him off his feet and tore off his clothes. He stood naked inside the jet, humiliated by the body search. He stared straight ahead. After what he went through last night, this was inconsequential.

One man wore an amused smile as he grabbed his dick, lifted, and cut the leather sack laced under his balls, nicking him.

"So that's your preference, eh?"

The man sneered, spilled the contents into his palm, rolling the large stones. The other threw his clothes at him. Rohki dressed as the man spoke to Zidane in an unfamiliar dialect. Congolese?

Zidane's dark gaze flicked up, pinning him. They couldn't know one was missing, Rohki thought, staring back. He held his hand out for the sack and stones. The guard eyed him, refilled the pouch and returned it. Rohki tucked them into his pocket, wondering when he could conceal them again before the final stop, and if the buyer was powerful enough to skirt customs there too.

The doors closed, the engines whined louder as he lowered gingerly into a seat and exhaled. The aircraft moved, shaking everything inside. He glanced around, pausing on the shifting curtain. Shock jumped through him when he saw shackles and chains anchored to the wall.

They were occupied.

Sam stood outside the ICU unit in Colombo, staring through the glass.

Logan had set Riley's shoulder, removed the bullet, and stabilized him as best he could. Then Sebastian ordered Riley on the jet along with several locals who needed intensive care in Colombo. The team's cargo plane, Dragon Six, lifted off as a hospital jet. Surgery had taken hours and Logan assisted the government surgeons. Riley hadn't regained consciousness.

A coma. Logan tried to convince Sam it was the body's way of healing itself, but seeing him hooked up to tubes, with a machine pushing air into his weak, perforated lung, it looked doubtful.

Sam wanted him to just wake the hell up.

The vigil felt weakened without the missing members. Dragon One's leader, Killian Moore, was off on his honeymoon and, typical of his former CIA wife, they hadn't told anyone where they were. Sam didn't blame them, if this was the news waiting for them.

He didn't see Max nudge Sebastian, then motion to him. The men stepped out and closed the door. Sam continued to stare through the glass.

"He survived Belfast, he'll be fine."

"Sure, he's just itchin' to rip off those wires and go dancing."

Sebastian Fontenot was silent for a moment. "It's not your fault."

Sam tensed, as Sebastian voiced his feelings. "I went after the runt, if I'd stuck closer—"

"The dam would have broken anyway."

"I was his backup. I left it unguarded."

"He didn't get shot in the back, either. That hit was at point-blank range. Intentional. And if the dam hadn't caved, you and Max were next."

Sam's lips tightened and he fingered his hat, then suddenly turned away.

"Where are you going?"

Sam didn't break stride. "To find a bar, or the bastard that shot him. Whichever comes first."

"He's miles away or probably dead."

"He better hope so."

Sebastian muttered a curse. "Wait, take this."

Sam stopped, half-turned, eyeing Sebastian's approach. He held out a palm sized, grayish-white rock. "Riley's fingers were locked around this so tightly it cut into his hand."

Sam plucked it, holding it up. Prisms of light shot through it. A conflict diamond. Uncut, bloodstained.

And from the look of it, the biggest puppy the market had seen in a while.

Two

Archaeological Restoration Dig
Udon Thani Caves
Northern Thailand

"Xaviera, I found something."

Viva flinched, smacking her head on the tunnel ceiling. If she didn't recognize the voice, she'd have known who it was instantly. No one ever called her that anymore. Viva backed out of the narrow tunnel, giving the dig workers and Dr. Nagada an embarrassing view of her butt in shorts. Clearing the tunnel, she rolled to her rear, pulled her scarf off, then blotted her face.

"More pottery?" That's all there was here. Aside from heat. Spending long, humid days brushing at powdery bits of dirt to reveal a single shard was, well, a real snoozer. Probably why she never did it for very long. Face it, you never do *anything* for very long.

"Would I truly bore you with something so uneventful as that?"

"Yes. You would. Remember the dig outside Giza? The third one," she said before he could ask. "I trekked through the Sahara to see some pieces of a sarcophagus."

He looked adorably affronted for a wizened old man. "For a queen to Ramses I."

"Whoop-dee-do. He had hundreds, and just as many kids.

Which is so the way to go if you're a pharaoh, but if you'd found the rest of her, that would be something to crow about." She stood and didn't bother to untie the rice sacks strapped to her knees.

"You were more fit and eager for the discovery then."

"Yes, well, so were you." She tugged a lock of his long white hair. He had a dashing look about him: white hair, dark brows, rugged features, and she adored Salih. He let her join his digs whenever she had the urge. "So what's this find?"

"Come see."

"The suspense is killing me." Probably a *whole* pot this time.

He handed her a bottle of cold water. She cracked it open, drank and when they stepped out into the sun, she poured half over her head, shook like a dog, then wiped her face. Then she dumped a bit down the front of her shirt.

He stared at her, neither frowning nor smiling. "You are such an odd woman."

She fanned the material. "I don't see you in the tunnels baking like pita bread."

His face, weathered from years in the desert sun, wrinkled like a dried apple as he grinned. "I promise, this you will like." They walked.

"You're so sure?"

"It's jewelry."

"Will it go with my shorts?"

He laughed, guiding her to the second cave. A portion was a dwelling where they'd found more than pottery—a rudimentary hearth, sleeping quarters, and even a drainage system. Got to love those ancient Thai, she thought. They were quick on the draw. Imagine, plumbing in the BC days. They didn't even have plumbing on the dig. That was just wrong.

She ducked under the canvas tarp and into the cave. Low rock ceilings tickled her hair, the corridor lit with electric lamps, yards of cables leading to the generator outside. She wished they had enough juice for air-conditioning. Wasn't in the budget.

She almost ran into Dr. Nagada as he squatted, pointing to the corner of two blocks. "See? And it appears to be gold."

Viva knelt, pulling her brush from her back pocket and swiping lightly.

"Your technique has improved."

"I'm trying the Van Gogh style of brushwork. Oh, wow, this is incredible. Get that side, it's sandwiched between something else." She glanced up to make certain she wasn't going to pull the whole dig down on top of them. Which would be so *her*.

She brushed and worked the rocks loose, and was suddenly touched that he'd let her do this. With Salih's direction, she gently pulled the item out, then handed it to him. He brushed it, blew off the dust, and she stood, then moved with him to the lights.

"It's a bracelet, a cuff. Excellent condition, must be gold." The two inch wide band was hammered and etched with markings almost too worn to see. "It's particularly small. A child's perhaps."

"In here?" Viva said. "This was just the average Joe's cave dwelling, and we haven't found anything like that before."

"And we are not done, either."

The man had the patience of a saint. No, two saints. After years of excavating around Egypt and Israel, and digging up all there was, he'd offered his services elsewhere. Cambodia, Laos, Thailand, and once on the island of Timor. If it was lost, he'd find it. Even if it took years. Viva admired that kind of diligence. She could barely find her panties before breakfast.

Salih walked toward the entrance and Viva dogged his heels. At a worktable shielded with a shade tarp, he brushed the cuff some more, then dipped it in a solution, rinsed and dried it.

He met her gaze. "It has stones." He held it out.

She took it, tipping it to the sun. The gleam of old gold blinked greenish in the morning light. "Small ones, but look at the faceting. And two cabochon cuts. Rubies, you think?" Thailand was famous for blood rubies and sapphires. "And if these are sapphires, they're good ones." So blue they were nearly black.

"Even more rare."

"But how could they have cut these? They didn't have the equipment, not to facet, create a bevel like this. Amazing." She stared at it for another moment, then handed it back. "So what are the markings?"

"That, my dear Xaviera—" She loved the way his Egyptian accent made her name sound. "—is the real question. I think they are Thai royalty."

"No kidding." She glanced back at the cave, and noticed a couple of dig workers listening to the conversation. "Hiding during an uprising or something?"

"We are near the Laos–Cambodian border and there are four temples in a straight line right to this area."

"A summer home, how lovely for them."

"I was thinking a pilgrimage. These markings are Thai, but the design is Cambodian. Though I am not well versed in its ancient text." He frowned at the piece a moment longer, then drew a small box onto the table, filled it with shredded material, and set the bracelet inside. "I want you to take this to Dr. Wan Gai in Bangkok."

Her brows tightened. "Okay, I give up, why me?"

"You've had that look lately."

She made a sour face. "Darn, I thought I was hiding it so well this time."

"You have been on five digs with me since you were in college. It is not hard to recognize. You stop chattering constantly."

"You say that like it's a bad thing."

Smiling, he pressed the box into her hands. "Take it to him, see the city while he makes his findings. Then perhaps you will come back and enjoy yourself."

She doubted it. Viva knew herself well, and her biggest flaw, her indecision, her complete and utter incapability to stick with one thing for longer than a year—no, wait, six months—was embarrassing. At her age, she should have a real paying career in *something*.

She looked at the small wood box, then up at Dr. Nagada, and thought, *Oh, goody,* Bangkok. Great hotels, a decent shower, food, and some real girl clothes were just too wonderful to turn down. She leaned over and kissed his cheek. "I'll make you some babaganoush when I get back."

He grinned. "I am already missing you. In the morning?"

"It will take me that long to scrape off the dust. Get all dolled up." She turned away, still talking. "And look fashionably cute for the train ride."

He frowned. "A *plane* ride, Xaviera."

"Is boring. On, up, down, off. What fun is that? At least with the train I get to commune with the locals, see more of this country." She walked backwards, smiling.

"And the dangers."

"Well, you know what they say?"

"No, what?"

"You're the expert on old stuff, figure it out."

"Tree!" he shouted and she turned, smacking into it.

"I meant to do that." Rubbing her forehead, she kept going to her tent, and Salih thought, she'd be lucky to survive the trek.

Twelve hours later
West of Chao Phraya River
Thailand

Sam parked his ass on a mossy rock at the river's edge, pulled off his hat, then scooped up some water. He poured it over his head, but wasn't dumb enough to drink the bacteria-infested stuff. To make the point, a lizard slid into the stream a couple feet away. Instead, he pulled the tube from his *Camelbak* water supply and drank fresh. Texas heat had nothing on Thailand, he thought. On so many levels. The air hung, and in the darkened jungle it dripped with humidity. Damn beautiful, though. Kingfisher birds darted overhead, as if warning him of their presence, then dove into the water for food. Hornbills, the bullies of the bird pack with thick, colorful faces and long, hawkish bills strong enough to chop a finger clean off, weighted branches overhead. And then there were the monkeys. Food for the local hill tribes and an annoyance. They threw stuff, mostly their own shit.

Sam fell back, then noticed banana trees a couple yards away, bright yellow fruit in the blanket of green. He shouldered off his pack and stared up at the trees, contemplating how to get up there. The locals could do it in a heartbeat, kids shimming up the trees and cutting down bundles. He stood, took several steps back, then pulled the whip from his belt, and unrolled it.

He raised and snapped it, the crack soft in the dense forest. The rawhide whip caught the bundle, ruined a few, but had a good hold. He yanked. It tore free and dropped to the ground.

"Like roping a calf," he muttered, crossing to the cluster and ripping off a banana.

He peeled and ate, then checked his GPS. A couple more miles to the meet, he figured, then glanced the way he'd come, pulling the shotgun over his shoulder to aim with one hand. "Come on, Max, show yourself."

"Don't shoot, my mom will be pissed at you." Max Renfield strolled into the open, splashed through the stream. A slung Uzi bounced against his side, and he stopped a few feet from him.

"Go away."

"You like pissing off all of us at once?"

"I don't need backup."

"Yeah, sure, and if I was someone else?"

"You'd have a hole in your head. I could hear you a mile back. You tromp like my dad's prize bull."

Max shrugged, not the least bit ashamed that he lacked the quintessential silent-and-deadly skills. "I'm not Recon, just the go-to guy."

"Then go-to somewhere else."

Max's lips tightened. "You need me, two heads are better."

"Like we have a clue where the bastard is, or the diamonds?" Sam offered a banana.

"He's here, we know that much." Max squatted, removed his pack, and fished in his gear. "And the next buyer." Max pulled out a small packet, tore it open, and squeezed peanut butter onto the banana.

Sam shook his head, amused. All former military, Dragon One was a retrieval team for hire, and Max was logistics and supply. A damn good mechanic, he could find food and equipment where no one else would look, and amazingly, knew where he was without a compass. A GPS had nothing on him.

Max shoved a wad of banana and peanut butter in his mouth and Sam thought, the guy's a bottomless pit, never without some chow.

"You were right. Happy?"

Sam sat, his back against a tree. "That I missed the jet? No. Rohki'd be dead if I'd found him." He was the only one close enough to have shot Riley at that range.

Yet word was out that the diamonds were for sale and the Sri Lankan government's threat—that anyone dealing with the Tigers or anyone else for the stones would end up in a cell in Welikada Prison—wasn't much of a deterrent. Just the image of that hellhole should be, but there was enough intel traffic in the Congo, Sierra Leone, and Angola to know that more than one terrorist group has stones mined on the backs of babies.

Evidently, someone had found a large geode and was hot to sell.

Sam would get the stones back and find their intended purpose. He had a sneaking suspicion it was Turkish missiles, made in the USA. Buying the stones off the market was still an option. Well, they hadn't planned to actually *buy* them in the first place. Confiscate was a better word. If all else failed, then they'd fork over the cash. Riley had developed a plan to intercept the cash too. It made no sense to take the stones off the black market and give the assholes the money they needed to buy weapons.

But the dam break destroyed that and everything else in its path. Which meant they had to start from scratch.

"If Rohki had washed up in the debris from the flood, this still wouldn't be over. Pisses me off they got in the air so fast." He arrived in time to see the small jet cross the sky.

"We had other priorities."

They were both quiet for a moment, Sam thinking of Riley hooked up to tubes, and a machine helping him stay alive.

Max broke the silence. "Someone paid to get the jet off the ground ASAP. No customs search, and no manifest. Who's got that kind of pull? Never mind, forget I said that," he added at Sam's sarcastic look.

"Aside from the fact that the stones are worth millions, and those were just the ones we tracked, Al Qaeda has cells all over the place." Add the Thai mafia, the Chinese–Thai Chiu Chow mafia, gunrunners, drug cartels, prostitution, and human trafficking. "There's plenty to choose from around here."

"We go nosing in their business, it's going to get really hairy."

Sam waved that off. "We find Rohki, we find the stones and the weapons," he said, climbing to his feet.

"You plan on beating it out of him?"

"For starters." He wanted Rohki to pay—so bad he could taste it.

Max stuffed the leftover bananas in his pack and stood. "Your confidence overwhelms me."

"Nowhere to go but up."

And the climb would be tough. This meeting was the easy way to Rohki. And risky. Jumping in bed with the Thai mafia gangs would get him inside fast. Finding the jet, the manifest, anything on the dealers from the locals was . . . hell, it'd be easier to open a can with a fork. Behind him, Max adjusted his pack and knew Sam was taking this far too personal. A damn good reason to be close. Sam had a tendency to seek the quickest and most deadly route into a situation. "Lead the way, I got your back."

Sam stopped, let out a sigh, and after a moment said, "Thanks, Max. For showing up."

Max smiled widely. "Man, bet that had to hurt."

Sam's eyes narrowed.

"You're welcome. One of us has to be smart. And for a flyboy, you weren't easy to trace."

"Yeah, but *you* were." Sam walked, hacking through the jungle. "Let's find this snitch."

Max withdrew his machete, spied a palm, then cut a thick frond. He drank the sweet liquid from the stalk as they walked.

"Quit eating the damn flora," Sam said. "You're leaving a trail."

The southbound train from Udon Thani wasn't the fastest way to the next stop in Ayutthaya, but it was certainly colorful. Viva cradled the box, watching the scenery roll by. The river paralleled the trains, another line, a bit more modern on the opposite side. They ran so often it was more productive to have both in each direction. Her side was more scenic, like a throwback in time. Rural, vast stretches of jungle between cities so modern, they put the US to shame. Yet here, clusters of villages lined the river and jungle, wood homes on stilts half on the water. Children played despite the threat of crocs, snakes, and the really gross water monitor lizards.

At the dig, she'd had one crawl into her bed during the night and settle warmly against her back, till she rolled over and squashed it. She cringed at the memory, and braced her feet on the empty seat across from hers. To say the express train was the no-frills version was an understatement. Another train with all the comforts ran later, and as much as she'd have enjoyed air-conditioning, this felt adventurous. Warm wind poured through the open windows, blending with the odor of sweaty flesh, fruit, and the rapid sound of Thai chatter. It wasn't that bad, she told herself, considering she had no choice for another few hours. She leaned to the window, letting the breeze cool her and saw monkeys swing through trees, then skip deeper into the jungle.

Bet he has a good career in nut gathering, she thought, leaning back in the seat. She wiggled into the lumpy cushion, and had just closed her eyes for a nap when the train suddenly lurched, then slowed rapidly. Viva stood, leaned out the window with the rest of the passengers.

"Bie nie hkrap?" she asked. What's happening?

"Jao Pho!"

Good God. Bandits. Or more literally, a mafia gang. She glanced at the box left on the seat, then grabbed it. She couldn't let them take it. It was a piece of Thai history. Wearing the cuff was out of the question. They'd strip it off her. Her own valuables were in her waist belt, making a sweaty trail down the crack of her butt, but she couldn't let them find the cuff.

Quickly, she pulled her duffel from under the seat, stuffed the box behind it, then put it back. She glanced to the right, and a man just shook his head, and smiled piteously.

"Never walk with your gold," he said in Thai.

Her smile was tight. Wasn't my gold, she thought, it's your country's.

She waited for the inevitable. For the men to empty the train and search. She could see people standing on the knoll, huddled in the sun as men with big guns yanked off jewelry, emptied wallets, purses, and grass-made sacks, then threw them back at the victims. Salih was right, the plane was safer.

Well, you wanted adventure.

She had a few bhat in her pockets, nothing more than she needed for the train tickets and some food. It wasn't long before they reached her car. She filed out; none of the passengers spoke. When she stepped out into the blazing sun, the first two cars of passengers were already collecting up their belongings and boarding.

Maybe this will be quick and painless.

A man with half an ear walked a line, stealing, shoving, threatening when people hesitated. She kept her eyes forward as he passed closer. Then Viva noticed his men go inside the train. Baggage and items flew out the windows. A crate with chickens broke and the birds scattered. An old woman in colorful hill-tribe clothing tried to catch them, but the leader pushed her down, then kicked one chicken into the air. Before it landed, he shot it.

Blood and guts rained down on top of them. Viva flicked at something on her bare arm, trying not to look. Gross. One of the men called out to Half Ear, and he crossed the clearing. Viva's heart clenched when she saw the lesser man hand over her little box.

"No! That's mine." She darted forward, shaking off the old man trying to grab her back. Half Ear tossed it like a ball.

"Yours?" he said, offering it.

She ran, grabbed it, held it to her chest. "Please don't take this. Take anything else you want." She pointed to her small suitcase.

He put a hand on his hip and regarded her, then muttered something. His man moved quickly and reached to take it. Viva batted his hand away and looked at the leader.

"You gave it back. You can't take it again. Law of the jungle." She knew that made no more sense to him than it did to her, but she only had so much to work with here.

His henchman made to backhand her. She ducked. His expression contorted with anger and he lunged, grabbed the box, but she rolled to the side and sent her elbow into his stomach, then her fist smacking into his groin. He howled and stumbled back, grabbing himself, cursing.

"I told you *no*."

Half Ear walked near, glancing once at his man still hunched over, then to her. "You cannot fight us all, woman."

"Clearly. But this I have to keep, it's not mine."

"No, it is mine." He reached and she swatted at him. He holstered his weapon, then grabbed her by the arms. Viva head-butted him, and as she reeled at the impact, he wrestled the box from her. It took her a second to realize she didn't have it and charged him, jumping on his back. She knew this was stupid, really stupid.

"*Farang ba!*" Stupid foreigner.

Oh, yeah, like that hurts. She held tight to his hair, but it was greasy and her fingers slid. So she grabbed his face and half-eaten ear. People watched, even his men, no one came near them as he tried to dislodge her. Then he dropped to the ground, rolled till he was squashing her into the dirt. She screamed, kicking wildly.

He wasn't much bigger than her. Strength was another matter, but that he was laughing at her made her furious. She fought the only way she could, like a woman, clawing his cheek, biting. But when he got to his knees and flipped her over on her back, Viva suddenly realized she might not get out of this alive.

Then he straddled her hips, and reached for her waistband.

The little Thai man stood between Max and Sam. Sam was doing the talking and Max could almost count the moments before his patience snapped. They'd been at this for a half hour and Phan wasn't saying enough. Not wise.

Sam latched on to his shirtfront, hauling him close. Phan's eyes went round. "Tell me," Sam said in deadly voice.

"Many hiding. Lots of talk-talk."

Max wasn't fooled, and neither was Sam. The little shit could con an old woman out of her teeth and he wondered where the source came from. Sam hadn't said.

Phan, if that was even his real name, had few teeth and those that remained were black and decayed. Bet dining with that mouth is an adventure, Max thought. Small and tightly built, Phan was barefoot, yet wore clean dark clothes and an expensive diamond pinky ring. Thief, con, a vagrant. All they wanted was information.

"What talk?" Sam pressed.

"Phan do not know. Hear things. Many people want to buy, only few get to—" he stalled, frowning, searching for the words—"be speaking to."

Sam frowned. "Get asked?"

Phan just stared with the same blank look he'd been giving him for the last half hour. No wonder the enemy used this guy. He gave nothing away.

In the distance, the train moved over the tracks. Phan

glanced in the direction and Sam tightened his grip, bringing his attention back. Then he lifted him off the ground. "Where is Rohki?"

"No Rohki. Phan swear, *swear.*"

"Listen up, pal, I came all the way out here for information. My source says you're the man. You tell me where he is, or I swear to God, I'll carve you a new mouth."

"No Rohki. I not see buy-man here."

No buyer. Disgusted, Sam released him. Phan landed in the dirt, whined a bit, then climbed to his feet. He stepped back into Max.

"I got no problem with giving you to him," Max said. "You can see he's pissed, and right now, I'd cooperate."

Phan remained silent.

"Oh shit, he's going to string you up by your thumbs."

Phan twisted, staring up with wide eyes. Max nodded ahead. Sam pulled out his whip, and let it slither on the ground like a snake. "Now that's gonna leave a mark."

Without much effort, Sam cracked the whip and took off a branch above their heads. Max admired his precision and over Phan's head, grinned at his teammate.

"No buy men, only chop man near! Chop man!" Phan blurted, nodding violently.

Chop man? That could mean a number of things, and he was tired of Phan playing illiterate when he knew from his source he wasn't.

Sam rolled in his whip, meeting Max's gaze. They heard the squeal of the train wheels grinding to a stop, then shouting. Max frowned, eyeing Sam. There wasn't a train stop near here.

Max leaned down, his mouth near Phan's ear. "What do you mean by chop? Hack, dice, slice, cut?"

At the last word, Phan tensed.

"Cut man," Max said, looking up. A diamond cutter.

"Who hired him?" Find the cutter and they'd find the stones and the source.

Before Sam could interrogate Phan further, a scream, very female and long, cut through the jungle like a machete.

Phan dropped to the ground, rolled, but as Max reached for him, like an acrobat, the small man dove into the jungle. Max instantly followed, the vegetation closing in around him. Sam was about to go after Max when he appeared, sweaty and winded—and empty-handed.

"No trail, not even a bent branch or a damn footprint." Max looked back the way he'd come, confused. "It's like someone plucked him out of the forest."

"I have another way to find him. Kashir!" Sam called out. "Show yourself."

From the branches off to the right, a man swung down, dropped to the clearing. Sam introduced Kashir Fokhouri.

"Interpol?" Max said, staring at the narrow man who needed a bath.

"Alexa's contacts," Sam said. He was undercover to stop gunrunners, but from what Sam had seen, he didn't excel at his job.

"How is the beautiful Miss Gaylin?"

"Married."

Another scream split down Sam's spine.

"We can't ignore that." Max turned in the direction.

"I would advise against interfering. Local Jao Pho stop the express train all the time." Kashir withdrew a thin knife and cleaned his fingernails. "They are just stealing."

"Sounds like more than that."

Sam was heading in the direction Phan disappeared when the shouts came again. He stopped, let his head loll forward, then met Max's gaze. "I know I'm going to regret this."

"It sounds bad." Max started toward the noise.

Sam pointed to Kashir. "You stay put."

Kashir shrugged. "I have nowhere to be, cowboy."

Sam and Max grabbed up packs and jogged toward the train. The noise grew louder and when they reached the edge of the forest, they hung back enough to get a good view of the express train and the group of armed men robbing the passengers.

His gaze locked on the woman. "She's nuts," Sam said.

"She's an American."

And a redhead. "Figures."

"A plan?"

"Nope. You?"

A man had her down on the ground, straddling her hips. He ripped a small box from her hand, tossed it aside, then delivered a grin laced with retribution as he copped a feel of everything she owned, diving his hand between her legs.

"Be ready to shoot something," Sam said, then stepped out into the clearing. "We got a problem here, fellas?" he said, aiming his rifle.

Guns aimed, the bandits, who were watching the show, took a couple steps toward him.

Sam leveled his shotgun. "At this range I can get half of you in the face."

The man on top of the woman looked up. At that instant, she kicked her leg high, hitting him in the back. Her attacker lurched forward and she grabbed his nuts, squeezed and rolled him off. She was agile, in a low squat, little fists primed to hit.

"Not nice, is it?" she said, straightened. "My body, my temple, touch me again and I'll—I'll—"

"What, lady? What the hell do you think you can do?"

Viva flicked her gaze to the man, and her first thought was *great white hunter*. A jungle guide. He seemed completely at ease, his relaxed curiosity utterly annoying. "I'm thinking of something."

"Give him what he wants."

"No. It's not his to take."

"Twenty guns say it is."

"You're condoning this?"

"Check the odds." The weapons were trained more on her than him. How could they be scared of *her*?

"He can take any *tangible* possessions he wants," she enunciated, taking her body off the list. "But not that box."

The man with half an ear reached for the box. Sam snapped the whip, hooking it and dragging it toward him. When weapons cocked, he sent the group a thin look, then bent to pick it up. "What is it?"

"An ancient bracelet. It has royal Thai markings on it."

"Is it worth your life?"

She looked at him, into dark eyes so penetrating, she lost her thoughts. "It—it's an artifact, history . . . *priceless,*" she said when he just stared. Didn't he get it? This was like the Holy Grail of Thailand.

Sam broke open the box, pulled out the bracelet and showed the leader. Half Ear laughed with his men.

"She's stupid to fight you over it."

"Please try not to insult me. We've just met."

Sam glanced. Jesus. She understood his crappy Thai. Sam held it out.

"Don't give it to him!" Viva tried to grab it.

Sam held it out of her reach, then caught her arm and in a soft voice said, "Shut that mouth and we might get out of here alive."

"Just so you know, you won't be stealing it either."

"Just so *you* know he wants to kill you to save face."

She looked at Half Ear. "He wants to do something to me, but I don't think it's kill." Half Ear was working his hand over his testicles, and she hoped they stung.

"It's your culture, a royal artifact," she said to him in Thai, then switched to English. "I apologize for grabbing you, but you gave me no other choice."

Out of the corner of her vision, Viva saw the passengers herded onto the train. "Give me the cuff," she said, out of the side of her mouth.

"Shut—*up*."

In the rear of the group, Sam noticed Kashir move up behind the armed men. Damn the man, he was supposed to stay hidden. Then Kashir inclined his head ever so slightly to the leader.

"Maybe we can help each other out? I want in on the deal." Buying in was the fastest way to find the weapons.

Half Ear's eyes flared. He looked between Sam and the woman. "Give me the woman first."

"Tempting." Behind him, she inhaled sharply. "She'll eat you alive, man. And you don't want the US government down on your ass."

Half Ear considered that for a moment.

The train started moving. Viva grabbed the cuff from the American and ran. Behind her, Half Ear sighed tiredly and gestured. A bandit took off after her, and Sam winced when he tackled her to the ground. She didn't go down easily.

Sam pushed his hat back and rubbed his forehead. Didn't she realize they'd kill her just for resisting?

"I'll pay." Sam pressed as the flunky brought her back. No one noticed that she still had the bracelet.

"Show me."

Sam withdrew the rough diamond from his pocket and held it up.

"Wow, is that real?" Viva asked, wrestling the gofer's hands off her.

Half Ear scoffed, turned away, reaching for the woman. Sam pointed his rifle. The man backed off and Sam yanked the woman behind him. "More? How much?"

Half Ear eyeballed him for a moment, then relaxed his posture. "It will cost you more than that—"

He stopped in midsentence, his expression confused, his hand raising sluggishly as if to swat a fly.

Then Sam saw the small dart protruding from the man's throat.

Half Ear was dead before he hit the ground.

Three

Viva inched closer to the American, staring down at Half Ear. "Is he dead? He really *really* looks dead," she said, horrified and curious.

Sam pushed her behind him and cocked his rifle with one hand. "Now would be a good time to run, lady."

He fired a warning shot into the air, and she bolted into the jungle. At least she had the cuff, and put it on before jumping over a low stream and splashing up the other side.

Then she heard the heavy thump of footsteps, the thrashing. Oh God. Bad guys. *Bad guys*. She pushed faster. Her legs burned with the strain, her body weeping sweat. Anything in her path sliced at her legs, her arms, then through the trees, she saw the rise in terrain, and headed toward it.

She hadn't taken ten steps when it hit her, the hard impact to the back of her legs. Strong arms clamped around her knees and she went down. Her chin hit the ground, her teeth clicking. The collision pushed air from her lungs and she collapsed, dizzy, gasping for air and wondering how this day had turned so bad so fast. She inhaled dirt, blew it out, then pushed up.

She twisted. Jungle guy. He was breathing hard and had lost his hat somewhere.

"You make it really hard to help you, lady." He backed off her.

"Thank you for your assistance, but did I ask for you to butt in?" God, the sheer idiocy of that hit her and she faced him, her head ringing too much to stand yet.

"You can go back. I'm sure they'll be interested in a little payback."

"I won't dignify that with a response." She sent him a brittle smile as she brushed off leaves. "I'm quite done with adventure for the day, thank you very much."

Sam sighed back on his haunches, then pulled the bandana from his throat and wiped his face. Shapely, red haired, and a nutcase, he decided. Anyone who'd take on the Thai mafia without a weapon was two jacks short of a full deck.

Then she eased back like a crab.

Aware of her intentions, Sam grabbed her ankle, yanking her close. "They're still out there, along with tigers, snakes—" *And whoever shot that dart.*

"And you."

"I'm not going to hurt you, for crissake." Sam let her go and stood, dusting off his clothes.

"I appreciate your interception, really, but I have to go to Bangkok."

He gave her a tight glance that said, *We'll just see about that.*

She saw right through it. "Who made you king of the jungle? While you look real cool with that rifle and whip, I'm sure you can see the wisdom in a hasty departure. And I'm not about to join your little band." She motioned behind him as another man walked up. Jungle guy didn't take his gaze from her as the other handed over the hat.

"Ma'am, I'm Max Renfield." Max held out his hand to help her up.

She didn't budge, and glanced between the two. "Where were you when all that was going on?"

He patted the gun at his side. "Backup."

"Effective, was it?" Viva brushed her hair back, took a deep cleansing breath, but the tension refused to leave her body. All my fault, she thought, and wondered where her sanity went to play this morning to antagonize all the wrong people. She fingered the gold cuff that hadn't been worn in a few thousand years, and knew it was worth it. She wore history on her wrist, though she hadn't planned to be a part of it today.

"I'm going to look for Phan," Sam said to Max. "Stay with her."

"I don't need a guard."

"No, you need a brain."

Her smile was nothing short of acidic. "Chivalry isn't your strong suit, I see. If it were, you'd at least be seeing to the wounds you made." She modeled her bloody knees.

They were a mess, but considering the bandits wanted to put two bullets in her head, she shouldn't be complaining. "Sorry, lady, no medical supplies."

"I have something to fix that," Max said.

"Figures."

As Sam walked away, Max moved forward, and knelt. "Don't mind him, he's in a rotten mood."

"I couldn't tell, his effervescent personality just blew me away." Max ripped open a packet and started to clean her knees. "Oh, it's not that bad," she said, taking the antiseptic towel.

He frowned.

"Well—" She flushed. "He knocked me down when a 'hey you, wait' would have done the trick. That man is *extreme* in every sense of the word."

Max sat back, grinning. She had Sam pegged from the get-go. Interesting. She finished cleaning her knees, pulling her leg up to her face like a dancer to blow off the sting. Great legs.

"Thank you, Max."

He frowned, glanced the way the other had gone. "Come on."

"Shouldn't we wait for him?" She really didn't want to trek through the jungle. The dart had to come from somewhere.

"He's been gone too long."

"Well, that can't be good."

He helped her off the ground and she followed him as they moved into the forest. Max hacked their way through the jungle for a considerable distance when he stopped, and called out softly.

Viva peered around him and she saw his partner.

He waved Max on. "You stay there," he said, pointing.

"Anyone ever mention you have control issues?"

His look was deadpan, and when Max approached, he dismissed her.

Max bent to look at something on the ground. "Good God."

Curious, Viva moved forward a few steps.

"I said stay back." Sam tried to stop her.

"You really need to work on your attitude, mister. And you can ask my father, I rarely do anything I'm told." She moved around Max and Sam threw his hands up in resignation. "Besides, I've seen a lot of interesting things in my life—" She stopped short. "Oh God."

The body of a small man lay in the underbrush, not hidden, but not in clear view. Yet it was the condition of it that stunned her. All Viva saw was blood; on his throat and his crotch, his knees, and feet.

"I take it back." She turned away, into Sam's chest and gripped his shirt.

Sam blinked, then closed his arms around her. Her trembling vibrated into him, clinging down to his bones. He murmured something useless, hoping to soothe and praying she didn't cry. Women and crying wasn't something he handled well.

"I'll just be a minute," she mumbled into his chest, and Sam thought, *take your time, honey*, enjoying all the soft curves pressed into him. Man, it's been a while.

Viva breathed deeply, the image of the mutilated body flashing in her mind as if once wasn't good enough. Then she felt his arms tighten, his hand cup the back of her head and massage it a little. She suddenly breathed *him* in, a stranger, dangerous enough that none of this seemed to affect him at all. Another stupid move, she thought.

"Are you okay?" he asked in the deepest voice on the planet.

She tipped her head back and met his dark gaze. "You were right. I should have stayed put."

His gaze roamed her face as if trying to scrape away the layers and see deeper. She felt suddenly hemmed in, as if a drape descended over them, closing out the jungle, the danger. It made her nerves keen, sentient, her body shift into his as if that's where she belonged. He didn't back off, frowning down at her, and she had the urge to rub the lines between his eyebrows.

"Will you obey my orders till we get to the city?"

"Sure." She pushed out of his arms. "Though I'd have to trust you for that, which I don't."

Max observed the exchange, then said, "Think Kashir did it?"

Sam lifted his gaze from her. "Don't know." He squatted, inspected the corpse. "The back of his knees are cut, and his toes are gone."

"That's just nasty." She looked everywhere except there. "Who would do something like that?"

Sam met her gaze. "A collector." And it was ritualistic, he thought.

"Half Ear, no toes. Bodies dropping—" Viva's hands never found a comfortable place to be and she turned away. "I can't be here with you two. I just can't."

Sam latched on to her arm. "But you can't be out there alone, either. I won't be responsible for your safety."

That got her. "Who says I want you to?" She yanked free, her hands on her hips. "You know, I've traveled all over the world and didn't have a bit of trouble till I met you." Well, never the dead kind of trouble, she corrected.

"Me either. So what is so special about this?" He grabbed her wrist, studied the cuff for a second before he let her go.

"This was found in the Udon Thani Caves, where it shouldn't be. Since cave homes and temples form a line over the border, it's entirely possible the royal family could have originally come from Cambodia or Laos."

"That'll ruffle a few feathers," Max said.

She nodded. "Makes the bloodline suspect, and the royal family here rules. What would happen to this society if it were known? What will it change? This is a very important piece."

"Then perhaps you shouldn't be flashing it around."

"I wasn't. I hid it, they found it. Can I help it if they're nosey? Oh, man."

"What now?"

"My bag. It's back there."

"Next to the other body."

"Thank you for that visual."

Sam eyeballed her from head to toe. "Who *are* you, lady?"

"Xaviera Luciana Dominica Fiori."

Sam blinked. "Jesus, you could choke on that."

"Call me Viva."

"Sam Wyatt, this is Max." He tossed a thumb toward his pal.

"We've met." She smiled kindly at Max.

"They couldn't ship that?"

"Sure. But we didn't. Not that it's your business, and since we're sharing, tell me why you look like Alan Quartermaine in bad need of a haircut and are dealing with those awful men."

Max stifled a laugh.

Sam turned away. "Come on, we need to move."

Clearly, he wasn't being responsive. "Thank you for your help—"

He glanced at her. "You know where you are? Which direction to go?"

"South to Bangkok." She pointed.

Sam inclined his head to his left. "That way."

"Thank you." She marched off, but didn't get far. Sam caught her around the waist, lifting her off her feet. She struggled and he shook her, her feet dangling.

"It's about two hundred miles," he said close to her ear and it sent a chill down her throat. "Want to meet more like the guy with the dart in his neck?" He set her down.

The realization hit and Viva turned sharply. "They'll be looking for me."

"I would."

Alone she'd be dead. "I accept the offer." She saw the wisdom in traveling with armed men, as much as her practical side was telling her to run like hell. These guys could be gun dealers, thieves, or worse, the enemy of that bandit leader. Which meant they'd hunt her just for being with them. Circumstances were crummy, but she didn't have any choice.

Sam took a few steps away, then said, "This time, stay put."

"Yes, certainly. Go visit the body." She waved him off, watching him move back to the corpse and with Max, cover it with dead leaves and logs. Don't anger this one, she thought, forcing a pleasant smile when he glanced her way. His hands soaked up the blood as he repositioned the body, and he looked more dangerous than the bandits. Dark hair poked out from beneath an old brown cowboy hat, the five-finger pinch molded with sweat and dirt. It's a favorite, she decided, and let her gaze slide over him. His jeans were a worn light blue, molded to his long legs, a pistol riding his hip like a gunslinger, low and loose. She almost expected it to be tied down. The man had style, she thought, his sweat-soaked T-shirt sculpting ropey muscles. Nice shoulders.

She cocked her head, watching, then, as if he could feel it, he looked up. His gaze slammed into hers, and Viva was struck again by his dark eyes and that he exposed nothing in his expression. He didn't say much either. That was never a problem for her.

He stood, spoke to Max, and came to her.

"Why didn't you bury him?"

"No point, it's fresh meat, fresh blood. The animals will smell it and dig till they find it."

Viva's stomach rolled at the image. "Sorry I asked."

He drew the slung rifle over his shoulder, loaded it again, and she realized it wasn't a normal shotgun as she'd first thought. Though shaped like one, it had a high-tech look about it. And a double trigger. "I've never seen a gun like that."

"Seen many, have you?"

"Today's been a veritable festival of weaponry."

He gave the rifle a hard shake, once, then slid it to his back, barrel down.

Sam felt something fly by his cheek and his gaze zeroed in over her head. He yanked her to the ground, shielding her. "Max, down, down!"

Max dropped without hesitation, drawing his gun. Then Viva heard the soft swish, like a soda can opening, only shorter. And rapid, one after another. Over her head in the trees were teeny spikes and it took her a second to realize they were darts.

Sam dragged his hat off and aimed. "Crap, they're back."

"Party crashers are so rude."

The crack of his rifle made her flinch, the smell of it hanging in the air. Birds squawked and rose into the treetops. She peered around him and where he'd aimed, a thin tree keeled over. Whoa. Max held down the trigger, cutting the trees in rapid succession with his automatic weapon. "Show off."

Sam went low, signaled to Max, slipped something into his ear, then drew a small, thin, bendable rod near his mouth. Max did the same.

They're in contact now, she thought. Radios? Cool. This was all suddenly exciting.

"Cover me, buddy," Sam said, then eased back, pushed her beyond the trees, his attention never leaving the terrain surrounding them. Max offered cover fire in spurts, Sam and Viva quickly shifting backwards.

"We can't leave him."

"Not happening, and be quiet."

Sam came to his knees, his weapon sweeping to his left. He unloaded and she heard something hit the ground hard. *Someone's dead out there.*

"Want to smoke them out?"

Max shook his head. "There are at least six, I think. Maybe more."

Outgunned, and he didn't have any explosives to make it simple. Where was Sebastian when you really needed him.

Viva heard movement over the wild beat of her heart in her ears, and tapped Sam, pointed. He swung and fired. The glow of return muzzle flash marked positions and Max opened up on the location as Sam moved, pushing her ahead. Bullets hit the trees, the ground.

Viva smothered a yelp.

Sam fell on her, flattened her to the ground. "We have to make a run for it."

"They'll follow."

He rolled off her, his body nearly sandwiched to hers. "We just have to be faster."

"And me without my Keds."

Sam's lips quirked. At least she wasn't crying. "Don't stand, crawl." He urged her. "Go now."

Viva obeyed, moving on her sore knees. Her palms slipped on mossy rocks and she fell, pushed up, and crawled.

Sam put a hand on her butt and pushed it down. "Drag yourself."

Max fired, ripping up the jungle, and crouched low, he backed up. "Meet you at the stream," he said.

"Roger that." Sam rose slightly, and took off. "Come on, woman, put a fire under it."

"Tyranny is so unattractive, Sam." She ran, clawing through the forest, barely flinching as the jungle shredded her exposed skin. The ground grew soft under her feet, slowing her, and when she stumbled, Sam caught her, practically carrying her toward the water.

He jerked her back before she went into the stream, and

forced her to the ground. He aimed from behind a cluster of trees, sliding the rifle barrel between the foliage.

"Drac, we're at the rendezvous, where the hell are you?"

Viva tucked behind him, still as glass. Sam didn't have to look; he could feel her warmth on his spine.

Max burst from the forest. "We have company!" he shouted, hurdling. "Move! Move!"

Sam took off, pushing her ahead to the river, and she shifted to the left, darting over rocks instead of through the black water, Max coming alongside. The bandits weren't far behind, the ground squishing with wet footsteps.

Christ, at this rate, he'd get her killed.

"We need to slow them down." Sam glanced at Max running a few yards to his left.

"I've got two clips," Max said into the mike, checking his pockets.

Sam slowed. Viva noticed. "Why are you stopping?" Oddly, she suddenly recognized the look; pure macho determination. "Don't do this!"

"This is risky, pal."

"Is there any other way? On my mark." Sam stopped, and in one motion with Max, turned, and fired. They emptied into the forest, and all Viva saw was blood on green, men bursting through the trees and instantly thrown back off their feet. The bodies bounced.

Viva turned away, covering her ears, wincing with each blast. Then strong hands were on her, dragging her up the stream's bank onto higher ground.

The figure moved through the jungle, soundless, eyes bright with awareness. Above the treetops daylight shone, yet the thick Thai jungle trapped the moisture and air in a vise. Sweat trailed her temples, down between her breasts, yet she kept moving, leaping dead logs and pausing only to slip through a thin outcropping of bushes. They'd been cut, then trampled. The path had already led her to the traitor, then to the *tho thahan*. Her body shivered with the memory of killing the mafia soldier, a warm heat brewing low in her belly. He'd betrayed the silence.

Now, the path to her master was wiped clean, the only evidence tucked inside a skin pouch dangling at her hip. None could be trusted, and she was the only one to see it so.

She followed the sound of gunfire.

Project Silent Fire
US–UK Command Post

Major General Al Gerardo rarely showed his emotions. It's what made him the consummate professional and well respected from the president down to the corporal who answered his phones. Gerardo never did anything halfway and for him, there was always a better solution, some tiny point that could be improved. It drove his staff crazy, but to work with him on this project, they'd learn to accept and respect it. His small idiosyncrasies had often foiled disaster.

Even in the most desperate moments of the nation's defense, he showed unquestionable authority and control. Only those who'd known him for years could recognize his anxiety.

Lt. Colonel Mitch Callahan was one of them. Gerardo rolled a quarter over his knuckles without looking, as if it was a part of him. All while he watched the video feed, the camera mounted on a Marine's helmet, the U.S. team backing up British Royal Marines.

"Be advised, the target is our only source right now."

The night vision lens glowed green as the feed went smooth for a moment, then staggered as it focused. Royal Marines had been posted around the small house and though there'd been no movement for over an hour, they knew who occupied the home.

"Execute," the general said. The team moved in, Royal and U.S. Marines covering the small house like a blanket. Gas went in first, masks down, then a Royal Marine broke through the front door, just as another team came in through the rear.

"Clear," echoed through the head mikes and to Gerardo's console. They watched the mission unfold. Each room was swept, floors checked for traps before the men moved to the last door, the bedroom where Hassan was hiding. All exits were covered, the second floor spotted with the red dots of laser scopes.

A U.S. Marine kicked in the door, men quickly sweeping the room. Several suddenly gasped and groaned. "Room secure, Jesus, it stinks in here."

They turned to the source. "Mother of God."

Gerardo leaned forward as his man got close. "Damn." He dropped the quarter on the console.

Mitch leaned for a better look.

Hassan was strapped to a chair, every inch of his clothing stained with blood already turned black. There were so many cuts on the man's body it was hard to tell what was a wound or a blood trail. Blood congealed on the floor beneath him. *Dead for days.*

A warning came, men lifted NVG goggles and the lights came on. The glare of light focused on just the victim.

The room was sparse, a bed behind the chair.

Gerardo said, "Those wounds aren't fatal." Each near a vein but not an artery. Enough to slowly bleed him dry.

"Yes, sir, I noticed," a Royal Marine said. "But these are." He tipped the helmet, the video relay showing that the man was missing his toes.

"The back of his knees are cut," one Marine observed. "What's the point of that? He's strapped to the chair."

But Gerardo knew. In many cultures, it was a final disgrace that the victim would never walk in the next life with his ancestors. Whether it meant anything to the victim was inconsequential. It meant something to his killer. But the lead, the most viable one they had, was lost.

"Secure and let MI-6 techs in there." Gerardo pushed

away from the monitor and stood. He picked up the quarter again.

"Maybe we'll get something from the house," Callahan suggested.

Gerardo waved that off, rolling the quarter. "Perhaps, but they're thorough."

Whoever had the weapons schematics was long gone by now. Gerardo looked at the surveillance printouts. Their people had gone over the photos of Hassan and any associate several times, trying to digitize the shots and pull something for identification. Hassan led a small, lonely life. A janitor with a security clearance, for the love of Mike. The man had no idea what he'd done, the danger he'd let loose when he stole the plans. Gerardo looked back at the monitor, video frozen on the victim's tattered face.

Perhaps he did.

Hassan was betrayed by his contact, obviously, and it hadn't been difficult to locate the man. That kept Gerardo up late. Someone knew the Standard Operating Procedure, the SOP of how reactionary forces worked. And that meant they had help—from the inside.

He looked at Mitch. "Wake everyone up."

"Sir?"

"Get every watchdog we have out there. I want visuals on the worst."

"Counter intelligence is already working on this, sir." They had visuals of several known terrorists.

"Not good enough. Get them in the trenches. We need photos, movement, associates, and if we have to dig into the gutters, we will."

"That's usually where they are, sir." Mitch reached for the phone, and dialed.

"Not this time. This group, they have financing, and damn good intel. Or they wouldn't have made it past the door." He looked back at the still video on the screen. "They're cleaning up their trails."

* * *

The jungle opened up, sunlight pouring down. With good reason. It ended.

Viva skidded to a sharp stop, slipped and flailed to keep from going over the cliff. Sam's arm snapped around her waist, drawing her back.

She clung to him. "We're trapped."

Max rushed to a stop beside them. "We missed some." He inclined his head the way they'd come, reloading.

"And the river is in front of us," she said, peering over the edge. "It's a forty-foot drop to the water and no way down."

"I have one." Sam pulled his whip from the lashings and cracked it. It looped around a branch extended over the water.

"Oh, you have got to be kidding." Even as she spoke, Sam pressed the handle into her palms, then drew her far back from the edge. "Ya know, I'm as adventurous as the next woman, but do you know what's in that water?"

"Snakes, crocs, pit vipers—and escape." With her tucked into his body, he pointed to the small boat. "That's our only way."

"Oh geez," she groaned, gripping the handle and staring at the wide open *nothing*. "That thing's not seaworthy, it's river garbage!"

"It's floating."

Max had his back to the river, his Uzi aimed. "ETA less than one minute, guys."

"Go, Viva."

"I am, I am. Can't you see I'm preparing to die?" She took a deep breath, backed up a step, then bolted. When her feet left the edge of the ground, she thought, *Life was a lot better before Thailand.*

Sam shouted to let go, and she obeyed, dropping into the water like a coin. The impact stung her arms, and she refused to open her eyes until she felt the sun on her head. She broke the surface as Max hit the water.

She headed toward the boat, looking back for Sam. "Where is he? He's not there!" The whip was gone too.

Max swam past her and climbed into the boat. "Come on, swim, swim!" From the bottom of the boat, he scooped up fallen branches and wet leaves, hurling them into the water.

Self-preservation slammed into her and she swam to the small boat. Max helped her over the side and she instantly sat up, rocking it. Max steered the rowboat away from the bank.

Viva's attention was on the cliffs. "Why hasn't he jumped?"

"Outlaw, you there? Outlaw, come in!" Max tapped the thread mike at his ear, then yanked it off, cursing. "It shouldn't be out of commission, dammit."

"Try to be upbeat, Max, really."

The men appeared on the edge, almost falling over it. Viva grabbed the second decaying oar and dug it into the water. Bullets rained, peppering the water like jumping schools of fish. Max returned it in deadly blasts. Viva ducked low, paddling faster, harder. The boat jolted and she stilled, exchanged a glance with Max as something amphibious rolled barely below the surface before it disappeared into the dark water.

"A croc?" she asked and hated the fear in her voice.

"It's a big one."

Max cocked the Uzi and aimed. Viva watched the water, poised with the rotten oar like a bat. "If you surface," she muttered to the bubbling river, "you're luggage."

Water fountained, the boat lurched sharply, throwing her back. She yelped, and twisted to strike.

"Whoa, darlin', take a breather." Sam hung on the edge of the boat, wiped his face, then threw himself in.

"I ought to hit you with this." She still brandished the oar.

"Row for a little while first, will you?" Sam lay there, breathing hard, and Viva realized he had to have run a half mile to get this far downriver.

"You okay, pal?" Max said, paddling smoothly and watching the terrain.

Sam waved halfheartedly. Viva sank into the watery bottom, tiny minnows pecking at her knees. “God, I’m really starting to hate you two.”

Sam opened one eye to look at her. “Now there’s a surprise.”

“You owe me an explanation.”

“No. I don’t.”

“Really?” She grabbed his gun, pointed it. “Think again, *Outlaw*.”

Sam rose up on his elbows to look at her. Covered in muck and a brownish-green cast to her clothes, she was still a gorgeous redhead. “It’s out of ammo.”

She fired. It wasn’t.

Four

The gunshot went past his hip and into the bottom of the boat. Sam was on her, tearing the pistol from her. "Christ, woman!"

"Oh God. You lied! Why would you lie?" She backed away from him. Man, he looked scary right now. "That was really dumb."

"Don't point a weapon unless you plan to kill something!"

"From what I've witnessed, that's your job."

"Do you ever shut up?" He popped in a fresh clip. He'd miscounted, dammit.

Viva reddened with embarrassment; it was a phrase she heard often.

"Guys, we're sinking."

A slow fountain of water bubbled in the side of the boat. Viva lurched across and stuck her finger in it.

"Oh, that helps."

"It stopped, didn't it? God, you're such a pessimist."

Sam rubbed his mouth and looked ahead. "Head there."

"I see it."

There was a house on stilts, nearly in the water, its dock half sinking below the surface. Two children fished from the end, sitting more in the water than on the wood. The men rowed toward it and in range, Sam grabbed the post and swung them closer. He leapt from the boat, then reached for her. She was still stretched to keep her finger in the hole, and staring up at him, mutinous.

"Give it up, Viva."

She climbed out under her own power. "You're irritating, Sam Wyatt, and not very nice."

"You shot at me, for crissake."

"But I missed," she said as if that made all the difference.

It didn't. She was an accident waiting to happen, Sam thought, and couldn't wait to get rid of her and find Riley's shooter.

"Besides," she kept on without missing a beat, "after what I've seen today, you're a walking testimony to bad karma all the way around."

Max stepped onto the dock, and within seconds, the boat went nose up before sinking beneath the surface. Brown-skinned boys on the platform barely noticed them, as if they'd seen men with weapons every day.

Viva knelt near the children, asking if they'd caught anything, how long they'd been out here, did they see any bad men with guns pass through here? The boys answered until the last question, then peered around her at the two men. "I know they look scary, but they won't hurt you. The train to Bangkok is near?"

The boys answered in rapid, choppy Thai, pointing out directions. All up hill. They spoke for a few more minutes before she slipped them a couple bhat, then straightened.

Sam looked at her like she'd grown another head, or in his case, a new brain. "What?"

"You're fluent."

She laughed. "There are about forty dialects. Nobody is fluent in Thai." She walked off the dock, finger combing her hair. Her boots squished with water, the butt of her shorts sagging. "The road is this way, a few kilometers. I'm going to hitch a ride or something. Thanks for the rescue." She waved over her head.

"We shouldn't let her go alone." Max frowned at her as

she moved past the house to the left toward the barely visible path that rose nearly straight up the hillside.

Sam was examining his rifle. It was useless until he could clean the sludge out of it. "You want to keep her around? She's trouble."

"We didn't get them all. They'll hunt us and her."

And she'd be noticeable. A redhead in Thailand. Worse than a Yankee at a Texas barbeque.

"And we brought her into this," Sam admitted, rubbing the back of his neck. "We have to at least get her wherever she wants." He looked up as she peeled off her wet shirt, then wrung it out. Beneath it, she wore a sports bra thing that showed off her tan and narrow waist. For a moment, he wanted her to face him, let him see what that baggy shirt had hidden, what he'd felt pressed to him.

Why did she have to be a redhead?

Then she shook her head like a dog, the motion making her lose her footing. She righted herself, then walked more stiffly. He imagined her cheeks reddening, and Sam's lips curved. Damn if she wasn't the most entertaining nightmare he'd ever had.

"We're stuck with her for now." He called out, but she didn't respond, melting into the forest, alone. "Christ, see what I mean?" Sam stormed after her, muttering, "God gave a frog a brain and shared half of it with her."

Max didn't follow immediately, his amusement dying as his gaze slid over the terrain, the way they'd come. They'd just pissed off the Thai mafia.

Viva was the least of their problems.

Inside the dense branches, she hid, watching the small boat slide to the dock on flat water. She couldn't hit them at this distance, but knew where they'd go. They had little choice but to cross the jungle. She studied their faces, put them to memory. Her master would make certain they'd never speak of this. She lingered a moment longer, then began the careful climb to the ground.

Below her, the bodies of *tho thahan* were like tumbled matchsticks, spent and useless. She'd take nothing from the soldiers. They weren't *hers*. Her foot touched the ground, soundless, and she quickly shifted beyond the dead, her ears tuned to the predators prancing slowly from the darkness to come feast on the still warm flesh.

The jungle wrapped her like a lover, her body glistening with its liquid touch as she moved quickly, her destination preordained, her task far from done.

The river vanished behind Viva, closed out by the dense tropical forest.

She didn't hear him move up behind her, but she felt it. His presence like a whisper, sensation without substance. It was the most amazing feeling she'd ever experienced, and she tipped her head slightly, acknowledging him, yet she said nothing.

He moved quickly abreast of her, hacking mercilessly at the jungle when the path narrowed. "Keep moving, Viva." He walked backwards a couple steps, weapon aimed.

She glanced, stumbled. "They're still out there, you think?"

"Definitely." Sam hurried her forward.

"But you put the fear of automatic weapons in them."

"We were just lucky. This is their playground." He signaled Max to stay to the left.

Hurriedly, she slipped her shirt back on and started buttoning it.

"Now that's just a shame."

Her gaze jerked his, confused till his gaze flicked to her breasts cupped in tight spandex. "Back off, Wyatt."

"No problem there, ma'am, you bite."

She blinked, then smiled brightly, making her eyes light up and turn her expression from pretty to downright electric. The power of it hit Sam dead center of his chest and left heat snaking down his body.

Man, he didn't need that, not now.

"This hasn't been a normal day."

For her, maybe, he thought, watching his six.

Viva noticed that though he appeared to be relaxed, he wasn't; his gaze darted around them, picked a new spot at each new scan. The machete was slung at his hip, and his finger was on the trigger of the rifle. And without touching him, she knew his shoulders were tight. "Who are you, Sam Wyatt?" she asked softly.

He simply watched the land, not responding.

"Listen, Sparky, I'm not stupid . . ." Viva pushed on ahead of him.

He blinked. *Sparky?*

". . . so don't play dumb. You bargained with at least a hundred fifty, maybe two hundred carat diamond back there. Although . . . cut it would be about half that. Which is still very substantial and worth several million, but that's if the cutter could find the table and split it with the least amount of fragmentation and—"

He caught her arm, keeping her with him. "Lower your voice. What do you know about gems?"

"Not much." At his scowl, she whispered, "I worked with a gemologist for about a year."

"How'd you go from a dig to gemology?"

Trying to meet his long strides, she gathered her composure for the assault she always received when people learned how many different jobs and career starts—and failures—she'd had. "Unemployment."

Sam saw the humiliation in her pretty face and wondered how someone so sharp could ever be out of a job. "You have a degree in archeology?"

"No, paleoclimatology."

"That's as useless as it gets."

"Not if you want to know the weather conditions a million years ago." And be bored to madness, she thought. "It was wet everywhere, by the way, then got surprisingly cold."

Sam went to push back some vines and she grabbed his hand before he did. "Don't touch that!" She found a stick and pushed up the leaves of a tall plant. She showed him the millipedes covering the leaves. "They secrete a fluid that will blister your skin."

His expression questioned.

"Two semesters of tropical botany." She walked away. "And I've been here long enough to experience my own stupidity."

Sam's brows shot up. A woman open to her faults, he thought, rare, yet more closed about her assets. His gaze lowered over her spine to the tight curves of her rear. Sweet. She had assets. In one form or another.

"Now that you're done inspecting my behind . . ."

His gaze flashed up. "Who said I was done?"

She flushed delicately. "You're changing the subject."

"Man, you're slick." Sam looked the way they'd come, frowning.

"I don't let go of a bone I want to pick either. So what are you, CIA, NSA? Some sort of secret American 'if I tell you, I'll have to kill you' Intelligence?"

"None of the above."

She blinked. "You really *are* a criminal?"

Sam stopped abruptly, turned, his gaze raking the hillside again. He nodded to Max, then touched his ear. *I hear them too.* He signaled, then grasped her arm, hurrying her up the hillside.

"Sam?" She ran with him.

Suddenly, he jerked her to the ground, put a finger to his lips, then, squatting, he rotated. Max was only a couple yards down the incline. Max pointed, and Viva saw figures moving up the hill. There had to be five at least, spread out and combing the ground. Crouched behind him, Viva's heartbeat picked up. It wasn't over.

Sam checked his ammo, signaling to Max. When he made a cutting motion across his throat, she thought, that can't be good. He pointed to his eyes, then to them as a pair. Max nodded, and backed up the hill.

Slowly, he mouthed, then tapped his lips. *Quiet.* She obeyed, watching her steps. They were coming for her. That she hadn't killed Half Ear wouldn't matter to those men. They wanted revenge. Oh God, if Sam got hurt—she swallowed, fear chasing up her spine and pumping adrenaline.

Ahead she could see the sunlight where the jungle thinned, the roasting sun already cooking her skin under her wet clothes as they climbed. Freedom is up there, she thought, then felt his hand on her back, warm and pulling on her shirt. She stopped, keeping low. Sam's gaze shifted downhill, to Max, then to her.

"We're toast, aren't we?"

He leaned close. "When I signal," he said into her ear, "I want you to run like hell and keep running."

She gripped his forearm. "Alone? Without you?"

Something clamped deep inside his chest just then, squeezing. "You have to. We're nearly out of ammo and this isn't your fight."

"It is. I started it," she whispered. "I'd be dead without you. Don't you think I know that?"

He leaned back enough to look her in the eyes. Tears welled in them, smoky green and desperate with fear. He slid his hand to her hair, pushing it back. "You're so damn brave, you can do this."

"From your mouth to God's ears." Then she looked down the hill. They were creeping closer. Max was nearly abreast of their position. She met Sam's gaze, the softness in his dark eyes comforting. *Another fine mess I've made.* "I wish I could do something to help."

"You can get away from this." He turned toward the jungle, taking a position deep inside a cluster of bushes. "Be ready."

Beside him, Viva saw the men approaching, the top of a head, the swing of a machine gun. And he was going to face them alone? Courage like that simply stunned her. "Sam?"

"Yeah."

"Outlaw or not," she whispered, then met his gaze, "you've made an impression." Her lips curved in a message that vised down on his heart.

"Darlin', you can't help but make one." His gaze combed her features, and suddenly, Sam couldn't let her go, not yet. He cupped the back of her head, and kissed her.

The contact was electric. Shocking him. And trapped in the hot jungle, he tasted pure energy, a quick heat crackling down his body as her mouth rolled eagerly over his. Her fingers slid into his hair at his nape, turning it intimate, personal. Then her tongue pushed between his lips and Sam was lost. Caving in. He devoured as much of her as he could and she made a little sound deep in the back of her throat. Sam drank that in, too—till it was dangerous, till his senses clouded, and a second longer would get them both killed.

He drew back abruptly, like the tearing of a limb. "Jesus." He swallowed. "Don't talk," he groaned when she opened her mouth.

But Viva couldn't, her breathing labored as her gaze raked his face. Her thumb smoothed his lower lip. Her heart would never pound the same again.

He forced his attention down the hill. "Get ready."

Viva eased away, reluctant to leave him.

She glanced back one last time. He sighted down the rifle, adjusted his stance. Blindly, he reached behind himself, and Viva gripped his hand for an instant, quick and tight.

Then, when his next shot came, she bolted up the hill.

Kukule Ganga Dam
Kalawana, Sri Lanka

Engineers and construction experts crawled over the ruins of the dam, trying to find the source of the fissure that sent eight hundred million gallons of water through the valley, killing thousands. Help came from everywhere—England, the US, Germany, Spain. Dr. Tom Rhodes wasn't stunned by the outpouring, only over the break in the dam. It was far left of the southern side, an area well fortified. He'd been on the first survey team before the construction at the request of Dr. Risha Inan.

Squatting, Tom glanced up as Risha made her way toward him, her hair looped through the back of a baseball cap, her shirt and shorts already dirty from crawling around the ruins. She still took his breath away, he thought. Her flawless skin, the smooth mocha color of it, and her eyes—she had the most expressive eyes of any woman he'd known. And he'd known her well.

The attraction was still there, though she'd married someone else, someone Hindi. Tom took it as a personal affront then, but knew now that she'd been right to break it off. His career was in the US, hers was here, helping her people. Neither of them would bend and for a love that had grown quickly, it had died just as easily.

He watched her approach and swiped a cloth over his forehead and throat.

She stopped a couple yards from him, adjusting her footing on the wet, broken concrete. "You will never grow accustomed to the heat, Thomas."

"What's your secret?"

"Don't fight it."

He made a sound of impossibility, and stood. They'd been sidestepping their personal feelings since he'd arrived after the flood. It was good, he thought, this barrier, because he wasn't here just to help the engineers find the problem. His position gave him access to vital information the Sri Lankan government might not pass along so quickly. Though the government was doing its best to get aid to the victims, intelligence was slow and the US was interested. But it wasn't enough. Tiger rebels were in the hills near the river when the dam broke. Several bodies had been identified, along with many Sri Lankan soldiers.

"Are you ready for a preliminary report?" she asked.

He shook his head. "There is nothing wrong with this dam, the concrete strength, the metal skeleton. I was here during the construction. It's sound. It shouldn't have broken."

"Thomas, you know a small fissure, given the pressure per square inch, could very well have worsened in a short time."

He was already shaking his head. "There are no cracks, no residue left from explosive charges. A dam this size doesn't just break. Your government has an inspection team go over this dam a couple times a month. You have crews watching the pressure and water flow. If something changed in the days before the break, why didn't they see it?"

"Charges could have been set recently. And we've considered that because some Tigers were close, they were perhaps waiting for the blast, and wanted to witness their destruction."

"Possible."

"The residue likely washed away with the water flow."

Again, he shook his head. "But the break in the section is still intact." He rose and gestured below. The dam had broken from beneath the rim. "And I've done a dozen chemical residue tests."

She frowned, suspicious. That wasn't his job.

"Do you want my help or not? The US is prepared to pour funds into helping your country, Risha, and I'm the first wave."

She looked over the broken dam. In spots, the water still flowed and farther inland workers struggled to create a levee in the basin. This was the water supply for the entire region.

"Without a crack, the only thing that would have caused this type of damage—"

She looked at him sharply.

"Is a drop in temperature, and I'm talking near freezing."

She stiffened. "Impossible."

"Yes, I know. Or sensors would have gone off. They didn't."

She frowned and he still adored that intense expression. He could see her thoughts ticking off scenarios.

"We built it and people are dead. It is our fault, Thomas."

She finally looked at him, the sadness in her eyes clear and bitter. She felt too much, he thought, but it was hard not to. Below them, workers sprayed the area with a bacteria killer before they unearthed more bodies.

"What do you need?"

He pointed to the concrete. "We have to get into the tunnels. That would be the best place to start."

"Not up here?"

"The dam break didn't have anything to do with construction."

Her look said she doubted that. "Then how?"

"That's our job. Come on."

Risha pulled her radio from her belt and spoke, informing her team that they needed pumps and workers to empty the tunnels. It would take days, but Thomas was a brilliant man and she trusted his judgment.

Viva met the top of the ridge and hesitated when she saw more jungle. A mile to the road, she thought and ran into the forest. She batted away branches and prayed they'd survive, yet felt they wouldn't. There were too many of the bandits. A hundred yards or so in she stopped to catch her breath, then pressed on. She didn't get more than a few feet when a man appeared in front of her.

Instantly, she darted in another direction and confronted another small man. She turned and was surrounded, men dropping from the trees. Hill tribes, she thought, by the look of their clothing and old weapons aimed at her.

Sam's going to be really pissed if I get killed today.

She put her hands up. "Help, *Jao Pho,* two Americans are trapped." She pointed and the first man, wearing a perpetual frown, followed the line of her arm. "Help, please!" She closed her eyes briefly and prayed she got the dialect right. When she opened her eyes, she was alone.

Sam aimed carefully and fired, swiveling to match his sight on the bandits. They'd taken cover at the first shot, but a few were bold. Max had his automatic off, firing one shot at a time to conserve ammo, moving closer to Sam's position with each blast. A shot spiked leaves above his head and Sam ducked, taking deeper cover, but the muzzle flash gave his position away. And theirs.

Max backed up, signaling and Sam mimicked. They couldn't get them all, but enough for them to escape. He counted time, giving Viva plenty, and in tandem, Sam and Max raced up the steep hill. He heard a grunt, a rustle in the bushes, then Max was moving with him. They stopped, turned, and fired, then overtook another twenty yards. Sam prayed he didn't find Viva anywhere near here. He glanced at Max, his pulse staggering when he realized he was covered in blood, but still moving.

Sam had a couple bullets left, his headset and radio wet. They were pretty much screwed. A bandit ran out into the open, and Sam aimed, but never got off a shot. The man went still and stiff with shock, a dart in the center of his throat.

He twisted sharply—and saw Viva. Damn woman. She waved, and on either side of her was a line of locals, covering them. Sam took off, racing up the incline, grabbing vines and propelling himself forward. She reached for him.

"I told you to run!"

"Yeah, well, that wasn't working for me."

He dove over her, then pulled her back with him as the tribesmen opened fire. He pushed her low, then, on his stomach Sam moved up beside the tribesmen.

Sam spent his last rounds, taking out a man who wouldn't give up. Alongside him, the tribesmen aimed slow and careful, expending precious rounds and getting the job done. As good as a squad of Marines, he thought, as they watched for movement. The leader nodded, then signaled. The men eased away from the edge, then rose, hurrying backwards into the jungle for a few yards before turning into its darkness.

The leader grabbed Viva as he passed, pulling her with

him. Sam was on him, prying his hands off her. The man scowled, let go, urging them on, and went farther into the jungle.

Max approached, and when Viva saw the blood, she was on him, patting him down for the wound. "I'm not hit, he just got close enough to bleed on me."

"Jesus, and you call me a thrill junkie," Sam said, pulling off his hat and rubbing his head before replacing it.

"Got my radio, though." Max held up a tangle of wires and shattered plastic. He tossed it.

Viva looked between the two. Their calm was amazing.

Sam checked his weapon, one bullet left, then motioned Viva ahead. This wasn't over yet. The tribal leader kept looking back at them, more specifically at Viva. "Got your own tribe now?"

"They found me. The hill tribes rarely get involved with outsiders." She didn't know what changed their minds, but was more than grateful for it.

"You're certifiably insane," he said.

She cocked a look at him, smiling. "We've established that."

Sam chuckled shortly and didn't know what to make of her. He wouldn't be breathing now if she hadn't disobeyed him. "Did your daddy paddle your butt a lot when you were a kid?"

An odd look flashed over her features, then turned to a smile. "No, he spoiled me. Which is probably why I'm here and not married with children in the States."

"And why aren't you?"

"I suffer from eternal boredom. Except today, of course."

"You could have been killed."

"You too." She leaned out to look pointedly at Max. "My backup was better than yours."

"Go ahead, gloat." Max edged closer, inclined his head to Sam. "He's too stubborn to admit it, but you saved our collective asses back there." Max moved on ahead.

Viva stole a look at Sam. He was just staring and the look had power, moving over her and almost stripping her bare. She was right before. The man was intense.

They broke eye contact when the tribe leader made a noise, gestured.

Viva smiled. "I think we're invited to dinner."

"Good, I could use a beer," he said.

The land cleared, and they stepped into the small village. Surrounding an old community well were large huts without doors, the roofs thatched with palms. People came out slowly, smiling and greeting the men. A few dropped dead monkeys into a pile. Women came to her, touching her hair, her clothes. Viva chatted, took the offer of water, and glanced back at Sam. Through binoculars, he sighted the way they'd come.

"Does he ever give an inch?"

Squatting, Max shook his head, removing his pack.

Sam lowered the glasses, glanced, and couldn't help his smile. Though the women pulled her toward a thatched house, her gaze was on him.

"We're going to have a girl chat, you know, makeup, hairstyles. Exchange a few recipes." The women chatted incessantly, tugging her along. "Don't leave without me, Sam."

Her plea was laced with a little fear. No, he wouldn't leave her till he could get her to Bangkok to deliver the bracelet. After that, it was just too dangerous for her to be near him. Today had proven it.

Sam pulled off his hat, swiped the back of his wrist across his forehead. "Phan's death, it was almost ritual. They didn't kill, just cut him up to bleed to death."

Max pulled smashed bananas from his pack and tossed them aside. "And whoever shot that dart was protecting whatever information Half Ear was going to offer up. Or Rohki."

Sam agreed. "Just before Half Ear died, he said, it will cost you more than . . ." Sam shrugged, trying to fill in the blanks.

". . . more than diamonds," Max said. "More to find Rohki, to get information? It could be anything."

"I'm thinking more than that to get into this weapons deal."

Max's head came up. "Possible. It's just rumor."

"Hear a rumor often enough and there has to be some truth to it. I say we back up and regroup, start with the jet. It was high-priced transport. I'm betting they're transporting a lot of shit under the wire." Sam slid off his Camelbak and tipped the clear pipe into his mouth, squeezing the pack. The water was hot, but wet. He handed it to Max, then patted himself down for extra bullets, coming up empty.

He straightened away from the tree, his gaze on the sky. "Great, they have air support." A chopper.

The pair dropped to the ground, taking cover, and Sam aimed his pistol. Villagers looked to the sky and scattered, grabbing children and melting into the jungle.

Viva came out of the hut, running to Sam. "Oh, tell me that's not what I think it is."

"It is," Sam said. The sound of blades beating the air sent an almost euphoric feeling through him, yet he wondered how he could get it to set down so they could overtake the craft. One bullet put that thought in the stupid-and-deadly pile. He readied to take out the gas tanks.

Viva was beside him under the trees. Behind them, the village was deserted. "Shouldn't we be hiding? Running with them?"

"Too late, they'll pick us off."

"You have one bullet left! What do you think you can do?"

"Get ready for a big explosion."

Viva felt that uncontrollable fear rise up again, tightening her skin, pushing her heartbeat up several notches. She was really tired of this shoot-run-shoot business.

Then the big, sleek black chopper came into view, low and slow over the area. It was armed with some dangerous-looking guns, aimed directly at them.

Five

"I can't watch." Yet Viva peeled one eye open.

"Just what I wished for," Max said, then winked at her. "The cavalry."

Sam instantly recognized the helicopter. It was his.

Landing gear unfolded as the black chopper lowered to the ground, a longhaired man standing in the doorway, armed and ready to fire. Sam scowled. Who was this guy?

"You Wyatt?" the man shouted.

"Hell, yeah." Sam pushed Viva ahead of him to the side of the chopper, helping her in before Max threw himself onto the deck. The chopper lifted off and Sam sagged against the jump seat. Before Sam could ask what he was doing here, the longhaired man handed them headsets, then pointed to the pilot.

Sebastian twisted long enough to flash a smile. "Thought you could use a ride out of the hot zone."

"You're a sight, Coonass, thanks. How'd you find us?"

"GPS marker, made it myself," Max said, tapping his belt buckle. Sam examined his buckle, then eyed Max. "You didn't think we'd let you go all commando without something, did you?"

"You two are damn lucky. You know what it took to get this chopper in the air over Thai air space?"

Sam looked up at the other man. "Lying through your teeth?"

"Shit-can it, Beech, you love breaking the rules," Sebastian said.

"Nigel Beecham, British intelligence," he introduced, and no one noticed Viva looking between the men, completely confused.

MI6, Sam thought, shaking his hand. Beecham had a crushing grip to go with his big shoulders in the flowered shirt. In shorts and sandals, he looked right at home, tanned enough to say he'd been here a while. Sam didn't want to know what he did for MI6. The British counterpart to the CIA were a deadly bunch, just like their own. And Sam didn't trust any of them, ground support or not.

"Will someone please tell me what's going on?" Viva demanded.

"When you Yanks shag the wrong people," Nigel said right over her words, "you don't even stop for a smoke, do you?" Nigel stood inside the chopper, his hands gripping the straps lacing the ceiling. The headset pushed on his face, making him look chubby.

"Not unless it's a Cuban cigar." Sam opened an ammo can and loaded his pistol. The rifle took custom-made shots. "Riley?" Sam said into the mike.

"Alive. And still in Never Never Land. Logan's on his way here and Killian and Alexa should be in Sri Lanka in a few days. But there's a hot-looking nurse who's sitting vigil over him. Too bad he doesn't know it."

Sam shook his head. Even in a coma Riley's Irish charm worked on the women, he thought, hunting through gear for a rag.

Viva grabbed his forearm. "Hello? Remember me? Clueless." She gestured to the men around her.

He looked at her as if just realizing she was there, then grasped that she'd heard too much.

"Yeah, who's the babe, Outlaw?"

Viva twisted to the pilot, poking her head between the seats. "Viva Fiori, hello. Thanks for the compliment, considering I know I don't look my best, and do you have a real name? Coonass is terribly unattractive."

He grinned, his attention on flying. "Sebastian Fontenot, *chéri,* and how did you get mixed up in this?"

"Because she's damn stubborn and has no idea when to keep her yap shut," Sam said.

She sent Sam a bitter look. "I brought you backup and you're complaining?"

"I wouldn't have needed backup if you didn't fight the Thai mafia."

"Well, sure, but we won. We're alive."

For how long? Sam knew one thing for sure. You could count on bad guys to hold a grudge. They'd given them several good reasons today. The diamond cut into his thigh and Sam pulled it from his pocket, handing it to Max. Then, finding the rag, he used it to pull the thin stick from the padded neck of his boot.

"Good Lord, Sam, and you call me certifiable?" Viva said, staring at the tiny dart.

"That's too close to the skin for my comfort," Max added.

Sam explained where it came from. "Someone was shooting these off like wildfire. I pulled this one out of my hat before I went in the river." Beecham reached for it. "Don't touch the end. Poison. We need to find out what it is and who has this poison."

Beecham sniffed the tip. "That's easy."

Sam frowned.

"It's local, *ya pit.* A mix of poisonous plants and the bones of the *hao fai,* fire cobra. Some venom. Jungle magic," he added, carefully handing it back. "Formulas are secret, passed down through women. Sorta warns you not to piss off a Thai woman, eh? It's usually ingested through food. Takes a couple hours, though."

Viva shook her head. "This was instant."

"Unusual." Beecham fanned his fingers under the day's growth of beard. "Refining it to kill on contact, well, that's an art."

Sam met Beecham's gaze. "Who's capable of that?"

He shrugged. "It's tribal magic. Nothing a *farang* can find." Gripping the straps, Beecham moved to Sebastian. "Set it down here, mate, I don't want to be seen with you guys."

Sebastian laughed and lowered the chopper in a field. Beecham tossed off the headset and jumped out, walking away as if he'd just left a taxi. Sebastian removed the helmet and slid into the copilot's seat.

"Who's going to fly this now?" she asked.

Sam gave her a lazy smile, then climbed effortlessly into the cockpit. Helmeted and hooked to the console, he took the stick and lifted off.

Viva leaned forward, poking her head between the seats again. "So what other talents are you hiding, Sam Wyatt?" He glanced, his expression driving a bolt of heat through her body. "Can I expect a demonstration?"

Sam made a frustrated sound, and looked at the sky.

"Sam can fly anything," Max said, oblivious. "Fast."

To prove it, he made a sharp glide to the left, heading toward Bangkok. Beneath, the land grew dense with homes, spreading to high-rise buildings that defied physics. He gunned it, climbing higher, and glanced to the side. Viva was enthralled, smiling brightly.

"This is so cool!" she said, rising up slightly for a better look.

Then Sam dove, curling to the right and Sebastian grabbed on to a handle. "Jesus, Sam, you trying to kill us?"

"Wuss," Viva said, grinning.

Sam lowered the chopper to a pad and she barely felt it touch down. He *was* good.

"This is where you get off, Viva."

She blinked, looking hurt, and Sam pulled off the helmet and climbed out, then opened the side door, offering his hand. Viva glanced, then handed Max the headset.

"Thrown out of another party," she said tiredly. "Nice to meet you, Sebastian," she said, then kissed Max's cheek. "It's been real." She took Sam's hand and hopped out.

"That was my first chopper ride," she said. "It's a real turn-on."

He arched a brow.

"Almost like foreplay."

Sam's body instantly clenched. He didn't say a word, talking would just get him in trouble with this woman.

"You aren't a criminal, are you?"

Sam didn't answer. But then, Viva didn't expect a confession. He barely knew her and whatever he was doing here involved all the wrong people. The British intelligence guy was a real eye-opener.

"We have to get off this pad."

"I won't see you again, will I?" The words stuck in her throat.

Sam stared down at her, memorizing her wild red hair, her lit-from-her-soul smile, and deep inside his chest he felt a tight, hard pain. Damn. "It's for your own safety."

"I'm thinking it's more for yours."

His lips quirked. He adored her honesty.

Men in jumpsuits rushed out of the small building alongside the helo pad, shouting. Viva frowned at them, then Sam. "You weren't supposed to land here."

"I wasn't supposed to do a lot of things."

Viva wondered what it meant when he kissed her, and suddenly she wanted those incredible feelings again. Let's be frank, she thought, he's dark and dangerous, and you want to know this man inside out, slowly, in the most biblical sense. The thought made her insides lock while her heart slowly broke.

"We gotta go."

"Who's stopping you?"

"You."

Her gaze ripped over him, hiding nothing of her emotions, and it felt like a claw raking his soul. She backed away a few steps, the chopper blades slowing.

Viva drank him in one last time. The beat-up cowboy hat, the whip lashed at his waist. The pistol and big bowie knife—his long legs in worn jeans. She was going to have some really great fantasies about him, she thought. "Bye, Outlaw."

Sam motioned for her to keep moving. The officials of the pad were yelling and Viva spun, chewing them out. Sam wasn't sure what she said, but they backed off.

She looked at Sam, shrugged. "People need to just get over themselves sometimes."

"Take care of yourself, Xaviera."

Her heart slammed in her chest.

Sam turned to the door, one hand gripping the frame. He closed his eyes briefly, wanting more and knowing it would put her life in terrible danger. It already had. He started to climb in.

A tap on his shoulder made him turn, and she was there, against him, her hand sliding up his chest, her fingers at his nape and pulling him down to her.

"You're not getting off that easy, cowboy."

Her mouth covered his and Sam trapped her against him, his entire body igniting like a warhead as his mouth rolled over hers. His fists bunched in her clothes, pushed her into him, and he felt it, that crackling current between them, the heat peeling off her in waves. Intoxicating, leaving him useless and hungering for more.

Then, abruptly, she pulled back and moved out of his arms. Sam felt suddenly stripped, empty. Then she walked across the cement pad toward the building, never once looking back. Sam watched her go.

Behind him, Sebastian whistled softly, then Max said, "Let her go, buddy. She's a civilian and we have a job to do."

"Yeah, yeah." For the first time, Sam hated his job. He climbed in the chopper, powering it up, refusing to look in her direction. "Contact Logan, we need some satellite photos to find that jet." The diamonds were out there, with the weapons. And Rohki.

* * *

Kashir pulled a swiftly made traverse bearing Najho's body. The dart was still in his neck. No one dared touch it or the body for fear of poisoning, and the belief that evil spirits were at work. Kashir had no such fear and led the procession.

Men flanked them, aiming toward the jungle as they followed the long path to the village. The American had done enough damage that they carried four dead. A half dozen others chose to continue the hunt. Kashir knew they would not survive.

Dragon One's reputation predicted as much.

Yet the men blamed the woman, and were determined to learn her identity. Kashir could do nothing to stop them. She was inconsequential to his objectives. The lines blurred often, and Najho had been his friend, of sorts. But Najho's death was not the American's doing, and Kashir's gaze flicked to the jungle, expecting another dart.

Watching his own back meant more to him than the assignment. But then, he was not a lifelong professional agent. He'd fallen into his career choice by accident. Lebanese born, he had connections that interested MI6, CIA, and Interpol. Recruiting him wasn't difficult. He was young and already inside when Interpol had come to him. Threatened him. It was best to be on the strong side of the law, though there were days he doubted who had control. He knew he was inconsequential, a voice from the inside. Only a few levels above Phan, he thought, and the image of Phan's mutilated body burst in his mind.

It wasn't the first time he'd seen such a massacre.

Ten years ago, several businessmen in Kuala Lumpur were found in just such a manner. Their testicles and toes taken, and some with their eyes removed. The flat in the high-rise had been a whorehouse, but that all the men were in the living room, positioned like an audience, had authorities scrambling to smother the murders from the news and find the killer. There was no trace. Phan, he thought, had met the same fate. From the same person.

That it could be a woman—there had been boys in the same whorehouse—twisted his stomach. It was punishment, a vile retribution. Yet as Kashir shifted the stretcher made of fronds and thin trees, he knew she was selective. None of their dead had been touched.

At the camp, he set down the travois and flexed his fingers. In his pockets were the uncut stones their leader had had on him. Just a few, he thought. For his own future. Kashir wasn't giving away information without a price. Finding Rohki for Dragon One was low on his list. Survival was first.

He moved into the village, the women rushing to the bodies of their beloved. Kashir stopped at his hut, removed his weapons, and sat on the low porch. A woman brought him water and a banana leaf filled with spicy chicken. Three men approached him. He simply stared up at them, then he knew. He'd been chosen.

He tossed aside the chicken bone. "Prepare the dead." Grooming, shrouding, and preparing the meal for the ancestor would take a day. The rituals of stories, and calling the spirits of the dead to take up residence on the ancestral altar, another two. "When their families are satisfied, then you may do as you wish."

And seek revenge.

The sun was bright in the sky when Viva took a cab to the Palace of *Wang Na*, the Bangkok museum. But her mind was locked on Sam and what he was really doing here in Bangkok. Best she didn't know, she thought. Tiredly, she walked up the steps to the pagoda-shaped museum, not even admiring the beautiful tilework before she went to the guard at the desk. She asked for Dr. Wan Gai, the curator.

The guard inspected her, making a face at her muddy boots, and Viva didn't want to see herself in a mirror. She felt bad, so she knew she looked worse. The guard made a phone call and she waited. Nearby were beautiful silk brocade chairs for visitors, but she was too filthy to sit. She heard crisp footsteps, and knew the moment Dr. Wan Gai saw her.

His steps slowed. "Miss Fiori?"

She nodded, primped her hair, and knew it was a disaster.

"I am Dr. Wan Gai." He held out his hand and she grasped it.

"*Sawatdee khrap.*" Hello. "You're not what I expected," she blurted, then mentally kicked herself. "A pleasure." Wan Gai was tall for a Thai man and handsome, his features angular, his eyebrows like black wings over piercing black eyes.

"Salih Nagada told me to expect you, and he was very worried when you had not yet arrived." His gaze moved down her body.

Her clothing was ruined, her boots so muddy she left trails. "I had a rough time. Salih was right, though. I *really* should have taken the plane."

Dr. Wan Gai frowned, coming closer.

She stepped back, eyeing his tailored black suit. "I wouldn't get too close. I've been in the river."

Regardless, he swept his arm around her, guiding her toward his offices. "Come, we will see to your comfort, have you a hotel room?"

She laughed to herself. "I don't even have luggage anymore."

He snapped his fingers, delivering orders in a soft voice. Food, coffee, water, and towels for Miss Fiori to clean, and Viva felt as if she'd found sanctuary after a prison of trouble.

"You'll want this." She pulled off the bracelet and handed it to him. Job done, she thought.

"Thank you." He didn't look at it, guiding her still, and inside his offices, he pushed her onto a plush sofa. She popped back up.

"It will be ruined. Look at me."

"It can be cleaned." He tsked and pushed her down again, then drew a chair in front of her and sat. "Tell me of your trip that put you in the river."

She gave him a vague story, leaving out Sam and Max's names, or that they were American. Her last image of Sam, a second before she kissed him, sent a burst of hot memory through her body. I'll miss his stubborn, overbearing self, she thought.

Wan Gai listened, pouring her a cup of rich black coffee, then withdrew a pair of glasses with small lenses attached to the outer rims and examined the bracelet.

"It got wet when I went into the river."

"It is unharmed." He glanced up, bug-eyed through the glasses. "Rebels?"

She shrugged. "I guess. They wanted it." But then, they wanted her underwear in her suitcases too.

"You are to be commended for keeping this from them." He stared intently down at the gold cuff, making pleased noises.

"Dr. Nagada thought those were royal Thai markings and from the big painting in the lobby, I'd have to agree. But isn't that Cambodian?" She pointed to the first marks near the closure.

He stilled for a moment. "I will make certain, be assured."

A servant entered the room bearing a tray of miang kum, and a bowl of steaming water and cloths to wash. She set it down on the table nearby, then left without a word. Dr. Wan Gai slipped the bracelet into a velvet bag, then into his pocket.

"Sit and rest yourself, my car will take you to the Regent."

She opened her mouth to protest. The Four Seasons?

He smiled patiently. "Salih insisted, and I do as well. It is the least we can do for saving such a prize. Order whatever you need." His gaze fell briefly to her clothing. "The museum will, of course, take care of the bill."

He stood, and exited the room. Viva watched him go, bewildered. The hotel was two hundred US dollars a night. But she wasn't going to balk. Her body and heart felt abused and all she really wanted was a bath and to sleep.

Viva washed her face and arms. Kneeling on the floor, she took a spinach leaf from the platter, pinched it to make a cup, then studied the samples, adding shredded dry coconut, red onion, diced lime, peanuts, dried shrimp, and a dollop of sweet sauce.

Behind his desk, a beautiful Chinese piece handcarved and embellished with gold leaf, was a TV. It was on a local station, and she found the remote and changed the channel to CNN. The reporter spoke in English, the Thai translation voicing over it. The camera panned the Kukule Ganga Dam, the destruction. My God. When did this happen? She focused on the dam, the people crawling over it like rock climbers. Viva moved closer to the screen, shoving a piece of miang into her mouth, then gasping at the spicy bite. Her gaze flicked over the camera shot, wishing they'd hold still, but the broadcast ended. She surfed the channels until she found it again, studying.

"That wasn't a pressure crack," she said to no one. She'd been working with the U.S. Geological Survey when that dam was constructed, mainly because there was a really hot-looking engineer on staff and she'd wanted him. He'd been a dud, in bed and out, reminding her looks weren't everything, but she'd learned enough from him to know how and where pressure cracks would start.

The door opened and she turned, food halfway to her mouth.

"My car awaits."

"Thank you so much, Dr. Wan Gai. Did you see this?" She gestured to the TV.

"The dam, yes, so tragic. All those innocent people."

"When did it happen?"

He looked confused for a second.

"I've been on the dig for a couple months and the only news I had was a radio." And her Thai translation skills weren't that fast.

He smiled like a patient parent. "A few days ago. In the middle of the night, I believe."

She nodded, frowning at the screen for another moment, then, after she washed her hands and sipped tea that was so sweet it'd give you diabetes, he led her out through the museum offices to the curb. Wan Gai's assistant, a tall man with a scar running down the side of his face, stood near the open car door.

The curator handed over a receipt for the bracelet for Dr. Nagada.

"Thank you. It's been a pleasure." She stuffed the receipt in her pocket before his assistant ushered her solicitously into his car.

Viva sat back in the leather seat, and let out a long, tired breath. Holy Grail delivered into safe hands, she thought. Now I can enjoy some me time in Bangkok before heading back to the dig. Her mind instantly went to Sam, and what he was really doing here that he needed British intelligence guys. Dangerous man stuff, she thought, and leaned toward the window, looking at the sky for the helicopter.

It was empty.

Tashfin Rohki sat in the luxurious room, feeding on grilled prawns and drinking strong Moroccan coffee. His favorite. It was placating. The generosity extended to the value of the stones and the people he represented. He procured weapons, handled finances and operations for the LTTE Tigers of Sri Lanka. A large portion of his organization's money was riding on this deal. And he'd been late to this meeting, stalling for time to find enough stones to compensate for the one the Irishman had stolen. It was his largest, and alone worth millions. How the Irishman had slipped it from the sack still confused him. He died for it, Rohki thought as he remembered the flood.

He tossed down a shrimp tail, wincing at the gust of pain from his broken ribs, then cleaned his fingers as he rose and walked around the room. It was all familiar now—and tiresome.

"Mr. Rohki," a voice said, and he turned sharply, his gaze shifting over the room, then centering on the speakers mounted near the ceiling. "Please be seated."

Rohki frowned as he obeyed. Theatrics, he thought, then a large screen on the wall blinked on.

For a moment, he couldn't see anything, then the silhouette of a shoulder told him there was someone in the shadows. "The stones are not as promised. You may leave, Mr. Rohki."

Rohki scowled at the screen. "You have what you demanded."

"You offered a large stone. One you failed to produce."

Rohki frowned at the man's concern. "It was lost in the flood." He'd spent days since gathering more to compensate for the loss.

The figure in the darkness went rock still. "You tried to sell it."

"They're mine to do with as I see fit. What do you care? You have the fee? Go back on your deal now and my people will spread the word."

A stretch of silence that was almost painful eased by. "You have met the requirements."

"And?"

"While you like to believe you are an intrinsic part, you are not. You wanted to bargain, you have opened the door," the man said succinctly. "Yours is not the only group that wants my product."

"Then I want proof of this weapon."

The man hesitated, then said, "In eight days"—the tone was ripe with arrogance—"the world will see its power. Now you may leave."

"A million in diamonds and I'm supposed to walk out with nothing?"

"You do not have a choice."

Rohki stiffened when he felt the cold barrel at the back of his neck. He turned slowly, his gaze rising from the Sig Sauer to the man holding it. Zidane. The man who'd brought him onto the jet. Bloodthirsty bastard.

Zidane flicked the gun and Rohki stood, wiped his mouth, and followed. Zidane stopped at the door and produced a hood, saying nothing. Rohki put it on. More theatrics, he thought. He heard the door open, and felt a push. He held rigid, testing the ground before him. He wouldn't be so shocked if he were being pushed out a window several stories up now that they had the stones. A ride in an elevator, they handed him into a car, the sound of engines telling him there were more participants. No one spoke and he was tired of this secrecy. The promise of a weapon beyond all weapons had a potential he wanted, yet each additional buyer bidding on it risked failure.

Eight days was a long time to wait for power over his enemies.

Zidane perspired in his dark suit, the concrete sweating against the cooler stone of the underground parking garage. He stood back as the hooded man was pushed into the car. The car pulled away.

"He has departed," he said into the mike poised at his cheek.

"Bring in the next."

Zidane signaled for the car, a smooth dance to keep the Pharaoh's identity secret. It had been ongoing for three days. The buyers were contacted via e-mail, then picked up at a remote location, hooded, then driven in the maze of Bangkok streets before coming here.

Only Zidane and two of his men knew each of the buyers by face. They were expendable, Zidane was not. The Pharaoh trusted few, and he did not take it lightly. The men, and sometimes women, who dealt with him were warned. Breaking his strict guidelines would have dire consequences.

Zidane exacted them. Clean up. He kept secrets, buried them deep.

Like Noor. His mind instantly filled with the dark, exotic beauty. Appearances were deceiving, he thought bitterly. While she was sleek and feminine, there was nothing womanly about her; no nurturing spirit, no need for anyone, except the Pharaoh. The man used her to his utmost advantage, knowing that she was nearly obsessed with pleasing him. A father figure, perhaps—Zidane did not know or care.

Zidane shook himself, his unspoken attraction for her disturbing. She was a strange creature and considered sex a weapon of manipulation, torture, to be used to her advantage. Or misused. She had no concept that men would be grateful to find pleasure with her. To Noor, it was punishment, degrading to them. In that, she lost and didn't know it. A weakness she hated and punished herself.

Two men helped the buyer out of the car. The man adjusted the sleeves of his jacket and tried for dignity. Blinded by the hood, it was impossible. Zidane grasped his arm, ushering him into the lift. He knew who stood beside him, the tattoos across his knuckles a calling card. Law enforcement of the free world would like to see this man tortured for his crimes. Yet Zidane would keep this, another secret, and escorted the man into the suite, a controlled environment where the Pharaoh had every advantage.

Above stairs, he pushed the candidate into a chair. As instructed, the man felt for, then removed the large pouch from inside his coat, and set it on the table. Zidane opened it, spilling the contents into a velvet-covered platter. The uncut stones looked like misshapen ice cubes. Worth more than a million. The fee to enter the bidding. He picked up one, and with a jeweler's loupe, inspected it, then he lifted his gaze to the cameras and nodded once.

Zidane took a position behind the buyer, removed the hood, then retreated into the shadows. He mulled over the thousands of secrets entrusted to him, the names and faces, the value of the stones. Should he betray the trust, he would die.

He almost wished Noor would do it.

Outside the museum, Dr. Wan Gai fingered the small gold cuff in his pocket, his gaze on the black car moving down Na Phrathat Road—and the woman inside it.

His personal assistant moved to his right, close but not crowding.

"See that she vanishes."

Behind him, the man stiffened, the only sign he'd heard correctly.

"She will sleep for several hours." He had seen to it, and the waking would not be pleasant. "Delegate, Choan. Let someone else take care of her." Wan Gai spun and walked back into the museum, his heels clicking.

With the bracelet in his possession, his king would never know his crown was threatened.

Six

Ramesh Narabi covered his face and waited inside the small room of the hangar. He breathed slowly, the air dank, a searing heat rolling off the walls and coating his already wet skin. Aside a table and the chair beneath him, there was a single bottle of water left for his comfort. He'd emptied it hours ago. He'd been here since the plane landed, since he was stolen away from Sri Lanka. How long ago, he did not know. Time was meaningless.

He leaned back, no less uncomfortable, the marks from the irons still fresh on his wrists, and sore. His throat still burned where they'd injected him with something. He'd remained unconscious through the flight and long after, yet he still could not understand why they kidnapped *him*. He had no money to pay a ransom, had no friends in the government. Blindfolded and bound till they left him in here. He'd no idea where he was nor what country. No one had uttered a word. The secrecy spoke of terrorists, the evil plague on all mankind. He wanted no part of it, had remained obstinate to the talk and violence. Now, he had no choice.

His treatment already spoke of cruelty. If he refused them, they'd surely kill him.

He stood and moved around the small confines, his chest laboring with fear, for breath, and he struggled for strength. His protection would arrive soon to take him on the next leg of this horrible journey. He knew because beside the water bottle was a slip of paper saying just that. The unknown terrified him. Who were these people? What did they want with him? What would they force him to do for their cause?

He heard a key in the lock, the rattle of the door, and he stepped into the corner, ashamed of his fear. *Vishnu, help me.*

The door swung open slowly. Silhouetted in the frame was a woman, slender, a black shape against the afternoon light.

"Come." She held out his work case. "Now," she added when he did not move.

Ramesh hurried around the table and took the case from her. Swiftly, she moved behind him and the skin of his spine squeezed down on his bones. She made no sound, not even breathing. For a brief moment, Ramesh glimpsed her face and he inhaled with shock. She was the most beautiful woman he'd ever seen.

With deadly black eyes.

Her lips hinted at a smile laced with pity and an anticipation so odd, the sight of it horrified Ramesh. Then she blindfolded him.

Viva woke with a splitting headache despite the air-conditioning, a long, luxurious bath, and the best meal she'd had in weeks. She rolled over and looked up at the silk-draped ceiling, the rich Thai silk falling to the floor in soft puddles. The scent of fresh frangipani floated on the air, the silken feel of sheets sexy against her bare skin and making her think of Sam. What was he doing in Thailand, exactly? She didn't consider looking for him. Aside that she didn't have a clue where to start, he didn't want her in his very dangerous business. It was time to get busy on her own, and that screamed *girl clothes*.

She glanced out the window, disappointed to see that dawn was just breaking.

Waiting for anything wasn't one of her best qualities.

She threw off the silk covers and swung her legs over the side of the bed. Her head throbbed and her stomach rolled, violent and sudden. This would just top off the last two days. She bent, waiting for the nausea to pass. It didn't and she bolted for the bathroom and emptied her stomach in one horrible, wrenching purge.

She staggered to the sink to wash and brush her teeth, then left the bathroom, latching onto a chair back till her head and stomach stopped fighting each other. Bad shrimp miang kum, she thought, though it couldn't get any fresher than the docks a few blocks away.

She prowled the suite, slipping on the hotel's monogrammed silk robe, her sore feet pampered on the plush carpet. They'd given her one of the private cabanas on the grounds, a single story with a little sunning balcony above. The little houses were tucked inside a manicured spot overlooking a lotus pond and a pool.

"Certainly better than the tent and cot," she said, pausing to order tea and toast before she turned on the news. She plopped on the sofa, watching for news in the US, yet only hearing repetitive broadcasts about the dam break. Shutting it off, she climbed the short curved stairs to the upper balcony.

The instant she stepped above, the sea breeze coated her, rippling the silk. The cabana was not far from the hotel's main building yet even from this vantage point, the city stretched out before her, a subdued palette of white and gray. In the morning mist, high-rise buildings and small shops were sandwiched together, yet the noise of the traffic was muted, the Royal Bangkok Sports Club still glowing with night lights in the lazy rising sun. Bangkok was a packed metropolis, everything you could ask for within reach, waiting to be explored. It was hard to believe that just a few miles away lay the dense, dangerous jungle.

Here there were no men with guns, no mafia stealing from the poor. No mutilated bodies.

No luggage either, she thought, thinking she needed to shop today. She started for the stairs when movement to her left caught her eye, and she strained to look. The clouds shifted, bathing the side gardens in light. She inhaled.

Sam. Alive and leaning against the white stone wall of the hotel, one ankle crossed, arms folded. Excitement swept through her. Her next thought was *get a load of those bare arms*, sculpted muscle twisting tight over long bones and big hands. His head down, she stared unobserved, her gaze moving over his legs in jeans, that snug navy polo shirt contoured to his chest. Even from here, she could see his snakeskin boots were polished.

Then, slowly, he tipped his head back and across the distance, met her gaze. Her heart slid straight up to her throat, snagging her breath, and she felt trapped, that incredible, spine-tingling sensation trotting over her skin. When was the last time a man made her feel so much without doing a thing? She didn't think about it. It would be examining a long trail of mistakes anyway.

But this man had saved her life. A redeeming quality, sure, but Sam was just too badass to the bone. He'd proven it yesterday.

What are you doing here? she mouthed.

Seeing you.

And he was, his gaze moving with the command of touch. Under the silk, her nipples tightened, and he arched a dark brow. He's too aware of his power, she thought, making a face, wrapping her robe tighter. It was useless. Her body wasn't listening.

His lips curved in a bone-rattling smile that drove heat straight down between her thighs, gave her that tight pull low in her abdomen that she missed, and created all sorts of erotic images in her mind. Most of them of what he looked like naked, aroused and sliding over her. But whatever he was doing here was dangerous. *He* was dangerous, and her practical side spouted a dozen reasons to stay clear of him. None of them had to do with guns and diamonds, and all with wanting the feel of his hard body covering hers, that exquisite moment of penetration, the slow, hot friction pulsing with the push of his hips.

Please don't come closer, she thought. It won't take much.

Sam felt his groin harden in the worst way. Publicly. He shifted, uncrossed his ankle, and shoved his hands into his pockets. Christ, was she telepathic? Yet he didn't move, that sly look of hers turning him inside out in the space of a breath, making him vividly aware of his weakness for redheads. Especially that one, up there looking like a wet dream in ripe, round curves and the hot slide of sex.

Even if she'd screwed up his plans and was an accident waiting to happen, he wanted her. He had a hard time breathing around her, just looking into her eyes stole everything from him, including the logic that said he should leave right now. Yet he couldn't turn away, rooted to the wall and staring up at her.

The wind molded the robe to her body, the shiny silk thin and enveloping her down to the vee between her thighs, the lush shape of her breasts. It moved her hair, layers tossing that "just rolled out of bed" look women paid a fortune to achieve—deep red and just past her jaw. And those eyes—smoky green and so damn revealing.

She plowed her hand into her hair and gripped the back of her neck as if trying to keep her hands still. If she called him up there, he'd pole vault to the balcony. But she didn't.

Definitely trouble, he thought, and sex with her was just a fantasy he struggled to bury. Any more than just looking, and he'd put her in danger. There'd be no getting around it. Viva had already proven she was a woman who didn't take bullshit from anyone. Even if it threatened her life.

Sam let out a breath, acknowledged the forbidden fruit dangling in front of his face, and did the only thing he could. He touched the edge of his hat in salute and melted into the shadows.

* * *

When he turned away, Viva couldn't help herself. She rushed down the stairs to the front door and threw it open. She found a room service attendant with a tray. Her shoulders fell, and she gestured the young man inside. She stepped onto the patio, looked around, but saw only the sway of flowers in the sunlight. Behind her, the young man had already set the tray down, and poured. She went to tip him, but he refused, never once looking her in the eye, and quickly left, closing the door.

Viva sat at the table, disappointed as she ate a wedge of buttered toast. She frowned at the aftertaste, washed it down with tea and stood, then instantly latched onto the table edge as her balance vanished.

This is not going to be a good day, she thought, grabbing furniture on her way back to the bed. She found Mecca when she made it to the mattress, falling facedown.

And never once noticed the man with the camera outside her room.

"He sleeps."

The large leather chair swiveled as he faced her. She walked gracefully toward him, her short skirt tight, a perfect portrait to show off her muscled legs. Her gaze flicked around the large rooms for anyone lurking, though she'd checked the instant she crossed the threshold. Noor didn't like company.

"Well fed?"

She nodded, the waterfall of black hair spilling over one shoulder. "He does not know where he is, the time, and has seen no one but me."

He waved off any caution she might have. "He will not be alive that long to point a finger, my sweet."

Her expression remained unchanged as he studied her, admiring her beauty, the lethal edge of it. He couldn't see them, but knew she was armed with her favored knives. He never asked why she preferred them; she had to get close to her victims to use them, yet this little flower had weapons no man could see.

"Tell me."

In a dispassionate voice, she relayed her activities in the jungle, from eliminating a traitor to ensconcing his guest.

"Nicely done."

She perched herself on the edge, crossed her legs, and plucked a chocolate from a small tray. She savored it slowly, licking the edge, digging her tongue into the soft center, and he felt himself grow hard just watching her.

"I have seen a stone."

She would not mention it if it was not substantial and he sat up a little straighter. "Go on."

She popped the chocolate in her mouth. "A man possesses it. He offered it to Najho. To buy in."

And she killed Najho for speaking of it. "Did he know why? What for?"

She shook her head, holding her hair back to examine the tray again. "In that, your secrets are well kept."

"Who is this man?"

Her shoulders moved. "From his accent, an American."

"Noor," he warned and she looked up, her stare brittle and cold. It reminded him how much she loathed men and that her association with him—he would never call it a friendship—was a privilege.

"I can find him, but that will take weeks." She tipped her head, no smile, no inclination of her thoughts, yet a glitter of anticipation sparkled her eyes. "There is a simpler way."

He smiled to himself, fatherly proud of her sharp mind. "And that would be?"

"I have seen his weakness."

He sent her an arched look.

"A woman."

"Find her."

She hopped off the desk, walking smoothly to the doors.

"Don't bring her to me."

She glanced over her shoulder, awaiting his command.

"Just locate her, watch her."

With only the lightest dip of her head, Noor slipped out of the room. She would follow his orders with precision. Unlike the men in his employ. Zidane lost the stone in Sri Lanka and while he accepted his own part in that, it would not have happened if Rohki had not dared bargain with smugglers for quick cash. He steepled his fingers, and considered how to use this woman.

His smile was slow and he tapped the keyboard. A view of the lab, a man hovering over a worktable came into view. A vast array of calibration machines and electronics were spread out in front of him. He touched the microphone. "Mr. Brandau?"

The man flinched and looked around, yet he knew Brandau saw nothing. "Yes?"

"How is your progress?"

"Almost there. But until I have the rest, I can't make this work. Not at the capacity you want."

Noor would find what he needed, he was sure of it. "I understand. In the meantime, I have an extra job for you."

Brandau looked directly at the camera, skeptical. "Does it pay well?"

"Will a million be sufficient?"

"What do you want me to do?"

Sam let his eyes adjust to the subdued interior. Streams of sunlight through bleary windows cast shadows and showed the age of the place. Behind a scarred counter, wood shelves filed like old soldiers, their posture bent and twisted, yet honor-bound to hold the contents. At first glance, it was littered with junk, but as he took a step closer, he noticed the dust and cobwebs hid the true value of each piece. Sam fingered a glass sculpture, art deco, circa 1920 US, he decided. How the hell did this guy get this kind of stuff?

He dropped his pack on the floor near the door and hit the bell sitting on the counter. It wasn't long before a slender man hurried down the center corridor, smiling his best. Then he saw Sam and froze.

"You don't look happy to see me, Niran, I'm hurt."

Niran did an about-face and headed to the rear door. Sam didn't move, sighing, and when Niran flung open the door, Sebastian was on the other side, big and imposing over the little man. Grinning, Sebastian walked, forcing Niran to back step.

Niran turned to face Sam. "Is he a new guy?" He inclined his head to Sebastian.

"We save him for special jobs."

Niran snickered, stopping at the counter. "I'm not talking to you."

Sam went to a shelf and drew down a clay pot, the markings similar to the cuff Viva had. "Maybe I can change your mind."

"Careful with that! You break, you buy."

"What's selling this week, Niran?"

"What are you buying? You need a motorbike? I have four in the back. Maybe a car, this I can find."

"Not what I want to hear."

The little man kept quiet.

Sam let the pot drop, and Niran lurched, but Sam caught the vase before it hit the dirt floor.

"They come to me, but I no can help." He rushed to replace the pot on the shelf.

Sam sent Niran a disgusted look. "That pigeon English is degrading, stop it."

Niran was raised in a British mission, his English was better than Sam's and his accent was more Brit than Thai. This poor, uneducated act was for his customers, yet the shrewdness of his bartering skills, among others, was in demand in the underworld. And he freelanced to anyone for a price.

Sebastian strolled the shop, examining the shelves. It made Niran nervous.

"They're buying diamonds," he blurted. "A Chechen was here, and before you ask, I don't have any roughs. That's like strapping explosives to your chest, all it will do is get you and everyone else around you killed."

"Clever. But you've bought conflict diamonds before." Niran was once a jeweler, and this place, he thought, was a big step down.

"Now they are buying them from me, and no one wants them cut. Not by me."

Sam's gaze flashed to Sebastian's. That was odd. Uncut stones were extremely difficult to move. Like a red flag that they were blood diamonds. "Names."

"They don't offer names, but they did buy some handguns, not my best stock, the cheap bastards."

Because they weren't planning on taking them home, Sam thought. "What else, little buddy?"

"That's enough without bargaining."

"What do you need this time?"

"Fly a plane for me."

Sam scoffed. "With what you transport, I'd get shot out of the air." Not that he'd consider it.

"Bring my mother to England."

"You don't have a mother, you little shit."

"That isn't the point."

Sam glanced at Sebastian, and he moved up behind him. "You aren't dealing in the sale of people, are you? Tell me it ain't so." The look on Sam's face spoke volumes and Niran paled. "That will get you killed."

Niran gestured to his shop of contraband. "So would everything else."

"I meant by me." Sam moved closer. Niran backed up. "Cough it up, Niran, you owe me."

Sam knew he was playing on the last scraps of dignity the man possessed. Sam had saved his wretched life, pulling him out of a firefight with a Chinese Thai mafia gang a couple years ago in Indonesia. They coerced the man into helping them find a diplomat's daughter, a child held for ransom for weeks. When it went down, Niran was caught in the middle.

Save the girl, save the snitch, and get hired *again* by the girl's father, Sam thought.

"They want big diamonds."

"Tell me something I don't know."

He leaned his forearms on the counter. "Will you make it worth my time?"

"No."

Niran sighed. "Tashfin Rohki came here looking for stones." He made a face over his dislike of the man. "He's been bargaining, stealing, trading for stones for two days. Then he just stopped."

He got what he wanted. "Where is he?" Why buy stones with cash, and not use the cash to buy weapons?

"Hiding, if he's smart. He looked for any stones, some cut, some not."

He's making up for the whopper D-1 had, Sam thought. Rohki needed that to buy in for the weapons, Sam was sure of it. But why deal in uncut blood diamonds? Any cutter worth his weight would turn them down and call the cops. The certification and authentication papers would have to be forgeries, the cutting done in secret. Damn hard way to go to get money.

"Who's got the weapons?"

"Look, cowboy, I don't know."

"You're really trying my patience, Niran, and you know I have little of it to start."

Niran shook his head. "You don't understand, *something* is for sale, weapons perhaps, maybe information." He shrugged. "No one speaks of it. Whoever has it wants only diamonds as payment."

Sam figured that much. "Any ideas why?"

"Who knows why they do things?" He made a crazy head motion at his temple. "But the identity of the seller is secret. I hear no one has seen this person, ever. A man spoke about it, and he was found in the river with his toes and nuts cut off the next day."

Sam's gaze shot to Sebastian's.

"Ahh, you know of this, the fight in the jungle over the redhead, perhaps?"

Sam tensed. Word traveled fast in the underworld. "It was over a robbery, not the woman."

"But revenge is such an ugly emotion, you know."

"The woman is innocent." Well, partly, Sam thought. "And the killing was by a dart."

"Ahh, see—a woman's weapon."

"A *Thai* woman's," Sam clarified. "And if anyone harms the redhead, I'll make sure they get some good-old American payback. Am I clear?"

Niran's features went slack. "Yes, perfectly."

Sam had seen her earlier this morning; he wasn't worried. Yet. His concern now was lack of information and the shield around getting more. Tempting the badasses to his door might be the only way to go. Dangerous, but doable. "I know you'll keep your mouth shut, right, Niran?" Sam went to his backpack.

"Or you will shut it for me, yes I know. You forget that I have seen what you can do to a person."

"Now would be a good time to practice that closed-mouth deal," Sebastian warned when Sam went still.

Sam closed his eyes for a moment, beating back the memory. He'd always been in the air offering cover fire, a pickup out of the hot zone. That time, he'd had to perfect his hand-to-hand combat skills in record time. Deadly force was a hard thing to swallow, and he preferred the thrills he could control.

He opened the backpack, pulling out a bundle, then tossed it to Niran. Niran caught it, frowning.

"I keep my promises," Sam said, almost in warning. He and Sebastian left.

Behind them Niran shook out the rolled cloth, smiling widely at the Dallas Cowboys jacket and hat. It was real, not a knockoff like the kind made around here by the thousands. Niran wasn't moved by many things, but that the Texan kept a promise made years ago, stunned him. He smoothed the embroidery and muttered, "This I will never sell."

* * *

Viva twisted on the sheets, her head pounding with pain as she dreamt. Yet the instant her eyes opened and she sat up, she felt different. Calmer.

"The finest hotel in Bangkok and I'm getting crummy sleep," she muttered, rolling off the bed and taking her time to stand. She'd never had a headache in her life and her brain felt swollen in her head.

She went into the bathroom, and after a moment, stepped under a hot shower, letting the steaming water rinse sleep from her body. Wrapped in a robe, her hair in a towel, she called the hotel clothing store and spoke to a pleasant woman. She told her the dilemma, that her luggage was lost and she needed something to wear. Giving her panty size to a stranger felt weird, yet by the time she dried her hair, there was a bellboy at her door bearing several boxes. She tried to sign for them, but he told her it was taken care of.

"Thank you, Dr. Wan Gai," she said, pulling out the khaki shirt and sleeveless blouse, then lingerie. She opened the last box. "Oh, she's a goddess. Makeup!"

She was out the door in fifteen minutes, hailing a cab, and walking in the heart of the river markets. The sun warm on her hair and she felt better than she had in two days. Around her shopkeepers hawked, throngs of people moved furiously through the narrow corridors. The scent of food made her mouth water and she stopped in a café, and ate lightly, yet was halfway through her meal when her head started hurting. She worried that it was something more serious than a simple headache, yet when she left the café it lessened.

Blowing it off as leftover food poisoning she walked to an internet access café, searching for anything on the bracelet. There was a vague mention of some legend in the north, but nothing conclusive. But the smelting of gold and bronze in the casting of the bracelet meant it was old. BC old. She left, pausing to chat and practice her Thai. Women paddling low-slung canoes filled with fruit passed on her right in the river, the concrete edge close to the walkway in front of the shops.

The sun felt scorching on her scalp and intent on buying a hat, she walked past several vendors, her gaze on her feet as if mesmerized by the tempo.

Then a sound jolted her, a loud crash of steel to steel. She stopped, looking up, and was stunned to see she was at the docks, alone. Her head whipped back and forth, her pulse suddenly rapid and short. *What in God's name am I doing here?* She didn't remember walking this far from the markets.

A forklift rolled by her, the man driving giving her a toothless smile as he drove past. She spun around and saw men everywhere, some rolling rope or operating machinery. A huge cargo ship was forty feet away.

And I didn't hear it?

Someone shouted and she backed up when a large platform laden with boxes swung from the side of the ship and started to lower. Instantly she turned back toward the city, and when several men started to follow her, Viva ran, her sandals slapping the asphalt and drowning their laughter. It was two blocks before the crowds thickened, and she slowed, moving between the people, checking to see if longshoremen were following her. No one was near, no one stared at her or did anything weird, but she still felt watched.

"How stupid can you get," she said to no one. She was reckless, she knew that, but not without *some* intention. This was just plain absentminded professor lunacy, and her heart was still pounding in her throat when she hailed a cab and went back to the hotel.

Leaving her shopping bags at the door, Viva dropped onto the sofa. She turned on the TV simply for comfort noise. A moment later, she got up and locked herself inside.

Sam and Sebastian left Niran's shop, walking the next two blocks toward the car and Max.

"Max, I need a visual on Viva."

Max's voice was soft in his ear mike. "You're really snagged by that woman, huh?"

He had no idea. "Niran mentioned her."

"Damn. I saw her down at the river market. She was shopping, chatting with the locals."

"Alone?"

"As far as I could tell, yes. Last I saw she was in a cab."

"Want to bring her in, lock her up at the CP?"

The command post was a house in the hills outside the city, a great spot for snagging intel out of the air. "Christ, that's not a fight I want to deal with right now."

Max slid the SUV to the curb and they crossed and got in. "What do you want to do about her?" He pulled into traffic.

A marker would have made him feel better, Sam thought. "She's in the best hotel, high security, hopefully she won't get into any trouble."

"Yeah, right," Max said dryly. "That works."

"Go by the hotel, I want to see for myself."

He kept his distance, yet his marks in his line of vision. When the marks stopped, he stopped, offering bhat for a soda, then kept going. He could pass them, and come up behind, he thought, until the pair slipped into a black SUV. He hailed a cab, the small green bug cramped and smelling like old shoes. He ignored the confused look of the driver as he directed him.

The SUV stopped at the Four Seasons cabana, and the man looked in the window before leaving. They ended up at a small restaurant. The men went inside.

"Pull over." He paid the cabbie and left.

In a low voice, he gave the address. Within five minutes another man moved behind the SUV, then crossed the avenue to wait outside the restaurant. His partner didn't glance his way, simply rubbing his nose in signal. The sun was dropping in the sky as he turned away, back to the offices to upload the pictures from his camera phone.

The pair weren't on the list, but they'd been in the same circles.

He needed to know why.

Seven

Sam had company.

It wasn't hard to notice. Anglos in Thailand sorta stood out. Who sent them was another matter. He'd noticed the man outside the restaurant this afternoon, then picked him up again when he was near the Four Seasons. Keeping tabs on Viva wasn't a job he needed right now, but he couldn't trust it to anyone except his teammates, and they were all occupied and short-handed this week.

This tail was a new one, and the man passed him, entering an apartment building. Another was back a block and turning in the opposite direction. Tag teams, he thought.

"Drac, you catch that guy?"

"Yeah." Max's voice rolled softly in his ear mike. "What do you want to do about it?"

Max was somewhere outside a bar up the street ahead, Sebastian nearby to the south. Sam didn't look. Fontenot had the skill to blend in with the locals, something Sam never tried to achieve. You could lie only so far and a slip-up would get you killed.

"Maintain, and let's see how far they take it."

"Roger that."

Sam stayed where he was, his shoulder on the stone wall, watching the human traffic slip past, stall, then move again. There were men off oil rigs for the first time in months, construction workers for the high-rises springing up all over the city. Locals were heading home as the sun set, to safety. This wasn't a bad section of Bangkok in the day, but at night, the potential for trouble floated on the salty air. He spotted more than a few ill-concealed weapons. A few yards away, the river moved slowly, small boats with lanterns flickered dim light on the water. In one, an old woman slowly paddled with the current, a child riding behind her and looking more alert than a cop.

He glanced at his watch, then pushed away from the wall, moving through the congestion of bodies, pausing to let people pass. The heat was only slightly less than at high noon, his overly long hair heavy and concealing the ear mike. This week he was a weapons smuggler in need of a plane. Some cash laid out and whispered words to some pretty degenerate types and his presence was noted, avoided. The locals eyed him covertly, then moved on. A few stared openly and he saw debate in their eyes, questions.

He wanted the badasses to come to him. While the team thought flashing the diamond around would bring some action, Sam wasn't risking Thai officials or Interpol snatching him, and then having to explain his ass out of prison for possession of an uncut diamond. He didn't have the time for roadblocks. There were enough around him already.

He slowed his steps. "Drac, ahead, half a click." Three men left a high-rise and got in a large town car.

In his ear mike he heard, "Getting pictures. Looks familiar. Chechen we met in Spain?"

"Jesus, I hope not." Those guys were brutal sadists and the cells of Islamabad were just too many to track. But if Niran was right, and the money handlers were in town, this problem just went global. "Send it to Logan." Max used a telephoto camera linked to a satellite phone to Logan. "This is the second Most Wanted in two days." Where the hell was Interpol in this?

"Everyone wants in the party."

But according to Half Ear, Riley's diamond wasn't enough.

"I'm getting that really bad feeling," Sam said.

"You're thinking big guns," Sebastian said. "I'm moving west. Nukes? Ballistics?"

"Christ. How do they get these things?" But he knew: blackmail, torture, kidnapping, and enough money could sway even the most honest of men. If he could find the jet maybe they'd get some names, fuel bills, manifest, cargo. Sam could read a jet-fuel invoice and know where the jet had been and its next destination. All he needed was one mistake to open a new door.

After a few minutes he heard through the ear mike, "Outlaw, be advised. You're a popular guy. Rabbit closing in fast."

"Roger that," he said and didn't look back, yet slid his hand inside his jacket.

"You look like shit, Outlaw," he heard, and Sam turned sharply.

Russell Dahl.

"I heard you were here somewhere." Sam lowered his hand from his weapon and eyed the man. Dahl had been in flight school with him. He'd washed out when he crashed a four-million-dollar fighter jet because he didn't listen to the flight leader. It was potential down the tubes, Sam thought. The man was a natural. He'd heard he was flying a Lear filled with wealthy businessmen from Bangkok to Kuala Lumpur, Singapore, anywhere there was jet fuel—and making money hand over fist.

Money meant something to Russ. It didn't to Sam. Hell, the guy was wearing Armani, for crissake, and sweating in it.

"What? No pleasantries? No, what have you been up to?"

"I know what you've been up to." Sam tsked softly. He had a dossier on Russ and he'd bet the CIA, MI6, and the Thai police did, too. Just not as thorough as Sam's. Logan could get information out of the dead, and there were a few bodies lingering around Russ.

"Good, keeps me from rehashing my sordid past. But you? You dropped off the face of the earth."

"Not really. Just off your part of it." Sam pulled a cigar out of his shirt pocket, bit the tip, and spit it aside before he stopped to light up. The cigar tasted smooth. He used the moment to look the way they'd come.

The man who'd tagged off the last guy was back, looking like a student with his backpack and scraggly hair. "Drac, you got a bead on him?"

"Negative, gimme a minute. Jesus, it's midnight, these people need to go to bed."

"Coonass?" Sam asked.

"I got your six, Outlaw. He's moving, your three o'clock. He's armed."

Russ frowned, then his features pulled tight when he realized Sam had comm gear he couldn't see. "You want to tell me what's up?"

"No." Sam handed him a cigar.

"Monte Cristos, man," he said, drawing it under his nose. "I can get these cheap if you want."

Contraband. "Don't tell me that, Dahl." Sam eyed him, then dragged. "I need to keep moving."

"Word is out enough about you."

"Easiest way to bring the nasty people close."

"You want confrontation?"

"I can only hope. Coonass, I'm going for the hippy," Sam said.

"Bang away, Outlaw. I got number two."

Sam clenched the cigar between his teeth and grinned. "It's a good night to beat the shit outta someone."

A chuckle came through the earpiece as Sam walked past the alley, and out of his peripheral vision spotted the man in the doorway. Jesus, he must be new at the job, he thought, too obvious. Sam motioned Russ to stay put, dropped the cigar, and walked into the building, drawing his pistol as he found his way to the side entrance. Sam looked down at the jamb, shaking his head at the shadows and light cast through the space between door and threshold.

He threw his shoulder into the door, breaking it open. On the other side, the watcher flew across the alley and into the brick wall. He groaned, whipped around, and scrambled for his comms.

Sam aimed and he went still. "Who are you and why are you riding my ass?"

No answer. Christ, he couldn't be older than twenty-five. "An answer would really help your situation."

"Fuck you."

Slight British accent, or Australian?

Sam slid back the glide. "You're not my type." Sam saw fear, a flare in his eyes, and moved closer. "Drac, got one." He searched him for weapons, pulled the gun apart, tossed aside the pieces, and kept the ammo.

"Got the other. No ID," Sebastian said.

"Who sent you after me?" CIA or Interpol, Sam considered. Which didn't tell him much. CIA wouldn't waste manpower on conflict diamonds. It was too big a problem to cap unless it directly involved the USA interests, and if he was offering a plane for his smuggled weapons, he should be talking now.

"I can beat it out of you, ya know. Right here, right now."

The man stiffened, his shoulders going back. Great. Stupid and brave. "I don't have time for this."

Sam holstered his weapon. The man made a break for the street, but Sam bolted, catching him by the shirt, yanking him back. He fought, and Sam hit. Two punches, the temple and solar plexus, and the kid staggered back. A roundhouse sweep, and Sam clipped him behind the knees. The man landed on the ground hard and didn't move.

"I'm done." At least he was out of his path.

"Number two down," Sebastian said in his ear.

"You guys get all the fun," Max put in. "What do you want to do with them?"

"Leave 'em." They weren't giving up anything, and he didn't have the time to interrogate. Sam left the alley and found Russ at the edge, smoking the cigar.

"You're a lot of help."

"You didn't need it," he said, exhaling a long drag. "CIA?" He inclined his head to the unconscious man.

"Who the hell knows? See ya."

"Something I can do for you, Wyatt?"

Sam eyed him, remembered his dossier, and said, "Not unless you can give me Tashfin Rohki." For some payback.

Russ's features went taut. Sam narrowed his gaze and Russ spilled it. "Tashfin Rohki, LTTE Tigers money man. Brawny, ugly, and rich. And yes, I know him."

"How well?"

"I flew him to Singapore." Russ scowled. "Don't look at me like that. It was before I knew who or what he was."

"Yeah, sure."

"I'm legit."

"In what hemisphere?"

Russ dug his hand in his trouser pocket. "Ya know, fly a known terrorist to Bali, then have the place blow up, killing hundreds, and I spend months in jail for it."

"Shouldn't you have?"

"Fuck no. Just because I wasn't F18 doesn't mean I'd betray my country. I did my years, paid them back for the flight education."

Though never enough. It cost over a million to train an F18 pilot, in Russ's case a bit more, since he ditched the jet over Miramar. But that didn't mean he didn't owe his homeland some loyalty. Sam had a feeling it was damn thin lately.

"I need the jet and where it landed. It came under radar."

"That took some doing, even in Thailand." Russ frowned. "You try the abandoned airstrips?"

"I must really look stupid to you, huh?" There were thousands of airstrips out of commission in the west after the tsunami. Slipping in through the area wouldn't be as closely guarded.

"Maybe I can help." Russ inclined his head and they walked, turning a corner and when Sam thought it would be another alley, it opened up to Nai Lert Park surrounded by high-rises in the business and diplomatic district. Streetlights lit the square, cars budging along toward the Hilton International Bangkok hotel.

Russ strode to the second building a good two blocks away and said nothing, then went inside. Sam grabbed his arm, halting him. "Fill me in."

"You find the jet and all it will get you is where it landed. You need to know who owned it, who paid the bill, and where Rohki is right now."

Sam doubted he could find him. Rohki didn't evade capture for the past ten years by being stupid. Russ entered the elevator and, with Sam beside him, he touched the tenth floor.

"I'm in the building, slow down," Max said into the comm link.

"What's here?" Sam asked Russ.

"Entertainment."

Sam's brows shot up.

"These women know everything."

Sam was game enough to try anything to get his hands on Rohki. He strolled into a wide foyer, the tile floor glossy. They passed a wide glass desk, a young woman sitting behind it clad in traditional Thai clothing, the waterfall of straight black hair contrasting the vivid pink.

"Hello, Russell."

Russ smiled. "She in?"

She glanced at something on the desk. "She'll be out in a few minutes."

Russ moved into the room, smiling, snatching a flute of champagne from a roving waiter. Two exotic-looking, black-haired women played chess, another curled on a sofa, reading a book. The place was a sea of brightly colored Thai silk, and no one had to tell Sam where he was; he could feel it, smell it.

The woman from the desk walked to him, her spike heels

clicking on the tile floor. "She's ready for you." She escorted them through a door marked NO ADMITTANCE, then down a hall lined with doors, she opened the last.

While Russ was grinning, Sam was watching the exits.

They entered a salon, empty except for the homey and very American style furnishings. A door on the far side opened, a woman wrapping her robe as she walked inside. She was beautiful, Sam thought. A delicate Thai flower. Yet mentally he compared her to Viva. No contest. Viva, hands down.

"Russell," she said in a throaty voice, tiny steps taking her to him. She kissed his cheek, smiled, then looked at Sam. Her gaze was direct and penetrating as she waited for an introduction.

"Mali owns this business."

"You're the cowboy."

Inwardly Sam swore.

"A man who kills a half dozen Thai mafia doesn't move quietly."

Russ looked at him. "Jesus fuck, you could have told me!"

"Slipped my mind."

The woman moved away from Russ, and sat in a chair, one leg beneath her. She leaned over a tray of canapés, selected one. Then gestured for them to join her. "Would you like some wine, or a beer perhaps?"

"No, thank you, what I want is Rohki."

"He landed a few days ago from Sri Lanka, on a jet with many others. Somewhere in the west." She waved a manicured hand. "He isn't staying in one place, which is his preference." She chewed, swallowed, then sipped a pink cocktail before she spoke. "He watches his money and his back carefully."

She wasn't telling him anything he didn't know. Tashfin Rohki might look like a small-time player, but he wasn't. He supplied half the mujahdeen with weapons, and diamonds were his currency. Logan was already searching for cutting equipment, new arrivals, transfers of old equipment, but Thailand was ruby and sapphire central, and a major area for the diamond cutting. Hell, the Jewelry Trade Center a few blocks away was fifty-nine floors of pure gem dealing.

"He is not the only one of his kind in my city."

"So far you're batting zero."

"There is a Russian gentleman, older, odd tastes. I turned him away. He leaves too many marks. He'd seek pleasure elsewhere, and not the willing woman."

Russian or Chechen, Sam wondered, there was a fine line between. He looked at Russ. "You brought me here for a who's who of bordellos?"

"The jet, Mali." Russ's gaze warned her.

Sam saw something pass between them. He almost missed the subtle exchange and a thought occurred to him. They'd need a skilled pilot to land on a crumbling airstrip. "You flew the jet."

Russ's gaze snapped to Sam. "Like hell."

Sam was across the room, slammed him against the wall, his forearm across his throat. "Try again."

"Back off, Wyatt. There are a thousand pilots around here who could land a jet in dirt, for crissake. You included."

Sam pressed harder. "But none of them knew to contact me."

"I didn't."

"Then how'd you know I was on that street tonight? Bangkok is a very big city."

Mali was there, not touching them, but her voice pleading. "Don't hurt him, please."

"Those were *your* people in the alley."

"I had to make sure you weren't tailed."

"What are you into, Dahl?"

"Transportation."

"Please let him go." Mali touched his arm.

Only Sam's gaze shifted. Mali retreated quickly.

Russell choked, clawed at his throat. Sam disarmed him, making a face at the small handgun. "Rohki."

"He was in the Baiyoke Tower, the Viengtai, and the Pan Pacific. In that order."

"Now?"

"I don't know, dammit, I'll tell you what you want."

Sam didn't move.

"Rohki hired me to fly him out of here in a week."

Sam thrust back. Russ rubbed his throat. "Tell me about the jet you brought him in on."

"I'm not sure he was on it. I was hired to fly in, fly out. I sat on the flight deck till right after the flood."

"You were in the cockpit, Dahl."

"Yeah, with the pit door locked from the outside, and they brought the passengers up from the right rear, out of my line of vision. They made me leave before they unloaded. These guys are slick, Sam. They cover all the bases."

"Where?"

"West, Ratchaburi. It's not an airstrip, just a field with a couple buildings under the trees. It's converted to a hangar, looks like a warehouse though. There isn't even a road anymore, you can't drive on it without an ATV."

Sam pulled out his cell to dial Logan for a search.

"You won't find it in computers, it's the dark ages. No paperwork. No traces. All in cash right then, and whoever pays the bills isn't visible. Ever."

They had to buy fuel, Sam thought, and write a flight plan from Sri Lanka. "Who paid you?"

"An envelope slipped under the cabin door when I landed here. And I was contacted at my shack by an encrypted phone delivered to me, then taken back before they locked me in the cockpit. I saw only the hangar. No people."

"Christ." Getting the number wouldn't matter, encrypted wires jumped through no less than a half dozen links before they hit the origin. "So what was your price, Dahl?"

"Half a mill."

"Your honor comes cheap," Sam said.

Russ took a step, but Mali pulled him down to the sofa, glaring at Sam. "Leave. It's bad enough you're here. Men come here for confidence and pleasure, not to be beaten."

"I haven't even started."

"Tell him what you know," Russ said tiredly, rubbing his throat, then downing her cocktail.

She touched Russ's face and nodded. "Rohki complained to my girls about delivering a fee and having nothing in return."

"Go on."

She shrugged. Russ pressed, grabbing her wrist. "Tell him!"

"Let her go," Sam ordered. Though when he did, she smiled at Russ, pleasure in the look. Takes all kinds, he thought.

"Rohki did not mention what he was buying, only that it was like no other out there. But his bed partner said he was almost afraid to have it."

What would scare a hard-ass like Rohki? Sam headed to the door.

"I'm sticking around here."

"I wasn't inviting you along."

Dahl scowled at him. "You got what you needed."

Sam slung a glance over his shoulder. "Yeah, and found a traitor."

Dahl's features pulled taut. "It's just money."

"And the people they kill, it's just their lives, right?"

He paled.

"You betrayed your country, the Corps, and worse, the men and women who are fighting these terrorists. Turn you in?" He scoffed. "I'll let America's best come after you."

Alarm lit across Russ's expression before Sam stepped out, closing the door behind.

Max and Sebastian heard the entire conversation and when Sam left the building, they gave him a wide berth. He walked in long strides, eating up the pavement for a block. Then he stopped, inhaled a lungful, and let it out. "The airstrip is in the West, Ratchaburi."

"I'll get a location. Sorry about Dahl."

"He isn't getting away easy. We clue in CIA first chance."

"Roger that."

He glanced back at the building, disgusted, then looked to

the sky. His gaze moved over the shops seated at the base of the high-rise, a sudden movement snapping his attention to the low roofline. Sam frowned, a chill running down his spine.

A rifle barrel?

Sam ducked into the alcove of a doorway and hit the walkie-talkie on the cell. "Be advised, we have a shooter on the roof." He gave the address. "Coonass, get west of my position."

The rifle barrel moved, sliding for aim.

Then it fired.

The wall of glass shattered inches from his head and Sam bolted toward the building, then down the alley, looking for a way up. *Shoot at me, God dammit.* He circumvented the rear, and found a fire escape ladder attached to the wall. He climbed. Who did Dahl tell about the meeting? Why shoot at him? At this hour, who were they aiming for? He flung his leg over the rim of the building, vaulting onto the surface, then stepping lightly. The roof wasn't stable, beat to hell from typhoons, and he moved along the edge, closer to where he'd seen the shooter. The air-conditioning units blocked his view. Sam edged across the uneven rooftop and around it, drawing his weapon.

Someone knelt on one knee, and aimed down into the street. The figure was motionless, dressed in dark, loose clothing, a baseball cap covering his head, face wrapped in cloth from the throat up to his eyes. Ninja clothes, Sam thought bitterly.

He inched around, aiming. "Drop it."

The figure didn't move, didn't shift.

"Drop the weapon!" he shouted.

The man rippled, like black heat in the dark night.

"Hands up," he called. "Back away from the weapon!"

The figure moved to the edge of the roof.

"I wouldn't, pal. It's a long way down."

Sam moved closer and heard heavy breathing, and nothing else. Then the figure dove over the side of the building.

Jesus. Sam rushed to the edge. The man landed on an awning, slid down to the ground, and hit hard. He rolled to his feet and took off.

"Drac, he's coming your way."

"I see him. I'm on it."

Sam slung the rifle and hurried to the ground.

Stones cut into her feet, the road burning her soles. She didn't stop, not to breathe, not to think, driven to advance. She heard the rapid footsteps behind her and ran down the block, then darted right, and ran through the wet, narrow alley. She was over the chain fence and running for freedom, a little smile curving her lips. She heard the shouts, the vehicle, and saw a stone wall in front of her. She expected it and leaped, climbing to the edge, and reached for the thick, gnarled branch overhanging the wall. She held still, hidden in the dark confines, cloaked and melting into the shadows as she watched the man hunt. He gripped the rifle, his speed and agility intriguing. She knew the moment when he gave up and she unfolded from her perch.

Colombo, Sri Lanka

Logan sifted through the newspaper, his laptop beside him. He waited for Max to send him more intel. Watching Riley sleep wasn't helping anyone and for the first time since he was board certified, Logan felt useless. On the other side of the glass wall, Riley was motionless, his condition unchanged.

His wounds were healing, yet he was still in a coma. Beside the bed, a young nurse sat reading Chaucer to him. Logan had worked in the hospital with patients until the Sri Lankan government stepped in. Legal issues, they said. A waste of manpower, he thought.

The laptop pinged. He folded the paper, and drew it to his lap. A photo message appeared, text beneath it.

Who's crashing the party? it read.

Logan clipped the photo, and dropped it into his data file, then started a match search. It would take a minute, the world had a lot of bad guys to choose from. The newspaper slid from the chair beside him and he picked it up, folding it roughly. He watched the computer glide through pictures, matching facial structure, and while it worked, he glanced to the right, a headline making him linger to read.

Dam break unexplained. He read a few lines. Thomas Rhodes, an American who was on the original construction, claimed the dam had not cracked from pressure, and was structurally sound. When asked why it broke, killing thousands, Rhodes could not yet offer an explanation. Dr. Risha Inan, Sri Lanka's top engineer, said her government would not allow the basin to be used and would route water supplies to nearby tributaries. That'll put a strain on the water supply in the areas, Logan thought, remembering the thousands of dead and dying they couldn't save.

The computer pinged with a match and Logan tipped the screen.

Immediately he sent a return text message. Sam needed to know the party crashers were big league. And deadly.

He closed the laptop, then looked up to see Killian and Alexa rushing toward him.

The rifle beat against his back as Sam followed the figure in black. Agile and fast, he barely made a sound as he ran, and Sam pushed harder, following the wet path around buildings. The man moved as if he'd practiced this run, avoided potholes and puddles, grabbed a low-slung fire escape, and vaulted over debris in the alleys. Sam lost sight of him for a block, then found the shooter rolling over the top of a chain fence. The fence rattled and the man dropped to the ground, landing on the balls of his feet, then bolted into the dark.

Sam used the trash cans like stairs and overtook the fence. When he landed, his gaze rocketed over the area. He was alone. "Be advised. I've lost visual at Prai Cho." Sam went left of the shooter's last direction, hoping to cut him off.

"We're coming up on the south end of there now."

"I'm north, but I've got the rifle and on the streets with this thing is going to get me arrested."

"Chinese brand of the day?"

"A Russian Dragunov SVD." Lightweight, accurate, with IR detection capability scope.

"Infrared scopes, geez," Max said. "Whoever had it, had a specific target."

"Yeah, me. Blew out the glass on the first floor near my head." He gave the street address, then picked up his pace.

"Shit. That's Thidan Graphic Systems," Max said. "It's a CIA station front."

Eight

A figure stepped into her path and Noor crouched, her knife ready. Recognition was instant and she relaxed, replacing the razor-thin blade in her sleeve.

Zidane eyed her from head to foot, then flicked a glance at the hotel in the distance.

"Do not spend your conscience with me, Jai."

She seldom called anyone by name. He supposed it made any meeting personal and Noor kept her distance from more than just people. She tried to move past him and he stepped in her path. Her gaze rose, locking with his.

"He will discard you as easily as me, or that woman." He inclined his head toward the hotel.

"She is his plaything."

"And you are not?"

Her eyes turned hot and angry. "*I choose.* I choose to do as I must or as I wish!" Her words bit softly.

"That includes fucking him?"

"Sex is meaningless to me."

Zidane neared, crowding her and knowing she didn't like it, but her pride kept her still, her small body locking with tension. He could smell it. "You let it be. You have risen above your past,"—he touched his fingertip to the knife in her hip belt, concealed as decoration—"Yet you keep it with you. Sex is not a weapon."

She cocked her head. "Do you want to fuck me, Jai? Come, find a spot." She reached for him.

He slapped her hand away, his face hot with frustration. "I do not want a woman who has nothing but her rage for comfort." He stepped back, disgusted, and finally, accepting her for what she was. A cold-blooded killer. At least he had a conscience. He left her.

Noor looked away, swallowing hard. Then she let out a long breath, before she headed back to her master.

Viva sat up sharply, her breath racing into her lungs so fast her chest ached. Her fingers dug into the sheets, panic flowing through her. A dream, it was a dream, she told herself, and looked around the room. The lights were still on, the doors closed. The air was almost too cold. She let out a long breath and gripped her head, the pain excruciating in the back of her skull. *This so sucks.*

Exhaustion beat at her body. She hadn't meant to sleep. Sleep was very unpleasant lately and just weird. Nothing made sense or order, and the more she probed, the more it hurt.

She looked at the clock, shocked to see that hours had passed since she returned from shopping. If she'd slept, why didn't she feel rested? Why did her head still hurt like a brigade was marching through her skull? She wasn't a stupid woman, dreams had a certain feeling, omniscient, like you knew they were dreams and let yourself be outrageous and far-fetched. She scoffed to herself. Hers were out of control. So this is what it feels like to be a space cadet, she thought, pushing off the bed and calling room service. Food would help. She hadn't eaten much in two days.

Her feet felt sore and she sat examining them and found cuts, then snapped a look at the sheets, and could see speckles of blood from there. Okay, okay, shopping, docks, sleep, bad food, sleep, bad dreams, nothing else. She sure as heck didn't remember turning her feet into hamburger.

Confusion twisted down to her soul, and a quick solution sent her off the chair to the mini fridge. She grabbed a small bottle of wine, broke the seal, and drank. It didn't help. She wanted to get tanked, pass out, forget everything for a while. She was reaching for more when a knock thundered through the little house. She whipped around, nearly dropping the bottle, then rushed to the door, peering through the peephole.

"This isn't a good time, Sam. Go away." She was just too messed up to deal with his sexy self right now.

On the other side, Sam scowled. "Open the door, Viva. We need to talk."

"Please, not now. Go away."

Something was wrong. "I can break it in, you know."

She sighed, threw the lock and flung open the door. Part of her was so glad to see him and she wanted to spill her guts. Another said, don't give the guy more headaches. "Why are you here?"

"I was in the neighborhood."

She stared, unamused.

"The wrong people know we were in the jungle and I killed Thai mafia." Sam frowned. She didn't seem concerned. "You're in danger because of me."

"No, it's because of my asinine behavior." The jungle felt so far away, and almost better than what she was experiencing now.

"They won't see it that way, though my contact was killed before you got into it with that gang."

Viva's forehead wrinkled as she thought about feeling followed, but she didn't trust her instincts, they were pretty much playing games with her lately. "I'll be a bit more cautious then."

"It's better if you left Thailand, and went home."

"There you go with those control issues again." She scoffed and waved him inside. "And there is no home." He moved in and she shut the door. "I have an apartment in New York that's sublet for another ten months and everything I own is in storage. Or still scattered on the side of the train tracks."

"Family?"

She hesitated. "Unavailable. I'll leave Bangkok." God

knew this was just getting too weird. "But I'll return to the dig."

"That might not be enough."

"You know what, Sam Wyatt, why don't you fill me in on what you're doing here and maybe we can pin the blame on you!" She dropped onto the sofa.

Sam scowled, noticing her hands wouldn't be still. Where was the woman who faced danger like it was a treat to be had? He knelt in front of her. "What's wrong? I can feel it." She looked incredibly pale and tired.

"I don't know." Her shoulders slumped. "I haven't slept well since I got here and when I do, it's just lousy. I got a little food poisoning from bad shrimp, I think. It hasn't been a good two days." Boy, was that putting it lightly. She didn't say anything about the dreams, the curtain thrown down over her mind. If she could just push it aside, she'd see what was really happening to her.

"You're not leaving the country?"

"Not this minute, no, but you're right." The farther away from Thailand, the better, she thought. "I'll contact Dr. Nagada, he'll understand, believe me." Didn't she fly from one project to another, one job to the next? Now she had inklings of being a schizophrenic? Bad career move.

She lifted her gaze to his. There was a hollowness there he hadn't seen before. "Promise me."

She crossed her heart and tried to smile. He looked so concerned right now, that scowl actually soothing to see. She flinched when the glass door rattled. Sam went to it, sliding it open.

Max stuck his head in. "Hi, Viva, glad you're okay," then frowned and added, "You look tired."

"That isn't a compliment, Max."

"Sorry." He shrugged, then looked at Sam. "Coonass has the rear. Everything okay?" He glanced at her again.

"Yes, it is," Viva said testily. Then her gaze fell on the rifle in his hand and she shot off the couch to ask what he was doing with that, but one word flying through her brain stopped her. *Dragunov*. In an instant, she knew how to load it, sight it in. Jesus, where was this stuff coming from?

"What's the matter, Red? You look like you've seen a ghost."

Her gaze flicked up and clashed with his. Sam's eyes narrowed. Her face was drawn and pasty, yet her eyes held almost a vicious glare.

"You need to leave."

"What?"

"Leave. I'm tired, you need to leave."

She was practically shoving him out, and Sam grabbed her arms, held her still. "What the hell is the matter with you?" He could feel it, an energy in her, her skin was hot, her eyes darting. As if she'd explode.

She wrenched out of his arms. "Go, please." If he stayed, this wouldn't end well.

Sam moved near. "Viva, you can trust me."

That hit a mark, a spot inside her heart that ached with confusion and uncertainty. She threw her arms around his neck and kissed him. Sam trapped her against him, feeling a strange desperation as her mouth savaged his, almost as if this kiss was their last touch.

A war raged inside her, heat and hunger and the desperate need to get far away from him. Fear, she realized, fear for him, and a blade of shock ripped through her when her fingers unconsciously closed over his knife. She jerked back. "Go, Sam, please."

Sam frowned at her for a moment, hearing the begging in her voice. He didn't want to leave her, not like this. He could feel the twist of emotions on the surface and wondered what had happened in the last couple days. Yet when she pushed, he stepped out. She shut the door and he heard the lock click, saw the lights blink off. Max came around the side and Sam looked at him.

"She just kicked me out."

"That's not like her."

"Something's wrong." Granted he didn't know her that

well, but that wasn't the woman who ran through the jungle with him.

"She didn't look so good."

It was more than that. For a moment there, Sam felt an uneasy chill from her.

Sam looked back at the door, deciding to check in on her tomorrow, and somehow get her safely out of Thailand.

Inside the room, Viva sank to the floor, tears flowing. What did I do? She wanted to take his knife, and the ugly thoughts she had—it hurt to have them. She swiped at tears, vaguely noticing an oily smell to her hands, then pushed off the floor, impatient for the room service. She went to the bathroom, splashed water on her face, washed her hands. She stared at her haggard reflection.

You're stronger than this. Smarter than this. Buck up. Figure it out.

She dried her face and pushed the towel into the hamper, her hand coming away slowly. She frowned, then flipped off the rattan lid and grabbed the black bundle. She shook it out. A tight-fitting shirt and pants, a long scarf. It wasn't hers. She sniffed them, a creepy feeling pouring over her when she smelled her own perfume. *But they're not mine.* She dropped them instantly, stepping back, looking around as if the room offered an excuse, a reason.

They *were* dreams. They had to be. Then she looked down at her feet, red and cut. It *felt* like a dream.

The knock startled her and she smothered a yelp. Hurriedly she stuffed the garments in the bottom of the hamper and let the waiter in. Again, he wouldn't look her in the eye nor let her tip him. She was closing the door after him when she saw someone beyond the trees and stepped out, scanning the wild gardens, movement in the palms and tall flowers. She started to investigate, but when she saw a waiter bustle by with a tray, she backed inside and sealed out the world.

Paranoia was new to her. Sam was right. It was time to leave the country. Packing would be easy, she thought, distracted as she brought the sandwich and tea to the sofa. She had one clean outfit. Her gaze on the blank TV, she ate without tasting, feeling her loneliness, her isolation. Sam's image popped in her mind and she knew he must think she was nuts. Well, more than he already did. She should have told him. He could fix this. She hated being saved, but today, she'd make an exception. She finished off the club sandwich and with her tea, pushed off the sofa. The room swayed. The cup slid from her hand, spilled, and rolled on the floor.

Viva's legs went numb and the sensation climbed rapidly up her body. Oh, damn, she thought, and never felt her legs give out beneath her.

MI6 Surveillance Post
Bangkok

Nigel Beecham tapped keys and the encrypted file began its deciphering program. He turned away, pouring another scotch. It would take a bit, he thought, and was in the middle of a sip when the door opened.

Abernathy rushed in. "I have pictures. Take a look." He handed them over.

Abernathy was an eager pup, full of the 007 of MI6, and hadn't fully realized that time and patience were the key to good intel. He'd swear he was American sometimes, the way he wanted to rush into things like a posse on the trail of a desperado. Patience would bring in more than one man. Killing off cells would only sprout new ones. It was a fight he was tired of making.

He sifted through the photos.

"Seen these guys before?"

Nigel recognized Sebastian, Niran's shop, and the other, Wyatt. "Can't say as I do." He handed them back. "Why tail them?"

"They were in Mali's place, seen with Dahl, and beat the stuffing out of a couple of Dahl's boys."

"So?"

"And my snitch says he's looking to buy into whatever weapon is up for sale. He's been in the same places as the Chechen's men. Need more?"

"Again I say, so? That leads nowhere; we must first learn why Brigaders are here." His pious tone irritated Abernathy.

"To buy weapons, dammit. It's what they do. Why are you giving me roadblocks, Beecham? Too tired to work for a living?" He gestured to the glass of scotch.

"I could drink a case and still be sharper than you, Abernathy. And what's the weapon? Home base hasn't given us specs, anything. We're chasing blind without more."

"Then I'll get more."

Beecham sat, sipped, and saluted with the glass. "Carry on, then."

Abernathy glared, then dropped in front of a computer. "I'll find out who they are."

"If you had a clean photo. A camera phone? With all the equipment we have." The office was amass with surveillance gear. His back to him, Abernathy's shoulders tensed. "You chat with Niran?" Nigel asked.

"He wasn't forthcoming. Not with anything we didn't already know."

I'm betting he was to Wyatt and Fontenot, Nigel thought, and decided to keep tabs on his old pal.

The sun had fallen hours before, blanketing the isolated airstrip in inky black. The buzz of flies and the odor of rotting trash cloyed the humid air, mixing with the exotic fragrance of flowers. Near the field that served as a flight deck, garbage cans were tipped over, debris spread over the ground and reeking in the heat.

It made the building look abandoned.

The armed guards said otherwise. That and the steel doors with hard locks and a five-inch thick bar.

Carefully, Sam moved up behind the guard and tapped him. The man turned. Sam slammed his fist down on his gun hand, and with the momentum of his body, drove three fingers into his throat, crushing his larynx. The man choked, the weapon tumbling from his grip. Instantly, Sam locked his arms around the guard's neck, pushing his head to the side and down. He pressed till he stopped struggling, then lowered him to the ground, and relieved him of a nice assortment of small weapons. He secured and gagged him.

"Clear," Sam said in barely a whisper.

His gaze swept the darkness, zeroing in on Sebastian as he knelt near the doors. Sebastian put up two fingers, then continued setting low percussion charges. A restaurateur now, the man made the best crawfish stew this side of the Mason-Dixon, and set a close-quarters detonation so precise you'd lift your fork and be blown to hell while your plate stayed right where it was. An art, Sam thought, moving past Sebastian to the rear of the building.

"Drac?"

"All clear in the west," Max replied.

Sam edged around the rear of the building, peered, then jerked back. "Be advised, Drac. A guard, your six."

Max was in the front near the hangar doors. "I can take him."

"Negative. Eye the west, I'm on it." Sam rolled around the edge, aiming his MP5. The guard dragged on a joint, inhaling and holding it. Sam approached, waiting till he blew it out. The guard turned, scrambled to aim. Sam threw, the small knife imbedding in his throat. He slowly crumbled to the ground, gurgling.

"Be advised, one ghosted." Sam pulled the body into the forest, then flattened to the wall.

"Charges set," Sebastian said.

"Blow it."

The sound was soft, like a hissing snake, then a quick, short pop. Sebastian ran to the door, catching the metal bar before it hit the ground, then pushed on the door. It was out of its frame and falling. Sam darted to help and they lowered it to the ground.

"All yours, buddy. We have twelve minutes till shift change." Sebastian set his counter, and backed up to guard the perimeter as Sam went inside.

He snapped on the light attached to his rifle and scanned the hangar. The jet was an old Gulfstream, circa fifteen years ago from the look of it. Sam ignored the jet for now and canvassed the perimeter of the hangar, stopping at a door and nudging it open. He shone his light at all four corners, then backed out and went to the desks in the far left. Lowering his rifle, he pulled out papers, old liquor bottles, and in the bottom drawer found film rolls. With digital cameras so cheap, and the ability to delete anything incriminating, why use film? He pocketed them, clicked on his penlight, and kept searching. He'd liked to have hacked into the files via computer, but it was impossible. Dahl hadn't lied, they weren't on any mainframe computer systems, not one they could hack into. It kept them out of the loop, smart, but slow. And that meant paperwork.

"Outlaw, anything?"

"No manifest, but fuel charges, flight out from here to Sri Lanka. Two days before the meet."

"Rohki was already in country then," Max said. "For weeks."

"Dahl didn't know for sure if he was on this jet. We know he was expected and probably not the only passenger."

Sam rifled, his penlight between his teeth and sliding over the papers as he read. Food? Bills for food and delivery, no address, only a trail of numbers and letters. Pocketing it, Sam searched for more, pulling everything out and laying it on the desk.

He found another fuel bill, dated for a flight three days from now. Quickly he calculated the pounds of fuel to the distance. It would get them all the way to the Middle East. Shit. They're making another run. Or was it for their escape?

"Drac, get in here, disable the jet."

Behind him, Max and Sebastian slid around the door frame. Max went to the jet, climbing inside. "This thing's an antique."

"Just make sure it doesn't lift off."

"Dahl's story checks out," Max said. "Locks on the cockpit door."

"He's still going down."

"I hear you."

Sebastian moved around the hangars, inspecting the only other room. "Someone's been held prisoner," Sebastian said. "There are ropes under the tables."

Sam turned, knocking papers to the floor. "Only ropes?"

"Yeah, and be advised," Sebastian said, "if these guys are duty bound, ten minutes to shift change."

"Guys," Max said cautiously. "You aren't going to believe what's in here."

Sam pressed the earpiece tighter and glanced over his shoulder. "Try me."

"Shackles."

Sam frowned and met Sebastian's gaze. "Come again?"

"Leg irons lining the walls of this thing. It's like a damn flying prison."

Sam signaled Sebastian to keep watch before he hurried to the jet. The smell hit him first, heavy and foul.

"Back here."

He overtook the seating area, then brushed back the curtain.

On one knee, Max held an iron brace and looked up. "And there's blood everywhere. Someone didn't make it out alive." He pointed to the rear.

Sandwiched into a spot where it didn't fit was a bare mattress heavily stained with blood. "Jesus, they cut their throat." The blood was black and congealed in the center top. His stomach clenched as his gaze moved down the interior of the aircraft. The irons were old, as if taken from Alcatraz, meant to be heavy and painful. Punishing.

"What kind of monsters need leg irons?" Sam asked. "You could knock someone out with drugs for hours and not hurt them."

"I'm thinking human trafficking."

"Slavery? Christ." His gaze moved over the mess again. It

was rank with the smell of feces and blood. They did this to break their spirits, he thought, then pulled out a small, round film case. "I bet they took pictures."

"I heard they approach the women with job offers, the kids they just steal."

From his position outside, Sebastian chimed in. "Beecham said it's the biggest crime here, worse than drugs."

"Search it, and put this thing out of commission—permanently."

"That won't stop them from getting another jet."

"At least this one won't be leaving the ground." And might delay any escape.

Checking his watch, Sam left the aircraft, returning to the desk, gathering anything viable, then picked up the fallen folders. He was going to return it all, but after seeing the jet, he didn't give a damn. Let them come for me, he thought, and tossed the last file on the desk. Papers slid out, and he turned back, frowning. Shining his light, he opened the file and fanned the sheets. Photos.

He flipped through them. They were shots of young women, and boys, school age. One was a little girl about twelve in a uniform, walking down a dirt road, swinging a book satchel. The faces were circled, several shots of the same person during their lives; shopping with family, talking with friends, leaving school and waving. Beautiful children, and young women. All marked for kidnapping. A sickness welled in him.

How many of them were already taken?

Sam gathered them, then searched the floor for the rest. He lifted a stack, his movements slowing as his eyesight tried to register with his brain.

"Oh, Jesus."

It was a picture of Viva standing at the loft of the cabana. At dawn. The morning he was there. Three days ago.

And her face was circled.

Viva heard muffled crying first, then felt the pain in her head. She struggled to open her eyes, move her fingers. Yet several moments passed without success. She forced herself to relax, to not panic, though her blood felt sluggish, her heartbeat slow and pounding in her ears.

Everything was wrong.

No smell of the sweet flowers that filled her room, no soft carpet beneath her. She'd fallen, that much she figured. The last thing she recalled was her legs feeling numb. She didn't know how much time had passed before she could open her eyes. The first thing she saw was the ceiling, a grid of thin metal, missing tiles, cracked or water stained.

Clearly, you're not in Kansas, Dorothy.

Her gaze flicked down to her body, and she was relieved to see she still wore the robe. How much of it was covering her, she didn't want to know. She couldn't feel the fabric on her skin. Viva turned her head, but her neck muscles were sluggish, trapping her in slow motion. She glimpsed a young girl crouched in the corner. She couldn't be more than ten years old, her clothing torn at the shoulder, her hair wild and half in a barrette.

She strained to see more, but even her eye balls hurt. From her position, flat on her back, she couldn't see anyone else, but she heard them. Feet shuffling, a cough, the scrape of chairs. The air was stifling hot.

Then she heard the rattle of chains.

"Unfriendlies, east side," Sebastian said, and it galvanized Sam. "Time to split."

Sam stuffed the photos inside his flak jacket, then swung his MP5 forward. "Drac, come on."

"I'm done, I'm out." Max darted across the hangar, shoving wires and components in his leg pockets.

Back to the wall, Sam was on the opposite side of the doorway from Sebastian.

"Left side, near the road," Sebastian said. "Green car."

"I can smell exhaust," Max said, then they heard car doors slam.

"To the right, then rear, and outta here."

Sebastian and Max nodded.

Sam peered, then pointed to his eyes, and held up four fingers. They'd go radio silent from here, their black ops clothing blending them with the darkness. Sam slipped around the edge of the doorway, and went right, darting into the trees, then turned back to cover his teammates. Sebastian moved past, Max coming up fast to his left.

The guards were visible, armed, and walking to the door blown off its hinges. They stopped short, some wild gestures, then a pair darted inside, the other scanning the area. One pointed to footprints, then they headed toward their positions.

"Time to fly." Sebastian touched Sam's shoulder. He backed up quickly, then turned, racing toward the truck. A few yards shy, he slid to one knee as Sebastian ran to his position, tapping his shoulder again as he passed to the van tucked in the forest.

Gunfire sliced through the trees, chunking into the ground. Sam didn't return fire; they were off the mark. "Max!"

"I'm on it," he said, threw open the side door and vaulted inside. Sam moved backward, the van's silhouette barely visible.

"Sam, get in!" Sebastian called.

"They're coming." He unloaded half a clip, heard the screams, then backed into the van. "Go, go!" He rode shotgun for a block, then slid the door closed, and sighed against the wall. "Head to the Four Seasons."

Max frowned into the rearview mirror. "You need to see her now? It's one in the morning." Max dragged a cloth over his face, wiping off the black face paint.

"Someone's after her." He pulled the photos out of his flak jacket and handed them to Sebastian.

He flipped through them, then lifted his gaze to Sam. "Oh, hell, your redhead."

Sam nodded, breaking down his gear to light and quick. He packed his pockets with ammo.

"And the others?"

"Max was right, human trafficking. Look at those girls,

they're babies, for crissake." The inside of the jet flashed in his mind, the gruesome cruelty of it.

Max reached a hand back and Sebastian put a picture in his palm. He glanced as he drove. "Why Viva? She hasn't been in Bangkok that long. Forty-eight hours maybe. How'd they find her?"

"Who knows? But we have to stop this." And he didn't have much time.

"I hate to be the bearer of lousy intel, but Beech said it's rare they ever find them after they're taken."

Sam took the picture back. "She isn't gone yet."

"We have a job to do," Sebastian reminded him.

"And we will," Sam snapped, and slapped papers he'd taken from the desk in Sebastian's hand. "They're not sticking around. They have fuel orders that will take that jet as far as Iran."

Viva came first.

Viva opened her eyes and saw a man standing near her feet. He wore a suit, his arms folded over his chest, but it was his eyes that had her, pawing over her body. She lowered her gaze. The robe was open. Humiliation swept through her, leaving a bad taste in her mouth. He inspected her, glanced to the side, then nodded and turned away. He said something to another and she turned her head. Money exchanged hands and then a small man came to her, covering her and kneeling.

"Help me," she croaked, her throat dry. "Please."

The man didn't look at her, didn't stop in his task. Her gaze lowered to his hands as he injected her with drugs. She didn't feel the needle, her skin without sensation, her body paralyzed. Tears blurred her vision and fell. Where's a high-powered rifle when you really need it, she thought, before she sank into oblivion.

Sam was out of the van before Max brought it to a stop, running to the doors facing the pond, and entered the bungalow. Only two lights were on, one in the bedroom, one over the entrance that led to the side yard toward the hotel.

He stilled when he saw the tray of tea and touched the pot. Cold. He moved to the bedroom, turned sharply when he heard noise. Sebastian and Max were inside. They didn't have to voice it. Sam knew. He was too late.

He went into the bathroom. The clothes she'd worn in the jungle were in a pile next to her boots. He picked up a belt, and frowned at the width of it and realized it was a money belt. Inside were her passport, US driver's license, and money; a considerable amount in bhat and American currency, some British pounds.

Max and Sebastian stepped into the bedroom. "She can afford a place like this?"

"I don't know. She has the cash and she's a world traveler. The woman's been in more countries than all of us combined." He handed Sebastian her passport while Max searched the drawers, the closets, and under the bed.

"She's got one set of clean clothes, some makeup, and a small flight bag, empty. There's nothing else here except that." He gestured to the waist belt.

Sam put everything back inside and stuffed it in his leg pocket. "Call the desk, see if she's checked out."

"Why would she with her cash here?"

Sam eyed him. "Cover all bases."

Max sighed and pulled out his cell and dialed. He put his finger in his ear, moved away as he spoke.

Sebastian walked back through the main room, then knelt. "There's blood."

"Shit." Sam rushed to him as Sebastian swiped his fingertips over the corner of the coffee table and held them up.

Sam stared at it for a moment, wondering if she'd just fallen and hurt herself. Perhaps someone came for the tray and found her, and she was in a hospital somewhere. But the blood was dark, hours old. And the tray was still there.

Sam went to the sofa and stood still, putting himself in her position, the plate left with just crumbs. She'd eaten and drank. He moved toward the blood as if replaying her steps.

"She didn't get that far, maybe three steps from the sofa." Sam touched the floor and felt the dampness of the tea stain.

Sebastian went to the carafe, removed the lid and sniffed. "It's the same scent as on the dart. Like cut grass."

Ya pit.

Sam sank onto the sofa, cradling his head, his fingers still wrapped around his gun. "She's been gone for at least twelve hours. Those pictures, the slavers were watching her while I was right here!"

"But why her? She hasn't been in town long and she said last night that she'd been feeling crummy," Max said.

And behaving very oddly, Sam thought. Did she know this was coming? "Hell, I found her easy enough." He lowered his hands. "Through the museum. She had to give over that gold bracelet." He'd caught the guard just after his shift and he'd remembered her. "The curator put her in a limo and sent her here."

Max came close, closing the phone. "That makes sense. The charges for this"—he gestured to the elegant suite—"are on the museum's tab."

Sebastian frowned. "All for bringing in a bracelet?"

Sam pushed off the sofa and strode toward the doors. "Obviously it was as priceless as she said it was."

Dr. Wan Gai moved into his office and poured himself a small drink, then took it to his desk. He didn't sit, but turned to the safe and slightly tapped the keypad. The door sprang open and he removed the velvet sack, laying it on his desk. He sat, sipped, and stared at the lump, wondering whether or not he should inform his majesty or simply destroy it.

He grasped a rock paperweight. The gold was fragile and while shattering it would make noise, the museum was closed and he was alone. He raised the rock.

"I wouldn't."

He dropped it, lurching out of his chair. "Who are you? What are you doing here?"

"Not important." Sam moved out of the shadows, staring at the man. "Where is she?"

"I don't know what you're talking about."

Sam leveled his handgun. "Guess again."

"If you are here to steal—"

"Sit," Sam said in a low voice, and the curator dropped into his chair.

Sam's first instinct was to beat the dog shit out of the man. He had enough evidence to know Wan Gai had something to do with Viva's disappearance. He was the last person, aside from Sam, to have any contact with her. No one else knew she was in that hotel. Or in the city. But it was the room service waiter who, with some pressure, confessed that a man had stopped him at gunpoint and sprinkled powder in her food and tea.

"You have two choices. Tell me where Miss Fiori is, or lose something vital."

"You are mistaken. I don't know who you are talking about."

Sam moved forward, snatching the velvet bag, and slid out the cuff. "Really? She had this when I met her, she nearly died trying to protect it."

Wan Gai's eyes flared. Another who knew?

Sam glanced over his head, and hands clamped down on Wan Gai's shoulders. Sam screwed on the silencer, slowly, then pointed it to Wan Gai's kneecap.

"Last chance."

The man said nothing. Sam shrugged and pulled the trigger.

Wan Gai screamed, jerking violently in the chair. It took him a moment to realize the bullet went into the floor. Sam leaned down in his face. "Let's be clear, pal, I don't care what happens to you. I don't care about the bracelet, the museum, or whatever it means. All I want is the woman."

Wan Gai understood he would not walk away from this. It was painted in the man's features, in the eyes. His life held no value there. "I don't know where she is."

"The next one will be your elbow." He let the sentence hang, and pressed the weapon into the bone.

"My man, he did it!"

"Call him." Sam picked up the receiver, handed it to him. Wan Gai leaned forward to dial, his hand shaking. When he finished, Sam hit the speaker button.

"Choan, what did you do with her?"

"Why do you ask?"

"What did you do with her?" he said more sternly.

"It is best you do not know."

Sam dug the barrel harder.

"Tell me now!"

"Voslav. The Serbian."

Wan Gai paled and looked at Sam. "Where?"

"I do not know. He took care of it. Just as you wished."

Sam leaned and whispered, "It's tough to walk without kneecaps, try harder."

"How did you contact Voslav?"

"A phone number."

"Give it to me, please."

There was hesitation on the line. "But sir, you did not want any traces."

"Give it to me."

Silence for a moment, then he gave the number. Wan Gai started to cut the line and Sam grabbed his wrist. "Where is he?" He inclined his head to the phone.

Wan Gai hesitated, swallowing. "I will need your help, Choan. Where are you?"

"In the Keb mall, but I can come to you."

Sam shook his head.

"Remain there till I reach you, please."

"Sir, what is wrong?"

"I have changed my mind."

"That's a shame, she's already sold."

Sam's heart bucked violently, fury beating it harder. Savagely, he cut the line, pointed the gun at Wan Gai's head. His fingers worked the grip.

"Don't, buddy," Max warned.

"Give me *one* good reason." Sam ground the gun into Wan Gai's temple.

"Murder. And she's still alive."

Sam stared down at Wan Gai, the man's fear so intense it gave off a rancid smell. Yet he thought of Viva, the terror she was suffering at the mercy of slavers, and he wanted to ghost this fucker. God, he *needed* to, but killing him now would bring trouble and Viva's life meant more. Finally, he tipped the barrel up. Wan Gai sank into the chair like a deflated balloon. Then Sam took the bracelet, stuffing it into his pocket.

"No, please, do—" Wan Gai reached for it, but the barrel in his face stopped him.

"What's this Choan's full name? What's he look like?"

"Lon Choan. He is tall and big like you, he has a scar right here." He made a slash down the left side of his face near his temple. "And he likes American food."

Sam debated taking him with them, then decided against it. The curator was trapped, and if he talked, he'd incriminate himself.

He braced his hands on the arms of the chair. "If I don't find her alive and well, I will come finish this." Sam pushed back, then grabbed the phone off the desk and ripped it from the wall. "Warn him and you'll wish you didn't."

He tossed the phone aside, and backed out of the office through the west doors.

Wan Gai rubbed his face, his hands shaking. He reached for the untouched drink and tossed it back in one gulp, then poured another. He would retrieve the bracelet later and knew Choan could handle the American. The word please in the conversation should have alerted Choan. Wan Gai never *asked* for anything. His family stature afforded him much, and now he would use it. He drank the second drink, then reached inside his desk drawer and pulled out a cell phone.

He dialed, relaxing back into the chair. As to the American, he would regret ever seeing the ancient bracelet—and its secrets would be safe.

Nine

While Max circled the three-block-long mall, Sam was on foot, hurrying toward the service entrance. Workers in black and white uniforms moved swiftly, unloading boxes and baskets of fruit even at this hour. Sam stilled, scanning the area, moving past a truck. The workers spared him a glance, yet continued their duties. Sam was coming around the front of the truck when he saw a tall man leave through an employee door. Choan gave himself away instantly, constantly looking around as he walked. His steps were a near run, and Sam followed him through the rear parking lot filled with trucks.

He kept his distance, moving laterally as Choan made a quick phone call, then pocketed the phone. Wan Gai had described him accurately, at least: tall, thick shoulders, a weightlifter, probably.

Sam stopped behind a food-service truck, the odor of raw meat radiating from the rear. He watched the man as he crossed the street to the massive, four-story parking garage. Sam signaled Max, and he drove the van into it from the opposite end. Choan hopped the fence, and stopped, checked his back. Sam was on his heels, slipping behind the small cars, keeping his footsteps quiet when everything inside the garage echoed.

He heard the blip of a car alarm, and moved low and fast. Max drove slowly as if searching for a parking spot. Choan stood beside a black sedan, and Max stopped behind it, blocking him in. Choan started for it, shouting for Max to move as Sam crossed quickly, coming up behind him.

He pressed the gun into his spine. "How's it going, Choan?"

He stiffened, and Sam searched him, relieving him of a small handgun, a cell phone, and a knife tucked behind his back.

"What do you want?"

"I'm sure Wan Gai told you, the woman."

He gets to die for that, Sam thought. "You will never find her."

Sebastian threw open the door, grabbed Choan, and yanked him inside. He fell forward, then rolled around to look at them. Sam climbed in and Max drove.

Choan adjusted his jacket, smoothed his hair. Sam aimed for his face. "Voslav. Find out where he took the woman."

"Fuck you."

Sam's arm shot out, the heel of his palm connecting with Choan's nose so hard his head snapped back. Choan grunted, and blood oozed. "Reconsider."

Choan started to reach inside his jacket. Sam aimed at his head.

Glancing between the two, he carefully pulled out the white square, shook it, and blotted his nose that was rapidly turning purple. "He's been paid, he doesn't care."

"Convince him."

Viva's life hung in the moments. Sam had the phone number, but the sellers of human beings would be overly cautious. Caller ID and a familiar voice were the only ways inside fast. He dialed, and held the phone to Choan's ear.

"Where is the woman? We want her back," Choan said.

Sam listened to the reply as Sebastian worked a computer, then paused to adjust the small dish. "Keep him on the line."

"She is gone," Voslav said. "At a hefty price I will enjoy spending."

"Ask who bought her," Sam said to Choan. He put the phone to his ear again, then listened to the reply.

"I would be out of business if I did that!"

"Tell him you'll pay to have her back."

Choan made a sour face, then spoke. He shook his head. No deal.

"Double the offer."

Choan did, then nodded.

Sebastian watched the screen, tracking the cell call, and gave a thumbs up when they had Voslav's position.

"Tell him your buyer is coming now," Sam said, covering the receiver with his thumb again.

Choan spoke, and Sam heard the accented English. He'd be waiting. Gave a location. One hour. Sam ended the call, pocketed the phone, then secured and gagged Choan, sandwiching his burly ass behind some gear.

"Damn, the cell signal died," Sebastian said, frantically tapping keys to get it back. "He shut the phone off."

Choan had the balls to snicker, and Sam whipped around and struck, a hard chop to his temple. The man remained conscious for about two seconds, then slumped, his bleeding nose staining his pure white shirt.

Project Silent Fire
US–UK Joint Command

Major General Gerardo sat before a large screen, the view was of the members of the joint chiefs and his boss, three-star General McGill.

"I don't need to know how we lost the plans," McGill said. "Just how to get them back before they use them."

A British Royal Marine general leaned forward and spoke into the microphone. "We take full responsibility, sir."

"America appreciates that, but it was a joint command."

"What have you got in ground intel?" an Army colonel asked.

"Sightings of Chechens, LTTE Tiger, Balinese, it's a damn party."

"Haul them in."

Gerardo shook his head. "Suspicion won't hold up in a tribunal, courts, or with the UN. They're experts at torture and would die for their cause, so interrogation methods don't get us much. We need evidence, and someone in the lower ranks. Someone we can break." Gerardo had people looking for just that right now, and didn't have time for reports and discussion.

"What is the Thai government doing?"

"They're assisting but really don't have the manpower and resources for this," Gerardo said, and they all knew that giving them too much intelligence would destroy their operation. Half the Thai police were corrupted by mafia ties. "They've relinquished authority to Interpol and the US–UK Joint Command."

"Good, but that doesn't take us any further, Al."

"We have CIA officers on the ground pulling all resources, but there is little to be had. We get close and they're dead."

"So we have nothing?"

"Not exactly. Sources tell us one man is running the show. But he wasn't reliable."

"Tell me something good, Al."

"I don't have it. Every trail we pick up is obliterated. As if they know our next step. Someone took a shot at the CIA station front in Thailand. No casualties but a window. However, that cover is blown."

"We have a leak? Then it's higher than terrorist factions."

"Agreed, but that means searching for a needle in the ocean."

McGill sat back and glanced at his colleagues. Their looks were as grim as the situation. "This weapon, if they create it, how bad can it get?"

"It's capable of several tasks," Gerardo said, uncomfortable with revealing top secret information regardless of the security measures. They wouldn't be in this fix if they'd been impenetrable. "We are using it on the caves in Afghanistan now. Even at ten percent capability, the force of it makes it impossible for anyone to not react."

"The result?"

"Any illness of our choice, the brain vibrates as well as the skeletal structure. It's an amazing defensive tool."

"Line of sight?"

"Two hundred yards."

"That at least limits it."

"For now, yes."

On the screen, McGill's features tightened. "Tell me they can't modify this thing."

"We already have."

Viva's eyes flashed open as if she'd never slept. Instantly she knew she wasn't in the same place as before. Beneath her was downy soft, above her, a paddle fan spun from a gold ceiling.

No crying, no chains. No numbed body.

How do I get myself into these situations?

The thought of being carted around barely dressed, by men no doubt, sent a flush of helplessness through her. She stared at the bed's canopy, a wood rectangle carved and gilded, the posts painted light green. The patterned green and gold wallpaper gave her eyes a workout and despite the mounds of gold pillows surrounding her, she couldn't move, her arms spread wide and tied with thick silk ropes. She tested them, enough slack to bring her arms in a little, but not enough to touch anything. She wrapped her fingers around the rope and yanked. They didn't budge. The bed creaked.

She shifted, glad her legs weren't secured, and bent her knees. She saw green silk. Okay, dressed was good, but the loose pants were ballooned, and she wore a sheer cream top with sprigs of bamboo embroidered in the fabric. And that's not all, she thought, feeling the tight bra beneath and tried to get a look. Low-cut and embroidered, it was clasped in the center with nothing more than a couple gold chains.

Jeez, I look like *I Dream of Jeannie*.

She leaned forward and instantly choked, something soft

and thick around her throat. She twisted, her gaze following the gold rope and ending on the bed frame. Oh crap, she thought, and tried not to panic, reaching for the lamp near the bed and coming up a yard short. Screaming was out of the question. Someone did this to her and they had to be outside those doors. She dropped her head onto the pillows, and tugged on her wrists, trying to stretch the silken ropes.

A hotel somewhere, she thought, by the service card on the room door. The suite was large, oriental furnishings and a little gaudy, yet looked familiar. Three rooms from what she could see from her vantage point on the bed. In the living room area, a laptop sat on a carved desk, open and running, beside it a webcam, and facing this direction. Great. Just what she needed. A video of her humiliation.

She kept tugging at the soft ropes, hoping to loosen them and tensed when the door rattled. She heard it open and close, saw a man pass before the wide doorway, and she understood the Scheherazade getup. He was dressed as a sheik, in period clothing, tailored, not robes. She'd seen men wear something like it for formal state occasions. He strolled around the room, doing God knew what, and she kept still.

He thumb-dialed a phone, tossing a leather sack like a ball. He spoke, and she caught only the murmur of it, something about an appointment time for discussions. He checked his watch. As he closed the phone, he faced the bed, a little smile curving his lips.

"Ah, my *kadine*, you are awake."

Sam strolled into the darkest pits of Thailand, beyond the temples, the restaurants, the kind people, and into the cavity that gouged every country. He turned into a narrow, wet alley, hookers near the streets, sliding their fingers over his shoulder. He shook them off and continued. So where is Voslav, he thought, nearly at a dead end. A man moved out of the shadows. Small eyes, was Sam's first thought, lost in the squat face. He looked as if he hadn't seen a laundry or bathwater in at least a week. The man inspected him and

Sam knew what he saw. Wealth in a suit and tie. He couldn't spend millions without looking like he had it.

"Are you alone?"

Sam inclined his head and Voslav looked past him. Sebastian was at the end of the street, armed and looking his dangerous best.

Voslav was amused and came forward. "Raise your arms."

Sam did and he patted his torso. Voslav gave him a "you're stupid" look. But Sam couldn't come armed. Voslav had to believe he had every advantage.

"So you want a woman?" The man snickered. "Or a child?"

Sam remained silent, noticing Voslav's accent was distinctive, a faint mix of Thai and Serbian. How long has this bastard been a slave runner here?

"You have money?"

Sam held up a fat wad of cash. Voslav practically salivated, reaching.

Sam held it back. "The redhead."

"You keep that handy, eh?" He motioned. "Come, take your pick, then."

Sam followed several steps behind, and in his ear, he heard Max.

"It's an old school." In the van, Max was jumping MI6 satellite feed surveillance. "Four exits, the alley, one at the street front, a gym, and service platforms at the rear."

Sam cleared his throat, indicating he'd heard.

"Coonass, once they're inside, move to the gym," Max said.

Voslav unlocked a side door, and gestured. Sam stood back, waiting, and the man shrugged and went inside, looking back to check the street. They went through a couple more doors, down a long hall littered with trash, and broken school desks, then stopped at one with a small window. Sam glanced around what looked like a lunchroom, then moved up alongside and looked in.

What he saw sent a wave of revulsion through him.

Darkness, the foul smell and heat radiating through the old classroom door. Children and young women were tied up, some gagged, and they weren't all Thai. Their defeat lay in the lack of movement, the stillness. He didn't see Viva.

Sam stepped back. "I came for the redhead."

"Ahh, her. She is gone, probably already fucked stupid."

Sam ground his teeth. Killing this man would be too good for him. "Find her."

"Fuck no, there are others here. You want, you choose."

Sam's right hand shot out, gripping Voslav's Adam's apple and squeezing. "Where is she?" Sam relieved him of his gun, pushing it into his own waistband.

The Serbian choked and Sam let up pressure. "Gone already, get off of me!" He clawed at his hand, but Sam squeezed harder, locking out his air supply, and blood to his little brain.

"Where!"

"Fuck you," he croaked, frantically pulling at Sam's hand.

Sam shook his left arm, a blade falling into his palm and he ripped it down Voslav's face. Blood bloomed as the man howled and tried to grab the wound. Sam wouldn't allow it. "That's one."

Voslav stared, his breathing fast, but otherwise unaffected. "Kill me and you'll never learn anything."

"Not a problem." Sam jammed the knife into his thigh, then ripped it forward, cutting tendons.

Voslav screamed and fell to the floor. "You motherfucker, I'll kill you! God dammit!"

Sam wiped the blade on his sleeve. "The redhead." At the noise, people pounded on the door from the inside.

"You'll never get to her. He's got a dozen men." Voslav spit at his feet, gripping his knee, blood oozing between his fingers.

Sam secured Voslav with slip ties, searched him for keys, then left him facedown before he opened the door.

People looked up, cowered, and their desolation just about killed him. "Coonass, get in here."

"No can do, he's got men, I count four. One looks familiar. They're doing the divide and conquer."

Shoot the bastards, was his first thought, but that would put these people in the crossfire. "Drac, track them." He touched his ear. "There are at least a dozen people here, guys, we need to get them out first."

"You won't." Voslav chuckled, bleeding all over the floor.

Ignoring the slaver, Sam entered, cutting the bonds of a few, then handing the knife to a young boy and gesturing to the others. He looked at each face, hoping to see Viva's. His gaze fell on a mattress, empty, yet still holding the impression of a body, and his chest tightened as people filed out, stiff and battered, but eager for freedom.

"Run," Sam told them. "Go home." He pointed to the exit, and one woman stopped, grabbed his arm, yet said nothing, her thanks in her battered face. "You're welcome, but go." He stopped a young boy. "A redhead, American," he said in his best Thai. "Did you see her?" The boy pointed to the empty mattress and nodded.

Jesus, no.

Fury poured through him and Sam was outside the room, hauling Voslav up enough to look him in the eyes. "A name!"

"I don't ask names!"

Sam ground his foot on his bloody knee. "*Where is she?*"

"The Baiyoke!" He swore in Serbian.

Rohki had been there too. Did he buy her? Sam shoved him aside as people filed out, one woman stopping to spit on Voslav, then run, dragging a child.

"She'll be dead or so used up she'll wish she was." Voslav managed to prop himself against the wall.

The taunts hit their mark, brewing terrible images of Viva being raped, yet Sam watched the gym doors as the last prisoner, a beautiful teenager in her school uniform, ran into the streets.

"Civilians clear." Sebastian hurried across the gym.

"They're clear of the building, and scattering," Max said. "Thai police on their way."

"Excellent."

"Why do you hurt me?" Voslav said behind Sam, his breathing labored. "I just provide a service. Some want a mistress, or nannies and cooks. Others want the softness of virgin children."

"Jesus," Sebastian said, disgusted. "Shut him up."

His outrage long passed the breaking point, Sam stepped closer, staring down at the man. He cared about a lot of things, a dying slave runner wasn't one of them. Voslav snickered, blood bubbling from his broken face. Sam knelt, and with the heel of his palm, he hit, sending his shattered nose into his brain. The bastard never moved again. He straightened, wiping blood on his leg.

"One dirtbag down, we're coming out."

"Negative," Max said. Sam stilled, met Sebastian's gaze. "His goons are inside somewhere."

"We'll bypass them." Sam accepted a handful of ammo from Sebastian.

"Negative, one saw the victims running and they're halfway to your position now."

Instantly, Sam flattened to the wall and inclined his head to Sebastian. They checked the two corridors. They were wide, lockers on the right, three doors spaced out on the left. Sam didn't bother searching each, the glass was knocked out, and a quick sweep showed nothing but debris. No exits.

"Last location?"

"Hell if I know. No city plans for this building."

Well, hell, he was used to flying blind.

"I'm going in behind them," Max said.

"Smoke them toward us."

Sebastian watched the first corridor, and Sam turned back toward Voslav. Alongside the prison room were three more classroom doors, then another corridor from the loading bays. Sam edged the hall, peering. "Two, my twelve, moving fast."

"One my way," Sebastian said. "No visual, but I can hear footsteps."

In the ear mike, Sam heard a grunt, then a deep breath. "One ghosted," Max said. "Green shirt with a Uzi coming your way. Sorry."

In the hollowness of the corridor, he heard rapid footsteps, the jingle of change, and he waited, listened. Sound was their best defense.

The gun barrel appeared first, slowly, and Sam grabbed it, yanked down, then drove his elbow into the man's face. Cartilage dissolved under the impact, and he shoved the man back into his partner. They fell like dominos, and Sam ducked back as the man sprayed the walls and ceiling with bullets. Before the dust settled, Sam peered around the edge of the wall. The pair were struggling to stand, one holding his bleeding face.

Sam stepped out, aiming. "Drop the weapons, guys."

The second man pulled the trigger, and Sam double-tapped the two and turned away in time to see Sebastian standing over a body, the green shirt bloody.

"We need to get out of here ASAP."

Sebastian frowned. "What'd he tell you?"

"She's at the Baiyoke Towers." Sam stripped Voslav's body of everything he could find.

"And you believe him?"

"No, but I don't have much choice."

They maintained caution as they left the building, checking rooms and closets for survivors. When they were satisfied no one was left behind that shouldn't be dead, they headed to the rear doors. Police barreled down the roads, sirens loud in the warm night air. Max gunned the van, and slid to a stop. Sebastian and Sam dove inside and he pulled away.

Sam drew out Voslav's wallet, prying through the contents. "Cash." It was crumpled, and Sam plucked through, leaving a pile. "There's nothing, dammit." Sam gathered the blood money, then found a slip of paper between folded bhat. He tipped it to the light. "It's a receipt for a water taxi, to the Oriental. Dated today."

"That's four separate buildings."

"And our best option." If they were wrong, they'd never find her. Sam couldn't wrap his brain around it.

In the rear, Choan stirred. "We need to dump him," Max said.

"Not yet. He knows more than he's saying."

"Well, that's a given."

Sam looked at Sebastian. "Can you cook?"

The Cajun smiled. "How big do you want the blast?"

Commander Anan Isarangura walked into the old school, remembering when it was set on fire by terrorists months ago. They'd hit eighteen schools in a year's time, each condemned and scheduled for demolition, yet he knew they would not be done for years unless the businessmen wanted the land for another skyscraper. He followed his men, motioning for them to fan out.

The rush of young children in the streets warned him that what he would find would not be pleasant. He was not disappointed. He stared at the bodies littering the corridor, then stepped over them to the one he'd hoped to find.

A young officer came out of a room, his complexion pale. "You were correct. Slavers." His gaze fell to the body.

"Ivan Voslav." He gestured. He'd been sought for two years now, evading capture and all evidence washed away before Anan could take him. He bent, checking for a pulse, knowing he was dead and wanting to be certain. "Remove the bodies and board the building."

"We should leave them to rot." The young man kicked Voslav's body.

"Their stench is already in our city, we do not want to make more."

Anan plucked a gun shell from beneath a body, turning it over in his hands.

"Do we go after the people who did this?"

"You are certain who it is?"

The younger man's features tightened with embarrassment.

"We are oddly grateful, but yes, we need to trace them," Anan said.

He pocketed the single shell. The bullets in the bodies said there had been more shots fired, but they had missed only this one.

An officer rushed in, offering a cell phone. A leash to the men with power, he thought, taking it and stating his name. "The museum has been robbed, Dr. Wan Gai is waiting with a photo of the assailant."

Anan said he would be there by sunrise, but that didn't satisfy his superiors. Wan Gai had influence. But that only one article was missing made him instantly suspicious.

Viva felt a strange calm settle over her, terror submerged beneath righteous anger. What kind of sick person did this to people? She thought of the children in that room and the other young women she couldn't see, like flowers hidden from the light to slowly die. The degrading horror of it drove fury up her spine.

She wouldn't make it easy for this guy and tried to think of ways to turn this to her favor. As much as she wanted to spit and shout at him, she kept her face impassive, her eyes wide and innocent. Let him believe she was terrified, she thought. Get him to lower his guard. Then what? She was tied and leashed like an animal.

"You came all the way to Thailand for an American?"

He smiled. "No. You're a distraction till I complete my business."

Russian accent, she thought. "And what's that?"

He frowned slightly. "Your only concern is pleasing me."

"That would be difficult since I'm tied like a dog."

She never thought she'd have to decide between rape and life, but knew no one would help her, and she'd no intention of dying today.

Then he strolled closer. Dark haired with a salt of gray, he didn't look capable of whatever he had in mind, nor did he look the least bit Arabic. His gaze moved over her clothing, ending on her breasts. When he reached the side of the bed, she noticed little things, the ring on his little finger, the biggest Burmese ruby she'd ever seen, then the gold chains dangling with medallions. Expensive bling-bling. The fabric of his black clothing was hand embroidered with gold threads. Even his buttons were made of gemstones. Money to burn and he spent it on slaves?

"You say nothing more?"

Language she'd never considered uttering went flying through her brain, yet she bit it back. No sense in enticing him, he looked pretty worked up already. She lowered her eyes demurely, and wondered if fighting would rile him up, or if submitting would deflate the erection she could see pushing against his garments.

He reached over her, and started to unbutton the over blouse. "I will see all I have purchased."

She twisted away, kicking out at him, and his smile widened. She had her answer. Fight and he'd like it.

He spread the fabric wide, and stared, his breathing increasing as he touched her stomach, his hand sliding upward toward the genie bra. Viva realized the pants she wore were open at the hips, held together by thin gold chains.

He pressed a knee to the bed and cupped her breasts. She faked a moan, trying not to spit in his face.

"You like that? There will be more, my *kadine*."

Not on your life, sajin. She pulled on the silk ropes, her palm folded. Freedom had to come; she'd rather die than be raped by the sheik wannabe. Then he moved to the foot of the bed, and grasped her ankles, his grip punishing as he slowly spread them, but before she could jerk free, he looped them with ropes.

"You don't have to do that."

He looked doubtful.

She sat up as far as she could, the rope around her throat holding her back. "I will submit."

"You speak lies, woman."

You think? God, he was a bad romance novel in the making.

"You'll never know till you try," she said, then gave him a shy look that was so rare her friends would laugh if they saw it. Viva kept at the ropes, feeling them give a little. They weren't that tight to begin with, but she still couldn't slip her wrist free.

"Try you? I plan to have you in every way I can."

Her gaze lowered pointedly to his crotch. "We'll see."

He laughed softly, crawling toward her, his hands sliding up from her ankles, dipping under the fabric made to fall away with the flick of a knife. The heat of his knees between hers drove another wave of panic into her blood, and she discreetely pulled the cords harder, the bed creaking with the strain. Then he lay on top of her, humping, his thick crotch pushing on hers, and she thought, oh, God, bathing for a week would never clean away this violation.

He kissed her stomach, her breasts, cupped one and squeezed hard. Pain bloomed in her chest, and she struggled, her gaze flicking to the ropes as she worked them farther over her palm. Then his hand wrapped her throat, tightening slowly as he rubbed against her, vulgar and heavy. Viva gasped for air, panting in his ear when she wanted to bite it off. Stars scattered in her vision. Breathing grew harder.

His hand found its way between her legs, stroking against the fabric and she twisted to avoid contact, hoping to dislodge his grip on her throat. But he chuckled, fumbled between her legs, and she realized he was opening his trousers. *No, please no.* The chains on her pants loosened and her vulnerability drove rage to monumental proportions.

This is not *happening to me, dammit.*

She yanked, yet couldn't pull her wrist free, and strained to reach his jeweled dagger. It was inches out of her grasp. Then he put both hands on her bare skin, nudged her legs wider, but they were secured. She inhaled deeply as he suddenly rose up, twisted to his right, and unhooked one ankle rope.

The angle put him within reach, and Viva grabbed the curved dagger.

"Hey! Lawrence of Arabia."

He turned back sharply, right into the blade. His body jerked, his expression glazed with unexpected pain.

Oh God. Oh God, she hadn't meant to—her gaze rocked between his face and her hand on the jeweled hilt.

"You will die, *cyka,*" he gasped, his hands locking around her throat. He squeezed hard, his body falling on hers.

"You first." Her world fading, Viva jammed the knife deeper.

Ten

In the deep cushioned chair, Constantine Jalier twisted his ring, his gaze on the wide-screen television. The sound was off. On the six-foot-long coffee table were three laptops, all in screen-saver mode. Behind him, the door opened and closed, no other sounds, and he marveled at her skill to be so silent. Her hand slid over his shoulder, then lower. He grasped it, kissed the back of her hand, then let her go and patted the space beside him.

She did not sit. "Forgive me, I've failed you."

The loss of the woman, bait for the man with the stone, was unfortunate, yet nothing could be done about it now.

"Zidane has people searching for the gray-haired man."

He glanced at her, again patting the cushion, and she hopped over the sofa back, sleek and slim, then sat erect.

"Be patient, they will find them."

"If her man finds her first?"

"Then we will change our plans. Now we wait."

Noor lifted her gaze to his, and he knew she was angry with herself. "I have forgiven, my sweet."

He slid his hand over her dark hair, marveling at her beauty. Having tasted her, he knew what to expect when her hand went to his belt, aptly flicking it open and sending the zipper down. Her small hand, a deadly weapon otherwise, worked inside and closed over his flesh. She stroked him a few times, then bent her head and took him into her mouth.

"No biting," he warned and settled back, watching his cock slide into her mouth. His gaze flicked to the screen, knowing he had only moments before his meeting with his next buyer. He moaned as her sucking grew stronger, tighter, and he pulled her from him.

"You have done nothing that warrants this."

She neither confirmed nor denied her motives as she slid over his lap, pulling up her skirt. She wore nothing beneath, her body shaved clean, and she immediately guided him inside her. He knew he'd come, she would stop at nothing till she made certain of it. Sex to Noor was a weapon as lethal as her blowgun. His gaze lowered to the black leather pouch at her waist, yet he did not touch it. She was immune to the poison, having suffered injecting herself over a hundred times so she could easily handle the darts. He pulled her skirt higher, her trim hips thrusting harder and harder.

"You are coming," she said, her face expressionless. She gave nothing, almost robotic. He didn't care. She was efficient and if she wanted to pleasure him, he'd take it.

She gripped his shoulders and pumped harder, and he flicked his fingers over her clitoris. It was then her expression changed, shocked, offended, yet he kept at it, wanting to see her climax, to see her vulnerable. He didn't succeed. She came, holding herself rigid, refusing to let herself succumb. The only difference was in her breathing. But he felt it, her grip of him, and he grabbed her hips and thrust, spilling into her. For an instant he thought of his wife, dead years before, and what she'd think of him, and disgust tried to work its way into the moment. He dismissed her image and fell back onto the sofa.

Noor didn't collapse on him, but instead stared at him for a moment, then crawled off and went to the bathroom. She tossed him a towel, then disappeared behind the door. He cleaned himself, zipped, then reached for his drink. His gaze went to the still dormant screen, and he glanced at the clock on the wall, then leaned, tapped, making the connection. The webcam blinked on and his brows rose when he realized what he was seeing.

In time to see the woman grab the knife.

No, he thought, do not! Yet when the man went stiff, he understood. He cursed, shot off the sofa, and cursed again. Then the screen went blank, and he kicked the table.

The bathroom door opened and Noor stepped out, perfect in every way. She didn't frown, nor do more than tip her head and say, "You are upset with me?"

"She's killed him!" He lashed a hand at the computer.

Noor went to it. "The picture is gone."

He drew the computer forward and tried to bring up the image. The stream was still in the hard drive and he hit REPLAY. An image blinked on, and Noor leaned closer.

"That is the woman."

"She just killed my biggest buyer!"

The woman had cost him far too much and he would get it back. "Go to the Oriental, bring her to me, and his stones."

"His men will not allow me that close."

"Find a way! Kill them all if you must."

Noor simply smiled, feline beautiful as she touched his chest. He gathered no assurances from her confidence, yet he brushed his fingers under her chin and kissed her. "Tell Zidane his lack of results wears on our timetable. Protect the buyers."

Silently, she turned to the door and found it open. Zidane stood on the threshold, his gaze moving from the Pharaoh to her. He arched a brow, and she continued toward him.

"You are out of favor," she whispered, and he closed the door behind her.

"And you have done nothing more than pleasure an old man."

She continued down the hall. "But it will give me more."

He grabbed her by the arm, jerking her back. "You'll never control him with that," he said with a glance down her body. "He's stronger than you, than both of us."

She wrenched free. "Jealous of my results, or scared?"

* * *

At four in the morning, Bangkok did not sleep. Lights spilled from the restaurant on the first floor of the Mandarin Oriental and lit the terrace, more lampposts shining on the pier and docks. Sam avoided them, his attention was on the author's wing: the original section, only a two-story Victorian with lavish suites named after James Michener, Joseph Conrad, Noel Coward, and Somerset Maugham.

She's got to be in there.

Registration was under a John Smith–type name, and the area restricted to foot traffic. Guards strolled the edge of the grounds, the waiters searched before they were allowed to enter told him security was high. The question was, which suite? Whoever rented the wing had the entire building under his control.

He touched his throat mike. "Any ideas?" They were going in blind again, no time to plan. Sebastian was between the old section and the new, Max near the terrace. Sam was close enough to the building to catch the aroma of food and cigarettes.

"What makes you think she's in there?"

"Not a damn thing. But this guy is paranoid enough to have four guards, and rich enough to select this place for its 360 view, least accessible from the street. If anyone wanted to shoot in, they'd have to be on the water." The second wing was behind him, running as normal and blocked by rows of tall, narrow trees. "And the guards haven't done anything but walk, no one going beyond the lounge area."

"Good point."

"That's why they pay me the big bucks."

"So what's a good decoy?" Max said.

"How about a drunken fistfight?" Sebastian suggested.

"As long as I get to win this time," Max groused.

Sam watched the upper floors. A couple windows were blocked by trees, and he considered climbing one, but it wouldn't give him enough time to get that far onto the grounds without being seen. He scanned the area and he picked a point of entry.

"Going in the balcony, west side, keep them busy."

A guard passed beneath it, his cigarette tip flaring briefly, lighting his features. Not Asian, he thought. "Go."

Sam couldn't see his friends, but heard them. They were singing, a moon doggie howl of old college fight songs.

Move away, little commando, he thought, eyes on the guard. The man spoke on the radio, tossed his cigarette down, and with a long-suffering sigh of smoke headed toward the noise. Sam hurried across the terrace to the side of the building, unwound his bullwhip, aimed and lashed it softly. The end curled around the rail. He climbed, tall banana trees shielding him from the lights.

He hoisted over the rail and flattened to the wall, peering into the room. Curtains closed, he couldn't see anything. He knelt, drawing a thin pair of wires from inside his jacket. It was the best they could do on short notice. Makeshift lock picks. He tried the knob first, then got to cracking. It sprang and he was glad this place was historically correct. Everything else opened with magnetic cards. He gripped the knob, turning slowly.

The air-conditioning hit him first, and he waited a few moments, then pushed back the drape. He slipped inside and shut the glass door. "I'm in." He heard grunts and shouts from his friends. He looked around and knew he was wrong. The room was empty.

From the living room, he could see into the bedroom, the four-poster bed untouched. Sam searched anyway, then went to the outer door, opening it a fraction. Great, a guard outside it and another one near the service staircase. Taking them out was not an option.

He fell back against the wall, thinking. He was traveling light, a load-bearing vest and a pistol. No Kevlar, and his backup was downstairs beating each other up for the show. A sudden blast of icy air swept around him, and he turned. An AC vent was above him. He grabbed a chair, stood on it and pried the vent off, then hoisted himself inside the shaft. He headed in the direction of the suite with the guards.

He crawled, using his elbows to propel himself forward. Slow going, and it was hot inside the steel tunnel. To his right vent shafts parted off to other sections. He paused to catch his breath, feeling like a spud in the oven. The pop of the metal vent corridor would give up his position. It was several minutes before he reached the vent he hoped was in the next suite. Sam curved his body, and looked down into the darkened room. The living room. Empty. Gourmet food covered a glass table, settings for two, and just as he noticed the laptop computer with a web camera, it went into sleep mode.

Then he heard one voice, deep and definitely male. The response, if there was any, was too soft to hear. Sam strained. *If it's you, baby, call out.*

Suddenly, the vent filled with air again, pulling hot air from the suite, and drowning out the voices. Now was the time, the AC covering any noise he'd make as he pushed on the grate, easing it out and carefully letting it slide to the carpet. Then he grabbed the lower portion of the cover, judged the distance and did a forward roll onto the floor. His landing soundless, he drew his weapon. Sam scanned the room, noting exits, then edged around tall pedestal planters dividing the bedroom from the living room. He looked into the bedroom.

Oh, sweet Jesus.

A man was on top of her, between her legs. With one arm and her knee, she held him back, trying to shove him off. Sam rushed to the side of the bed.

"Sam! *Sam?* Oh God, help me, please."

Sam put a gun to the man's head, and violently yanked him back. Lifeless eyes stared back, and his gaze dropped to the knife in his chest. *Oh hell.*

He looked at Viva, but she was frantic, twisting and yanking, trying to reach the rope at her throat. "Untie me, oh God, untie me!"

He grabbed her hands, staring into her wild eyes. "Baby, it's over. You have to calm down and be quiet." Sam swiftly cut the bonds, then severed the one at her throat. She launched off the bed and into his arms, gripping him so tight Sam felt it to his bones. He crushed her to him, pressing his lips to her temple and for a brief moment, closed his eyes.

"Oh, thank you, thank you! I know this looks bad, but I swear, he was—"

"I know what he was doing, honey." He stroked her hair, held her tighter. "Shh, shh." Over her head, Sam looked at the dead man and wanted to kill him again for touching her.

"Outlaw, Outlaw!" sounded in his ear.

"I found her, she's alive. Give us two minutes." He eased her back and when she kept looking at the dead man, he cupped her face. "Focus on me, okay?" She nodded and he noticed the marks on her throat turning purple. "We have to get out of here. Now."

She nodded through her tears. He kissed her greedily, then got a look at her clothes. *Whoa,* he thought, yet his gaze went to the splatters of blood on the blouse and her throat.

Viva grabbed at the half-falling garment. "Some fantasy, huh? Give me a hand here." She tried to secure the slacks at her hip, but her hands shook and Sam took over as she buttoned up the blouse. "Oh forget it, let's go, please."

Quickly, Sam urged her to the vent shaft. "This is our exit." He pulled a chair near to give her a leg up, then disengaged the laptop and camera, shoving it in the shaft before he reached for her. She wasn't there. Viva rushed to the dining table.

"Viva, we're out of time." She grabbed something off the bedside table, stuffing it down the back of her pants as she hurried back to him. She slapped her hand in his and Sam pulled. "I swear, woman."

"I know, I'm irritating."

Sam moved faster this time, pushing the laptop ahead and Viva right behind him. He slid into the empty room and when he turned, she rolled down and fell into his arms.

"What was so damn important?"

"I don't know, but it was important to the sheik wannabe."

Sam moved to the balcony doors, pushed them open, pulling her outside.

"You're always making me jump from high places," she whispered hoarsely, looking down.

Sam lashed his whip to the rail and wrapped her hands around it. "Crawl over and down. I'm right behind you."

"What about that?" She gestured to the laptop. He looked for a way to secure it and Viva reached inside the room, yanked the silk drapery panel, wrapped it around the laptop and made a sling. Sam slipped it on. "Now you're stylin'."

Sam cupped the back of her head and kissed her hard. She responded wildly, the slip of lips and tongue primal and greedy. He drew back, and she stared up at him, a feline smile on her lips.

"Bad guys, your three o'clock," he said, pointing right.

Viva eased over the balcony, gripped the whip, then slid down. She dropped the last couple feet. A moment later, Sam landed nearby in a crouch beside her.

He touched his throat. "We're out, break it up." He looked at her, so damn glad she was alive. "Stay low and right behind me."

"If you insist."

They edged the building, and Sam pulled mini NVG's and sighted. "They're getting the shit kicked out of them, dammit."

"Get—her—out," he heard Sebastian say with each punch.

Viva grabbed his shirt and yanked him back. But it was too late. A voice called out, and Sam looked to the front upper-window.

"Intruders!" the man shouted, pointing.

Sam pulled her toward the street side, but men came around the side. He heard it seconds before they appeared and backed her up against the wall, his body shielding hers as he aimed.

"This isn't working out like I planned." He leaned out and fired, then instantly ducked back as shots came. "Okay, not an option." He flashed her a smile in the dark.

"No argument here."

"That way." He urged her with him to the water.

"God, I really don't want to swim in that again," she said.

"We aren't." He held tight to her hand, and moved northward along the riverfront, yet stopped short when he saw a wedding party spilled onto the terrace of the next hotel. "Well, dammit."

"Gorgeous bride, though." She turned on her bare feet. "I don't suppose—ouch—you have a chopper coming again."

"I wish. Get down." They dropped behind some benches, and Viva winced when a bullet hit wood. Sam shot out the light hanging over them, then aimed, but didn't fire. "Too many civilians. "

"Don't these people know to run when they hear gunfire?" Viva looked around for an escape. No ferry, no small boats, only a thirty-foot cruiser floating at the end of the lit pier. She took off toward the cruiser.

Sam whipped around as she ran to the end of the yacht to the pair of jet skis floating in a tow rack. "Oh, smart girl. Coonass, get cooking!"

Sam darted low as she unwound the ropes and straddled a jet ski. She released the lock and the jet ski floated back from the tow with the current.

"You can drive it?" Sam jumped on behind her.

"Like a motorcycle on water." She turned the key and the engine roared. "Then again, I've never actually ridden a motorcycle."

Men rushed toward them and Sam fired, knocking one off his feet. They opened up with a hail of bullets as Sebastian's charges went off. Screams and debris flew into the night with orange fire as bullets hit the pier, the water, one striking the nose of the jet ski. "Go, go!"

Viva gunned it, the front tipping up for a few yards like a bucking bronco. "Sam!"

Reaching around, he pressed the trim button, and the machine leveled out as it shot across the water. Sam twisted, aiming, but she was going too fast for a clean shot.

"Don't stop."

"Oh yeah, I wanna meet those guys real bad."

Watching behind him, Sam saw a figure move to the edge of the pier, and aim something. "Faster, baby."

Viva pushed the throttle to the max, wind and water blistering her face.

And all she thought was, spared from rape only to be shot?

On the dock, Noor stepped from the shadows, her gaze following the jet ski with her blowgun. Yet she did not fire.

For that man to find her before Noor said he knew where to look. She turned, her gaze following the men as some rushed to the explosion while others ran to the edge of the dock and fired blindly. Stupid. It was too dark and they were long gone—as were the two men who were fighting. She circled the hotel and with surprising ease was inside.

The men were still trying to figure out what happened, she thought, staring at the buyer sprawled on the bed, his expression frozen. She searched the room, tearing it apart for the stones, and found nothing. Then she saw the web camera on the table. Alone.

He will not be pleased, she thought, moving into a vacant room and out the balcony doors. She was over the side and on the ground before his men entered the suite. She dialed her cell, walking in the opposite direction, north up the riverfront.

"He has his laptop." A string of curses filled her ear, and she waited till he was done ranting.

"Let us hope he was wise enough not to put anything leading on it."

Noor did not comment. The buyer stole an American from her bed. His actions so far were driven by his arrogance and his need for sex. Wisdom had no part in either.

Whatever was on the laptop would lead them to her master. It was time for him to leave the country, she thought, and briefly glanced back at the water. The wake of the jet ski had faded, and Noor knew she could have easily killed the woman. She was exposed, in her sights. She deserved the chance to redeem herself, and while her master was angered over the buyer's death, Noor was pleased the woman had the strength to kill him.

CIA Station
Bangkok

Adam Kincade watched the screen stretching for several yards. Surveillance from three locations played. In front of him, officers ten years younger than him worked the computers, wearing headsets and sporadically whispering into wire mikes, sending intelligence, then eagerly waited for confirmation. On the ground, speaking wasn't an option. Too much chance of distortion. And there were just too many listening devices out there to risk it.

Adam's concern was the hunt for Silent Fire, schematics for a weapon prototype stolen from a US–British training area. That someone even knew of its existence said they had a traitor within. The US wasn't going to accuse the Brits and vice versa. You don't piss off your best allies. But the traitor wasn't his main concern, he'd leave that to the Pentagon. As a weapon, he'd only heard, it was untraceable. As a danger, it was catastrophic.

He sipped coffee, thinking of other avenues, other options. His people weren't aware of the real dangers, told only to locate and watch known terrorists. It was a who's who of the world's most wanted. Ground intel was the only option now. His gaze moved to the surveillance post on the Chao Phraya River, then flinched when the video feed lit up with a night explosion. For a moment, the night vision lens went white, nothing visible. The room went instantly quiet, and Adam pulled on a headset, then tuned in the surveillance team.

"Show me that, now."

The officer on detail turned to the camera, using the infrared scope to narrow the focus. "A live one and he's moving." Film recorded and Adam watched the jet ski maneuver up the river from the Oriental.

"He's got a woman on the front, sir."

"Yeah, I know tits and ass when I see them," an officer said.

"Keep down the chatter," Adam ordered, then turned back to the table littered with papers, and pushed some aside. He'd seen that man before and found the MI6 photo log. Same man, he thought, then heard a second explosion.

"Jesus, the place is lit up." A body was midair, then hit the ground and bounced. "Somebody's pissed." The scope swung left.

"They're headed into the canal, harbor police on their tail."

"He's out of our range, start a new recording on the hotel." Adam wanted to see the aftermath, how they moved.

The video turned it from night vision to day-clarity. The hideout of known terrorists.

"Who the hell has the pull to get the harbor police on the water that fast, sir?" an officer asked.

"Port Authority. They patrol the main tributary, rarely here. Only in the harbor." It was like a Vegas strip of hotels on the water, and miles away from the port, Adam thought. "Harbor police can't get that big boat down the canal, he's long gone." He looked to the second screen, then called up his field agents and gave them the area. "Intercept them."

Max and Sebastian slipped away in the chaos of the explosion, and walked casually down the street as Thai police and locals swarmed to see the damage and be nosey.

"You hit hard, Max," Sebastian said, working his jaw.

"Sorry, it wasn't meant for you."

Sebastian cricked his neck and when they were out of sight, they ran toward the black van.

"I saw them get on a jet ski. Headed downriver, south."

"You see the woman on the dock?"

"Yeah, she had a whole daughter-of-death thing going on with those clothes," Max said.

"She aimed a small blowgun."

Max's expression went slack. "At them?"

Sebastian nodded as they got in. Max tried to raise Sam on the headset. "They're out of range." Throat mics were on close-quarters' frequencies. Sebastian drove south. "Good bomb, buddy." Three guards went up with the benches, the building untouched.

Sebastian glanced at Max. "The benches and streetlamps they can replace. A hundred-and-fifty-year-old hotel wing, they can't."

"Glad to hear you have your priorities straight." After a few miles, Max tried again. "Outlaw, this is Drac, what's your twenty?"

Sam directed and Viva obeyed, her fear driving adrenaline up her spine. In the dark, she maneuvered the jet ski between large boats, the wind snapping at her clothes and spraying her with water. The jet ski running light was small and she could barely see more than a few yards ahead.

"Red, you can slow down now." She didn't, and Sam covered her hands, prying them off the controls and slowed the craft.

She leaned her head forward on the handlebars, and let out a long breath. "I'm sorry to cause so much trouble."

"Baby, that's your middle name."

She straightened, twisting. "You looked for me."

The astonishment in her voice cut through to his soul, leaving a mark. Her hand trembled as she touched the side of his face. "You made an impression."

"As a first-class pain in your ass, sure," she said, laughingly.

Her smile sent tears down her cheeks and his expression softened. "You're safe now, don't cry." Her tears felt like little slices to his heart. She was so damn strong, resilient, and he admired the hell out of her, and hated that anyone brought her to this point.

"Thank you, Sam." She brushed her mouth across his and he groaned, sinking deep into her kiss and almost forgetting he was driving. One touch and he was oblivious to the rest of the world, he realized.

When she pulled back, her gaze went past him. "Apparently, it's not over."

He twisted. Thai harbor police. "Hold on."

He gunned it, dodging between pleasure boats and the ferry. Sam knew he could hit debris in the water and end this in seconds. The jet ski bounced over wakes, slamming them down onto the seat.

"Oh, for pity's sake, Sam!" Viva took control, side-winding around the boats and avoiding the wake of others. He admitted she was better at it than he was.

Then the harbor police fired on them.

"We have to get off the water." He pointed toward the mouth of the river, and Viva slipped the jet ski sideways into the canal. The harbor patrol was still hot on their tail, maneuvering to get the heavy draft boat into the canal.

"Run it aground."

"You're joking!" It was pitch black nothing out there.

"There, run it aground!"

Viva pushed the throttle, trimmed and raced toward the shore. Sam held her tight as he cut the engine a few yards in. The jet ski hit bottom, jerked to a stop, and tipped.

Viva slid off and splashed to the shore, Sam grabbed her up, carrying her over the ground to the street, then set her on her feet. Traffic zipped past and Viva started to put her hand up to hail a cab, but Sam grabbed it.

"They aren't going to stop."

"Then we'll steal one." She ran up the road to a line of parked cars, and tried each door, setting off alarms. She threw one open, and dove under the steering column.

Sam was there, and saw her pop off the column cover and pull wires. "You can hotwire?"

"Product of a misspent youth."

"Man, this I wanna hear about."

Static charges sparked and the engine started. Viva crawled over the console and Sam climbed behind the wheel, handing her the laptop.

"I think the car's owner is coming."

He yanked the wheel, pushed the gas, and the car shot into traffic. "We can't do this for long."

"Far enough from here is good." She looked behind, and could see the car owner waving his hands. Oh yeah, buddy, like that helps.

Sam drove with traffic, and glanced and grinned.

"Please don't tell me you like this outfit." She wrung out the wet pant legs.

"Under other circumstances maybe, but I was just thinking you certainly have grace under fire, darlin'."

Viva felt the warmth of his words, and smiled. "How did you know to find me?"

Sam really didn't want to talk about this now. It would only hurt her. But she'd pester. "Dr. Wan Gai." She frowned. "He sold you."

Her eyes flared. "No, you must be wrong." But the look in his eyes said otherwise. "Why would he do that?"

"The bracelet."

"It's just an artifact. Ancient, sure, but not world class."

"Would he have gone to this extreme if it wasn't?"

"I guess not." She sighed back into the seat. "Sold me . . . the disgusting little bastard. I ought to—"

"You can do what you want to him, I'll make sure of it." He grasped her hand briefly and squeezed.

She sent him a look that was downright sadistic. "You won't want to witness it." If anything, for the people left in that smelly room.

"Probably not. Drac, Coonass, where are you?"

"Damn man, I was getting worried," blasted in his ear and Sam winced.

"We're fine, meet us at the south end of Nerti."

"You're *driving?*"

"Yes, I'm driving."

"Not very well." Viva pointed and Sam jerked the wheel.

"Jeez, I hate ground level."

"It's not too fond of you. Sam, left, stay on the *left.*" She banged the dash. "Oncoming headlights give you a clue? Pull over, at least I remember which side of the road I should be on."

"Too late, our ride's here." He pulled to the curb and got out. Viva started to leave the car, then reached over and yanked the wires. The engine stopped.

She was just coming upright when she saw bright headlights barreling toward them. She waited a split second, expecting them to stop. They weren't. "Sam!" The car swerved sideways, slid and hit, jolting their car backwards.

"Start the engine." Sam dropped behind the wheel as Viva ducked low, working the wires again. Two men spilled out of the black car, weapons rising to aim. "Bug out, Max. Viva, hurry!"

She struck the wires against each other, got a spark, once, twice.

"We can take them," Max said.

"Negative, you're too far away and they have range." Right at them—or the gas tank. "Viva!"

The engine caught. Sam threw the car in reverse and hit the gas. The motion set her forward.

"Jesus, Sam!"

"Sorry." Sam drove backwards, swerving and correcting, taking out a vendor's cart and making the few people out at this hour scatter. "Seat belt," he warned.

She buckled in. "They're coming after us." The two men jumped back into their car.

"Yeah, I figured that." Who they were was the big question. The men at the hotel were dead or nursing wounds and hadn't followed by water. So how'd these guys know they were on the road?

"It would be wise to turn this around." They had the advantage of not traveling backwards. "They aren't shooting. People around you always shoot."

"That says something. One of their own is dead, they'd shoot to kill."

"You think that's comforting? Oh man, they're gonna hit again!" She braced herself.

Sam looked forward just as the impact drove them backwards. He braked, but the tires smoked as the other car ground into theirs. "Okay, you wanna play, you son of a bitch!" He jammed on the gas and told Viva to lay on the horn.

"People? People?" she shouted and waved. "Get out of the way. It's a chase!"

"You tell 'em, honey. Drac, the tiger has our tail."

"We're heading them off," Max said. "Go right down the next street."

In reverse? "I need a place to turn around, too many civilians," Sam said.

"There's an alley." She pointed. "Back in there, let them pass us."

"You've definitely seen too much TV." Sam's gaze shot around and he realized she was right. It was the only one without human congestion and vendors. He jerked the wheel, rear end into the alley. There was a good reason. It was blocked with garbage cans and they collided, trash spilling before he shifted gears and eased out. But the other car was there, stopped, engine revving.

Sam considered shooting out their tires, but aiming would bring gunfire and he wasn't at an advantage here. "Max, we're cornered."

"You can outrun him," Viva said. "He's in a Toyota, we're in a BMW. Go. Go!"

Sam shrugged, gave it gas and made a sharp left, the rear fishtailing as the other car climbed up his ass. "You were saying?"

"So I was wrong. At least you're not backwards. God, you're a shitty driver."

"Max, where the hell are you guys?" He needed to ditch this car. On foot in the tightly packed city, they'd have better odds.

"West, Rajprarop Road and oh yeah, the Thai police are coming."

"Great."

Suddenly, the car stalled.

Eleven

Viva's gaze snapped to the wires. They'd uncurled and she bent to try again. The other car pushed from behind. Tires squealed. Sam had both feet on the brake.

"Viva, get out!" Drunk people were in front of them, just staring.

"I almost have it."

When the car backed up to ram them, Sam opened his door. "No, now!" He pulled her upright.

They rear-ended them, her shoulder hitting the dash. She grabbed the laptop and shot from the car as Sam rolled over the hood, taking the computer from her and grabbing her hand. Sam ran, pushing between people who should be in bed, and hurried her into a bar, moving swiftly between the drunks and pole dancers. Her bare feet slapped the cement floor. A waitress shouted, a man came to defend her, and in one motion, Sam turned, shielded Viva, and aimed his gun. The guy threw his hands up and sat, and Sam headed out the back, checked the area. They went left. The street was half as wide as the avenue, clothes hung from lines strung between the buildings. A drunk sat in a doorway, and watched them run past.

"Max, Max, get to Rhaiji Street, east end." Sam looped the sling over his head and shoulder.

"It's one way," came back with static.

Viva glanced back as the two men spilled into the passage, looking left and right. Instantly she grabbed Sam's shirt and pulled him down an alley. "They're here."

He moved ahead, the alley so narrow his shoulders brushed the walls. At the end, he stopped short and Viva plowed into him. A rickshaw hurried past.

Sam's gaze followed it, then he grasped her hand. This is gonna hurt, she thought as they took off after it. Viva called out in Thai and the man slowed the small motorbike. Sam jumped in, Viva tried and hopped a few feet, wincing, and he grabbed her by the waist and yanked her in.

"Your life is painfully exciting." She sank down on a sigh.

Sam held her tightly against him as he peered behind through the carriage hood. The two men were searching, parting in two directions. They had radios.

"We lose them?"

"For now." He sighed into the seat, both breathing hard.

Sam spoke to the driver. The man twisted a look over his shoulder, frowning.

Viva smiled. "You just told him to take you into the river." She spoke quickly, directing him toward the river market streets.

"Max, head to the market, east end."

"Thai police have the streets blocked. And they're doing a search."

"For what?"

"Well, since they're grabbing anyone with the slightest shades of red hair, I'll give you one guess."

"Wan Gai pulled some strings?"

Viva looked at him sharply.

"I meant to tell you that."

Sam pressed the earpiece tighter to hear over the noise in the streets. "What?"

"I looked into his background. He's part of the Thai royal family."

"Oh, hell." He told Viva, and her eyes rounded.

"Maybe that explains the Thai police, but over a bracelet?"

"He's covering his back. With you locked in a Thai prison, he won't have to worry."

It was the worry part that had her confused. Wan Gai's actions were extreme and unnecessary. It told her the bracelet was more than a really great archeological find.

The rickshaw stopped and Sam inspected the area carefully before getting out. He paid and he and Viva walked quickly toward the docks, the crowd thinning out.

"Sam, slow down, I'm barefoot."

His gaze darted to her feet, then he gave her his back, adjusting the laptop in front before squatting. "Hop on."

Viva leaped on his back, and he pulled her legs around his waist and trotted.

"A monkey on your back. Sorta says something about our relationship."

"Gee, I just can't see it." She nipped his earlobe. "There they are."

The van slid to the curb, and the door popped open. Sebastian stuck his head out. "Come on, we've got company."

"Again?" She glanced. Blue lights of Thai police cars were headed toward them, but the people traffic held them up. "Why aren't they after the other guys?" she said as she slipped off his back. Sam hurried her into the van.

"Glad to see you're okay, Viva." Max grinned in the rearview, waving as he pulled into traffic.

"Nice to be alive. Thank you. Good backup this time."

"Any idea who the rabbit was?" Sebastian asked.

"They were determined, but sloppy. CIA?" They snickered. "They didn't want to kill us, just stop us." There were a lot of badasses in Bangkok this week, Sam didn't doubt the intelligence community of several nations were out there watching and waiting to make a move. Hunting them though, said they didn't have any more of a clue than Dragon One did.

Sam lifted his gaze to Viva. "You okay?"

On her knees, Viva pushed her hair back and the longer she stared, the more the tears welled in her eyes. His throat felt thick, and he couldn't decide if he should stay clear of this woman, or drag her into his arms and say the hell with it.

She solved that for him as she launched into his arms, covering his mouth with hers. He devoured her, his fear and rage at the past twenty-four hours bleeding into desire as he kissed her and kissed her.

"Thank you for looking," she said between kisses. "Thank you for even *thinking* to look. I never thought I'd get out of there and a life of servitude was just not my calling."

Sam grinned against her mouth, tightening his arms around her, then drawing her across his lap.

"What about me? I helped." Sebastian smiled.

Viva drew back, staring at Sam for a moment, running her thumb across his lower lip before she looked at Sebastian. She slid off Sam's lap and kissed Sebastian's cheek.

Behind her, Sam pulled the pouch from the back of her slacks and she flinched around. "So what's in this?"

"Heck if I know, but he made an appointment to discuss that. It was all I heard."

Sebastian frowned, and Viva opened the sack. Her eyes went wide and she lifted her gaze to Sam's. "I think I made a big mistake."

"With you, that's the norm."

Viva tipped the sack and spilled uncut diamonds into her palm. Sam looked at Sebastian, who merely arched a brow.

"The man who bought you, who was he?" Sebastian asked.

"I never saw him before I woke up tied to the bed."

"Tied? The son of a bitch tied you!" Max said, disgusted.

"I recognized him," Sam said quietly.

Max peered in the rearview. Sebastian waited. Viva looked at him, pouring the diamonds back in the sack.

"It was Ryzikov." Sam unfolded the damp fabric, showing the laptop.

"Who?" Viva said, then noticed the pasty look on Sebastian's face.

"He's Chechen, and handles finances and operations."

"For what?"

"The Riyadus-Salikhin Battalion."

Viva's brows knit and she looked between the two men. She was afraid to ask. "And that's who, exactly?"

Sam let out a long breath. "Chechen Islambouli Brigades." He rubbed his mouth. "Al Qaeda."

CIA Station
Bangkok

Adam Kincade cursed. "You didn't think that merely approaching them wouldn't get you a better response?"

"They were running from Thai police, by car."

"*I'd* run from the Thai police!" He pushed his fingers through his short hair and swore it went gray. "You people need to go back to the Farm. How long have you been in this country? Don't answer that."

He drew a breath, paced, and watched the screens that tapped into the airports, the main hubs of business districts, hotel cameras. Each section, a four-person team watched a large area of the city around where they suspected the worst of humanity was in Thailand.

"Find them," he said into the headset. "They were in Ryzikov's hotel, they saw something, they know something about why he's here, and we need to know it because, boys and girls"—he looked at the room full of surveillance analysts—"we need an advantage. And we need it now."

A young man approached, a baggie in his hand. "Only one shell, a Dragunov, SVD." Adam only glanced at the bag. Beyond the secured room, workers were replacing the shattered glass. Looters had taken most of the equipment, and though it was for looks, it was expensive. He was busting the budget in manpower already.

Adam nodded, refraining from waving the man off. The

officer didn't know about the weapon schematics, didn't know the danger it posed. He wanted to tell them, to give them the lead, and he wished the hell someone in Langley would get with the program. Working blind would only leave them stumbling in the dark.

And the terrorists had the light.

The jungle canopy hid the dirt road, torchlight brightening only where he stood as Kashir watched the line of Land Rovers be swallowed by the darkness.

He'd been anointed, given control by the Chow leaders. And that dropped him in deep trouble. He didn't want the job, yet wisely refrained from saying so. A gang leader, territory to work and protect. None of the Chow seemed concerned that Najho was killed by a dart. It was a concern to him. Kashir had seen it too much. Najho had said too much.

Certainly the treatment was better, less work, more catering to him, yet what he heard from the Chow was enough to make his skin crawl.

He had to contact Dragon One. The danger waiting for Wyatt wasn't a concern. The Texan had already proven himself resourceful and skilled. Kashir's conscience nagged him enough to actually do his real job for Interpol, and warn the man that Rohki was just a cog in a big wheel. His final adversary was more powerful—without a just cause or personal stake—and that made him deadly.

Viva heard Al Qaeda and tossed the sack at Sam. "Count me out."

"I don't blame you, but you're stuck with us now."

"What do you mean? I'm heading out of here on the next flight . . . oh hell, my passport."

Sam dug in a bag and handed the money belt to her.

"See, now I'm all set, some clothes and I can leave, be out of your hair." Sam shook his head. "No, don't do that," she warned.

"Viva, you killed the man."

Her features went slack, the color draining, and in a tiny voice she said, "It was self-defense."

"Yes, it was." He could still see the man's fingerprints on her throat. "But he's got friends in low places. They'll come after you."

"It's true, *chéri,*" Sebastian said. "Your best chances are with us."

"Okay, okay, just exactly who *are you people?* What are you doing mixed up in this?"

"I'll explain later, but we're the good guys."

"I think you've proven that a few times." She smiled at Sam, then beyond him in the rear of the van, she saw movement. "That's Dr. Wan Gai's assistant. What's he doing here? And tied up and bleeding."

Sam tossed a thumb in Choan's direction. "He's the one who actually sold you."

She was about to argue the point, then realized Choan wouldn't be in here if he *didn't* have anything to do with this. She looked from Sam to Choan, then suddenly lurched across the gear bags and punched Choan over and over.

Sam let her have at it for a minute, then pulled her back. "Get that out of your system?"

"Not really." She blew on her knuckles. "He's got the bracelet, so what's the big, hairy deal?"

Sam dug in a bag and handed her the gold cuff. She turned it in her hands and then met his gaze. "I missed out on a lot, didn't I?"

"You said it was priceless."

"It is, to find something like this in those caves is phenomenal. I'm betting it's older than even Dr. Nagada thought, but what was I going to do with that information? Go to the king? I'd never get an audience."

"What would the curator be required to do with it?" Sebastian asked.

She shrugged. "Catalogue and display it. I don't know the Thai protocol for artifacts. Probably inform the king, maybe turn it over to him. He's Thai royalty, so he's got a lot of leeway."

"Apparently whatever it represents is detrimental, or Wan Gai wouldn't have risked this coming back on the king," Sebastian said.

"I intend to find out." She put the cuff on.

"Home sweet home, guys," Max said, pulling to a stop.

Viva looked out the front window, but all she saw was more jungle. Sam slid the door open, hopped out, then reached for her. Beyond him was a one-story house, very Thai with a sloping, pagoda-style tile roof and beautiful gardens.

"Boy, you guys know how to live," she said, then turned back to the van. "What're you going to do with big and ugly?" She inclined her head to the back and Choan.

"What is your preference?" Sebastian said devilishly.

Viva mentally debated that for a second or two, but didn't want anyone's life on her conscience. One was plenty. "I'll leave that up to you, but selling him into slavery would be an option I'd consider." Sebastian grinned as she turned away, and with Sam, walked toward the house.

The front door opened, and Sam reached for his gun, his footsteps faltering for a second till he recognized Logan. "About time, pal, we could use your help." Sam held out the laptop.

Logan took it, but his attention was on the woman, his gaze sliding admiringly over her. "What did you do, Wyatt? Steal from Ali Baba's harem?"

"Yes, and the forty thieves will be right along," Viva said, sweeping past him into the house.

"Bathroom is to the right," Sam called out. She waved overhead, and Sam and Logan followed inside.

"Prisoner or plaything?" Logan asked.

Sam scoffed. "Neither." He didn't expect her good mood to last. "She killed a man tonight." And when it sunk in, nothing would console her.

"Her?" Logan glimpsed the beautiful redhead before she disappeared down the hall.

"She's tougher than she looks. And a fighter."

"So who'd she ghost?"

"Andrei Ryzikov."

Logan whistled softly. "What's he doing here? Last I heard he was hiding somewhere in northern Chechnya with Russian Foreign intelligence hot on his ass."

"Diamonds brought him out, and I'm hoping the answers in there."

Sam stood outside the room, and knocked softly. She didn't answer and he figured she was sleeping. Yet when he opened the door, she was curled in a chair, staring out the bank of windows. The sun was just coming up. "Viva?" Her back to him, she brushed at her cheeks and the muscles around his heart tightened.

"I'm okay," she said.

He gripped the towel hooked around his neck and debated leaving her alone. "Are you?"

"Well, killing a man today was a first. I'm sure I'll get over it."

He crossed to her and felt a jumble of emotions. Anger that she'd suffered, that she was forced to take a life, yet mostly he felt sympathy. He understood what she was feeling. The first time he had to kill a man, he'd puked. His other feelings, his attraction to her, which was nothing short of startling, had no place right now and he knelt before her.

Her arms wrapped around her bent legs, she rested her chin on her knees. She looked so desolate, not like the woman who fought off bandits in the jungle.

"You won't get over it, just used to the idea."

She pressed her forehead to her knees briefly. "I didn't have a choice, I know that, but when I grabbed the knife all I thought was—me or him. And I really didn't want to die."

"Ryzikov has a reputation for killing his women, baby. I would have killed him. Gladly."

Her head jerked up, eyes flaring.

"He had no right to touch you. The man who sold you to

him is dead, the people who were in that room with you are free."

She let out a long sigh. "Oh, thank God." Her voice rasped, remnants of the strangling. "I was thinking I was a really crummy member of the human race to be sitting here, feeling sorry for myself when they were all suffering." She bent her head again, yet said nothing.

He could tell she was crying. "Talk to me, Red." He stroked her hair.

"I'm scared."

His heart just plain ached for her. "You're safe now."

"No, of myself, of things I've done that will leave a mark and change everything." She tipped her head and met his gaze. A voice in her head said tell him about the rifle, the headaches, the dock, but it wouldn't come. More fear, she thought. "I've spent my adult life going from job to job, never doing anything more than six months, a year maybe. I changed jobs for men, for boredom, for a challenge. Well, that's what I kept telling myself, but the truth is, I just quit." She let out a breath as if letting go would change her world. "I don't want to quit anymore. And as ridiculous as it sounds, this past week has been the most exciting of my life." His brows rose. "Well, most of it. But at least I felt alive."

"The rush is temporary, trust me."

"I do."

He smiled, blushing a little, and she almost expected an "aw shucks, ma'am," then knew it wouldn't come. Sam didn't let anything so trivial hinder him. He jumped in with both barrels blazing or that bullwhip cracking, danger be damned. At least she knew to be scared, she thought, her gaze sliding over his bare chest, his hair still damp from a shower. The towel looped around his neck, he gripped the ends. Did it get any sexier?

"You're one terrific guy, ya know."

He smiled gently.

"I've seen courage before, but you take the cake." She let her feet fall to the floor.

"Give yourself some credit."

"For trouble, sure. But nothing like what I've seen." She pushed his hair back off his forehead. He had hero written all over him, she thought. "Do you *fear* anything?"

Sam stared into her soft green eyes, and saw the truth. "Only you."

"Why?"

"You do things to me."

Her lips curved. "Screw up your mission, force you to come rescue me, twice?"

"Who's counting." He leaned in.

Viva felt swallowed up by the look in his dark eyes, intense, for sure, but something else she'd never seen in a man.

"You make me want to crawl inside your skin and find out what makes you tick."

Tears blurred her vision and she inhaled sharply, a perilous feeling tumbling through her. "No one's ever tried," she whispered, touching the side of his face.

"Lucky me."

She smiled softly, a tear falling.

"Don't cry, it tears me up to see it."

"So now it's all about *you,* huh?"

He chuckled. He never knew what to expect from her. She was the most unpredictable woman he'd ever known, and she fascinated the hell out of him.

She grasped the ends of the towel, pulling him near, and his hands on either side of her slid along her thighs, her hips.

"This is dangerous," he said, his face nearing hers.

"Define danger." Her mouth lingered over his and she slipped off the chair, straddled his lap.

God. He could feel the heat of her through his jeans. "You, in *any* form, me hot as hell to have you."

"And time alone with no one shooting at us," she finished. "And let's not forget I'm naked under this robe." Her mouth trailed his throat, and she caught his earlobe and nibbled.

Sam felt himself go cross-eyed with desire. "Oh, Jesus.

You're making me come apart again, Red." He kissed her hot and quick.

"Is that all?"

He gripped her hips, ground her to him, and proved she had him in her grasp.

"You've had a rough couple of days, and—"

Her gaze flashed to his and he saw it, the memory, the moment when Ryzikov violated her, when she knew she'd die. "I know my own mind, Sam, and I think—yours."

But she didn't.

She had no idea how close she came to *not* dying today.

Ryzikov had plans for her, a personal brand Sam had seen once before. The bastard would take her to the edge of her life, then jerk her back; a reprieve that lasted only till the son of a bitch wanted to witness his control again. The marks on her neck were only the first layer.

Seeing them made him relive his fear, admit he'd never been so scared in his life than when he couldn't find her, couldn't protect her. It ate him alive. She had no training, no defenses, nothing to help herself, and then, she proved him wrong—again.

"Sam?" She frowned, wondering what he was thinking on so hard. "This zoning-out thing is not a good sign and my ego is terribly fragile. I might not recover."

He smiled slow and broad, then cupped her jaw in his broad palms and kissed her. Really kissed her. Not like he hadn't done a damn fine job before but this time, he was full of patience when she wanted to plow ahead. Each roll of his mouth made her toes curl, her skin tighten. Her soul opened.

"I can't ignore you, baby," he said against her lips. "It's physically impossible."

Her body reacted with quick shivers, her hands spread wide over his chest. "Mmm, command of the body. It's a good start."

He met her gaze, something battling behind his dark eyes. "You and me, we're more than that." His fingers flexed on her jaw.

Viva went still inside, and swore her heartbeat just plain stopped. Was he for real? No one had ever spoken to her like this. She covered his hands, pulling them from her face and gripping. "Seriously?"

"I don't say anything I don't mean."

"Me, either." Her gaze lingered over him, her hand spread over his bare chest, the contours of muscle defined and rippling. It made her hot to see all of that man, and know he was hers for tonight. She lifted her gaze to his as she tugged at the robe's sash. She'd never been shy, never let what she wanted escape.

Yet he hesitated. "Me or erasing his memory?"

She smiled with feline grace and spread the robe, exposing her breasts and loving his jaw-dropping look. "Oh, if you don't know that by now, we really aren't communicating well enough." Her hand went behind his neck, and she drew him close. "Let me fix that."

Her tongue snaked out and slicked his lips and he groaned as he sank into her. The terrorist's touch evaporated with each press of his mouth on hers, in the way he touched her, as if he'd never get the chance again. It was a rare sensation for her, and the bounty of it flowed into an empty place in her, in the scattered loneliness she'd lived for years. And she ached for more, greedy woman. There was no question in her mind when she slid the robe off her shoulders, and let it pool at her hips.

He swallowed, his gaze riding over her body. "Oh, man, you're—"

"Ready and willing?"

"Beautiful."

Her heart just got lighter, she thought, sliding her arms around his neck and sinking her fingers into his hair. Her breasts grazed his chest, and in his ear she whispered hotly, "Wanna rock and roll with me?"

"Jesus." Sam slammed his eyes shut.

Then she kissed him.

Pure heat and wild hunger. And more. Sam felt the power of it speed down his body and fight for escape. Instead it built, a need like sucking in a lungful of air that wouldn't come, and he struggled. It almost scared him, opened up feelings he'd buried for the missions—fighting it was impossible. Viva made him *feel.* Just by her very existence. She was her own adventure, her own ruler, and the thrills in a high-speed chase in a tight cockpit didn't compare to the ecstasy of Viva—naked—pressed against him, her mouth moving savagely over his.

His hands swept up her tight ribs, cupping her breasts, and the contact was electric, her kiss stronger, hurried. He thumbed her nipples in slow circles, and her shudder tumbled into his mouth. Strong thighs clamped him and he broke the kiss, and held her gaze as he bent her over his arm and closed his lips over her nipple.

She threw her head back, moaning beautifully, then watched him take her skin deep into the heat of his mouth. "More good man skills," she breathed.

He smiled against her skin, lifting her higher against him, his tongue sliding wetly over her breasts, his teeth deliciously scoring the plump underside. But it wasn't enough. He wanted her screaming, he wanted her weak and panting and vulnerable—only for him.

Her fingers dug into his shoulder. "Now, right now, Sam."

"Not a chance."

"Spoilsport."

He smiled and tasted her mouth as he cupped her behind and rose, carrying her to the bed. He bent one knee, hefting her onto the mattress.

Smiling devilishly, so natural for her, she crooked a finger at him.

Sam damn near leapt on her as he worked his belt, watching her twist with desire. He drank her in, her wild red hair, the ripe, round curves of her body. Her breasts were a thing for poets. But it was her eyes that trapped him, playful, sexy.

"Want help, cowboy?"

"You touch me and I'm all over like an eight-second bronc ride."

She laughed softly and came to him, gripped his belt and jerked him close. "That was just too much of a dare." She got it open, shoved the zipper down, then swept her hands inside. She cupped his tight rear, squeezing, then pushed the jeans down.

Sam kicked them off, but Viva wasn't done.

"Eight seconds, huh?" He flinched when her hand closed over his erection, fingertips sliding across the tip. "So much of you is big, and strong."

He chuckled but it never materialized. Her mouth was on him, taking him deep and he couldn't breathe, and could only watch the slide of her warm lips over him.

"Five, four, three," she teased, then licked.

"You talk too much."

She looked at him. "Then I guess you better shut me up."

His arms locked around her, his kiss driving her head back. He caught her knee, pulling it to his hip, and she rubbed against his erection as his mouth grew heavier, as if to drink her in, swallow her whole.

Viva loved it and said nothing. She couldn't. He was taking her down to the mattress, his hands and mouth trailing over her throat, her breasts. He paused to suck her nipples, draw on her skin, taste the curves of her ribs. His hands were busy, everywhere, and Viva knew Sam had more skills than pulling a trigger and flying. Then he spread her thighs over his, baring her completely and met her gaze.

"No comments?"

"More?" she said, breathing heavily. The anticipation was enough to make her come right now.

Then his hands roamed from her knees to her center, and he parted her, his fingertips dipping lightly, and he smiled as she twisted on the sheet, drew her knees up a bit. Then he pressed a finger inside her and she arched, and thrust into his touch.

"Do that again." He did. "Oh God, Sam." She cupped her breasts, arched deeper and slid her hands down her thighs. "Come to me, inside me."

"No." He introduced another finger and stroked her.

She whimpered, but Sam wasn't going fast, not when everything in him said take her right now like a thief in the night. This was just too incredible to rush.

Then he bent, slowly, his gaze locked with hers and Viva practically licked her lips as he lowered.

"Oh, goody." His tongue snaked, and her breath hissed in.

Then he laid his mouth over her center, fingers peeling her wider as his tongue slicked wetly. "You're not talking."

"My mind is blank, a first," she gasped, and he lifted her hips, his tongue flicking and circling fast, then slow. Viva gripped her thighs, her breath hissing through her teeth. "There's nothing more erotic than a man's head between my legs."

He chuckled. "That all you want between there?" He tasted her again and again, drawing her to the edge and letting her dangle. Her hips fluctuated and her hands swept to cup her breasts, her feet on the mattress and pushing.

She was wild, and damn vocal, telling him everything she was feeling, that she wanted to feel him pushing inside her, that exquisite moment when they were locked. And that this was just the start.

She was coming, he felt the pull, her inner muscles working his fingers, and he withdrew and thrust.

"I don't want this alone." She rose up, climbing his lap and closing her fist around him.

"Condoms."

"Don't need 'em." She turned out her forearm. Under her skin he could see a slim, faint mark of birth control. Then he wasn't thinking as she stroked him. "And I really don't want them." She kissed him and whispered in his ear, "Yee haw."

Sam's erection flexed in her hand. "Eight seconds and counting, baby." She pushed his erection down, sliding wetly across him, teasing him. "You're killing me."

"I was hoping to make you feel alive."

She did, more than a hot jet ride, touching her was exhilarating, feeling her wet and hot against him mind-blowing, and when she rose up a bit and guided him, her lids fluttering.

Her expression changed, her eyes going glossy.

"Viva?" He held her as she sank down on him, her body shivering in his arms, and Sam thought, I'm falling apart for this woman. For a moment, they just stared at each other, and with his thumb, he brushed the tear escaping the corner of her eye.

"God. I—I can't think."

"Then don't." Sam gripped her hips and gave them motion, filling her, and Viva clung to him.

"Sam, oh Sam."

"I know, baby. Kinda scary." Opposite as they could possibly be, they fit, matched.

She met his gaze. "You're the one thing that doesn't scare me." She moved and he cupped her behind, pulling her back. "Don't hold a damn thing back. Don't you dare."

"Now that would be impossible." He tossed her on her back, grabbing the headboard and pushing into her. He left her completely and slid back, loving the flare in her green eyes, the smile that never seemed to fade.

Tanned muscle and strength hovered over her, pleasured her. Her softness touching more than his skin, but also his soul. She reached up and smoothed her fingers over his jaw, let them dribble down his body to feel him plunge into her.

It didn't get any more erotic, he thought, and then it did. She locked her legs around him, her hands on his chest as she pushed him back and she straddled him, never stopping. Her hips curled in a rhythmic wave, letting him feel every inch of his erection sliding in her. For a moment Sam was mesmerized, her stomach muscles contracting, her spine bending and pushing her hips into his. His hands closed over her breasts, thumbs circling slowly, and her lids lowered, the tempo increasing with her breathing.

He let her keep control. She seemed to need it. She gripped

his arms, holding on and riding, faster and harder. She called his name, her look almost afraid. And Sam cupped the back of her head, forced her to look directly at him as his fingers slid over the bead of her sex. Her eyes glazed.

"More, more, more," she whispered, and he laid her back, and drove into her, felt the claw of her body on his, the rage of passion sweeping over his skin. He was uncontrollable, mindless need to drive harder, and their momentum pushed her across the bed.

Yet she matched him, her hips pistoned to his. Then his world split, his climax exploding and she gripped him, thrusting faster as his body tightened and rocketed with hard, exploding thrusts.

Viva arched, her back bending so deeply he thought she'd snap. She gripped his hips, grinding him into her. "Kiss me, hurry before the world hears—"

He did. Eating her mouth, his tongue thrusting. She came, her scream muffled and tripping into his mouth, her hot little center jerking and clawing his erection. He slammed into her, the rip of pleasure tearing over his skin, pulsing with her. They strained, held on, and let the sweep of it take them.

Sam groaned, the waves of pure ecstasy crackling through him for several moments. She collapsed on the bed and he'd barely caught his breath when she said, "Eight seconds, my ass."

He chuckled and looked at her. Viva touched his face, pulled him down on her, and he rolled with her to his side, drawing her leg over his. For a long moment they just stared, damp, a tangle of legs and arms.

"You're under my skin, Red."

"An itch you can't scratch?"

His hand slid over her hip. "I just did."

Her eyes danced with a snappy comeback, but instead, she leaned close and rubbed her mouth over his. What a guy, she thought, and she didn't even know why he was in Thailand. It didn't matter, not now, and Viva snuggled closer, staring up into his dark eyes.

"Think your friends heard us?"

He arched a brow. "Do you care?"

"There's little that could embarrass me, Sam." She shifted on top of him, and Sam reveled in her soft, lush, completely sexy body on his, his hand sweeping up her behind. They stayed like that, sinking into the sensations, the tender moment, then Viva braced her arms on his chest, her chin on her hands. He smiled.

"Let me know when you're ready to do that again."

Sam laughed, clamping his arms around her and rolling her to her back. "Now good for you?" With his knee, he nudged her thighs wide.

"God, I love a man of action."

A half hour later, a knock rattled the door.

"Go away," she said sleepily, too content to move.

"I'm going to beat the hell out of whoever's on the other side," Sam groused, leaving the bed.

"Don't answer it," she muttered.

"I have to." He pulled on his jeans. "We're here for a reason."

"And here I thought it was all for me."

Words faded as he glanced back. She was sprawled on the bed, asleep, every inch of her beautiful skin exposed. God, he was a saint to leave that, he thought, then the knock came again. He opened the door a crack. Logan was on the other side.

"You're walking a damn thin line right now."

Logan arched a brow and looked like he cared less. "You have to see this."

"It can't wait?"

"I found surveillance photos, targets, satellite images."

"Satellite? His connections are better than we thought." Google Earth would only take them so far. Someone let Ryz into some classified material.

"He's got a lot on the US and allies. And before you ask, no, I can't find which satellite they used."

Sam's expression tightened. "We need to get that to the CIA and Washington."

"Not till I get past the passwords and encryption. If I can get into his e-mail, we'll know who he was in contact with."

"The laptop was hooked to a webcam when I took it."

Logan's expression instantly changed. "Was it on?"

"Dormant, I think." Sam's eyes flared. "Crap, whoever was on the other end could have seen the whole thing."

Twelve

Project Silent Fire
US–UK Joint Command

He'd been trading intel with the Pentagon all day, so much that each time the link was possible, they were in conference. Yet when Gerardo saw the captain moving toward him, he prayed it was good news.

"Ryzikov is dead."

Gerardo's brows shot up. "We have photos, proof?" His head on a goddamn platter.

"Some, sir, they are uploading now."

The general addressed the assembly on two continents, then waved for the captain to take over.

He hit the remote for the screen. "These are photos taken by our surveillance of what we'd suspected was Ryzikov's location." The Oriental hotel popped on the screen. "Evidence later confirmed it. As near as we can tell there was a small explosion, three killed and little damage to the hotel, and these two men fled." The camera, blinked four or five times, narrowing the focus. "We have no identity as yet. However, a man and a woman also fled, moments before, by the water." Photos came up again. "CIA is loading up more."

"Dead is dead, captain. What's the point of this?" Lt. Colonel Maitland asked.

"Ryzikov's body was removed from the building a short while later and taken immediately to the airport for transport. No papers, no official red tape to remove the body, nothing. In the air and gone."

The murmurs in the room instantly stopped. Whoever had a hand in that had tremendous influence.

"Good grief, Thailand can't close its airports, how the hell can we stop these people?" a British general said.

"NSA intel traffic snagged some signal intelligence just before the explosion." The young man hit the speaker, and the Russian's accented voice played. It was a coded discussion, and around the room, people made notes, heads together in quick discussion.

Of course, I have the stones and we will discuss the bargain at the appointed time.

After the conversation stopped, the officer said, "We intercepted it via a cell tower."

"I don't care how, who'd he call?"

"We don't know. It's sending over twenty thousand bytes per second and the nodes are not identifiable because of an encrypted onion router."

Gerardo frowned at him along with half the men in the room.

In DC, the NSA director spoke up. "Onion routing provides anonymous connections that are strongly resistant to both eavesdropping and traffic analysis. It's our biggest challenge. Ryzikov might have used a cell phone, but whoever he was talking to was calling through a *computer*. The call can be acoustically distorted, and sent to another computer with a router, then splits it off and fans it out."

McGill put his hand up. "I get it." Give him a missile to track or a tank to target, but computer speak just gave him a headache. "We have this technology?"

The NSA director nodded. "We can find the source if he's not using a proxy server."

"And if he is?"

"It will take more time." The director leaned forward, looking solemn. "This information also narrows the field."

"How narrow?"

"Start excluding some Chechen rebels, Colombian, Congolese, they don't have this technology. It's costly, rarely available to the public, mostly government and corporate use, some of the ones under our government contract. Plus they'd need an expert to set it up. And we've hired most of them on our team."

"Apparently not all," McGill said as he stood, racking his papers. Tracking the software sales was pointless. There were thousands of people out there skilled enough to recreate the processors. "Analysis on this in an hour. I want to know who has this capability and what the hell *stones* has to do with this."

He looked at the screen and nodded to Gerardo. The man looked exhausted and considering it was pretty late in England, he silently commended Gerardo's stamina. "Get some rest, Al. I'll call you at seven your time."

McGill turned toward the door, a group of men following him. He didn't go to his office and stopped at Staff Sgt. Walker's terminal. The man looked up, then stood.

"Sir?"

While the clearance for the information was the highest, McGill knew he could trust this young man above all. He had the ability to take the most inconsequential bits of information and make connections. He inclined his head, and Staff Sgt. Walker followed the three-star general. Walker knew he'd face a challenge when the general kicked everyone else out.

Ramesh Narabi was escorted into a room. His blindfold had been replaced with a hood, and strong hands led him forward, then pushed him into a chair.

Then the hood was ripped off his head, the light faint, but no less startling to his eyes. Large hands held his head still.

Before him was a large blank screen. His gaze flicked but in his line of vision, he could see nothing and no one.

"Mr. Narabi," came from somewhere near the ceiling, and he strained his eyes to see the speakers. "You are curious as to why you are here?"

He said nothing. The voice held an accent he could not place.

"You are a craftsman, the finest diamond cutter in India."

Ramesh wasn't affected by the praise. He liked his job and therefore was good at it. Any less would make him unworthy.

"I want you to exercise your skills for me."

"No."

"I will pay handsomely."

His expression hardened. "With blood money. If you had legal stones, you would not have played this game to bring me here. And now you will not show your face?" He tried to shake his head, but the hand on it made it impossible. "No, I will not."

"Perhaps you might reconsider."

The screen blinked on, and Ramesh's eyes snapped wide. His breathing increased till he was hyperventilating.

"Calm down, Mr. Narabi. Your answer?"

"Yes." The word came out broken, tortured.

"I thought so."

The door security toned through the house, and Sam reached for his gun, then saw Max and Sebastian enter. "Oh, feel the love," Max said and dropped a few shopping bags near the sofa. "She'd better like it." He headed to the hall to get some sleep. Sam peered in one bag and thought, I want to see that on her, just so I can take it off. He looked up when Sebastian handed him an envelope.

"The film from the slave jet." Sam took it, but before he slid the pictures out, Sebastian said, "I hope you have a strong stomach."

Sam looked. Jesus. It wasn't the occupants of the jet, he realized after he got over the revulsion. It was the bombing in Bali. He sifted through the photos. They were taken from a distance, the police vehicles, the rescue, the broken bodies.

After a moment he got used to seeing it and looked harder, picking out details. "We need to load these to the Pentagon." Sam came to him.

Logan looked up, rubbed his face and tried to look refreshed.

Sam spread the photos out on the only available space on the table. "Ignore the bodies for a second, the debris. Here are three consecutive photos, each with this man in the background." Sam stabbed a finger. "He's fucking smiling." How anyone could with the death around him, was more than a clue he was involved. In the foreground, rescue workers were caught motionless as they removed a legless young woman from the blast site. "Can you do something with this?"

Logan took the picture, scanned it and loaded it in. He worked the keyboard, cutting out the distracting portions, refocusing on the man in the photo. It was only half an image, the man stood under a tin beach cabana. But what was there was showered in sunlight.

"I'm betting they're blackmail shots." Sam looked at the rest, trying to find the man again.

"Let's enlarge," Logan hit keys, "and redigitize." He clicked a program and they watched the pixels break apart, then come together again.

Sam sighed. "We can't get a good view of his face." Too much in shadow.

Logan highlighted one side and selected mirror image.

Sam stared. "Not ringing my chimes."

"Mine either."

"Run his face up the pole and see if it flies," Sam said, and glanced down at the photos again as Logan loaded it into the search database. "Wait, focus on his arms for a sec." The man had them folded over his waist.

"What are you looking for, Wyatt?"

Sam pointed to the screen. "Is that a ring?"

Logan was like a man driven, using his precious computers like they were extensions of his hands. "You know this proves nothing."

"Voslav was a sick puppy and he had a good reason to put photos on film and not on digital."

"More tangible with negatives. Digital is instant deletion."

"Sure, but leave them in that desk where anyone could find them?" Sam shook his head. "Voslav was a slob, but careless? DNA all over that jet, keeping slaves in an old school. That pig had been doing this for years, so much that he had a Thai accent." Sam shook his head. "No, he was certain the film would never be seen or he would have secured it."

Sam stood rock still for a long moment, and Logan knew the man wouldn't pace, wouldn't talk aloud.

Then Sam said, "Voslav knew this guy"—he flicked a hand at the screen—"*never* considered him a threat. Nor would he set foot in that hangar and find these photos, or get in his business."

"That doesn't tell us who he is and why he's in this photo."

"Insurance." Suddenly Sam picked up the photos, sifting through each one. "He's got a habit, and it shows."

A single lightbulb dangled from the ceiling, shining down on the naked and hooded man strapped to the chair. Noor studied him, for a moment admiring his powerful physique.

Beyond the door, Zidane waited, his part done. He knew what she would do in the dank room, yet never voiced his dislike of her methods. Zidane's emotions had no bearing on anything. She was not hired for her morals. She had so few.

Noor paced. The man in the chair was unaware she was naked, only able to hear the click of her heels on the damp cement floor.

"What was on the laptop?" she asked in his own language.

He shook his head, refusing to speak.

"I have no fight with you, but I will make one."

She straddled his lap, and he flinched at the contact of skin to skin, and turned his face away. She brought it back, her free hand closing over his cock. "Tell me and I will free you."

"Nyet."

She could break him. Men were vulnerable. They were ruled by their sex. Women could fake an orgasm, show desire that wasn't real. Noor knew how; it had been a skill she learned young. She stroked the man, listening to him fight his pleasure, and knowing he hated that she could control him. She understood. Men had done this to her. Because she'd been too weak to fight, to turn it back on them. But no longer.

"Did he use the encryption on the computer?"

"I don't know."

"Liar," she said softly, yet her hand squeezed. He grunted in pain, and she smiled to herself. His stomach muscles flexed with need and an attempt to stiffen against her touch. "Tell me." She leaned to press her bare breasts to his chest.

She let up on the pressure, and stroked him. He grew hard in her hand and she watched, amazed at the simplicity. "The laptop, my handsome man."

She slid off him, and squatted, taking him into her mouth with a vengeance. He elongated and flexed and she waited for the perfect moment, near the edge when his hips moved, then she stopped.

He cursed her, and she asked again, slipping a condom on him, then settling herself onto his erection. "The information," she said in Russian. She thrust on him four times, then left him. He groaned miserably.

"I will give you satisfaction, but he must know what others might see on that computer."

The man gasped, tried to reach her, but his restraints stopped him. Noor moved behind him, her hands sliding down his chest, and she let him feel her knife against his belly. "Who was the man who took the computer?"

The man only shook his head.

"I grow weary. Tell me and I will pleasure you." She said it near his ear, in a whispered tone that made him react. She knew what men wanted to hear. They'd told her many times, and now she tortured him with their own words, with a nimble touch till he was breathing hard and nearly climaxing. "Were the schematics on the computer?"

He nodded.

"Details?"

He nodded again, almost begging her.

Her master would not be pleased. "The rule of the bargain was that nothing tangible would be left to find." Ryzikov was lucky he was dead. Noor would have made his last hours unpleasant.

She slid around him, her breasts brushing his masked face, and she climbed onto his lap, then slid onto his cock. He groaned hard, and thrust upward, but Noor had control. Her hips worked fast with the pulse of her own need, and she heard the slap of flesh to flesh, the sucking sound of slick organs, but she did not look at his masked face, did not wonder at his appearance, his name, nothing. To her, the man did not exist, the moment did not. Yet she took it, climaxing, pounding on him, seeking her own pleasure in the faceless man. Her explosion rushed through her, and she hated that it heated her blood, stole her power to stop it. He was coming, too, telling her harder, faster—his talk vulgar and begging to touch her. She let him come, let him feel the pleasure that blinded him. Then she backed off before he caught his breath, before he reached that perfect summit, denying him. He called her ugly names she'd heard before and her gaze narrowed as she folded her hand around his cock. Then with her knife, she took his testicles as a prize.

Commander Anan Isarangura stared out the window, his hands braced behind his back as he listened to the police radio, and the ongoing search for the couple in the stolen car. He suspected only to himself that the explosion at the

Mandarin was the root of it, yet influence from his superiors would let him pry only so far. That the car was recovered wasn't important, the prints would tell them something, but it was who was chasing them that troubled him.

He glanced back at the desk, at the picture of the dark-haired American. It was hazy, from the surveillance inside the museum office. Yet it forced another suspicion to the surface. Why would Wan Gai not have a photo and records of the stolen artifact, nor reveal its nature beyond that it was a bracelet? And why, Anan thought, when there were thousands of valuable pieces in the museum, ancient jade and blood rubies, would an American steal only that one particular piece?

Sam flinched awake and realized he was on the sofa, papers still in his hands. The living area was dark and in the moonlight. Logan was still at the computer terminals, sound asleep in the chair. The room smoldered with the final rays of the sun as it fell into Bangkok Bay, the glow of the computers working a program. Sam stood and stretched, and Logan woke. "Sorry."

Logan waved him off, rubbed his face, and focused on the screen. "You know, if someone saw her on the webcam, we have to get her out of the country," he said as Sam neared.

"Yeah." Guarding her would leave them too short of manpower. "Whether she'll go peacefully is another matter." She wanted to find out about the bracelet and he didn't blame her. He had to break it to her, and moved toward the voices and music coming from the kitchen.

He pushed open the door, the scent of spices and frying onions rolling on the air. Viva and Sebastian were cooking, and laughing. Then he realized she was speaking French, so fast he couldn't catch it. All while she chopped onions with amazing speed. *She does everything in high gear.*

"Viva," Sebastian said, a flick of his head toward Sam.

Her smile was wide as she came to him. "You breeched the inner sanctum," he said. "He doesn't let anyone near when he cooks."

"I have skills."

"Don't show him any more," Sam said, his hand resting on her waist as he kissed her.

Viva smiled against his lips, the memory of his mouth elsewhere on her body playing through her mind. "You know . . ." she murmured, "we have some unfinished business, you and me."

Sam felt his body lock and go ballistic. Being inside this woman would stay with him forever. "Oh, yeah," he said, then deepened his kiss.

Viva was overpowered, no question, no doubt, the strength and greed in his kiss diving into her soul. Sam did everything with a sharp intensity and if there weren't other people in the house she'd coax him to make love to her again—right here.

"Get a room," Sebastian groused, his back to them as he sautéed.

Viva laughed against Sam's kiss, then reluctantly went back to the counter.

"I thought you'd sleep for days," he said, leaning against it, trying to get his breathing back to normal. She'd conked out fast.

"I never get more than five hours. Any more and I'm crabby." She didn't mention the dreams haunting her.

"So that's the reason." She nudged him. "You look good dressed, though," he said for her ears alone. In the deep purple blouse and black jeans, she looked incredibly exotic. "And not."

Viva felt that instant pull low in her belly. He'd left her a note with the bags of clothes. *As much as I like seeing you naked*—so very Sam, she thought, brief and to the point, and right now, she was ready to drop the knife and have at him.

His smile said he got the message and he snatched a carrot. "You go to culinary school, too?"

"No, I was a cook, Florida Keys after college. No jobs for a paleoclimatologist. Who knew?" She brought the cutting board of onions to Sebastian, and Sam heard French again.

"How many languages can you speak?"

She started loading the dishwasher. "A few. Learn a couple non-romance languages and the rest is easy. Except Farsi, that's a tough one."

Sebastian turned, glancing at her, then Sam. At the silence, Viva looked up and between the two. "What?"

"Why didn't the CIA or FBI snatch you up?"

She looked away. "I never applied. So what's with the *National Geographic* logo on the chopper?" She had seen it in the driveway, parked like a car along with the beat-up van and the SUV.

"Keeps us from getting shot out of the sky."

"And the guns don't help?" She scoffed. "You need to aim better." Sebastian chuckled to himself as she dried her hands. "What's next?" He shook his head and she leaned on the counter, soaking Sam up. "You're a team. I get that, and you used to be military."

Sebastian served chicken onto a platter. "I did not tell her," he said. "Though she is persistent."

"I tried torture, see the bamboo under his fingernails?"

Sam slid onto a stool. She had a right to know. Niran and Dahl's woman both knew of Viva's association with him, and if the webcam was on when she killed Ryzikov, someone else did, too. "Dragon One"—he made a circular motion, collective—"is a retrieval team for hire."

"So, you're bounty hunters."

Sebastian glanced over his shoulder, a little startled, a little insulted.

"I never thought of it that way," Sam said, smiling.

"I could split hairs and say mercenaries." At his dark look, she said, "Oo-kay, I guess not. Ex-military?"

"*Former* Marines."

Marines. She should have known. That snap-to attitude was a giveaway.

"Except me," Logan said, coming into the kitchen. "I went Seal."

"Logan is a field surgeon. Sebastian is an explosives expert."

He owned a restaurant in New Orleans, that much he'd told her. "Max is the get-everything guy." She plucked at her clothes.

"Logistics, gear, supplies, the best navigator, and he can fix anything."

"Sounds like he works the most."

"Thank you, Viva, you've endeared yourself to me for life," Max said, from the door, yawning. She backed away from the counter and brought them cups of coffee. Max gave her a grateful smile, yawning again.

"We're hired by the private sector, sometimes," Logan said. "A UN Security Council member this time. Sulak Krahn."

"Heavy." Arms on the counter, she leaned closer to Sam. "What did you do in the Marines?"

"F18 attack fighter jet pilot."

Whoa. "And?" He frowned slightly. "I've seen you fly, so there has to be a good reason you aren't doing that now."

"I was shot down in Serbia, had to eject, and broke my leg and wrist," Sam said. "The area was too hot to airlift me out, so I walked." She cringed at that image. "Without authorization, Riley infiltrated enemy lines, paid a crap load of bribes, and damn near carried me back to secure territory."

"That's a real friend." She'd never had one like that. Did most people? Viva pushed off and started setting the kitchen table.

"Riley's in a coma in Sri Lanka right now," Logan said. "Killian and his wife are with him."

She twisted to look at him. "Sri Lanka? The dam break? I saw it on the news."

They sat at the table, and Logan filled the silence with telling her about Riley, his wounds. She could tell they were all worried that he'd never wake up. "This job, or mission or whatever you call it, is for the big fat diamond, right?"

The men exchanged glances between bites.

"Okay, be silent and deadly, I'll talk."

"Now there's a news flash," Sam said, and she jabbed him playfully.

"The stone is uncut, so it's a conflict diamond. You've been very bad boys." She tsked, amused. "A stone that size, everyone and no one would want it."

She got a communal frown that was intimidating as hell.

"A diamond over ten carats doesn't go unnoticed. The minute it was unearthed, its existence went global. That's nearly as big as the Cullinan, or the Star of the East." At Sam's look, she sighed and said, "I'm betting that rock was a couple *hundred* carats. It was long and narrow, yet very clear, even uncut. I'm really surprised the Half Ear guy didn't snatch it up, but then, anyone fencing it would have big trouble doing it."

"She's right," Sam said. "I think someone killed that guy to keep him from talking about it."

"We weren't excluded, either," Viva said. "Anyone look into people dying from those darts recently?"

"It was a woman," Max said. "We saw her on the docks, she was aiming at you two."

Viva went still. "Then why didn't she fire and what was she doing there?"

"Covering the dealer's tracks," Sam said and they looked at him. "Phan talked and was killed instantly. Half Ear, I'm not sure about him, but he was going to talk. Ryzikov and Rohki, both had diamonds and were in on this deal. This woman is the armed cleanup for whoever is orchestrating it all."

"I don't want to meet her in a dark alley," Viva said, pausing to sip water.

"Do you know what's necessary to cut the stone?" Logan asked. "Sam said you worked for a gemologist."

"Aside from laser machinery and polishing equipment, the best cutter in the world." He made a rolling motion for her to keep going. "The cutter would have to study the stone for a while to get the largest stones with the best quality. The least flaws. Cutting a stone that size would be like slicing skin, one fraction too deep, too far to the left, right, whatever, and it would split the stone incorrectly and ruin the quality."

"I'm impressed, *chéri,*" Sebastian said.

"Don't be, it's common knowledge." She picked an apple from a bowl, holding it up. "Say you want this to be a perfect stone, maintain the large size, and achieve the most brilliance. Big rocks don't always mean big stones. The cutter has to consider the widest point of cut. The table, that makes the top." With her knife, she lopped off the top. "The crown controls the fire. It draws light in from all sides." She cut away the sides so they slanted. "and the girdle, that's the diamond's edge that's beneath the crown and stands above the pavilion culet. The small facets at the bottom of a diamond and tapers off what would otherwise be a sharp and brittle point."

"Now I'm really impressed," Sam said. The apple was shaped like a diamond.

She flashed a quick smile, blushing. "Maybe there's a flaw in the center or to the left, so you figure out how to cut two perfects, with the lesser quality falling to the floor, so to speak. That's *if* they care about what's left."

"Why wouldn't they?" The people they were dealing with wouldn't care, Sam thought. They were selling stones for lower cash value than they'd get in a jeweler's market.

"Quality and size versus more stones. Though no good jeweler would ever let diamond dust go down the drain. They sell every aspect of a cut, some made into the blades they use, drill bits for granite."

"I've checked out diamond-cutting equipment, but it's a commodity here like the gems," Logan said. "Lots of new and used, refurbished, impossible to trace." He mentioned the article about the diamond cutter kidnapping in Sri Lanka.

She ate, listening to them talk about the stone and their mission, trying to pick up on the acronyms they tossed around. "What weapons have been stolen lately?" She speared chicken, the fork poised at her mouth.

The men scoffed. "The sixty-four-dollar question. Arms dealing is big business, aside from the countries, *not* our allies, who'll sell them on a regular basis."

"Then who's the richest bad guy you know?"

The room was quiet and she looked up. They were frowning at her again. "Well, you said yourselves that whoever is in charge wants only uncut diamonds. Which is black market, dangerous, and a passion to him. To risk everything with *conflict* diamonds, he's got to have a lot of power and pull."

Sam thought of the plane getting off the ground without notice, that they were one step behind finding anything tangible.

"You've got my attention, Viva, keep going," Max said, leaning his forearms on the table.

"You, Dragon One—cool name, by the way—know weapons. This Rohki guy, what's he dealt with before?"

"Rifles, bomb materials, mortars, RPG's. Rocket propelled grenades," Max clarified.

"Scary to me, not him, right? Sam nodded. "Was Ryzikov dealing with the same kind of weapons?"

"What are you getting at?"

"Must be something not only dangerous, but different. So much that a single leak would alert the authorities as to who has it."

"That takes out rifles and mortars."

"Christ, ballistic missiles again?" Sebastian groused.

"The dead man in the jungle, your snitch cut up, the video feed from Ryzikov's hotel." Sam noticed her fingers tighten on her fork before she said, "This bad guy is careful to the point of paranoia."

Sam thought of Dahl and the extremes they went to, to get him to fly the jet.

"Cutting the stone isn't important. He wants them uncut for a reason," she said. "But you're still back to square one, sorry."

Sam watched her chow down like a marine at boot camp. "When was the last time you had food, Viva?"

She looked up, chewing, then swallowing. "Sorry, I must look like a Viking. This is great, Sebastian, and other than a sandwich on the river market, and some toast in the hotel, my last decent meal was at the dig."

Looking concerned, Sam held up three fingers and Logan left the table. He was back in a few minutes with a syringe and stood near Viva's chair.

"I'm packing away the protein and carbs," she said in protest. Logan simply waited. She sighed and rolled up her sleeve, their protectiveness touching. He swabbed, then injected her with some vitamin concoction. "Pretty great that you have your own doctor. Everyone want to show me their scars?" She wiggled her brows. "Chicks love scars." They laughed, and she went back to eating up a storm.

When Logan didn't return, Sam stretched a look into the living room. He was staring at a computer screen and didn't look happy. "Logan?"

"We have the fingerprints."

"Who's the bastard that shot at me?"

Logan rubbed his mouth and met his gaze. "Sitting next to you."

Thirteen

Sam turned his head slowly. Viva was eating, oblivious. "That's impossible." He shot out of the chair, coming to Logan.

Logan gestured to the screen. "Young and Goth, but it's her. Maybe sixteen, seventeen."

Viva felt the sudden silence and looked up from her meal. She was alone and left the table, hunting them out in the living room. All four were entranced by the screen.

"That's got to be wrong," Max said as Viva approached.

"No, it's not," Viva said, and they turned. "I was really hoping it was all a nightmare, my imagination. I guess not." She shrugged.

They waited for an explanation. She wished she had a good one, but she didn't.

"I was on the roof, I don't know how. One minute I'd finally fallen asleep, the next I was kneeling on a rooftop with that." She pointed to the rifle propped against the wall.

"Do you even know what it is?"

"A Dragunov SVD, Russian, gas powered, semi automatic." She picked it up. "PSO-1 with infrared resolution detection capability. Whatever that means. Range of four to five hundred yards, max rate of fire, thirty rounds per minute." She checked the load and shot the bolt home.

They just stared, dumbfounded.

Viva held out the nine-pound rifle and Sam took it. "Don't all talk at once." She moved to the computer. "The records are sealed. Stole a car when I was seventeen, a joyride, a dare." She stared at her face on the screen, remembering she'd done that look to piss off her father. "That's a really awful picture, huh?"

"Viva!" She met his gaze and Sam saw it, the confusion, and sudden helplessness.

She looked at each man, felt a little cornered. "I don't remember. I swear it."

"How can you fire a sniper rifle and not remember?" Sam asked.

She reeled back. "Fired! I fired it?"

"At me, dammit!"

She crumbled. Right before his eyes, she fell apart in little jagged pieces and Sam instantly regretted his tone. He reached, pulling her into his embrace, swept his hand down the back of her head. She trembled against him, and gripped him like a lifeline.

"Why didn't you tell me?"

"Oh, yeah, sure. Hi there, nice night, catch a bullet lately? I couldn't tell what was real or a dream."

"I believe you, I do." Over her head he looked at Logan, begging him to help her.

"Viva, let me check you out."

She turned in Sam's arms, unwilling to give up the comfort and safety. "What are you looking for?"

"Anything, everything."

Fear sparked her eyes and Sam rubbed her arms. "We need to know how you got on that roof and why."

"So would I. Lead the way."

Logan grabbed a black duffel and as they disappeared toward the other rooms, Sam turned to the screen. *Match* flashed at the bottom in red. Someone set her up, left that rifle for her. Why her? She was the least skilled at weapons. He remembered her tumble off the roof, the chase. Her strange behavior at the hotel. Did she even know what she'd done then?

He waited for Logan to examine her, a thousand questions racing through his mind and when Logan finally appeared a half hour later, Viva behind him, his gaze popped between the two.

"I'm totally embarrassed, doctor or not." There ought to be a law against good-looking doctors, she thought, dropping into a chair.

Logan smiled gently. "You're fine, except you have blood in your ears."

"Gross."

"That means your eardrums have ruptured."

She frowned. "I don't hear any different. Wait, no, I *did.*" She shifted to the edge of the seat, excited. "I heard stuff, well, not . . . it's hard to describe. I'd sleep and it was so real, but you know when you dream, you know it's not real so you just go with it? This felt patterned, more like I *heard* it, not envisioned it. Just weird."

"Do you remember the dream?" Sam asked.

"Only pieces." And they scared her. "But it felt familiar, like I'd been through it before."

Logan's gaze shifted to Sam's.

"What?"

"I'd like to run some tests."

She made a face. "Doctors always say that when they don't know what to tell a patient, Logan. Tell me, I can take it."

Still, he didn't give a diagnosis. "I'll take some blood, urine, and maybe try some hypnosis."

His last word didn't faze her. Anything he could do to learn what had happened was fine with her. "Voodoo, spells, whatever. I'm cleaning the kitchen."

"No, right now."

Ramesh Narabi hovered over the worktable, the tight focus of light passing through the stone and showing him the table. His hands had stopped shaking hours ago. His fear turned to his work and what he must do to survive.

He lifted his tools, positioned the bore, and made the cut.

He kept his normal routine, yet the stone's cut was unusual, no facets, no refraction at all. He glanced at the pile already complete, the largest stones he'd seen in a long while. He had everything here to make them first water. But that was not required. He continued, feeling the bore of the cameras spying down on him. Whoever was behind this was cloaked in secrecy and Ramesh would rather not know more than he did. Yet as he continued to cut the blood diamond, he wondered, after he had completed the task, would they really let his family live?

Samples taken, twenty minutes later Logan was alone with Viva in a dark room. She was stretched out on a bed, her mind in a deep, tranquil place. Max had set a small speaker on the nightstand, rigged it to play out in the living room. Logan figured that Sam was hanging on to every word.

"What do you remember just before you were on the roof?"

"I was asleep." She told him how she'd felt, the fear, the images and knowledge that came to her without reason. Of walking to the docks and being shocked she was there. And the uncontrollable need to get to the roof. She'd felt ill constantly, headaches when she'd never had one before, and she murmured how the feeling lessened the farther she was from the hotel. Then Logan knew: someone had programmed her mind.

"Did you see anyone on the roof?"

"No. No one." There was panic in her voice. "Only the rifle. I picked it up, knelt and waited."

"For what?"

"My target!"

"Take deep, slow breaths," he said, trying to calm her. "What was your task?"

"Kill the cowboy, take the stone." Her tone was impersonal, cold. Logan coaxed her further away from their control.

"You had him in your sights."

"Yes."

"Yet you missed. Why?"

"I—I couldn't." Tears slid from behind closed lids and onto her temples.

"Who told you to do this?"

Her brows knit. "A voice."

"You saw no one?"

"No."

"Would you recognize the voice if you heard it?"

"Yes."

"Did the voice instruct you to do anything more?"

"No." Her lips thinned. "Yes."

Logan waited.

"To leave the stone in the fountain, near the temple at Wat Pho."

A massive temple with lots of people paying homage, Logan thought, sighing back into the chair. He asked her for details—the clothes, the rifle—but it all came back to the voice. It was the only tangible thing they had and finding a match would be impossible. The voice could have been distorted for the programming. How these guys got to her was a mystery. Programming was usually in a very controlled environment. That this worked well with such precision said they were up against something much larger.

As he brought her up from the hypnosis, he instructed her to remember everything, and to fear none of it. She was, and always would be, in control. Logan didn't have any doubt. That she didn't kill Sam said that whoever did this chose the wrong woman to manipulate. Logan would bet the *voice* hadn't counted on that.

Taking her to the last level, he woke her, and Viva sat up, sniffling. Then she looked up, eyes wide.

"Oh, my God. Your diamond, the voice, he wants it."

"And he knows Sam has it."

Winston Brandau heard the speaker hum before the voice called his name. He didn't bother to look up. He felt stupid talking to a black box. "Yes."

"Your progress?"

He spun the chair. "I've done my part. But it won't have the range." If his employer didn't want to travel to use the weapon again, then they had to give him what he needed, and it would be tough to get classified material. Not his problem. He could wait, the pay was good enough. "Coordinates?"

"I will have them by nightfall," the voice said.

The speaker clicked off and Winston scoffed. That's what he'd said about the stones. Whoever *he* was. Winston had never seen the face of his employer, their one and only meeting taken in the shadows, his identity so covert that only a select few would recognize his face. No photos had ever been taken, supposedly no DNA left to match.

Winston didn't care. Three men had broken him out of a Chinese prison camp. If this guy wanted him to make a bomb, he'd do it. The accommodations were a sight better than the wet floor of a cell, he thought, his gaze moving to the bed in the far left corner, then swept toward the ceiling to the glass window, eye-shaped and dark. They watched him constantly, if not from the glass perch, then from screens all around the compound. Even if he wanted out, it was too late.

Yet the Pharaoh—he smirked, doubting his employer was really Egyptian—had spared no expense. The cavernous room lacked for nothing except some style. The bland surfaces of concrete and steel, painted a soothing pale blue with black floors. A kingdom of equipment: circuits, tools, computers, even test subjects; humans corralled like sheep, helplessly waiting to have their bodies assaulted. If his conscience bothered him, the three million already sitting in a Swiss account was enough to soothe it; another five when he completed the job. As long as the Pharaoh kept paying him, the outcome made little difference. Though, it would to the rest of the world.

Sam stared at the speaker, anger rippling off him in waves. *All my fault.* She'd been used, programmed to kill because of him and that goddamn diamond.

"Sam?"

He turned. She stood under the pagoda arch of the room, her hands looking for a place to be, her expression drawn with worry. "I couldn't hurt you."

"I know." He crossed the room, his gaze on hers as he neared. "You're too damn stubborn to take orders. And if you really wanted it, I'd be in heaven."

"Don't say that!" she snapped, then jutted her chin up. "And what makes you think *you'd* go to heaven?"

"If I keep hanging around you, no chance of it."

Her smile was slight, strained, and she stood perfectly still. "Oh, Sam." Then he did what she wanted; he took her into his arms and held her warm and tight. "I'm sorry."

He pressed his mouth to the top of her head, and murmured, "It's not your fault, baby, it's mine."

Sam felt her release a hard breath, and he gripped a little tighter, unwilling to let her go. Who else would use her against him?

Someone cleared their throat and Sam ignored it to kiss her softly. Viva would have nothing of gentleness and demanded more, made him hunger and take. She dug her fingers into his back, her kiss taking on an almost desperate edge for his forgiveness when he should be apologizing for bringing her into this. When he drew back, her lids lifted slowly, her green eyes clear.

"Wanna finish this later, without an audience?" she whispered for his ears alone.

Sam laughed softly. He never knew what to expect from her. "Definitely." The memory of tasting her filled his mind and he clamped down on the rising need, kissed her forehead, then turned to the team.

"The only person who saw the stone was the Thai mafia man in the jungle and he's dead."

"The blowgun bitch saw it too." she said.

That made them smile.

"Now you have it, and the woman kills Half Ear to keep his mouth shut, *but* she's seen Sam with the stone, then goes after the three of us in the jungle. Failing that, she goes after the easy target—me. To get the stone and kill you." Her voice wavered and she met Sam's gaze, empathy in his dark eyes.

"I'll buy that," Max said, smiling.

"The person who messed with your mind is the same one who wants the big diamond. The blowgun bitch"—Sebastian winked at Viva—"is trying to get it back or protecting it?"

"Both, I think," Sam said.

"You know: you want in on the deal and you have the big kahuna of stones. That gives you leverage. A lure, and with Ryzikov's stones . . ." She picked the bag off the coffee table and tossed it at Sam. "It's plenty, right?"

"He doesn't know you're not a weapons dealer," Sebastian said, rising to the challenge.

"You have Ryzikov's work on the computer. I'll bet the answer is in there."

"I can't get past the passwords," Logan said, clearly angered at himself by that.

"You don't have a decryption program?" she said to Logan.

"Not in Russian or Chechen."

"So make one."

Logan scowled at her.

"Look at this sweet setup." She waved to the computers. "It's got to have a translation program."

"It does." His eyes flared. He hadn't thought of that. "I can copy the encryption program, translate it and run it." He got busy.

"Try both languages and for a password in Arabic, too. Sheiklike. He had a thing for role-playing." The memory pushed her anger to the surface, renewing her pain, and making her touch the finger marks on her throat. "What did you do with Choan?"

"Left in the jungle, right about where we jumped in the river," Max said.

"The monkeys were eyeing him for a date," Sebastian said.

"Did I mention he was naked, and smeared with bananas?" Max added.

"I was hoping you tortured him."

The room went silent, all four staring at her.

"Don't look at me like that. I was sold, *twice,*" she snapped, her eyes gone brittle. "To a sadistic fanatic whose only intention was to repeatedly attempt murder and screw me till I was dead. Put yourselves there, then we'll talk about sufficient retribution."

Her voice broke with the last words, and she left the room in a fury.

Sam dropped to the arm of the sofa and gripped the back of his neck. "Man, I've really done a job on her life." Ryzikov's men, the weapons dealer, the woman, they'd still come after her, each for their own reasons.

"We have to get her out of the country," Max said, and Sebastian agreed.

They couldn't protect her 24/7 and finish this mission. "Is that enough?"

"One more problem," Logan said. "Whoever was on the other end of the web camera saw her kill Ryzikov. If it's the weapons dealer, then he knows he's lost a buyer."

"If he's as greedy as he's been, he'll let one more in," Max said. "It needs to be us."

"Then you'd better break that code, Logan. We don't have much time."

"Now we're on a timeline, geez." The AC stirred papers and Max grabbed them, frowning at the food bills from the hangar.

"Dahl said that Rohki hired him to fly him out of here, in a week."

Sebastian mentally counted. "That's the day after tomorrow."

"Keeps getting better, huh?" Sam was already walking toward the hall. He really didn't want this confrontation, but he couldn't trust Viva's safety to anyone.

Kukule Ganga Dam
Kalawana, Sri Lanka

Thomas Rhodes repelled down into the tunnel, Risha a few yards above him. He hit bottom and waited, then they unhooked the cables and side by side, stared at the walls of the reserve pressure tunnels. The concrete was still damp, the pumping ending only an hour ago. Thomas squatted near the cavity, Risha bending to run her hand over the edges.

"You're right, this didn't crack," she said.

"No, it's been obliterated."

The wall of the tunnel holding millions of gallons of water had been pulverized. The force of the wash would have taken away debris, yet the hole was too clean to be faulty concrete or a pressure crack. Thomas had donned scuba gear and looked, too impatient for the pumps to finish. But Risha had to see it for herself.

Her gaze followed the normal flow of water, then back to the concrete.

"Why only here? If the pressure was that great, which we know it was not, why didn't it break in other spots, why haven't we seen any other damage?"

"It's as if something drilled this."

"Under four fathoms of water? How?" She lifted her gaze to his. Her features pulled tight. "That night the Army was here, Thomas, to capture Tiger rebels. Most of them died. Do you really think this was an accident?"

Thomas looked back at the hole. "No, I don't. But if there's something out there that could cause this, with this precision, how do we fight it?"

And who do we tell?

Viva heard the door open but didn't look up and continued to throw clothes into a duffel. "I heard." She pointed to the speaker still on the nightstand.

"Eavesdropping is a nasty vice."

"Not if I spied for a living. Hum? That would be a new career choice." She checked her money and passport, then met his gaze. "You don't have to explain, Sam, really. I need to be gone. People are using me to hurt you and you can't do your job with me here." She was damn tired of the bad guys winning and this was so much bigger than her. "I still want to pound Wan Gai into the ground, it will have to wait."

He came to her, forcing her to look at him. "I don't want you to leave."

That soothed her. "But some things never change, I'm trouble, and these awful people, they won't ignore what's happened."

Sam swallowed her in his arms, knowing he had to do this and hating that he'd forced this choice. He felt a deep slash in his heart when she said, "Can you help me get out of here?"

Satellite Surveillance Center
CIA Station
Bangkok

Kincade had cooled off and stood in the rear of the comm room, the screens video feed a bit subdued. Agents were on the phone, analysts furiously digging through information while the satellite feed from Langley was still operational.

"I have I.D." A female analyst glanced to the left, and motioned him.

He frowned and moved near, bending.

"The men the agents were chasing with the Thai police."

His lips tightened over that mess.

"I've got some visual, MI6 and our feed on the river. But it doesn't make sense to me." She looked at him. "They're Americans."

"And you think every American is the perfect patriot?"

"No sir, but this man"—she tapped keys and pulled up a photo of two men leaving a run-down shop, and pointed to one—"he's a patriot."

"You know him."

She shook her head. "Not personally, but I know one of his teammates, Max Renfield. They're Dragon One."

He frowned. "Never heard of them."

"Yes, you have. Russian missiles on Amianan Island? That arms dealer and the Chinese?"

His features went taut. Price's career fuckup.

"They helped stop them."

"Find out what they're doing there."

"It could be anything, sir, they're private hire."

"I don't care, use your friendship with this Renfield, or send people to bring them in for interrogation."

"If they don't want to talk, we won't get them in. They don't take a job that isn't ethical, we can trust them."

"Today, we don't trust anyone."

In the early dawn, Viva took the plane ticket and turned to Sam. "It leaves in a few minutes. Last seat. Probably next to the bathroom."

Sam only nodded and moved with her to the gate. "Call me when you land."

His cell number was tucked in her jeans' pocket. "I expect you to find me when you're done with this thing you do."

His lips quirked a bit. "You've been amazing help."

"A storehouse of trivia. Who knew?" Viva didn't want to leave, not now, but understood she was in terrible danger and it put Sam and the rest of the guys at risk. Sam wanted to take her to England himself on their jet, one she'd yet to have seen, but it was in Sri Lanka, and they didn't have that much time. She wanted to be with Sam more than she wanted to see the bastards pay, including Wan Gai, but she knew when to leave a party. Her only connection would be when and if Logan had voice imprints for her to identify. She was doubtful that would ever happen.

Over the loudspeakers, they called for the boarding.

Sam almost flinched at the sound, having a hard time letting her go and kept telling himself it was for her safety. Her life. She'd been used and manipulated enough, and beyond taking back weapons and chasing diamonds, someone wanted her dead. He feared that putting her on a plane wasn't enough. "My friends will meet the plane when you land."

"My own personal guards?"

"Sorta. Don't let the accents sway you, okay?"

She smiled. "I'm partial to a Texas drawl." Viva could feel it, the break about to happen, the moment when she knew she had to sever this and lose the chance of ever seeing him again.

"Sam?"

He met her gaze. "God, I didn't think this would be so hard," he muttered, and his hand slid to her waist. It took only a gentle tug to bring her close.

"I know." Her throat strained. "Find me or *I'll* hunt you down."

He tried to smile. "Count on it." She had a bio marker in her, just to be sure.

"Kiss me good-bye, cowboy," she said, and he bent, and gathered her closer, his mouth touched and rolled. His heartbeat was painful, a longing he'd never thought he could feel shattering inside him, and he crushed her to him.

"This is far from over, Viva," Sam said roughly, and she was moved that his voice was strained.

Pushing out of his arms felt like the tearing of a limb and Viva wiped her lipstick off his mouth, then turned away. She handed her passport and ticket to the agent, refusing to look back and have her heart broken, yet when she passed through the doors, her willpower failed. She glanced.

Sam was already gone.

Zidane stared at the man, barely listening to his rant. It was directed at Noor.

"If they learn his passwords, they will know everything!"

"Then I suggest you step up the bidding," Zidane said, knowing it fell on deaf ears.

"The field is narrow enough," Constantine snarled and

looked at Noor. She stood still and expressionless. "Was it necessary to leave so much evidence behind?"

"I got your information," she said plainly. "And it's in ashes." She nodded to the news broadcast playing, the sound turned down. Constantine turned to watch for a moment, then looked back at her and nodded, not at all pleased.

"You disappoint me, Noor," Constantine said.

She dipped her head. "Forgive me."

Her tone was not the least contrite. "You had a clear shot at the woman, yet you did not use it. Why?"

Her gaze flicked to Zidane's. "She may still be useful."

"Doubtful. You are obsessed with teasing the man, end it now." He looked at Zidane. "Assemble the buyers, you alone."

Noor looked insulted and left abruptly.

Before Zidane reached the door, Constantine called to him. "Watch her. I will not have her rage at the world of men destroy this."

They both understood that Noor was on the edge. Zidane was still confused over why she did not kill the woman when she was ordered to do so. She cared less for life than she did her own, and that was the real danger. If she chose to die, she would take them all with her. He left the suite and found Noor leaning against the wall, her arms folded over her trim waist. She met his gaze.

"You are tender for this one man?" That, he'd never believe.

"Why are you so concerned about the lives I take, Jai? We both do it for him."

She thought using his given name would alter his view of her. "Allowing them to live gave them the advantage with the laptop. You knew this." Zidane cocked his head. "You admire the woman? Or you toy with her life, waiting for her to change—like you, perhaps?"

She scoffed, pushing off the wall. "You try to analyze me. Don't."

It scared her, he thought, that he knew her better than she

did. The red-haired woman had killed once, but Zidane doubted she'd do it again. Taking a life did not make taking more any easier.

At the window, Max peered down the street side of the house, glanced at his watch, then turned away.

"Check Sam's GPS." In the belt buckle.

Logan glanced at the time, then quickly switched to another computer, and started the trace. "He's on the other side of the city."

"He's not answering his phone, either." Sebastian closed the cell.

Max went to the gear stacked in the corner. Logan stood to join him.

"We can handle it, Logan. We need to crack that computer and get it to the Pentagon. And that's out of my league."

Logan hesitated, then agreed, and turned back to the computers. "Keep in contact."

"Roger that, he may need a rescue." Within minutes Max and Sebastian were suited, supplied, and heading to the SUV.

"Okay, Max, what are you thinking?" Sebastian asked when they were inside the truck.

"Sam's in trouble and I think it's our guys."

"Come again?"

Max tossed Sebastian the GPS tracking unit. "The GPS says that he's near Thani Graphics, right where that shot hit."

"Then I'm glad I brought the Semtex."

Fourteen

MI6 Satellite Relay Station
East Asia Theatre

Lieutenant Stephen Darwood glanced at the clock. *He's late.* This was the third time in three months his replacement hadn't shown up for duty. He reached for the phone to call his girlfriend and cancel their dinner when the door opened.

"Giving up on me already? It's only a minute."

Andrew moved near and Stephen could smell ale on his breath. "You righteous ass. Drinking?"

Andrew stilled. "One pint with my cousin, that's it."

Stephen made a sound of disgust, then saved the satellite course photos and closed the program. Andrew could open his own, he thought, though it would take ten minutes and they shouldn't let it go unguarded.

He grabbed his jacket, slipping it on as Andrew dropped a paper sack on the desk that smelled like fried Twinkies, and sat.

He looked up from the screen. "Well, aren't we pissy today? Closing me out."

Andrew rapidly tapped the keys, opening the watch program. It was still booting when Darwood flipped him off, then left the building.

Through the window, Andrew watched him walk to his

car, open the door, and slide behind the wheel, but it wasn't till he was pulling out that Andrew reached for the bag. He withdrew a cell phone, slipped it out of the plastic baggie, then turned it on. He looked at the screen, then text messaged the numbers into the phone and hit send. He replaced the phone in the greasy bag of fried cakes, and thought, thirty grand richer than this morning.

Handcuffed and in a chair, Sam glanced around the Thai police station. He was in the private offices of the commander. They'd pulled him from the airport, and none too gently, he thought, stretching his neck and feeling the lump growing on the back of his head. His gun was on the desk between them, along with his comms.

"You are accused of stealing a Thai artifact." The commander's voice was soft with patience.

Christ, that's what this was about? "Nope, doesn't ring a bell, sorry."

Commander Isarangura turned from the window and plucked a picture off the desk. "This is from the museum surveillance cameras."

Sam was in Wan Gai's face. He should have shot the fucker for all he put Viva through. "I took a tour."

"Wan Gai said you broke in."

"I was anxious to see the silver exhibit."

Anan smothered a smile. Clever man. "The artifact, where is it?"

Sam kept quiet.

"Mr. Wyatt. Yes, I know your name, and your reputation. You do understand the advantage of speaking to the authorities now, before I lodge charges."

"Am I speaking to the honorable half or the good old boys who take orders"—he jutted his chin at the pictures—"from anyone?"

Anan stiffened. Wyatt was correct, the reason he was speaking to him in his private offices and not out with the others; where ears were pricked to the conversation and would travel to the wrong people. "Let me say that I am grateful you have cut an artery of the slave trade."

"Now you really have me stumped." Sam wondered how he knew anything, since Wan Gai kept himself clean and let Choan get his hands dirty for him.

Anan dropped the shell casing on the table.

He couldn't find the ballistics without the gun and that was at the CP.

"Wan Gai has a great deal of power and he wishes to exert it on me."

"Sorry for you."

"It will not work, sir, be assured."

Sam scoffed. "He's Thai royalty and that I'm here says he's exerted it already."

"I am obligated to look into all matters."

Like one of his men out in the other offices couldn't do this? Yeah sure, that washes, Sam thought.

"But the king believes and always has, that our laws rule more than he does."

"You're so sure?"

He gestured to a photo of the king of Thailand and himself. Golfing. To prove his point, he came to Sam, removing the handcuffs. "Will you tell me why you are here?"

"Ask your countryman on the UN Security Council."

Anan's features pulled tightly over his smooth-boned face. "Sulak Krahn?"

Sam nodded, rubbing his wrists.

"The artifact. Please," he said when Wyatt refused to answer. "I must understand the worthy fight."

Sam scowled. "Wan Gai didn't tell you what it was?"

He shook his head, humiliated he'd been kept in the dark.

"It's a bracelet, a hammered cuff. And it's the reason Voslav is dead. Wan Gai sold a woman for simply viewing it. So watch your back."

"You have seen this?"

Sam took back his weapons, concealing them, stuffed the small comm radio in his pocket, then grabbed a sheet of paper and made a quick sketch. "Rubies and sapphires, heavy gold and bronze. It had royal Thai markings as well as Cambodian or Laotian."

"Where is it?"

"In safe hands." The thought of Viva made his heart ache.

"It should be returned."

"It will be, I promise. But only when I'm certain Wan Gai will not hurt any more people for it."

Isarangura looked down at the paper. "You are certain the markings were Cambodian?"

Sam didn't understand the concern over the carvings, nor did he care. "I'm not an expert, but the woman was on the dig where they found it. Udon Thani Caves. And Wan Gai knew there was something valuable enough about it to sell a human being to keep it quiet."

A hard pound rattled the door, a Thai cop calling out excitedly.

Isarangura wasted no time. "This way, please." The commander stood near the water closet, and opened the door at its left. "My private entrance, hurry. It will take you to the street."

Crafty bastard. Sam didn't know why he thanked him, but he did. "How are you going to explain this?"

"No one questions me, Mr. Wyatt."

"Must be nice." Sam crossed the threshold and down the dozen steep stairs, then drew his gun, not trusting that the police wouldn't ambush him and claim he'd tried to escape. In the darkness, he searched for a door and his knuckles smacked a knob. He turned it. Dusky light poured down, and he slid out, then looked back as he closed the door. It disappeared into the wall. Neat trick, he thought, pulling out his comms.

He got Max on the wire. "Jesus, we damn near blew up the CIA station to find you."

"You need to work on your investigating skills. If I had to wait for you . . ." He let that hang.

"We were playing with Semtex."

Sam hailed a cab, glancing over the roof before he lowered himself inside. He was tempted to wave to the eyeball tailing him. The man needed to blend in better, he stood out like the last time.

Kashir hurried away from the train, glancing back to see if he was followed. He'd walked most of the journey from Chairyapham, slipping on the train when he got closer to Bangkok and changing lines twice.

He had to be certain the Chow did not follow him. He never was.

Kashir moved with the crowd, wanting to hurry, hoping they'd disperse, but knowing he was safer in the throngs of people. Outside the station area, he headed deeper into the city, passing a pay phone and wanting to make contact, but there was no time.

He'd had to leave his equipment behind, stashed in the jungle. If anyone found him with any of it, his cover would be blown and he'd be dead very quickly.

He crossed the street between high-rise buildings, pausing for cars and rickshaws, and tourists, and thinking he liked the peace of the jungle better. His clothing brought curious stares and he wished he'd had time to clean up. Hurrying, Kashir sensed rather than saw the small group of young men walking to his right. He looked ragged, an easy target, and when he turned sharply, the young men blocked his path.

"I am Chow." He named his boss, the Jao Pho leader. "Go find someone else to taunt." Worthless teens, he thought, then knew he was in trouble when one man sneered, whipping out a knife as he advanced.

Constantine twisted his ring, then reached for his coffee, smiling to himself. The assembly would be a fine moment, he thought, his gaze drifting to the locked box, the cache of diamonds that held his fortune.

The cell phone chimed, and he grabbed it, flipping it open and reading the text message. Finally. He set it and coffee aside to type it into the computer. He tapped the speaker. "Mr. Brandau, you have them."

He knew he did. "I'll load, but like I said, it won't have the range."

"Let's prove its value."

"You did that already. You know, too much of a good thing—"

"Do not think to advise me," he cut in. "I will see you back in that dirty little cell."

Constantine brought up the camera in time to see Brandau flip him off. He merely smiled. *I will destroy that cockiness when I am done with you.*

"Do you want to fire it?"

"Of course."

"Then you'll have to come get it."

"Think outside the box, Winston."

He cut the line and opened another. Zidane had the buyers online at remote locations, all to protect his identity. They had no real idea they were only a few floors below him, along with Brandau and his workshop. The squat, round face of a buyer came into view. The man looked impatiently at the webcam.

"What is your bid?"

The man offered seven million.

"A bit low, no thank you."

The Indonesian quickly increased it to ten. "I want proof, now."

"You shall have it when the other bidders have spoken. Is that your final offer?"

The man nodded. Constantine severed the connection.

His e-mail pinged, and he leaned over to open it, frowning. *I have a prize for you,* it read.

Constantine scrolled, then smiled at the still picture. He set a price, conditions, and a delivery, then hit send and sat back.

Like brokering commodities, he thought, then went on to weed out the low bidders.

* * *

Logan focused on the screen, impatient for the translation program to finish. It was like watching *Wheel of Fortune*, the letters turning to English, and yet, as they were literal translations, not making a whole lot of sense.

It finished and he read what he couldn't understand beyond the obvious.

Then he ran the translated decryption. Viva, bless you for this idea, he thought. He prayed Ryzikov wasn't up on the latest programs, nor had access. Logan had written his own. This had to work. He'd tried passwords in three languages and back doors, all with failures. *Access denied* was irritating him.

As decryption ran, Logan helped it along, sending the program to focus on the one group of files he couldn't even access to know how big it was.

He leaned back in the chair, scrubbed his hands over his face and, as he lowered his hands, his attention fell on Ryzikov's laptop. Logan had copied the hard drive because the Chechen's computer was too slow for his tastes.

The bag of diamonds Viva had taken were beside it, and he remembered what she'd said about role-playing. Sheik, scimitar, harem, Sahara. Nothing worked. Ryzikov was twisted and extremely arrogant. He didn't do more than handle money and weapons, but he considered himself the power of his faction. He'd stated it enough in videos after claiming responsibility for a bombing somewhere.

Logan typed in the first ruler of Islam, and the files opened.

It gave him a new set of problems.

Tashfin Rohki slowed his steps down the crowded avenue. Over the heads of the city dwellers, a familiar face grabbed his attention. Instinctively he felt for the small pistol tucked under his jacket. He kept walking, maneuvering between the throngs, and stopped before Zidane seated at an outside bistro.

"Sit, please." He gestured to the opposing chair.

Rohki didn't. "What do you want now?"

"Sit and we will discuss it." Zidane gestured to a waiter inside the restaurant, holding up two fingers.

"I don't deal with you, you're just a gofer."

Zidane arched a brow and waited. "If that is what you believe."

Rohki flicked his hand, dismissing the matter, and sat.

Without the long hair and the Manchu beard, Rohki would look less dangerous, Zidane thought, his gaze skimming his dark suit and ice blue silk tie. Little of the man he'd brought from Sri Lanka remained.

"Why would the Pharaoh give *all* the details of the weapon to the Chechen, and not to you?" Zidane noticed Rohki's eyes narrow, his hands clench.

"You're prepared to tell me," Rohki said.

"No, show you." From inside his jacket, he removed a CD.

Rohki practically salivated and reached for it, then hesitated. "He didn't send you."

Zidane inclined his head to the CD.

"He'll kill us both."

Someone would die, Zidane thought, but it wouldn't be him. "The large stone has surfaced. The one you lost."

Rohki's small eyes narrowed. They knew it existed because they'd seen a digital photo of it. Of all the stones. The Pharaoh had wanted proof before he allowed anyone into the bidding. Why he was obsessed with that particular diamond was a mystery, but then, eccentrics were as such. He said nothing till the waiter left the coffees. "Who has it?"

Slowly Zidane pulled a photo from inside his jacket and tossed it. It slid and spun across the small table.

Rohki didn't pick it up and stared, his brows knit. "I've seen him before, I think. In Sri Lanka." While the photo was clear, Rohki didn't recall the man's face well. He was nothing more than an armed guard. "The Irishman took the stone before the flood."

"And the flood—was made with the weapon." Rohki's head snapped up and Zidane enjoyed the shock.

"That's impossible. It's just the plans."

"It was created long ago."

Rohki was silent, pieces falling into place. He exploded. "I lost my men! My countrymen!" Just because he fought for the Tigers didn't mean he wanted to kill his people.

"He doesn't care, he has no cause, no sympathies, but for the stones and the money the bidding war will bring him." Zidane unfolded from the chair and stood. "What would you do to return the favor?"

"Kill him."

"Then prepare yourself." Zidane stepped to the curb and hailed a cab. "A car will come for you."

Rohki's gaze drifted down to the CD. Having the design was useless, he needed the weapon.

The team entered to see Logan standing, working between the three keyboards.

"Now that's an excited man," Max said.

"I got past the encryption."

"Outstanding," Sam said.

"This guy has his whole life on here. Photos of targets, known and unknown associates, bank accounts, future targets. He was even writing his memoirs. It's sick."

"They'll love you in Washington."

"You have to see this, though. It's the schematics for a weapon, I think."

"*You* aren't sure?" Sam said, moving to the screen. They were pretty much up on the latest warfare.

"Ever see anything like that?" Logan asked.

"It doesn't look like a weapon," Max said, hovering. "What's that square silver plate on the top? And the housing is too wide to be loaded with bullets." It would hold a .50 caliber, but the device itself would never hold up to the propulsion of it.

"Can you turn this view?" Sam asked.

Logan tapped keys.

"I've seen something like that before." The men looked at him. "An article in *Popular Mechanics*. The inventor was in on the development of the first sonograms."

"Woody somebody, he was a tech in the Air Force, I think, a radioman," Max said.

"It's HSS, hypersonic sound." Sam straightened and looked at his buddies. "It pinpoints sound. Commercially, investors would use it to say, give the sound of a soda opening when you passed a vending machine. As weaponry, it can make your skeleton vibrate, and you can pick the illness. At two hundred yards."

"And hear what's not there. They used it on Viva," Logan said with finality.

Sebastian entered, carrying a six-pack of beer, pulled four off the ring and handed them out. "Why this? If it's patented, it's for sale in the open market."

"It barely resembles the one in the article, except for that plate," Sam said. "This one is narrow and long. And what's this?" He drew a line from the base to the bulbous end. The mechanism had the streamlines of a rocket launcher, yet the components on top, the grid plate that looked like silver material, obstructed. It wasn't concealed or housed and very close to the end. The entire length of it wasn't more than a yard.

Then he noticed the tripod stand, collapsible.

"It stands," Sam said. "It's stationary, the others were handheld."

"That puts it pointing to the sky," Logan put in.

Sebastian studied it. "Why, when direction would normally be horizontal?"

"Who knows?" Sam said. "The military bought thousands of the other versions. They're using them in Afghanistan to empty the caves."

"Well, hell," Sebastian said, "that means it's ours." Stolen from a US project.

"We need more information. Someone's got to know it's missing. Load it up to the Pentagon, A-sap."

"Was just about to." Logan turned back to the computer. "Going to use up my favors on this one."

National Military Command Center

Walker hovered over the desk, then looked at the white board. He'd been trying to find a connection between the theft and the sightings of terrorists in Thailand enroute to the area—beyond the obvious. Who had the capability to use such clandestine software? The Chinese, sure, but they had their own resources. National security, yes—he twisted, frowning at his board. *Whose* national security, he thought and went to town.

Zidane canvassed her moves. Noor did not blend easily in the city. She was graceful and beautiful, but while men looked, she didn't notice, nor did she care. He advanced when she started to fade from his sight and he paused in a doorway. He should have given this job to one of his men, but needed no one to understand his motives. Noor hunted.

Zidane tracked her.

She searched for the American. For the stone so she would return to favor. It troubled her—probably the only thing that had in a while—that she had been lowered in the Pharaoh's eyes.

Zidane was surprised she didn't just fuck him again. Sex was the most lethal weapon in her arsenal. Even he had wanted to try the beauty, but not anymore. He'd seen enough.

Noor slipped into a skyscraper and Zidane proceeded, frowning at the address.

Noor didn't stop at the desk and when the receptionist tried to block her path, Noor shoved her aside. The woman sank into her chair, and quickly made a call. Noor kept walking, turning to a NO ADMITTANCE hall and stopping at a door. She knocked when she wanted to break it in. The door slipped open, the pretty face peered, first seductively, then with utter shock.

"You swore never to come here, ever."

"I need something from you." Noor pushed her way in, looked around the flat and smirked. "You can do better than this, Mali."

"And you have? Get out, I want nothing of you, you will destroy my business. They have not forgotten."

Noor's gaze slashed to Mali's. "I didn't want them to. Your lover, Dahl, who was his friend?" Mali would give up her own mother to save her precious porcelain skin, Noor thought.

Mali frowned. "I don't know, an American, a cowboy."

"A name." Noor slipped out a knife.

Mali backed up and reached for the phone. A kick and Noor sent it flying across the room.

"I beg you, do not hurt me."

Noor sneered. "You're pathetic, stand up."

Mali rose gingerly.

"A name, I know he told you."

"Wyatt, that's all I heard. Wyatt."

Noor didn't say another word and spun on her heels, leaving the room. Mali immediately grabbed the phone to warn Russell.

Zidane's gaze followed her as she left the building. She was so intent on her progress she did not see him standing near the bank of phones. He left the newspaper and the building, popping a lozenge in his mouth. He could easily learn what she had on the sixteenth floor. But trailing her would be much simpler—and beneficial.

Logan called his pal, Deets, at NSA. "I've got something you should see."

"How much?"

"About ten gig."

Deets whistled softly. "Let her rip."

"You aren't the only one getting it. I've sent this to the Pentagon."

There was a moment of hesitation, then, "What the hell is it, Chambliss?"

"Andrei Ryzikov's computer hard drive."

"Holy shit."

Logan could just barely hear him speaking to others.

"How did you get it?" Deets asked.

Everyone in there just went on fast alert, he knew. "Long story, but it involved Ryzikov's little death's-door fetish." He heard more muttered sounds and instantly knew they had intel on this. "You know something."

There was silence, no confirmation, no denial.

"What's your mission and for who?" Deets asked.

"I've got a sworn duty, too. No."

"Money making the decisions?"

"You know better than to ask that, God dammit. I was hoping you could shed some light on this."

"Logan, that's a flash."

Flash, flash, flash was the term used in emergencies by the higher ranking, old-school military. It cut all communications and allowed the info to travel to the right sources lightning fast, chain of command be dammed.

But NSA had their own priorities, and Logan needed to understand this machine better.

Sam prowled the house, unable to sleep. Even when she wasn't here, Viva kept him awake. *She should have landed by now*. He dropped onto the sofa and reached for the phone to call his buddy in the RAF. He was about to dial when a soft ping made him twist, his gaze searching the room for the sound.

A cell phone, a computer? There was enough equipment in here that it would take an hour to find what was buzzing. He pushed off the sofa, and went to the computers. He frowned as he tapped each one. Nothing on them.

He straightened slowly and turned toward Ryzikov's laptop sitting at the end of the table, away from the rest of the equipment. Scowling, he went to it. Any associate had to know by now that Ryz was dead. He hit the key and the dormant screen blinked up. He checked the e-mail and found a new one.

He switched on a lamp and brought the computer close. It was wireless, he realized. He opened the e-mail account; glad it was converted to English.

One new mail.

It was a video stream of someone with a black hood. One of Ryzikov's pals? Al Qaeda? The guy sure looked the part. The stream was erratic, and not all that clear. He unplugged a cable and inserted it into the back, then sent the stream to the larger screen.

It played for ten seconds.

Small shoulders, thin neck. A horrible, cold feeling slipped through him. His heartbeat slowed and his stomach instantly sank.

Sam woke everyone up. Logan was there first.

"Check Viva's marker."

"At this hour?"

"Check it, dammit."

Sam pointed to the screen. Logan didn't bother to sit and bent to work the keyboard. "The range isn't that far. Shit." He looked at him. "She's still in Thailand."

"She's right there!" He lashed a hand at the LCD.

The bronze cuff showed clearly in the picture.

Logan looked from the feed to Ryzikov's laptop. "I can trace it."

"That means they can, too!"

Sam caught sight of a series of black dots at the bottom and scrolled the message a fraction.

A single word was typed on the bottom.

Trade?

Fifteen

Sam stared at the screen, trying to see if she was injured.

"Man, this Pharaoh really wants that diamond bad, doesn't he?" Max said, pulling on a T-shirt. "Pharaoh" was the only reference they'd found in the laptop.

"We can't give it to him; he's done too much to get it," Logan said.

Sam looked at him. "Yeah, like using Viva. Because of us. I'll be damned if I let that bastard have her."

Sam grabbed the diamond off the coffee table. It had been a bowl all this time, like a ordinary piece of crystal and not a couple hundred million in conflict ice. He looked at his teammates. "This man has been one step ahead and killing everyone in his way. He won't hesitate to kill her."

"That stone is more than some obsession with him," Max added.

"Good enough reason not to give it to him." Logan was the team's pessimist.

"If you can think of a better way to handle this, I'm open," Sam snapped. He would not let Viva suffer for this. Never.

"Killian's on the wire." Logan hit the speakerphone.

"Riley's awake." Ooh rahs and smiles wreathed the team. "He's not talking yet and in a lot of pain, but he's going to make a full recovery. Alexa and I are taking him back to the US."

Logan apprised them of the latest developments.

"Let me talk to Sam, alone." Sam grabbed the phone and moved away. "The team might tell you not to trade for her, but I won't."

"It isn't going to stop the weapons' deal, Killian."

"No doubt. The bastard's got stones out the ass. This is your game, Sam. You call it."

"We trade," he said without hesitation. "It's our fault."

"Roger that. Next time, send the woman packing."

Sam heard what sounded like a smack and Killian laughed.

Alexa's voice murmured in the background, then Killian said, "Alexa tried to contact Kashir, no dice. He missed the contact point twice. She pulled a string with that kid, Lorimer. CIA is tracking your moves. Expect interference."

"More than they have already?" And damn near got them killed chasing them through the city.

"Yeah, well, she said if you need to trust someone there, it's Adam Kincade."

Killian signed off and Sam tapped the phone against his chin. He didn't realize he'd been gripping the diamond all this time till his palm ached. He looked down at it, possibilities forming. "She has a marker, we go in with the best advantage. Reply to that e-mail with a cell number." He tossed the diamond at Sebastian. "Rig it."

Less than an hour later, Sam's cell phone rang. He looked at the number, showed it to Logan, who copied and started a search. He opened the call.

"You received my message," the caller said without preamble. "Though you cannot see her beautiful red hair."

Sam ground his teeth, and gave the team a thumbs-up. "I'll trade."

"Good. You will join me on the twelfth floor of the Jewelry Trade Center."

"No, I choose."

"I have your woman."

"And I have your stone." Sam's temper flared and he drew in air, hoping he didn't lose it. He grabbed a map of Bangkok and ran his finger over a path. "Outside, Temple of Wa Phat."

"No. Too open."

"Look, pal, you accommodate me, or the consequences will give you nightmares."

Logan shook his head, still tracing. "It's an onion router, Sam, he's got his ass covered, he could be in Istanbul for all we know."

"You'd risk the woman's life?" the caller said.

Never. "Harm her and your stone goes in the Chaipya River." Sam could care less about the diamond.

"It's worth millions."

"It would help you to remember that."

There was a long silence and then, "I agree."

"Two hours. You call this number. I'll tell you what to do." Sam heard an irritated noise.

"You think to run me around the city? No."

Arrogant bastard. "Not an option. My way or the highway, pal." Sam cut the line.

"You're insane," Max said, but was already reaching for communications gear.

Only Sam's gaze lifted. "Viva has a marker. We'll see them coming."

Max shot over to the GPS programmed with the biomarker. "That's if she's with him. What's the advantage?"

"To make him so eager to get his hands on the stone, he'll slip up."

Sebastian came out of the kitchen, carrying a small wooden box. "It's ready. You sure you want it like this? Viva could get hurt."

"Not if our timing is good." He looked at Logan. "Be prepared, he's had her long enough to implant something in her mind again."

"I didn't get a trace." Logan yanked off the headset and

tossed it. "Dammit. The onion router, that's high tech. I made my own software, but for an entire system, it's expensive, and you need several networks that have the same capability."

"That's freaking Greek to me," Sam said.

"It means that he has a clandestine routing system that rivals the NSA."

"Then her marker is our only way to track."

Time meant nothing to Viva.

Her surroundings were merely a housing, leaving prisons only her mind could conjure. Telling herself that Sam would find her didn't ease her terror. He thought she was in England. A pinprick to her skin, a hand over her mouth before she made it to the jet hatch, and everything changed.

This was really starting to piss her off.

She couldn't see, her head wrapped in fabric. It was so snug she couldn't raise her eyelids. No one spoke to her, and she heard nothing beyond doors opening and closing. Of course, the tape over her mouth took away prime moments for some really good verbal attacks anyway. The only thing they'd allowed her was to pee. Try that with your hands tied, she thought, and didn't know if she'd had an audience. At this point, it didn't matter. She'd been inspected by slavers, dressed like a genie, and nearly raped and choked to death. Modesty wasn't up there with survival.

Amazing, she thought, that she'd killed one man and felt remorse, not regret. Right now, she could easily stick a knife in this bastard and feel nothing.

Sam stood at the end of a long carpet of grass. Temple devotees walked the grounds, cars parked alongside the road. In the distance, Max strolled, the image of a student tourist, taking pictures, wearing a backpack and grubby clothes. People would have to get close to notice he was well past the age of a college kid. His attention was on the people, looking for any clue to the bastard that had Viva.

Sam prayed he didn't hurt her.

"Outlaw, your three o'clock," came through the comms.

Sam glanced in Max's direction as he turned and focused the camera. "Roger that."

The sedan rolled down the street alongside the park, the windows tinted black.

Sam stepped into clear view. The car stopped, and his cell rang. "Show me the woman."

The door opened. A tall, swarthy man in a black suit stepped out, then reached into the car. A figure appeared, grappling for a handhold, staggering as the man pulled her in front of him.

She was hooded, her head wrapped in black cloth.

"That could be anyone," he said into the phone. The clothing was the same and she wore the bracelet, but that could be staged.

"You will have to trust me."

"Not a chance."

"I can see inside the car," Sebastian said from his position on the hill. "The guy is hooded, too. Paranoid, isn't he?"

"Show me her face," Sam demanded. "Now."

"Show me the diamond."

"And let you shoot me now? No. I have it and you know it. Your little dart hunter saw it. Now show me her face!"

There was a muffled comment, then the man who held her loosened the hood and yanked it off. He saw the red hair first and she blinked against the sunlight, tried to touch her face, but the man held her arms. Across her mouth was a wide strip of tape and her hands were tied.

She looked around, then across the expanse of grass, and saw him.

Sam's heart soared. She's okay. Her eyes flared, and even across the distance, he could feel her fear, her shock.

Then the man hooded her and pushed her back in the car.

"The west dock. Forty minutes," Sam said.

"No, we deal now," the caller said.

"If you're late, you can dive for the diamond in the river."

"And you can also do so for the woman."

And with her mouth taped, she'd never get a breath, Sam thought. "Guess you'd better hurry, huh?"

Sam turned away and his gaze drifted to the van, to Sebastian on the hill.

"There's only two in the car other than Viva."

"His voice isn't altered, you get the accent? He sounds French but with something else, Middle Eastern, maybe, it's guttural," Max said, the comms linked to Logan at the CP, recording everything.

"Sebastian?"

"I've got nothing on him, he stayed back in the seat and concealed."

And still no idea who they were dealing with.

The sedan pulled away. "They're on the move."

Sam hopped on a motorcycle and headed toward the docks. He wanted Viva in his arms before nightfall.

Inside the car, Viva waited for someone to speak again. Before now, they hadn't said anything she could decipher, just whispered words. Now the speaker was ticked off. The fury in his tone, his impatience meant nothing to her beyond the accent. Any doubts about who had her evaporated. She was at the mercy of the same person who'd violated her mind.

She hoped the next time Sam saw him, he shot the bastard in the head.

At the dock yards, Sam watched from the roof of a warehouse. This time Sam didn't show himself and forced the dealer to show Viva. They wouldn't allow her to move, to give him any signal, and that made him suspicious. Had they drugged her? "Roof of the Italthai. I'm waiting."

Inside the car, Jalier cursed rudely. "We take this man. He thinks to toy with me."

"No more than you have with her." Zidane gestured to the woman who sat perfectly still, her bound hands on her lap.

"You have sympathy for them?"

"Of course not. You must deal with him on his terms. Sacrifice your pride. The outcome will get you the prize you covet."

Jalier snarled something in French, then looked out the window.

Zidane's gaze drifted to the woman, and he wondered what she thought of this. For a moment, he admired her calm and confidence in her man, then added his own, for the cowboy had neatly cornered Jalier, giving him no choice but to deal on his terms. But the woman's lack of fear for Jalier, while an annoyance to the man, was unwise.

Jalier had no allegiance, even in this bargain.

It was several minutes before they reached the Italthai, driving into the lower garage. Zidane left the car and checked the area for bystanders before he opened the car door. A hooded woman would bring notice. The elevator was standing open and Jalier entered before Zidane bodily moved the woman inside. They rode to the top.

"The hotel roof is a helicopter port."

"And dangerously windy. Have your men ready."

"And Noor?" Zidane asked.

"Unnecessary." His gaze drifted over the woman. He had glimpsed her face once, when she'd stabbed his highest bidder. He didn't know her name, nor wished to learn it. He closed his hands over hers. She yanked back, protesting sounds muffled under the tape gag.

"If he tries to betray me," he told her softly, "you will both die."

She gave him a cocky pose that spoke loudly of her confidence. He wished he knew the man he was dealing with, but as with the woman, Jalier didn't bother. They wouldn't be alive long enough to matter.

In the top of the Italthai tower, Zidane gripped the woman from behind by the arms. She stiffened. "There are steps," he said near her ear.

She tipped her head to the sound of his voice, almost curious. His accent, he decided. She was a confusing woman, offering no fight, only her distaste for Jalier. She'd been delivered to them, hooded, bound, and unconscious. By whom, Zidane didn't know, yet since then, she'd been compliant, though Zidane felt as if he held uncapped energy. She fought her need to rebel. Prudent.

Zidane had kept her secluded, away from all eyes, including Noor's. Noor had learned the name of the man who had the stone and was eager to take revenge on him for her fall from grace with Jalier. She didn't understand that Constantine Jalier had no attachment to her. Noor was a necessary evil. For now.

Jalier stood on the small landing a few feet above them, then looked beyond. Zidane twisted. Noor approached.

Jalier scowled, and motioned her back. "Cut her bonds," he ordered. Zidane obeyed, and she rolled her shoulders, rubbed her wrists. Zidane urged the woman forward and she searched blindly for the railing, her hands moving without purchase. He placed her hand on the iron rail.

"That's Thai." Noor reached for the cuff the woman wore.

Jalier blocked her. "Leave it be, it doesn't matter."

Noor ignored the command and tried to take the cuff, but Jalier gripped her wrist hard, throwing it back at her.

"She wears a royal bracelet!"

Jalier frowned at the thing. It was thick and hammered with dark stones of rubies and sapphires, but of no interest to him. He was not a curator of antiquities, nor was it of any value to him. He wanted his diamond, and that, he'd gain without Noor's interference.

"Then perhaps you should bow to her," Zidane said and Noor glared at him. Then she spat in his face. He wiped the spittle, his eyes gone dangerously dark.

"I want it. You owe me this," Noor insisted.

Jalier's gaze narrowed sharply. "What?" The word snapped with ice.

If Jalier thought she would cower, he was mistaken. Her entire being went rigid, her hand lying on her knives.

"You defy me, now? For that?"

Noor said nothing, fuming.

"Don't." Disgust marked Jalier's features before he pulled on a black mesh hood and turned away.

Zidane helped the woman up the final staircase to the roof.

"Are your men ready?" Jalier asked.

Zidane nodded and he felt the woman tense under his grip, and make a sound, shaking her head. Begging them not to hurt anyone. It was pointless, she had to know that.

If it benefited him, Jalier would push her over the edge of the high-rise.

Wind howled around her, and Viva felt the sharp whip of it as she climbed the steps. *They're going to double-cross them.* She was unsteady as she felt for the next step, and the man held her firmly, and told her to take three steps forward. His voice was surprisingly gentle. Then he let her go and she tottered, hating that she was blind.

Viva held herself still and could do nothing. A pawn again.

Jalier ascended the final steps. Wyatt was there already, in the center of the roof. Jalier glared back at Zidane. "You stupid fool. Did you not think to check?"

Frowning, Zidane looked. Clever and curious, for he'd sent men up to check here only fifteen minutes ago. He scanned the nearby buildings, the rooftops, yet saw nothing unusual. At this level, the hotel was isolated from any other building.

Zidane turned to Jalier, waving him on. "You have no choice now. Just as he planned."

Jalier glared at him, then squinted against the setting sun.

Wyatt stood in a wide stance, heedless of the wind tearing across the pad. He held a small wood box, and Jalier's pulse increased at the thought of having the stone. Then his gaze fell on the gun and whip at Wyatt's hip. Americans, he thought, and stepped fully onto the platform. He twisted and pulled the woman forward and used her as a shield.

"You are alone, how will you leave with her?"

"Not your problem."

Behind his back, Jalier motioned to Zidane. *Be ready*.

NMCC

High-alert status sent a military base to scrambling. Fast-moving operations in the Pentagon, they tried for calm, except for one young lieutenant. He raced down the hall to the "tank," went through no less than three security checks and waited. When the general was alerted, they let him inside.

General McGill looked up as the lieutenant hurried around the desk. "We have Ryzikov's hard drive from his laptop."

A rumble of approving murmurs circled the room.

"How the hell did we get that?"

"It was sent to us via a secured program. From Thailand."

McGill frowned.

"Commander Chambliss. Dragon One?" The lieutenant said, clueless.

"I know who you mean."

"It's under analysis and loading up, but this was encrypted." He inserted the CD into the computer and tapped a few keys, bringing it up on the large screens.

The schematics for the weapon. "Can they build from this?"

"No, sir, for design and security purposes, Silent Fire was not a complete schematic in any one file. It was broken up into two parts. This is the main one, though, but the theory and reports are there."

"Gerardo has seen it?" The lieutenant nodded. "Get him on the wire. Now." It was several minutes before the satellite link connected them.

"I'll let you speak with the designer," was all Gerardo said, stepping back. A gentle-looking man lowered into the general's chair.

"The modification indicates that the thieves have altered the design to be powered by laser."

"That tells me little, sir."

"Instead of firing it with directional acoustics, the sound is modified by passing it along a laser, increasing the distance and accuracy. And the intensity."

Longer range and a lot more power, McGill thought. "What do they need to do this?"

"That's the concern. This is an impossible modification. It will not work without a clear substance for the beam to travel. No refraction or it will blow itself up. Glass, polymer, even crystal change in molecular structure or melt if hit with a laser. The only material that would withstand the heat of a laser is a diamond."

McGill's lips tightened. They'd heard Ryzikov's cell call, the mention of stones, and he looked down at the CIA report on conflict diamonds surfacing in Thailand right now.

"A very large one."

"If this weapon is modified, and they do have the diamond, what's the capability?"

"If it works, at the least, it could take down an aircraft."

Wyatt pulled out a cell phone, held it up. Jalier autodialed, confident the signal routed back and forth across Europe and Asia before reaching Wyatt's. He put it to his ear.

"Send her to me," the man demanded.

Jalier leaned close to the woman, nudging her. "Take ten steps forward." She didn't move, frightened. He pushed her and she advanced slowly.

The man walked, gripping the box.

Viva counted ten and stopped.

"Viva."

She nearly crumbled before his eyes, made a helpless sound. "Hold out your hands." She did, and Sam laid the box in her hands, curling her fingers around the edge. "Now, turn around and take it to him, then come back to me." She shook her head. "Jesus, baby, don't argue."

"He'll kill you," Viva tried to shout. *Get off the roof.* But it was just noise.

He forced her around, holding her upper arms for a moment. "No matter what, do not take the stone out of this box." Sam was wagering on this bastard being obsessed enough to want to fondle it.

This close to Sam she didn't want to move, but Viva had no choice except to walk, marking off her steps. She held out the box like an offering. The brisk wind made her unsteady.

Sam's heart jumped when a woman rushed from the lower steps and grabbed Viva's arm. Viva held on to the box and fought her, but the battle brought her close to the edge of the platform. It was a twenty-foot drop to the roof and nothing stopping her from going over the edge—nine hundred feet to the busy street.

"Stupid white bitch!"

I've about had it, Viva thought, clawing at the woman, felt her face under her nails, and put her weight behind a punch. Viva clipped her chin, sending her reeling back.

Sam's heart slammed to a stop as Viva's blind struggle with the blowgun woman put her close to the edge. His breath hurt. "Be still! Don't move!"

She froze, clutching the box to her chest. A tall, dark-skinned man appeared, armed and rushing the women.

Zidane grabbed Noor, nearly throwing her toward the stairwell. "You risk everything, woman. Leave it be!"

"You betray me when I need you!"

He scoffed. "You've betrayed your country a dozen times already. A bracelet is meaningless." He motioned to his men to hold her, then inched up the staircase.

Sam saw the armed man poised in the stairwell.

Behind the mesh mask, Jalier threw an angry look at Noor, then turned toward the woman. He righted her position in front of him, then said, "Open the box."

Sam saw Viva turn the box away from herself, latch out, and feel for the opening.

"Jesus, Sam," Sebastian said in his ear, watching the monitor, the coin-sized camera set up on the edge of the pad.

"She won't take it out." She opened it, showing the Pharaoh the large, long stone.

The man ordered her to give it to him. But she shook her head, offering it, letting the box teeter in her hands.

"Oh, holy Christ. If she—"

"I know! She's dead."

"Hand it to me!" Jalier shouted over the noise.

Viva refused, lifting the box higher, Sam's warning playing in her head. When the man didn't take it, she let it drop. It hit the platform and tumbled. He'll be pissed now, she thought, and backed away slowly, completely lost as to her position on the roof.

Sam shouted. "To your right!" She moved a step, but no farther. "Coonass, now!"

Jalier looked between the woman and the stone, then suddenly lunged, and grabbed her around the chest. He put the gun to her hooded head. His eyes widened when he saw blades at the edge of the platform, the whirl of a black helicopter rising in the glare of the sun. It rose fast and high, barely making a sound, yet the wind force of the blades unbalanced him.

Then the nose of the black chopper opened, metal plates folding back over the last and revealing machine guns. The guns rolled sideways and extended. The man in the cockpit smiled, baring his teeth like fangs.

"I'll kill her now!" Jalier dug the gun in, forcing her head to the side.

The woman went slack against him, sliding down his body to the ground. She rolled, came to her knees. Her hands out, she crawled, felt her way.

Jalier reached for her, but the wind sent the diamond rolling across the concrete slab.

Zidane rushed from the stairwell, aimed, squinting against the wind.

"Shoot them!" Jalier ordered. "Tell your men to shoot!"

Zidane refused. "They will cut you in half!"

A line dropped from the chopper, looped at the end and the cowboy grabbed it, slipped it over his head and arm as he ran toward the woman. The chopper swept forward with him, guns ready.

The diamond rolled and Jalier dove for it, knocking Viva. Half-upright, she tottered on the edge, reached out, and felt nothing but air.

McGill was on the speakerphone. "Commander Chambliss. We've seen the hard drive, excellent work, but we have another problem, the machine."

"We haven't located it, sir."

"We aren't certain they've manufactured one from the plans."

"Considering the situation, do you really doubt that?"

"Agreed." He frowned slightly. "NSA tells me your teammate was in Ryzikov's hotel?"

"Yes, sir."

"Did he have uncut stones, diamonds?"

"Yes, sir. They're right here. Our job was to trace the conflict diamonds to the weapons rumored for the purchase. We've spotted enough known terrorists to be certain it was going to happen here, within days."

"Well, this is it, Silent Fire, but our concern right now is that it's been modified and its capability depends on a large diamond."

"Oh, shit."

"Not what I want to hear, son." McGill swore he was ready to retire after today.

"Sir. We have a large stone. Our sources say it's over two hundred carats."

Men sat back, impressed and wary. "Uncut?"

"Yes."

He looked at the screen, at the designer, and his nod was a mark of doom. "We need that stone."

"Can't help you, sir. It's being traded for the life of a woman right now."

"Well, stop it!"

"Sir. This is the woman who killed Ryzikov."

"I'll give her a damn medal, but if they have the machine and that stone, they can magnify the weapon."

"I'll call you back."

The line went dead, and McGill looked at the phone. Worst thing in the world was former military. Shot all respect for orders to hell.

"Get them back on the wire!"

Viva started to fall.

Sam bolted across the helo pad as he cracked his whip, the tail snapping around her waist. He yanked her back, clamping his arms around her. Her weight took them over the edge.

"Oh, God," Max said, aiming the MP5, watching helplessly as they tumbled.

Sebastian pulled back on the stick and brought the chopper high. "Did he get her?" he demanded. "Jesus Christ, Jesus Christ!"

"He's got her!" Max shouted. "Fly! Fly!"

The chopper lifted straight up, dangling them over the roof.

The dark man fired, and Max returned it, aiming to kill as the chopper rose above Bangkok.

The force of the wind kicked the diamond over the edge of the pad. Amid gunfire, Jalier clamored for it, throwing himself on the cement, his fingers closing around the stone. He rolled, shoved it inside his shirt, then pushed himself up. He was on the edge. His vision blurred, the building almost swaying. The street was no more than a thin line eighty stories below. He yelped when heavy hands clamped on his jacket and yanked him back.

Viva felt the ground vanish from under her, then arms grab her. She screamed behind the gag, then heard Sam's voice close to her ear.

"Hold tight!"

She clung, her arms and legs wrapped around him, and the chopper rose, then swept across the city thousands of feet above the streets. It's a good thing she couldn't see, she thought. She'd be barfing right now.

She heard a grind of gears, felt the pull of their bodies against the wind, whipping them back and forth like a pendulum as the noise of the engine increased. Then hands grabbed on to her shirt, pulling, and she felt for the cable. For Sam. They pulled them inside.

Viva shrieked behind the blindfold, tearing violently at the cloth that wouldn't give.

"You're safe, Viva, you're safe!" Max shouted.

Hands held her still and the cold steel of a knife ran under the edge of the hood, cutting it. She couldn't catch her breath, couldn't rip it off fast enough, and looked up into Sam's eyes. He yanked off the tape.

She inhaled a deep breath, then said, "That was your plan? A joyride off the roof?"

Sam gripped her head, staring into her eyes. Grateful for the chance. "Viva, Viva!"

She swore in three languages. "Jesus, Mary, and Joseph, that man needs to die! He really needs to die!"

Her breathing was too fast. "Viva!"

"What!"

Sam kissed her. Hard and thoroughly, then pulled back.

She blew out a breath, calmer, smiling. "You'll have to work a lot harder than that before I'll forgive that lousy plan."

Sixteen

In the stairwell, Jalier yanked off the hood and backhanded Noor, sending her reeling down the staircase. "You stupid bitch! You could have ruined everything and gotten us all killed."

Noor rose slowly, her gaze darting to the men, to Zidane, then to Constantine. "The bracelet is Thai," she said calmly, wiping blood from her lip. "And you forget who you touch."

He'd done more than touch her, and ignored the threat. "What do you know of history?" Jalier moved past her down the stairwell to the elevator, the fat diamond clutched in his fist.

Zidane handed the box over to his man, and entered the elevator. They turned to stare at Noor. Blood collected at the corner of her mouth, her eyes black and savage.

"Compose yourself," Jalier said, disgusted. "Then we will discuss this new behavior." The door slid closed. "Assemble the rest of the buyers. Bring them to the compound."

Zidane's face showed his shock. "You're certain?"

Jalier slid him a cool glance and Zidane nodded.

Beyond the doors, Noor boiled with outrage. Pigs, she thought, and retraced her steps to the helo pad. She stood on the mark in the center, her gaze darting around the platform as she remembered Wyatt's courage, his desperation to save the woman so keen that Noor could still feel it—potent on the air. It left her steaming with jealousy. To have such devotion, she thought, then shook it off. She spun on her heels, wondering where the American had gone, for with him went the bracelet. A piece of her people, and nothing of her own past.

Only Sam and Viva were in the rear of the chopper, Max in the copilot seat as Sebastian flew them toward the CP.

His back to the bulkhead, both wearing headsets, he cradled her between his thighs, his arms wrapped tightly around her. He set the comms so they could talk privately. "Anything else you want to bitch about?"

"Lack of wet, sloppy kisses?"

"I think I can accommodate that." Sam laid his mouth over hers with exquisite tenderness and Viva curled into the warmth of his body, wishing they were somewhere else. Preferably naked.

Sam's heart instantly jumped and he gripped her tighter. *I almost lost her,* he thought, and knew that was an adrenaline rush he never wanted again.

"I really didn't want to go to England anyway," she said, between kisses. God, his mouth felt so good on hers.

"Can't trust you to behave." He couldn't get enough of her.

"I tried, give me credit. They got me before I even got to the jet hatch," she told him. Sam was groping her nicely when a ball of paper hit them and they looked up.

Smiling, Max motioned to turn the headset on to hear him. Sam reached above and flipped the switch.

"Cutter's on the wire. He was trying to reach us in the middle of that."

Sebastian flipped for all-comms. "We're on our way back with the package."

"Glad you're okay, Viva, but tell me you still have that stone," Logan said.

Inside the chopper, they frowned. "No," Sam said. "It was the trade, you know that."

"Well, NMCC's been beating up the airwaves, trying to stop us."

"For what reason?" There was an edge to Sam's voice.

"The HSS machine design on Ryzikov's computer was modified to increase its distance and intensity with the diamond."

"Oh, shit." Briefly, Sam told her about the HSS machine.

"Okay, now I feel really guilty," Viva said.

"Don't," Sam said. "If he didn't have that one, he'd get another. Rohki had a lot of big stones in Sri Lanka and he's not the only buyer."

"That's why he wanted uncut stones," Viva said. "He wasn't obsessed; he needed one to fit that thing."

"The bigger the stone the longer the range," Sam said.

"Hell if I know," Logan said. "So I get to tell McGill they're a day late and a dollar short?"

"Figures," Sam said. "This isn't over."

"It's like the Energizer Bunny, it keeps going," Viva said.

"I'm just glad you didn't put the diamond back in the box."

Viva twisted to Max. "Why?"

"It was rigged to explode."

"So was the roof," Sebastian said.

"You guys take way too many risks."

Collectively they said, "That's why we get paid the big bucks."

"Then I want a cut."

They laughed and Viva pushed her fingers through her hair, then went still and looked up. "That means the box could blow any moment."

"That tall guy took it," Max said with a glance back.

"Hopefully it will blow them to hell." Perfect justice, Sam thought.

"I can stop it from the shack, Viva," Sebastian said. "I never let an explosive device go wild."

"Besides," Max said. "There's a tracer in the box."

Kashir ran, half-limping in the dark, humidity clinging to his skin. He stopped, fell back against a stone wall, wincing at the jolt. He checked his surroundings, then peeled back the sticky rag from his ribs. Blood soaked the cloth he'd stolen off a line hanging between buildings, and he adjusted the folds, then pressed it harder, trying to hold tight pressure, but he couldn't. The longer he took, the less time Dragon One would have. He pushed off the wall, staggering for a moment, then focused his direction, thinking the knife might have pierced his lung. It was getting harder to breathe.

He'd left three dead in the street for the effort. There would be more seeking revenge. In his condition, taking a bus or a cab would bring the police and he didn't have time to deal with Thai laws. He was out of cash and options except to go by foot, or steal a car.

Kashir had only one person he could seek out at this hour.

Exhaustion made his eyes water as Ramesh Narabi studied the large diamond before making the next cut. This, he thought, was the true reason he was kidnapped from his home. The diamond was the largest he'd ever seen and after a preliminary examination, he knew the stone could be cut in one piece and would be nearly as large as the Cullinan. The thought of the prize of India stolen by the British and sitting in the Crown Jewels of England's monarch made his chest ache. A nearly two-hundred-year-old affront to his people, he thought, then glanced again at the instructions given with the stone.

His instructions had been simple, demanding nothing more than a flawless first water cut with no refractions. Like the last stones. While a faceted cut for this would take nearly a year, without one it would be a matter of hours. He left the stone on the table and went to the sink, splashing water on his face and the back of his neck before grabbing a towel to dry. He wiped slowly, unwilling to face the task ahead. Rebellion was out of the question. His family would suffer for it.

For Ramesh, all he had left in this world were his children.

* * *

Outside a buyer's hotel, Zidane heard the voice on the other end of his phone and tensed. "You are never to call me."

"I need your help. Now."

Zidane slid a lozenge into his mouth. "I can't accommodate you."

"Are you willing to blow this whole thing wide open? I've worked damn hard for it, too."

"What I am willing to do and what you must are not in tandem." He cut the line and waved to his man to bring the car. Moments later, he put another buyer into the sedan, and into the shell game of secrecy that was rapidly falling apart.

McGill didn't take the news well. "You didn't think to inform US intelligence sources of this, Commander Chambliss?"

Logan was tired of being raked over the coals because Viva was alive and the stone was gone. "You know, General, the last time we tried to help, the intelligence community tried to kill us, *sir?*"

In the Pentagon, McGill sighed, still feeling the ripple effect of Price's ruination. With trust obliterated, they'd had to rebuild the clandestine operations from the ground up. "Some notice would have been beneficial."

"I sent the damn hard drive as soon as it was decrypted, for crissake. What the hell are you paying all those suits to do?" Logan reeled in his temper. "It swings both ways, McGill."

On the other end of the line, McGill blinked. "What do you need?"

"Tell me what we're up against, because if you've got someone deeper inside, we need to know it. What's this thing capable of? Aside from being used to brainwash."

"That's classified."

"Really," Logan said dryly. "Then let's figure how much cash it would take for an MIT grad to reproduce it from these schematics, which, I'll guesstimate, about a half dozen terrorists already have?"

"You made your point, Chambliss. But since it's been modified, we aren't positive."

"Estimate."

When Logan heard the specifications, he thought, *They have the power to hold us all hostage.*

Sam was glad that Dragon One worked like a well-oiled machine or Viva wouldn't be sitting on the edge of the bed, letting Logan examine her.

"You really are anal sometimes, Logan."

Sam chuckled to himself as Logan checked Viva's ears and everything else she owned. He'd grabbed her the instant she was inside the house and wouldn't listen to any of her balking. They were all afraid the bastard had screwed with her mind again. Didn't seem that way and she kept her gaze on Sam, refusing to be parted while she sat through the exam. Sam didn't blame her. It had been a scary few days. His gaze swept her, searching for signs of torture. The marks on her throat had turned dark, the visual threats to her life.

"It was the voice," she said. Sam's gaze narrowed. "The same guy who did the mind thing on me, it was him. He needs to die."

"Bloodthirsty woman," Logan said, and she turned her head and gave him such a vicious look, he put his hands up in surrender. "I stand corrected, ma'am."

"Did you black out?" Sam asked.

"Other than when whoever it was took me from the plane, no," she insisted. "I didn't see anyone, ever, but I smelled cloves. One guy smelled like cloves." The lozenges were popular in the Orient like clove gum and clove cigarettes. "He was actually gentle. I heard the woman who tried to take the bracelet." Her gaze drifted to the cuff, too fragile to wear any longer.

"Blowgun bitch," Sam said, his lips quirking.

Logan stepped back. "Other than the marks on your neck, which have turned a lovely shade of green"—he said as Viva looked in the mirror over the dresser—"you're fine as far as I can see. Blood work will tell us what they used." He gathered his things.

"They wanted me off their hands for the stone," she said.

"Probably why they gagged you," Sam teased, and she sent him a sour look.

Logan moved to the door, glanced back. He started to say something, then clamped his mouth shut.

Sam dragged his gaze from Viva and frowned. "We get anything on that picture from Voslav's stash?"

The name made Viva cringe.

"I enlarged the ring up, but it's distorted, looks like a family crest. NSA is searching for a face match. I'm through about four layers of the onion router, in Istanbul, believe it or not. But it disengaged before we started the trace. No trail. We can only get so far. McGill agreed to give us help if we needed it."

"How about what the CIA station is up to?"

Logan scoffed bitterly and left them alone. Not that they'd notice.

Viva never took her gaze off Sam. "You gave him the means to fire that thing, you know."

He shrugged. "Like I give a damn about a few million in diamonds." Her life was worth anything he could give.

Viva was still amazed at that. "I didn't think for a second you'd find me."

"Underestimating me *now?*"

She rose and moved across the room. He leaned against a dresser, his arms folded, his head dipped down, and Viva thought, *No one would suspect the casual power in that stance*. He still needed a haircut, and when she neared, he unfolded, reaching for her. She loved that, the way his hand searched, caught, and tugged her close, like she belonged.

"I'm wild about you, Viva."

Then he'd shock her like that, say things that made her

heart roll in her chest. "I knew there was a reason you keep rescuing me."

Guilt drew on his skin. "You're missing my point intentionally."

"No, and the feeling is entirely mutual, but you want to take the blame, like you did with the sniper rifle, and Riley's injuries." He scowled, ready to protest. "I'm right, aren't I?"

"Maybe."

She smiled. Stubborn Texan. "I've got lots to feel guilty about, believe me. It gets really heavy after a while. Put the energy to better use."

"Suggestions?"

She wiggled her body to fit to his. "Got eight seconds?"

Her words slammed into him and sent his body into lock and load. So easily.

Her hands slid around his neck, her smile telling him he was in for some fun as she pulled him willingly—God, so willingly down to her mouth. He tried for tenderness, for less than what he was feeling, but it wasn't possible, not with Viva, not with the excitement she generated with just existing.

He couldn't live without her, without this, he thought, closing his arms snuggly around her, one hand molding her curves and under her shirt. She opened his jeans, boldly diving her hand inside, and a sphere surrounded them, encased them in heat, her kiss setting off the wild lick of flames down his body. Gentleness vanished and they were tearing at each other, at their clothes, laughing when he toed off his boots and they nearly fell.

He grabbed her back, his mouth trailing hotly down her throat, and he paused long enough to strip off her shirt, toss it with his before his lips closed over her nipple. He drew it into the heat of his mouth as if trying to devour her, his tongue circling and flicking.

Viva shimmered with desire, drank it in, the scent of him, the way he tasted her as if he never would again, his tanned, ropy muscles flexing as his hands roamed her roughly, almost desperately.

He pushed her jeans down; she tried kicking them off without stopping the kiss, then in a frantic scramble they stripped, and she was back in his arms, his hand sliding down her body and between her thighs.

"Oh, Sam," she breathed, thrust to his strokes and with her arms around his neck, she hopped, clamping her legs around his hips. He arched a dark brow and she thought, *I love it when he does that.* "You have some making up to do."

"It *was* a good plan." He worried her mouth, cradling her behind, and pulled her to him. His erection slid wetly against her center, and Sam loved the way her breath hitched.

"Yeah, right." She nibbled his ear, his throat, and felt him tremble with her with anticipation of him pushing inside her. She wanted him, right now.

"Next time, you plan it—oh, jeez, you feel good."

"There won't be one." Her breathing labored.

"Yeah, yeah, trouble follows you." From behind, he dipped his fingers deeper.

"Not if you stay this close to me—oh, God, don't stop that."

"Didn't plan to." He sank to the carpet, stroking her, and she grew more breathless, thrusting to him.

She managed to say, "There's a bed just there." Her hand closed over his erection, eliciting a dark, heavy groan.

"Too far." He pushed into her palm, his mouth rolling over the flesh he could reach, his hands combing a wild ride over the rest.

He felt the pressure on his thighs as she rose up, guiding him, teasing him mercilessly as she rocked on his erection. Her smile was sinful, her fingers sliding over the tip of him.

"You're *trying* for eight seconds?" he asked and leaned forward till she was on her back.

"Break a record."

He entered her on one thrust.

For a moment, he held still, her hands on his face, her gaze locked with his. Emotions swelled, tightening his chest, his heart pounding so hard he swore she could feel it. He'd almost lost her and the terror of it made him realize his feelings for her went beyond this moment, beyond this mission.

"I'm trying for a lot longer," she whispered, and leaned up to tear him apart with a kiss.

Sam quaked with the savageness of it, her impatience, and without will, he moved. Viva pushed back, her heat flexing around him, a tight, firm lock on more than his body. He laced his fingers with hers, as if being joined together wasn't enough. She smiled up at him as he withdrew and pushed, her hips doing that rolling-curl thing he loved, letting him feel every inch of him sliding into her. When she quickened, he knew he wouldn't make it, then it didn't matter. Her mouth was on his, her body pumping with his, and she stopped kissing him long enough to whisper, "Yee haw."

Sam chuckled and scooped her off the floor and onto his lap. Her eyes flared at the slick, wet length of him and she rocked, giggling when he gripped her hips and growled like a beast, and startled when she pushed him on his back.

She rode him, leaving him completely, only to shove back, her green eyes wicked and full of her power. She knew what she was doing to him. Unhinging him. She made wisecracks about cowboys, and sexy, erotic talk that would drive any man over the edge, and Sam thought, *She's got me, she's got me and I'm drowning in her.*

Energy rocked and pulsed—around them, between them, he could almost taste it on her mouth, and Sam sat up, their motions primal and raw. She was on the brink, her body flexing around him, clawed him.

"Viva, oh, Jesus."

"Come on, Sam. Take me home."

He rolled her on her back and hips pistoned. The explosion ripped, the pound of it pushing them across the floor and she bit her lip to keep from screaming, but Sam swallowed her cries as her slick, wet muscles pawed him, drew him with her. Into the tumble of pleasure. He watched her ride the eruption, savored the sight of pure satisfaction shimmering through her. Viva left nothing to chance, still moving, taking it all and glowing with ecstasy.

Before it was over, before the rapture faded, she clutched him, wanting his weight, and when she had it, the sound she made was exquisite. Perfect contentment.

And Sam knew.

He just *knew.*

"The Indonesian buyer is dead." Zidane said into the phone.

Jalier cursed. "How?"

"In his hotel room. He's been relieved of some organs. The backs of his legs cut."

"You're wrong."

He knew Jalier wouldn't believe it, and Zidane used his cell phone to take a picture. "Sending you proof now, sir."

A minute passed before Jalier said, "Dispose of it. Find the rest and protect them!"

Zidane scoffed. "I am but one man. It would do us more good to find *her.*"

"Then do it. The stones?"

"Gone." Zidane ignored Jalier's anger and closed the phone. His gaze moved over the body of the faction leader sprawled naked and bleeding on the bed. The kill was obvious, he thought, and left the room, and with a white handkerchief, wiped the blood from his hands.

Max drove, following the movement of the GPS tracker. When it was stationary, he stopped, sliding the car to the curb under a tree. Across the street, the building was old, neat, and well tended, sandwiched between new, larger buildings and almost hidden. At this hour the streets were busy, people strolling from bar to bar, and a block up he could see a tattoo parlor open for business. The scent of the sea rolled in on the warm air and he cracked the window a little farther and picked up the faint grind of engines as longshoremen worked the docks into the night. Music slipped on the warm air and he yawned, then decided he needed a sugar rush, and grabbed a candy bar from his stash.

He still couldn't pinpoint who had the box, only general movement. Too many cars and people going in the same direction and the only thing he could do was wait till it got out into the open. The tracer was just a beacon and had a hundred-yard radius.

He chewed, closing his eyes and thinking he could use a couple hours shut-eye. He was just dosing off when the sensor beeped and he shifted, turning over the engine and looking around.

The tone increased, indicating close proximity and his gaze zeroed in on the black sedan, its windows tinted dark. His gaze flicked from the car to the GPS.

"Gotcha," he said as he put the SUV in gear and followed, the candy bar clenched in his teeth.

The air-conditioning wafted the scent of death around the hotel room. Sirens blared in the distance and Kincade knew he had only moments. He touched nothing, the door wide open and likely left that way by the killer. He couldn't remember ever seeing such carnage in one place. Blood splattered the walls and furniture, the fat body slumped on the floor.

Someone beat me to it, he thought, and on his encrypted cell phone, informed the CIA station chief, verifying with pictures. Check this fucker off the list of America's Most Wanted. Hezbollah faction, he thought, pulling on latex gloves as he moved around the room, thoroughly searching it and the personal items. They'd never had a clear target of who was running the finances. Who'd take up the gauntlet of the dead was their next concern. Either way, the killer had the diamonds.

He read some of the files on the laptop, and while he wanted to leave with it, he didn't think he'd get out without notice. It was his job not to be seen. Instead, he copied the documents, sent them to his computer, then erased that one history. Then he deleted the weapon's schematics and logged off just as the sirens sounded outside. People gathered in the hallway. Time's up, he thought, and hurried to the rear of the room, glad this guy had a low profile or he'd be in a better hotel. He opened the window and looked down. It's only one story down, he told himself, then swung his hip over the sill, and vaulted into a pile of trash.

Max hung back behind the locals, watching the Thai police escort a body out of the building. He'd followed the GPS marker and lost track of the car in heavy traffic, but not the signal. The paramedics wheeled the gurney out of the building, the body jolting under the white cloth already soaked with blood, and Max suddenly appreciated the care American EMTs took with the dead. The men met the curb and shoved the stretcher, the body nearly toppling. In the grab, the sheet over the face slipped. He sidestepped the people to get a look.

Well, well, he thought. Ain't that grand. Chalk one up on the fight against terrorism. He headed back to the SUV, the GPS tone already steady and moving. Who are you? he wondered. Are you leaving a trail of bodies or tracking the killer?

He'd gone another mile when the tracer stopped. Max climbed out of the car and crossed the street, covertly glancing down at the GPS tracer as he headed toward the signal. *I've been made*. Or at least the box had. He knew it before the tone went steady and he looked down into the trash can.

Crap. Did it have to be outside a restaurant?

With a sigh, he went Dumpster diving. The box was covered with noodles and he shook it off, then used paper trash to wipe it clean. He couldn't leave it. It was rigged, though Sebastian had disengaged the detonator. With it, he turned back to the car, mentally marking the location of the last stop. He opened the car door, put the box inside, and was reaching in the glove box for a wet wipe when he felt the gun at his back.

Well after midnight Viva sat in a corner chair, sifting through papers from the hangar. The guys couldn't get a handle on it and offered it to her. "Sebastian, you own a restaurant." He looked up, nodded. "You get food delivered on a regular basis, right?"

"Every day, sure."

"Do you have to contract a refrigerated trucking company to transport it, or do the sellers do it for you?"

"Depends on where I'm getting it from. Shrimp and crawfish come from local fishermen, so I send a truck to pick it up. Why?"

"These invoices." She rose and came to him. "Could they be invoice or routing numbers from the company, a regular customer, their data in files, computers, whatever at the main warehouse?"

Sebastian took the sheet, then turned to his laptop. "The bill would go to corporate, like it does to me. The drivers would just have the address and contents, no idea what it cost, or who's paying the bill. Yeah, it works for me. Logan, I need you to hack this company." Sebastian had to call him twice.

Logan had on a headset and was tapping into the computers. She swore the man breathed megabytes.

He looked annoyed, and though she'd no idea what he was doing on those computers, he stopped and inserted a CD, typed a code. "Let it run, it will find a back door and cut through."

"You're a geek of the first order, Logan." Viva said, grabbing her coffee and watching them work. All three were doing something, Sam studying photos they'd taken in the past days, searching for Lord only knew what. Occasionally, Sam would look up and search the room as if he thought she'd be gone. When he found her, he'd smile, wink, and make her heart trip a little. I'm so loving that man, she thought, pouring coffee, then grabbing a pastry off the platter before they all scarfed them down. Max was usually first at the food.

"Where's Max?"

"You just now noticed he isn't here?" Sam teased, then frowned at his watch and reached for the radio. "Come to think of it, he hasn't checked in." He tried to raise him and got nothing, bringing Logan and Sebastian's attention. The same with the cell phone. "The radio is working, he's not near it."

Logan instantly pulled up the tracer on the screen. "Stationary, box tracer and his GPS mark are on top of each other." Which didn't answer why he wouldn't respond.

Sam grabbed his weapon and gear. "Load it to the chopper," he told Logan.

Viva met him at the door. "I'm going, too."

"Not a good idea. Too many people want to hurt you."

"And with you I'll be safe. Besides, I can watch the GPS. I'm good at directions."

"Someone knew you were getting on that plane when they snatched you. It takes some heavy pull to get a jet manifest. Stop being so mutinous, it's for your own safety." He leaned to kiss her and she took a step back and folded her arms.

"Don't treat me like I can't handle it."

"God love you, Viva," Sebastian said when the hacked program finished. "It is a trucking routing number, and the address is southwest. The food delivery is to a house."

Viva frowned, coming to him, and Sam looked too damn grateful for the distraction. "That's a lot of food for a home."

"Enough to cater a very large party, maybe two hundred, and the house isn't that big." He brought up the files. "Nothing special about it."

"Other than it's connected to Voslav, that jet, Rohki, and the diamonds," Sam said. "Check it out. Surveillance only."

Sebastian hurried to put some of the strangest gear she'd

seen in a pack. "The owner is a corporation. Can't get more than a name. Which means it's probably a dummy." Sebastian was already at the door when Logan joined him.

"I'm not sitting this one out."

Sam kissed her tight mouth. "Hold down the fort, Viva."

Within minutes, Viva was alone. The phone rang. "Set the alarms," Sam said. "Don't open the doors for anyone but us."

"Oh, gee, you think?" she said, irritated he wouldn't let her join him.

His deep chuckle filtered through the phone, lighting her insides. "I'll make it up to you."

By his tone, she knew exactly how, and she smiled. He gave her the codes and she punched them in. An instant later she heard the locks click around the house, a green light blink on the panel. She was surrounded now by sensors, explosives, and alarms. And weapons, she thought, looking at the array of gear neatly arranged in the corner of the living room.

She turned to the computers, watching the green dot representing the chopper move toward Max's last location. For a very long time she hadn't worried about anyone except herself. Now she had four men who meant more to her than her own family.

And they walked into danger like it was a trip to the market.

Seventeen

A moonless night was perfect for surveillance. No glare, no shadows. Perched on a hillside, Sebastian eyeballed the house through the night vision binoculars. There were no cars in the driveway, but the guards walking a post said this wasn't the average suburban home. Stretched out on his stomach, Sebastian pointed the directional acoustics device, a long name for a snoop machine. Max had redesigned it for longer distance.

Behind him, Logan adjusted the frequency, listening to the noise in the house.

They heard dishes clanking and the rapid trot of footsteps that could only mean children. Light and fast.

"Kids?" Sebastian asked and the hackles on his neck came to attention.

"You didn't see where Viva was kept. Voslav wouldn't be so kind as to house slaves for sale in a place like that. And if it is, then someone's already taken over his business. Heads up, we have visual." The lights were on inside the house and Sebastian had a decent view. It was modern, straight lines with balconies and built into the side of the hill. With three sides to watch, the guards had a view of the city below.

They saw a girl grab a little boy and pull him back from the window when a guard stepped in front of her.

"She looks like a teenager," Logan said. "Maybe seventeen?"

"I can't make out the language, it's not Thai, though." Logan whipped out his cell.

Sebastian glanced at him. "Who you calling?"

"Viva." She got the phone on the first ring. Bored, he thought. "I need your language help."

"Finally, some use around here. I've found something you should see."

"Later. Can you translate this?" He hit play on the recording. It was so rapid, he couldn't even pick out the tones. "Anything?"

"It's Hindi. Raibur, you must behave. They will hurt us," she translated. "Sounds very young. Whoever answers is a child. High, whining, he's crying for his father. And the girl says he will come. She says it over and over."

He thanked her, ended the call, then refocused the binoculars.

Sebastian saw a child move toward the windows again, the backlight of the house showing a young girl shielding the boy when a guard shouted at the kid. He shuttered off a few pictures of it. "They're captive, that's obvious, but why?"

Logan lowered the binoculars and looked at Sebastian. "That's the diamond cutter's family." He'd seen their pictures in the Sri Lanka newspaper. "We have to help them."

"Roger that." Sebastian searched for a good way to get inside. "Hold on. Look at the door, to the right of it."

Logan changed his position and adjusted the focus. "Hell. This just got really ugly."

A soft tone hummed and Sebastian twisted as Logan hit the remote he carried.

"Pack it up, something tripped the sensors."

Viva was the only one at the CP—alone.

Max straightened slowly. His gaze went to the shop window in front of him, but it was too dark to see the face behind him. The guy was big, this wasn't going to be easy.

"Hands on the hood."

Max lifted his hands and the man reached for his weapon.

Max cocked his leg and drove his heel back into a kneecap. The man groaned and Max turned, hitting his solar plexus, then his jaw before a leg sweep knocked the man off his feet and onto the pavement. Max drew his weapon, aiming.

"Hands up, up." He aimed closer. Max disarmed him, then searched his pockets for ID. When he found it, he looked between the man and the wallet. "Christ."

The man wiped at the blood on his lips. "God, I hate it when that happens."

"Get up. You're supposed to be clandestine."

He stood, brushing himself off, rubbed his knee.

Max handed back the ID. "Why are you following me?"

Kincade's eyes narrowed.

"I saw you a half hour ago. Was that your handiwork back there?"

"He was already dead."

"Someone ghosting the buyers."

Kincade tried not to show a reaction.

"As much as it gags me to say it, we're on the same team," Max said.

"Price was a first-class bitch," Adam said, leaning against the car and rubbing his stomach.

"Okay, now we can be friends."

Kincade snickered a laugh.

"We need to get out of here." Max frowned at the sky. The black chopper circled overhead, the spotlight sweeping the area around the car. Hurriedly, he opened the car door and grabbed the radio. "Outlaw?"

"Jesus, Drac. Check in, dammit."

This from the man who left Sri Lanka alone? "Nice to know you care, buddy. Had a problem. Got a prize for you." He looked at Kincade. "Get in."

"I'm only going because I have orders to cooperate."

"Yeah, sure," Max said. "And Price was the Queen of England."

The chopper lifted higher and Max and Kincade headed

south. He radioed the CP and didn't get an answer. He tried the cell. Nothing. "Drac to Outlaw, I'm getting no response at the CP. Viva with you?"

"No, dammit. She's alone."

Max heard the fear in his voice and Max sped toward the house.

Sipping a soda, Viva left the kitchen and headed back to the computer to keep searching. The entire system blinked, as if a power surge had hit. She moved closer, opening the programs Logan had running. Everything seemed fine. He even had messages.

Then a sharp, loud noise startled her and her soda went flying.

Immediately, she grabbed the 9 mm and cocked the slide, chambering a bullet just like Sam had shown her. It was heavy in her hand as she hurried to the panel and hit the screen. The red dots showed the triggered sensors. End of the driveway and walk. Great. She hit the camera, repositioning to the drive. Nothing there. Not even a breeze.

Then something slammed against the door and she lurched back, aiming, and hoped it was someone nice. "I really don't want to hurt you," she called out, but the alarms were louder. She hit the mute. That's when she heard the base radio.

"Viva. Viva! Answer me!"

She rushed to it. "I'm here, I'm here, Sam. Something hit the front door, but I can't see anyone."

"I'm touching down in one minute. Hold tight, baby."

"See, you should have taken me with you." A hard pound rattled the door and she spun, aiming.

CIA, Langley
Virginia

David Lorimer watched the satellite screen and wondered if a promotion meant he'd be bored. His job, along with tracking satellite alignment for intel feeds to operations around the world, was to sift through the visuals and send them to the appropriate analysts. Those people, who poured over imagery, could tell a rocket launcher from a stinger, a truck from a building, and pinpoint the slightest movement around enemy commands and training camps. Often it was a single analyst's insight that had stopped attacks around the globe.

The clock ticked off the seconds and his boss was impatient for the alignment feed to make contact in Thailand. "David?"

"Yes, sir, alignment in five, four, three, two . . ."

The entire system flickered, the computer screens blinking. Analysts cursed and David tried getting the link back up.

"The systems are fine." David frowned, confused at that. "But it'll be five minutes before we are linked again."

His boss cursed and left the Sat comm booth, tossing the headset aside. "Get the techs up here, find out what did that."

David made the call, then reworked the alignment feed to get the satellite link connected and confirmed. It shouldn't have done that. Nothing should have. Satellites were electromagnetic-pulse protected, and an EMP would have burned up anything it was connected with, too. Yet power here was fine, his links to other operations untouched. Energy bursts were unheard of.

He worked the keyboard, turning to another system. Where did it come from?

The slap to her face stung up to her eyes and Noor woke instantly. Her gaze shot around, and she was surprised by her surroundings—and the man looming over her. He dared strike her again.

"You have some definite personal issues, my sweet."

She glared at him, then kicked out, her foot connecting with his groin. Jalier folded in pain. "Now *you* do."

Jalier glared at her, agony climbing up his body, and he inclined his head. Zidane latched his hands around her upper arms and yanked her from Jalier.

"You killed my buyers, why?"

"I have done no such thing," she said calmly. "Look to the cowboy, or these people you want to trust with that." She nodded to the solarium yards beyond them. "I would not betray you. I have no reason."

Jalier moved in gingerly, touched his fingers beneath her chin, then tipped her face up. "The kills bear your touch, and that brings me short two buyers."

The edge to his voice made Noor inch back.

He tossed down computer photos. "Explain."

She glanced at the photos, her look speaking her ambiguity to the gruesome shots. "I did not do this."

"My buyers are afraid of you."

"They should be, my loyalty is to you, Constantine." She yanked from Zidane's grasp, twisting to glare at him.

Zidane merely arched a brow, calm, emotions concealed.

"You do this because I will not come to your bed," she said.

"I would have to want you first."

Hurt sprang in her features, then vanished. It was a brief encounter with the woman locked inside.

"One man could not do this to another." He pointed to the photo, the crotch of the man carved away.

"Not unless he didn't have balls," she said with a look down his body.

"Stop it! You jeopardize everything. *Now?* Lock her up."

Noor whipped around and Zidane knew it was her worst nightmare to be confined. She bolted, her feet almost soundless as she vaulted over furniture like quicksilver, agile, swift. She was out the doors and into the darkness before Zidane made it into the hall.

Jalier sank into the chair, knowing the man wouldn't catch her. It had taken months to bring her to him, and now, if she wished to be gone, they would never find her. His gaze fell on the photos. Zidane's men were searching for the others, bringing them to him for safety. Four were inside the compound, unaware of their location. He didn't want them here, this close, but he had no choice. He rubbed his crotch and pain throbbed in sharp points.

Noor was a liability and must be dealt with immediately.

Sam swooped over the land and touched down. He shut off the engines, hopping out of the chopper, his weapon drawn as he hurried to the side of the house, sliding along the wall. His heart was in his throat, the thought of Viva harmed tearing at his insides.

He peered around the edge to the front door. A body lay sprawled across the porch. He scanned the area, thinking it was a ruse, and moved back to check further on the property, then edged to the porch again. He knelt, searching the body for weapons, or triggers, then checked for a pulse. Thready.

Watching his back, he called out. "Viva, open up."

The locks sprang and she opened the door. "Oh, my God."

"Pull him in." Sam watched the drive and street as she grabbed the man by the shirt and yanked him over the threshold. Inside Sam reset the sensors, and knelt.

Viva grabbed a towel from the kitchen and rushed back, sliding on her knees on the floor. "Look at him, his leg, his ribs, he's cut up pretty bad." And a while ago, she thought.

Sam bent close, checking his eyes. "Kashir, Kashir?"

"You know him?"

"My contact in the jungle. He's Interpol."

She held the cloth to his side, and tried to check his wounds. "These are nasty." She looked for more, her hand sliding under him and coming away covered in blood. "He's been stabbed in the back."

"Christ." Who the hell knew he was Interpol?

Viva tore open his pant leg, washing the wound. "The tendons behind his knee are cut. How did he even walk?" With wet cloths, she washed the dried blood. "Get me some water, medical supplies."

As Sam left, Viva hurried to the kitchen washing her hands, then returned, breaking open the supplies and snapping on latex gloves. Viva cleaned up the man's wounds. "He needs Logan, he needs stitches, maybe surgery. It's deep. They're all deep." The man stirred when she pried off the blood-soaked rags. "I'm sorry, but we have to clean this."

"Kashir," Sam said close to his face. "What happened?"

His eyes opened, and he grabbed her wrist, startling her.

"It's okay, it's okay," she cooed, stroking his head. "Who did this to you?"

There was an irony in his dying expression. "Someone I trusted," gurggled past his lips. He choked and blood oozed from the corner of his mouth. "The dealer. He has power."

"We know."

Kashir tried to shake his head, but didn't have the strength. "*Right* power."

Then he said something Sam didn't understand and Viva leaned closer as the man repeated it, the words slurred. Then they faded, his breath rattling in his chest. Viva immediately started CPR, pumping his chest. Sam breathed into his mouth, then checked the pulse.

"Stop. He's gone."

Viva didn't, kept pushing, counting.

"Viva!" He gripped her shoulders and she lifted her gaze. "I'm sorry, honey, he's gone."

She looked down at the body between them and fell back on her rear, rubbing her forehead with the back of her wrist. Death still rattled her. "I wish people would stop doing that around me."

Sam closed Kashir's vacant eyes, then searched the body again. "He's got nothing on him, no money, no ID. An Interpol agent without his gun?" He looked at her. "Tell me you understood what he said."

She wiped a tear. "I'm not sure. My Farsi isn't great. It doesn't make any sense. He who concedes?" Viva recited the phrase over and over in her head, sure she was getting it wrong. Then her gaze flew to his. "Negotiation or negotiator?"

"You're right, it doesn't make sense." Kashir couldn't just give him a name? Or did he even know it?

"Who has power and negotiates?" she asked aloud as she repacked Logan's gear, wanting anything to focus on except the dead agent.

"Government. Corporations. Senate, national councils." Sam's voice faded as he went to get a blanket to wrap the body. "Ambassadors. To negotiate treaties, deals." Sam stopped short and met her gaze. "Diplomats."

She scrambled to her feet, almost lunging at the computer. "That ring in the picture. I bet it's a diplomat or consulate seal."

"Sir, there's something you should see."

David's boss, who was much more personable than Price had ever been, moved beside his desk. "That break in the link, it was an energy spike."

"Your point?"

"Energy spikes from a satellite are impossible. They are programmed to follow a pattern and the cells keep the power even. It's more than reliable, it's accurate. But with the spike, the systems didn't go off-line or they'd have rebooted. Which is automatic with a power flux. But it's not here. It's up there." He pointed to the big screen that took up the walls.

"Say again."

"The flux was with the bird, not these systems." David knew the satellite they used was connected to an entire network of the US government.

"You're certain? Absolutely certain?"

"Yes sir, I did a back check. We didn't lose any data, not even a reboot. Just a break in the contact. It lasted about fifteen seconds."

"Any idea of the cause?"

"No, sir, but it's happened before. Eight days ago. Right about the time the dam in Sri Lanka blew."

"Coincidence." His boss stared down at him long enough to make David feel like a bug under a microscope, then he said, "See if you can pinpoint it."

"I already tried, the only way we can is if it happens

again, and then it's a matter of seconds. If we can lock on to it, maybe a little more time."

"We can tell which satellite is affected?"

"Just the relay, sir. It covered line-of-sight hookup to the Asia Theatre."

His boss was quiet for a moment and was likely thinking as David was: that China had a lot of snoop hardware and maybe they were trying to tap into theirs. "See if there are any spikes elsewhere. Start with Arizona relay and work east."

A lot of ground to cover, David thought, flexing his fingers to prepare for the long haul.

Anan Isarangura watched the chief of the morgue pull the body from the river. It hadn't been there long, he thought, or it would be bloated horribly. But cause of death was obvious and his officer rushed up the incline and to his side.

"It is the same as the last."

Anan had seen the like before, several years ago. The ambulance workers lifted the body onto a gurney. Despite the heat of the morning, the young officers shivered beside him.

"Who would do such a thing to a man?"

"A very angry person, I suspect."

His gaze traveled over the crowd, searching the faces. Often the killer watched the discovery of their handiwork. He looked for someone in the background, someone almost eager to see how the police reacted. He found only onlookers who quickly turned away at the sight of the bloody body.

Anan understood the criminal mind better than most of his staff and his investigators. He'd worked for many years searching the world for the worst of society before coming home. Before this body was discovered, he knew that there were terrorists using his homeland as a haven. Law agencies from all over the world had sent their people here to search them out. Anan was not offended. He understood that in his own ranks, some officers were ruled by the Chow, the Jao Pho. Because of money, not for their cause.

Yet when dealing with the most vile, one often had to send their most deadly. Balance the scales, he thought, then wondered how deep the American was in this.

Viva lurched back when Sam whipped around aiming his gun. He released a breath, pointed to the ceiling as Logan and Sebastian came through the door. "*Chéri,* you okay?"

"I'm fine, he's not."

Logan holstered his weapon and examined the body. "This looks like a battle, but stabbed in the back." He pried at the deep gouge and Viva's stomach turned over. "Big knife. Might have pierced his lung."

"He said someone he trusted did that."

Logan looked up. "Another agent?"

"A contact who got a better offer," Sam said and thought of Niran. The guy would sell out his mother for a profit. He told them what Kashir had said, and the seal Viva found.

"Not so odd," Sebastian said. "The house has an embassy emblem near the front door. And it looked like that." He gestured to the printout.

"What country?"

"Algeria." Logan told them about the diamond cutter's children and his certainty left no questions.

Sam frowned. "Algeria assumed a seat on the UN Security Council. The same time as Sulak Krahn."

"Who?" Viva asked.

"The man who hired us to trace the diamonds," he answered, distracted. He was at the desk, searching for something.

Viva started toward the hall, looked at the body, then at Sam. "What will you do with him?"

Her sad expression made him hurt for her, her clothes covered in Kashir's blood. "Deliver him to Interpol."

"It seems so undignified. His life is over because he tried to get to you."

Sam moved toward her, seeing the stress in the lines around her mouth. "You okay?"

She looked away as Sebastian and Logan lifted the body out the door. "That's two people who've died on me." Strangers, she thought. One bad, one trying to do something good.

Sam frowned and started to come to her. She put up her hand. "Give me a minute."

He turned to the team. "Get the Big Cheese on the wire. He needs to know about this."

Kukule Ganga Dam
Kalawana, Sri Lanka

Thomas Rhodes cursed under his breath and ended the early-morning call.

"They don't believe you," Risha said, turning from the window and sipping from a bottle of water.

"Would you?"

"It is hard to believe, Thomas."

"But without proof, no one wants to listen." He pocketed the phone. "I left messages for everyone I know at the Pentagon. If I get an answer, then maybe."

"It changes nothing about the dam."

"If something could make that hole, it could do it again."

Horror shaped her expression.

"I think we have some big trouble coming."

Risha's assistant threw open the trailer door and ran inside, grabbing the remote and switching on the TV. "You are not going to believe this."

They watched the broadcast and Thomas slowly lowered to a chair. "That's impossible. Utterly impossible."

"If you knew where the buyers were," Viva heard as she came into the room. "why didn't you ghost them all, for crissake?"

"I don't know all of them, just the ones I had a visual of.

But the seller is the one we have to take down. The rest, we can pick off whenever we want."

Sam threw Kincade a narrow look. "If you could, then bin Laden would be in the ground."

"Someone else is doing it for us anyway."

"Max!" Viva rushed to give him a hug. "I'm so glad you're all right."

He looked over her shoulder at Sam and said, "She likes me best."

Viva laughed. Sam didn't.

"I heard you guys had a woman on the team." Kincade inspected her slowly from head to toe and Viva felt stripped.

"And I'm not her. I'm the troublemaker."

"Viva," Max said kindly. "Not your fault, but ours."

"Good, take the blame. Do I get a cut now?" She looked at the new face and Sam introduced Adam Kincade.

He was on the phone and waved. "You were right, it's a diplomatic seal."

"Big deal, did you match the face?" Viva asked.

"Is she always this demanding?"

"Yes," they all said at once.

Viva whipped around, flushing red.

"I like 'em like that."

The team gave Kincade a narrow look and he laughed.

But it was Sam who said, "Off limits, Kincade."

It made Viva feel giddy as Kincade went back to speaking into the phone, jotting notes. He ended the cell call and came to them. "You have more information than we do. Though I can tell you exactly which terrorists are in country."

Viva didn't know what the names meant, but the team certainly did. They went still as glass, and lots of "oh, shit" fluttered around the room.

"Sam, we have McGill on the line," Logan said, and Sam grabbed the phone, giving the general the latest development.

"Wyatt, do you know the political ramifications of entering a house of the diplomatic corps?"

"I imagine for the same reasons these guys brought them there, sir."

"We can't touch them."

"Sir, this man was kidnapped, and his family's hostage. We have confirmation. We've seen the children."

"Entering will set back diplomatic relations with Algeria five years."

Sam's fist clenched in a small effort to control his temper. "He has the diamond, when the cutter isn't of any use, he'll kill him and any trail."

A lengthy silence passed before McGill said, "The US government must claim no knowledge of what transpires inside the diplomatic corps of another country. It's *sovereign* foreign soil. We cannot interfere in domestic internals of diplomats. I repeat, you—"

"You don't need to say it twice, McGill, I'm not fucking deaf. So we leave this man's family there to be executed?"

"It's unfortunate, but we can't. Relations all over the world with the US will be jeopardized."

"And babies will be dead. Hope you people sleep well tonight." Sam cut the line and swore.

Viva looked at them all. "We can't leave those kids there. God, what Voslav did to those children in that abandoned school . . ."

That foul place flooded Sam's memory, and his rage over it went nuclear.

"Bending rules is one thing," Kincade said. "Causing an international incident that will put the US in a bad light is another."

"I can't believe you're even hesitating," she said.

"Viva. We feel the same way, but if we assault, India will be accused."

"Then India's government should be told!" Viva looked at Kincade. "You're CIA, do something. You do secret, covert stuff all the time."

"My boss agrees with McGill." He wiggled the phone. "I can't go against orders," Kincade said.

Viva looked around the room, the men solemn and silent. "You let something happen to those kids like it did to me and I swear, I'll never forgive you."

She stormed away from them and Sam knew she was right. What the hell did Washington know? They weren't here, hadn't seen the results of the slavery.

Conversation stopped, the silence falling hard in the large house, frustration filling the air. Adam sighed heavily, then whispered something to Sam.

Behind her, Kincade left.

Yet Viva continued to fume, seeing those poor kids locked away in the dark, the horrible things they did to the girls. Images multiplied and she stared uninterested at the TV. It took a second for what she was seeing to register. Viva approached, and dread washed through her. The sound was down, but she didn't have to hear it. It was a frantic scene, fire erupting in quick flashes, people screaming, and as she moved closer, the realization of it hit.

Volcano.

She grabbed the remote and turned off the mute. "Would you look at this?"

Slowly they came closer. "Sweet Jesus," Logan said.

Orange-red lava rolled down the hill, the TV camera jolting as the cameraman rushed to get out of the path. People bolted, frantically grabbing children and animals.

"Go west," she said as if the people could hear her. "Lava's heavy, it travels downhill." She gestured to the TV. "They won't get out of the path unless they get far away from the flow. It rolls like a ball and moves along the land, but the slightest elevation in terrain and it will change directions. Oh, God, where is that?"

"Guatemala."

"Impossible. That's got to be Tolimán Crater; it's been dormant for nearly two million years."

"Looks like it woke up," Sam said.

"No, no." She shook her head. "There are three volcanoes within fifty miles of each other. Dormant for millions of years and it erupts now? Without spewing ash? Without warning?"

"Who's to say it didn't?" Sam asked.

"I do. We would have seen something about it, and those people would have left long before lava erupted. Good God."

The cameraman jumped into the back of a Land Rover, still filming. The rush of molten lava was high, crushing and burning everything in its path. Trees, homes, people. Thousands were dying before her eyes.

"There's little ash in the air."

"People often wait till the last minute before evacuation," Sebastian said.

"Jeez, you guys. It's not like you can hide from that. It's not a storm, it's lava. There is no safe shelter." She watched the devastation, flipped the channels, and found more on other networks. The villages at the base were already gone. "There should have been a warning, weeks of it."

"What do you know about volcanoes?" Logan asked.

"I have a degree in paleoclimatology, weather patterns, and geothermal reaction to the Earth's core and crust. Not just what it did to dinosaurs and the caveman. And I worked for the USGS. I know that"—she pointed to the screen—"should *not* be happening. Not without some previous activity. It would take a major shift in tectonic plates to erupt like that. The water in Lake Atitlán would have changed temperature. Geologists monitor it with sensors. They'd have warned people. The lake is three hundred and twenty meters deep and smack up against Tolimán."

"What do you think it means?" Sam asked.

"This is not a natural disaster." She looked at each man, her skin paling to bloodless. "He used it."

Eighteen

No one said anything, three men staring at her as if she'd lost her marbles and they were rolling across the floor.

"Viva, it's a volcanic eruption," Logan said. "You can't honestly believe that HSS could cause a dormant crater to erupt."

"No, I don't. But a fissure crack, even a small one, is enough of a catalyst. The pressure builds, like a pot boiling over. With nowhere to go, it splits. You said it could take down an aircraft. How much power would it take to do that from the ground? Jets are up there at twenty thousand feet. I'll bet you"—she looked directly at Sam—"flying lessons that this isn't a natural disaster."

"Even if it were possible—and, sorry, baby, I'm not agreeing on this yet—in *this* short a time?" Sam said. "It's been maybe ten, twelve hours."

"The designer said it was larger, but portable, and he has the stone. What more do you want? And if it's not, then explain the eruption without ash spewing first."

"I can't. That's your department, apparently." Sam sat on the edge of the sofa, thoughtful.

"The plans were already modified, and that general what's-his-face said that they needed a diamond to increase its intensity." She waved at the TV. "There you go."

"But the HSS would have to be there in Guatemala. This

thing has a range of yards, not miles, even with the diamond. How could it reach from here?"

"That's saying it's still here," Sebastian said. "And if they are telling us its real capability." They agreed that was possible.

"They'd still need line of sight," Sam insisted. "That's halfway around the world and they can't get around the curve of the earth." Sam went still. "The only way to do that is with a satellite."

"Christ. There's thousands up there."

Sam wasn't buying it. "They'd have to know exact satellite movement when it passes overhead. That's precise coordinates to hit a bird and hope the beam shoots down in the right spot? It's risky, inaccurate, and damn difficult to obtain."

"What if it was rigged with one of those GPS things?" Viva asked.

Damn, the woman was quick. "Like painting a target with a laser?"

The boys, as Viva thought of them, bristled with the possibility. "I don't know what that means, but if they needed a satellite, then they've got their pick," she said. "SETI, astronomers, cable TV, and if they somehow used a satellite *dish?* There are fields of them all over the world, some right here in Thailand."

"Back up, regroup," Sam said. "Dishes are directional and immobile, pointed at one target in space. Maybe the HSS hit a sensor in Guatemala?"

Viva waved that off. "Sensors are designed to catch minor seismic activity and temperature change. It would probably burn out with something so intense."

"Scratch that, then, birds have a pattern. Certain ones are in range within hours of each other, overlap, and link. Some don't move at all." It's a wonder they didn't hit each other.

"What does it matter, if they can reach *one?*"

"But they'd have to have the present satellite movement over the one area and from here to have the means to bounce off one. Covering an area from Thailand to Guatemala?" His expression was wry with doubt. "Retasking one is a major deal, and it takes time. Won't go unnoticed, either."

"I still don't think it's capable of long-distance range," Logan said. "At least not in thousands of miles."

Viva tipped her chin up. "You're entitled to your opinion. It's wrong, but keep at it."

Logan's smile was slow, then he chuckled to himself.

"Listen to me, you know the capability better than me," Viva said. "During Desert Storm, they were running the show from the US via satellite, with intel, those unmanned aerial units. I watch the Discovery Channel," she said when they looked startled. "You can't tell me there aren't enough satellites to bounce it off?"

"She's right," Max said, a sandwich in his hand. "Corporate, telecommunications, air traffic control, banking. Heck, even FedEx and UPS have them with GPS to track trucks. They're all stationary."

Viva moved to the windows, below a lovely view of Bangkok Bay, estates on the far side of the water, testimony to the wealth in Thailand, spread out for miles. She didn't really see any of it.

"Viva, you're quiet, it scares me," Sam said.

She laughed to herself, yet her face was still marked with concentration as she twisted to look at them. "I'm trying to think like a sadistic diamond buyer."

"Now, I'm really scared."

She flashed Sam a smile. "If this is real, if it's capable of that"—her look dared Logan to contradict her—"then why fire it? He's got to know you're on the hunt. He knows we have Ryzikov's laptop, he e-mailed you through it."

"It doesn't make a difference, baby," Sam said. "He's got his ass covered ten ways to Tuesday and he knows it. As far as we know, no one's ever really seen this guy."

"Wait, wait," she said, thinking faster than she could talk and latching on to the identity of the seller. "The ring, the photo, and what Kashir said, the kids hostage." Her look said they'd better find a solution to that soon. "This guy is a diplomat. He's got to be."

"He's using the diplomatic corps as a cover," Sam said.

Viva shook her head almost wildly. "If he can hide inside his diplomatic credentials, what kind of information could he get?"

"They aren't privy to intelligence like satellites, Viva," Sebastian said. "They are like Kashir said, negotiators, using diplomacy."

"That's if they are using birds to bounce the signal," Sam said.

"What else could it be? And who's to say he followed rules, he's selling a dangerous weapon!"

Sam came to her, first laying his hand on her shoulders, then pulling her in close. He understood her feelings. She wasn't accustomed to seeing the goal within reach and having bureaucrats tie their hands. It was like asking permission to engage when the enemy was spraying you with bullets.

"We can at least get a face, maybe." Logan grabbed the phone, and Viva heard him make a call to a buddy somewhere asking for a face match within the diplomatic corps. "There's a lot of them."

"A face, a location, we need something more."

Logan looked doubtful. "He's using the encrypted router system."

"We know he's here, in Bangkok," she said.

"He's not in the house with the kids, there were only three guards and no cars."

"He wouldn't get that close to anything that would implicate him. Ryzikov was bidding through a webcam and online," Sam said. "It's safe to assume the others were, too."

"I don't get why he used it. Why not sell it and get lost somewhere?" Viva said.

"Maybe the highest bidder gets a test shot," Sam said.

"In Guatemala? There isn't anyone threatening there. Villagers. Tribespeople. God, why don't you just shoot these people and be done with it?" Viva said.

"Because we have to retrieve the schematics and the weapon before we can do that," Sam said. "If it went out there to terrorists' networks." He let the thought hang in the air, reminding them all of the risk to the innocent if they didn't get it back or destroy it.

"The stones were the path to the weapon, *chéri*."

"Well, I say you go commando on them and just take them out."

Sam grinned. "I'm with you on that, but we have to find them first."

"Then get your buddies working." She flicked a hand at the computers. "Call in some favors. My God, this thing will be killing people all over the world before it's over."

"Of course, that's saying you're right and it is a man-made disaster."

She whirled on Logan. "Go play with your computers, will you?"

He smiled and obeyed. Viva looked at Sam, her worry like a living thing inside her. Her gaze went to the TV, the continual broadcasts of the devastation. The lava was still moving, still killing.

She dragged her gaze from the TV to Sam. "If he can do this . . ."

"He can do anything. And we won't be able to trace it."

"No one will," Sebastian said. "It's sound."

"Then there is only one way to get close enough," Sam said. "We have to get into the bidding."

McGill carefully put the phone in the cradle. Sometimes, he wished he didn't have to follow orders and the thought of those kids, the same ages as his grandchildren, left his stomach in knots.

The buzzer sounded and his aide let Walker inside.

"Something good?"

"I'm not sure, sir. Three things." He spread papers out on the desk. "First, the onion router, high security, this one is, at least. It's the kind our embassy uses."

McGill glanced down at his notes on his conversation with Wyatt. "Tell me this isn't from our people."

Walker shook his head. "NSA has acoustic intel, and they picked up sound intensification so much that it registered as a malfunction on a satellite."

McGill perked up like a well-praised student.

"So I went back and looked through some Sat intel. Tai Pai monitors, the Holland relay, several others, but they basically just watch the path and make sure they aren't going to run into each other."

"I'm aware of that, son."

Walker flushed a little. "Going back to several days after Silent Fire was stolen, and I found an increase in seismic activity that registered with USGS. In Sri Lanka."

"The dam?"

"Yes, sir. Add to that, CIA Satellite Comm Center confirms and we've got a message from a Dr. Thomas Rhodes who is at the dam, but I'm not authorized to respond."

McGill picked up the phone and ordered a call to Rhodes. "You said two spikes."

"This one happened early this morning. Near Guatemala."

McGill swung the chair around to stare at the CNN broadcast he never turned off. Good God.

"Can you predict?"

"No, sir. In fact, we can't even trace its origins. The only way we could is if it would happen again and we knew when prior to an event."

"Jesus."

"We could find a link through the onion router system. It's used mostly for internal-to-country messaging. High-encryption block. Echo shield. NSA says it has to be up and running for them to track it. And even with that, we'd have the length of the hit to pinpoint, and that's saying our guys can do it. But that will take fast work and a lot of techs."

"We have them, they live for this kind of stuff."

"I also did a side search on the hypersonic sound."

McGill waited for him to continue.

"Harris had invented and perfected it, no question, but another man made the same claim when Harris went for the patent. It was in dispute for a while. He'd been a friend of Harris's, but never worked with him. He's got a degree in engineering and Harris didn't." The enlisted man smiled. "Bet that just roasted him when he tried to prove he invented it and lost. His name is Winston Brandau. He was in a Chinese prison for hashish possession."

"We'll never see him again. Wait. Was? No one gets out of there, Walker."

"He did, someone killed four guards and several inmates to get him out."

"Where did they take him?"

"Doesn't really matter. Thai intel says he turned up in the river last night." Walker slipped another photo in front of the general.

McGill frowned, recognizing the kill report from the CIA in the field. Good God, someone was angry at men. "The HSS design was only half of the schematics. This explains how they got the rest."

"Should we focus on embassies?"

"No, we can't touch them."

"But, sir—"

The general put up a hand. "No. Stay clear."

"Sir, we'll never find them if we don't."

"Then we need other options."

"Can we use Killian's alter ego?" Sebastian asked.

Viva's gaze bounced between the men, trying to understand, then realized Killian Moore masqueraded as a weapons' dealer, Dominic Cane. God, she thought, what they do for the job. Stepping into the underworld wasn't something she'd call a walk in the park.

"Possible, but he'd need to be here."

"I can set it up like Ryzikov had it," Logan said. "Through a webcam."

"Not close enough," Sam said. "If we get the chance to

get it, this guy might want to see him up close and personal and Killian's stateside."

"I'm betting this guy had each bidder checked out first," Sebastian said. "A reputation for killing is a requirement, no doubt."

"How do we get into this auction before they kill another thousand people?" Max asked, looking around for more food.

"Not a clue," Sam said.

"I do."

They swung to look at Viva.

"I have connections that might help." Her face flamed with embarrassment. "The kind that will open the door and maybe get you into this buy quickly."

"How? With who?" Sam said.

"Before I tell you anything, you've got to swear you'll keep this with the team."

"Jesus, Viva."

Oaths echoed around the room. Except from Sam. Her gaze fell on him and he was looking at her with such suspicion, it made her heart hurt. Finally, he swore.

"Logan, give me a line to the US," she said.

Logan routed the phone via satellite and handed it to her.

"Who're you calling?" Sam asked.

Viva hesitated before dialing. "My father."

Constantine wasn't comfortable with the bidders staying on his estate, but it was the only way to protect them. He strolled around the device, admiring the modifications. Money well spent. The diamond gleamed from inside the laser's track.

He turned back to the wide living room. Black granite floors so polished they reflected the light, and clean lines in furniture, glass, and stone. Zidane appeared at the end of a short, wide corridor. Behind him a single elevator led to the lower floor and the garage beneath the house.

"They are nervous."

"As well they should be with Noor killing their counterparts. Just keep them happy. They have proof enough now." His attention went to the large-screen TV, the sound turned off—more because noise irritated him than not wanting to hear the incessant chatter.

He smiled at the geologists interviewed on screen, the Americans and Latins rushing to help. The bidders for the weapon saw the same, and though he'd done this entire transaction by computer before, he truly didn't want to risk the bidders seeing his face. His entire goal was to escape this without any leads back to him.

"Noor will return," Zidane said. "You know this."

"Why should she?" She had to know he couldn't let her go unpunished.

"A matter of pride, to finish what she started, or to kill me." For her imagined betrayal.

"Then you'd best stay armed." When Zidane started to speak, Jalier cut him off. "No, you can't go after her. I need you here."

Zidane eyed him for a long moment before he disappeared into one of the halls.

Alone, Jalier reached for his phone, dialing. "I have a job for you."

"That depends on what it is and how much it pays."

Jalier turned to the curved windows offering a view of the harbor. His reflection showed the clean lines of his garments, the silver at his widow's peak. "I'll double your profits, only because this kill won't be easy."

"How can your father help?" Sam asked, completely confused and not liking it.

"Maybe not much, he's in prison."

Sam's brows shot up. No wonder her family was *unavailable* to help her.

"My father is Salvatore Fiori."

Max whistled softly. "The mob boss?"

She put the phone to her ear. "The one and only."

"Why didn't you say something?" Sam asked.

"Oh, I don't know, shame? The utter mortification that I *was,* not am, a Mafioso princess? I put him in prison, so we're not on the best of terms. This might not work." She spoke into the phone. "Warden Calloway, this is Xaviera Fiori. I need to speak with my father." She paused, listened, then said, "I know he doesn't want calls, but he especially doesn't want them from me so let's piss him off, shall we?"

Viva tucked the phone away from her mouth. "It wasn't until I was about sixteen that I realized how he made his living. I had lots of uncles, if you know what I mean. In some territorial vendetta someone had against my father, my mother was murdered. In front of me."

"Good God."

Her voice wavered when she said, "We were shopping for a prom dress, for pity's sake. It pretty much started a mob war."

Sam's heart broke for her, and he remembered the TV reports of bodies turning up all over New York and Boston.

"My father insisted she was well aware of the risks, but that didn't matter to me. The son of a bitch pissed off another mob boss and my mother was dead." Viva's eyes watered, and she blinked, then cleared her throat before she said, "For a couple years I made him pay, stealing cars, basic teenage trouble. I was in juvenile jail when the FBI contacted me. I was so angry I helped them. My dad is serving a life sentence for racketeering, drug traffic, conspiracy to commit murder." She waved, the list was endless. "Because of me."

"Why aren't you in the witness protection program?"

She made an odd sound. Of frustration or regret, Sam couldn't tell.

"My father would see to it that anyone who came near me would die. Most times, I use my mother's maiden name, but no one knows where I am. I left the country to be sure of it." She put up a finger and spoke into the phone.

Her Italian was lyrical, Sam thought, then she put the call on the speakerphone.

"*Mia cara,* you call after all this time?"

"Don't get used to it. You haven't had long enough to regret the errors of your ways, old man."

Sam frowned. He'd never seen Viva like this. Chillingly hard, detached.

"I need you to make some calls, talk to that overstuffed lawyer of yours, I don't care, but I need to get into a bidding in Thailand."

"Bidding for what?"

"For a weapon."

"You know nothing of weapons. I made sure of it."

Yeah, she thought, I learned on my own how that worked.

"Who do you do this for, a man?"

"No, I'm not doing it for a man, I'm doing it for my country. You know, the country that threw you in jail instead of putting you in front of a firing squad?"

There was a moment of hesitation before he said, "I am alone here, daughter, I cannot help you."

"Liar. You might be locked up, but you're still running the show." He protested and she talked over him. "I've never done anything great, except this."

"You, my daughter, I helped make you, you *are* a great thing."

Viva rubbed her forehead. "Set it up, old man, I know you can do this."

Sam noticed she refused to call him Father or Dad.

"Calls I don't get," he said.

"Bullshit! Pay someone."

In Italian, he berated her for her language.

"Get over it and listen to me. We don't have much time. Hours, maybe. I need to be a buyer for this weapon and I need it now."

Sam felt her frustration, the pain radiating in her expression. Especially when he started begging for her forgiveness, and to come see him.

"Stop that! Please! This isn't about you and me. There's a horrible man who has killed millions already, and he's going to kill millions more! He's selling to Al Qaeda."

There was an instant of quiet before her father said, "What do you want?"

"Now I know why you talk so much," Sam said.

"Who is that?"

She looked at Sam, the sympathy in his eyes touched her. Words tumbled from her very soul. "The man who has my whole heart."

Sam smiled.

"All of it, Xaviera?"

"Sí, all."

"You, young man?"

"Sam, sir."

"You love my daughter?"

"Papa, *sia calmo!*" Be Quiet.

"A father has a right to know these things!"

Viva opened her mouth, to lambaste the guy, Sam figured, and he met her gaze, knowing without a doubt as he said, "Yes, very much."

She inhaled sharply. Her eyes teared, hot emotion racing through her and making her heart crash in her chest. She wanted to scream, to ask if he was sure and to repeat it, certain she'd heard wrong, yet instead she flew across the space and latched on to Sam, kissing him.

Beyond her wild kiss, Sam felt only one thing: satisfaction in his soul.

Her father scoffed. "You must be a very strong man to handle my daughter."

Sam chuckled and leaned toward the phone. "No one handles Viva, sir."

Deep laughter filtered from the speakerphone. "Give me the particulars."

Viva was still staring at Sam. "Good. Listen to Sam, and do as he says."

Sam picked up the receiver and told him what they needed, giving him the e-mail linkage so they could get the information to the seller through Ryzikov's laptop.

When he was done, her father wanted to speak to her again, but Viva shook her head, sinking into a chair. He spoke to her in Italian and she made a tiny, pain-filled sound. She stared at her hands, tears dropping onto her fists.

Sam ended the call. All they had to do now was wait.

The silence hung like dampness, and Viva sniffled, hating that it still hurt so badly to speak to him.

"Your father is a Mafia don." Logan still sounded amazed.

"Was. He's nothing more than an inmate now."

"It must have been tough to turn in your own father," Sebastian said, and patted her shoulder as he passed.

"Not really."

"Viva, honey . . ."

She looked at Sam, tears still wet on her cheeks. "No, Sam it wasn't hard. My mother was cut in half by some hood making a name for himself. She died on the street instead of old age. Instead of surrounded by her family and grandchildren. Mom never hurt anyone and sheltered me from my father's *career*. He deserves worse than life in prison."

Sam understood her anger, sympathized, and thought, it's good the man is locked up. He'd reek havoc on her heart. "When was the last time you spoke to him?"

"Ten years ago, maybe." He slid to the spot beside her and pulled her into his arms. Viva wiggled into his chest, the weight of his arms around her, the sound of his heart against her ear soothing. "Know what he said to me when my mother died? 'These things happen.' Bastard."

"But you loved him."

"When I think of him, I try to remember the man who pampered me as a girl. It's not easy. His money came from all the wrong places."

"But not his love."

Viva buried her face in his chest, and he squeezed her tighter. He'd understood, roughly, what her father had said to her before ending the call. *'Be at peace with me, my beloved. For no matter what occurs, I will love you always.'* When she tipped her head back to look at him, Sam saw a vulnerable woman, uncertainty in her green eyes.

"What?"

"You never say what you don't mean," she reminded.

"Roger that. Just don't expect me to say it in front of a crowd again."

"You'd have to actually *speak* the words first," she teased, and didn't give him a chance to respond as she sat up, and reached for pen and paper. "Max," she called, scribbling fast. He came into the room again chewing food. Did the guy ever stop eating? "I need some things."

He looked at the list. "Sure, be back in an hour."

She twisted a look at Logan. "If I know my father, it shouldn't take long to set this up."

"I'll be ready."

"Give McGill a head's up. We'll need the NSA to decipher," Sam said, then looked at her sharply, scowling. "If you think I'm going to let you be the target of this, you're nuts."

She didn't go off on him, didn't get righteous when he revealed that he was worried about her. It had been a long time since anyone gave a damn, she thought, smoothing the lines of his forehead, her fingers skimming to his strong jaw. "Sam," she said softly. "You don't have a choice. Unless you can speak Italian, Russian, and maybe Farsi." He scowled, since she knew better. "And if you're in front of the camera when the geeks decipher the router to him, what then?"

She had a point. It would take all of the team to get this son of a bitch. "I don't like using you as bait."

"But you'd let that stop you when this Pharaoh is holding us all hostage?"

Sam's shoulders slackened. "Fine." He didn't like it one bit. "So what's with the list?"

She smiled slyly. "A little deception."

"Don't get all happy," Logan said, leaning back in the chair, swearing under his breath. "McGill says if we can't trace the last link to the router, then the only way to pinpoint it is when it hits another target."

Nineteen

Hitting a target was not an option. "I'll let the God damn machine go before it makes more casualties, General."

"The joint chiefs consider it an acceptable risk."

"I don't."

"Perhaps US and UK forces need to take over this operation."

"Fine, go for it, but consider that you don't have people with connections to get into the bidding, nor someone who speaks five or six languages. Who on your end is ready to move right this moment?" Sam asked, knowing the answer.

It would be at least four hours before they could get undercover operatives anywhere near these people and even longer to set up a deep-cover infiltration, which the CIA had been trying to do since Ryzikov stepped on Thai soil. They didn't let in any outsiders.

McGill finally agreed.

Sam wasn't satisfied. "We're going in, McGill, so how do you justify leaving two kids behind?"

"That diplomatic residence is official, paid for and run by the Algerian Embassy."

"So if this router location is his home, you're okay with that? Jesus, McGill. What difference—" Sam clamped his lips shut. "You need to find another solution. Or I will." He cut the connection and tried not to slam the phone down and instead tossed it into a chair. "Assholes. All those great minds and they can't come up with something better?"

"Military Intelligence is a contraction in terms," Max said, and Sam gave him a sour look.

"Sebastian, we need some surprises. If Viva has to be alone, then I want a fortress around her." Although MI6 and the Bangkok CIA station had agreed to have officers on the road and grounds, Sam wasn't comforted. He didn't trust them enough to be inside the CP.

Sebastian agreed and set aside the gear he was stocking, then turned to a silver metal case filled with his toys.

While McGill and the joint chiefs were assembled, more as spectators than participants, the Silent Fire project commander, Gerardo, would be online through a DIA intel link. England had Special Forces in country ready to move with the US and were helping with a face match to the photo from Voslav's film. It would help to know who they were gunning for, Sam thought.

The Algerian government and its embassy couldn't be informed. The joint chiefs agreed that since they didn't know exactly who was involved in the theft of the weapon that tipping their hand would not be wise. Whatever, Sam thought, kneeling to double-check his gear. Someone in the intelligence community had betrayed them again. Whether it was the US and her allies or another country, they may never know.

Sam watched Logan rewire his systems to meet the requirements.

NSA analysts were sitting comfortably in Virginia ready to decrypt the router system and find the last hop across the world to the man who referred to himself as the Pharaoh. Speed and communication were essential. One of our own satellites had been retasked to be certain the lines of communication didn't break.

Lots of people involved now, he thought, and Viva was taking the biggest risk. She had to keep the Pharaoh on the line and right now, they weren't even sure they'd get into the bidding. It all depended on her father and his willingness to call in one huge favor on Viva's behalf. He didn't want to think about how the guy was going to pay it back. Mafia had their own set of dangerous rules.

"NSA will try to trace the last link in the router system by keeping him on line," Logan said. "Let's hope it works. This Pharaoh planned this very carefully."

"And he's mine," Sam said, sliding his knife into the scabbard.

"Whoa, baby!" Sam heard from behind and turned. Shock tingled over his skin, and he understood what Viva meant by a deception. A different woman walked across the room. Dark, sultry, and hard edged. Her hair was dark brown, her makeup heavier, but the black suit and fake diamond jewelry gave off a completely different impression. Sophisticated, worldly. Don't-fuck-with-me powerful.

Viva adjusted the hem of her jacket. "Not one word."

"Guess I can't call you Red anymore, huh?"

"It washes out." She laughed lightly at the quick relief in his expression.

"You really look Italian now."

"Sicilian, big difference to *mia famiglia*."

A few minutes later, the phone rang and Sam answered, then he held it out to her.

She spoke in Russian for only a moment, giving them a thumbs-up. "Dah, dah." She smiled as she said, "No, I don't owe you a favor, Uncle Vlad, my father does." She hung up, smirking. "Let him try and collect. Vlad is my godfather, Russian mob. Ex-KGB, as a matter of fact. This will route through his network."

"Jesus," Max said. "Remind me never to piss you off."

Viva winked, really smiling for the first time since she'd spoken to her father.

"We have to keep him on line to get a location, the router systems have to be operating." Logan was tweaking his systems.

"That's cutting it close," Sam said. "Once the deal is done, then it could be disconnected."

"I'll keep him on there. I'll talk him to death."

Sam smiled, looking her over and his gaze landed on her neckline. "That's a lot of flesh you're showing, baby." Her breasts were nearly spilling from the fitted jacket.

"It's a distraction. Working?" She jiggled a bit for him.

"Oh, yeah." He practically smacked his lips. "I want to kiss you," he said.

"You'll smear my makeup."

He grinned and pressed his forehead to hers. She loved that he didn't care that the team saw them. He rested his hand on her hip and tugged her closer.

"Don't be a hero."

"You, either," she said. He was already suited up in black, wearing a load-bearing vest, a gun, and knives strapped to his thighs and calf. It was a terribly sexy look.

"Viva, I need to get you set up for this," Logan said.

For her part, Logan had set up a single computer with the webcam, the backdrop behind her a clean wall with no art. Nothing to give away their location. On his screen, and back in the US, they would see what the Pharaoh saw. She brushed her mouth over Sam's, then laughed when she had to wipe off the lipstick. She turned to Logan and inserted the tiny ear mike in one ear, then put on a headset microphone on the other. She'd be able to hear the caller, the Pharaoh, in the headset, and speak back into the lip mike curved to her painted mouth. Through the tiny earpiece, she'd hear instructions. From who, she wasn't sure. The team wouldn't be here for it and that scared the heck out of her. Too much depended on her alone, and she'd avoided that like the plague for years. Can't quit now, she thought. Time to step up to the plate and be counted.

She was on her own, attached only by microchips and a satellite feed.

"Hearing voices on both sides of your head isn't going to

be easy," Sam said. "You have to concentrate on one at a time."

"Before or after it gives me a migraine?"

Sam's lips curved. "Just be sure not to respond to us and only to the Pharaoh."

This guy had a ruler complex with a name like Pharaoh. "Logan, you have the translator up? Because I have to speak Russian for a bit for this to seem authentic." Trying to fool this guy wasn't going to be easy and the burden, unfortunately, rested on her.

Logan nodded. "US intel is getting the same thing now."

"Hello, General."

"Miss Fiori, we can't thank you enough for assisting."

"Hey, I'm thrilled to hold my father over a barrel for a good cause. Just put on your thinking caps and don't leave me out in the cold. I'm not trained for this."

"We'll do our best."

She rolled her eyes. "Logan, can you haze out this camera lens or filter? This guy will not recognize my voice, but the other tall guy that was with him, he might have seen my face. I don't want him coming after me."

"Hell, it's not like half the criminal world in Thailand wants you."

"I always wanted to be so popular," she said in a Valley Girl voice.

"If they knew who you were, they wouldn't touch you," Sam said and winked.

She took her seat, adjusted her clothing. The last time she wore stockings was at her father's trial. When the screen came on, Viva tensed, startled by her own appearance.

Sam was in her line of vision as was Sebastian. Once they had the final router point, she thought, all hell would break loose. "What happens if we don't get the original router point?"

"Then we have to convince him to meet with you," Sam said and her eyes widened. "You won't have to do it."

"No other woman here, Sam, who are you going to get to fill in?"

"We'll work around it, you're not getting near the bastard."

"Protective instincts aside, which make me feel all warm and toasty, we have to do what we have to do."

Sam came to her, cupping her face and taking her mouth with a ferociousness that left a mark on her heart. "I do, *you* don't. If you have to make him want to meet with you, then we'll intercept."

"And if he won't? He's been so clandestine so far, why would he?"

He let her go. "To get his money."

"Electronic transfers would cover that."

"We have that step, too," Logan said. "Fake money from a fake account. USA will handle it."

"He wants those." Sam nodded toward the bowl of diamonds she stole from Ryzikov.

"I don't think so, I think he wanted many uncut stones to get one to fit that machine, and he has that."

"Then it's one of those play-by-ear things, I guess." Sam swiftly loaded a 9 mm Beretta and laid it on the table beside her.

Viva looked from the gun to him. "You're making me nervous."

"I wouldn't leave you if I thought he could track you."

Sebastian had to fly the chopper, and since they didn't know what kind of firepower they were up against, or where, they needed Logan. Sam wished he had a platoon and some stingers.

"CIA sent three officers, they're on the lower road. Sebastian wired some extras in the windows and grounds and we'll set the sensors when we leave."

"Heads up, people, he's calling you," Logan said and nodded as the connection linked.

* * *

Gerardo watched a simultaneous cast with McGill.

Both men sat perfectly still, watching the green line trace the onion router connection, the first, second, then the third; a neon line raced over the world map, and turned back. It was a maze. Israel, Tibet, England, Ireland, then shooting into the Middle East, then across China province. He listened to the woman work the deal, heard the intel coming from Chambliss. They were still too far from finding the final signal.

"Hurry the hell up," he commanded, then leaned to tap the comm link. "Is Dragon One in the air?"

Viva stared at the screen that offered nothing more than a figure in the shadows, sitting behind a large desk. She could barely make out the room, yet noticed the gleam on the stone floors and arches behind him.

Then he spoke. The sound of his voice, the memory of him toying with her mind to kill Sam fueled her outrage. Who did this bastard think he was to hold us all hostage? A moment of greeting passed. His language skills were poor, and Viva wasn't going to attempt Farsi and spoke in Russian, yet when he couldn't understand her, she switched to English.

"You come highly recommended."

"You do not," Viva said coldly, affecting a heavy accent and hating this man with every cell in her body. "People die around you." She could see nothing of him, only his outline. Yet Sam tapped his ring finger. This was the man in Voslav's photo.

"Some things cannot be avoided."

"Dismemberment should be."

The Pharaoh sat up straighter, his hands folded on a green desk blotter, and Viva knew she'd struck a sore spot. "You're rather informed for a newcomer."

"We've been watching you, Pharaoh."

"Impossible."

Then, "Don't piss him off," whispered in her ear.

Antagonizing him backed her into a corner. "There are several of my counterparts in this country. When they start turning up dead, one wonders, dah?"

"It could be you. To get into the bidding."

"If it was, *we* would not have left a trail for others to find."

Beyond the camera and computer, Max, Sebastian, and Sam picked up the meanest-looking black rifles and slung them. She didn't dare take her eyes off the screen and Logan moved into her line of vision.

In her right ear she heard, "It's all locked in. Keep him talking. The visual and sound control is on that laptop," he gestured to the one in front of her. "In the lower right corner. Just click it once and it will black out if you need it, but will keep the connection locked."

She inclined her head, indicating she understood. Max and Sebastian were already out the door, Logan following. Sam paused, looking back, and Viva's chest tightened. It struck her that she might never see him again.

Her eyes burned, and the urge to rush to him nearly overpowered her. She squeezed the arms of the chair, her nails digging into the brocade fabric. He held her gaze for a moment, then he was gone.

Jalier sat back, rubbing his mouth. Arrogant woman. He had to cull her; she was his highest bidder with unlimited funds. He stared at the screen, seeing the beauty and well-rounded shape of her. She appeared to be alone, though he doubted that. A woman with such power wouldn't be left unguarded. His speakers gave off the murmur of discussion between the bidders and instantly, he cut them off. They heard only him for the moment. The mafia's representative, the woman, was the only one not within his grasp.

He admitted only to himself that he'd rather keep the connections through computers, but Noor's behavior had decided other plans. He couldn't get his money if they were dead. More's the pity.

The black chopper lifted into the night, the Sat comm link to NMCC clear in the headsets. He didn't want Viva to hear any of this, to add to her nervousness, and had Logan cut her off from their voice traffic for the moment.

"Dragon One to Command, we're airborne."

"We've almost got it, five minutes, maybe."

"It's just fuel, we're ready."

Sam made a cutting motion across his throat. Sound went off except inside the chopper. "Commander Isarangura is on alert. He's handpicked men he trusts to be discreet, and when we get the location, he'll secure the area."

"You didn't trust MI6 or CIA to do it?"

"Not when they won't get the kids. They have an agenda and this is his country, his jurisdiction. Algerian Embassy can be kept in the dark, but not this guy."

The light on the dash blinked and Sebastian hit it.

"We have the final link. I say again, we have the final link." They gave an address. "Bangkok, west shoreline."

Sam slid the door back and surveyed the black coastline with night vision goggles.

"I've got coordinates. Thirty-one degrees, ten minutes west," Max said. "Shit, he's right there."

Sam swung to look. Right across the harbor from them all this time. Fuck. Sebastian turned the chopper, flying over the glassy water.

"Slow down, Coonass," Sam said. "He'll hear us, we can't repel from the chopper. He's got his own troops, assume he's got more. We have to get him by surprise."

"You want to drop and swim?"

"I have a better idea." Sam grabbed the radio and tuned the frequency. "Commander Isarangura, this is Sam Wyatt." He gave him his location.

Max twisted in the seat, showing Sam the satellite imagery. "It's an estate, massive house, and a long road leading in, cliffs to the water, and he's got a couple acres surrounding him."

They could come in from the land side, but that would be a lot of running and a lot of time. The bidding was going down right now. Isarangura gave as much information on the estate as he knew offhand. It was plenty. Sam tapped a key and brought up the image of the building. There was only one way in without notice. "Commander, I need a favor."

"Begin, I've little time to waste."

"The bidding starts at one million in diamonds. You have been vouched for."

Viva nodded regally. "I want to see this weapon." The screen blinked and what looked like a telescope appeared. Oh, God, she thought, it's *that* small. Illuminated from the bottom, the big diamond glittered from inside a channel. Then she realized it was set up to operate.

The bidding rose; seven, ten, fifteen.

"If I may interrupt," she said, and the Pharaoh shifted in his seat, clearly annoyed. Big, hairy deal, she thought. "This machine could be a mere casing. We have not seen it perform."

"Yes, you have."

The screen changed, the devastation of the dam in Sri Lanka, the volcano in Guatemala. *I knew it.* She didn't have to see the guys to know they understood.

"I'll reserve judgment when geologists confirm. Your word, since we have no previous dealings, is not good enough." She could almost see the Pharaoh bristle on the screen. "I want proof."

"Each of you have a chance to see it work."

"Each? Those who fail the bid? You do not know the meaning of a worthy deal, Pharaoh. I am high bidder. This loses its effects when you destroy for a test. Careful selection is tantamount. And the authorities will certainly be hunting."

"It will take them years to understand and be assured,

they will not locate it." In the shadows, he cocked his head. "Or have you grown a conscience?"

Viva's eyes narrowed, dangerous with her fury. "I want *my* enemy to die, not theirs."

McGill stared at the neon green light on the large screen. It blinked intermittently. He turned toward the cheap seats, the men lined against the window and looking down. Dragon One had learned far more and faster than they had. He looked back at the screen, the satellite imagery narrow enough that they could see the lights surrounding the building.

Just because they had the location didn't mean this asshole wouldn't fire it. He'd done so twice, they believed. It was clear the consequences meant nothing to him. Therefore, letting the bidders test fire meant even less.

McGill made a call, then cut the line and dialed again. Gerardo picked up instantly. "I've scrambled AWACS."

Gerardo understood his intentions. "That's a long shot, sir."

The Airborne Warning And Control System's planes could trace everything from troop movement to signal intelligence. The ear of the US. "If this Pharaoh fires it, the only thing we can do to intercept is put a large barrier in its way."

"Then pray it doesn't do as our scientists predict."

And take down the aircraft.

Viva cut the outgoing voice to the Pharaoh. "Are you seeing this, General?"

"Yes, we are. This is Gerardo, Miss Fiori, and Mr. Harris."

The designer studied the machine. "It will work. The acoustic platform is the same, the pinpoint, but passing along the laser stream through the diamond's beam—"

"How can we stop it?" she interrupted.

"Breaking it can stop the diamond transfer but not the sound. It's three times the size of a standard. It would go mega. You wouldn't hear it more than a whisper but the intensity of it would cook your brain."

Oh, no, Viva thought, even if Sam stops him from firing, he'll be a vegetable.

In her left ear, the other buyers discussed her point till they argued. She opened the line. "Enough," she snapped. "What use is it if I cannot select my own target?"

"It must be aligned with a satellite. And this takes time." The Pharaoh chuckled, a dark, viperous sound, and she knew she was in trouble before he spoke. "Select a target, my dear. In fact, I insist."

"Allow me to confer with my people." She leaned, tapped the key, and closed off any outgoing sound or picture. "All right, you've got the smart people with you, now what?" It was like speaking to God, no one there, but you knew they were listening.

General McGill's voice flared in her ear. "We have people standing by with a geologist."

"Oh, forget it, General, you're a day late and a dollar short again." She stood and got a map from the desk. "Okay, okay, I can pick a target that will not hurt anyone, well, not many, unless they are in the Baltic."

"We have outposts there."

"Then I suggest you do something to get them away from it, and do it now. That's the only place I can think of that will not cause a tsunami, or an earthquake. Find these guys before I have to hit something!" She hurried back to the chair and hit the screen. Before she could say a word, a man spoke up, only his voice coming over the system.

"Here are the coordinates."

Oh, shit. "I am high bidder!"

"They all wish to see it work again."

"Then they pay the price or you forfeit mine. To do so, Pharaoh, you risk millions." She held up the bowl of diamonds. "Are you prepared?"

Bangkok Coast

At Wyatt's signal, Commander Isarangura cut the engine and let the boat coast on the waves. The house was in sight before they moved this close, now all they could see was a slight glare from the floodlight illuminating the grounds. No less than fifty meters above them. Isarangura watched curiously as Wyatt slung the nylon rope over his head and arm and moved his rifle higher on his chest. Then Wyatt turned, extending his hand.

"Thanks, buddy. Just cover the road, we don't want them running."

Isarangura gripped his hand and in Thai wished him a glorious victory. Within moments, the three men were over the side of the boat and becoming part of the darkness. The cliffs were rocky and blended in to the stone wall, the view to the sea open through the pilaster rail. On the west and north face, a twelve-foot wall offered the comfort of protection to the property, as did the long road. Wyatt was correct. A sea approach would not be unexpected.

When Isarangura could no longer see them, he turned over the engine and maneuvered the boat away from the shore cliffs and back to his officers.

Like most of the rich and depraved, they were also paranoid. As if the poorer part of the world wanted to look in and see what they couldn't have. There were cameras at each corner of the wall, moving in a pattern. The bay side was rock cliffs, steep and full of good footholds, Sam thought, gripping a rock, testing its anchor before pulling himself up.

Like mice over a chunck of cheese the team climbed, keeping distance between themselves. They each had a target. Cameras, guards, find the cutter, and take out the weapon. Anything else would be cherry. Sam would rather be coming in by chopper, guns blazing, but they didn't know if there were hostages. He hoped the diamond cutter, Narabi, was here and not housed somewhere else. Pharaoh liked to play it close to the vest, he doubted Narabi was far from his control. If he was still alive.

According to Isarangura, the incoming road was wired with laser sensors and fenced in with silent electrics, like homeowners had for dogs, all buried underground. No way for them to find the sensors and deactivate, though a good electrical shock would have done it. But they couldn't show their hand. Sam didn't doubt Viva was in for a battle with this guy, and there was the chance that he'd fire the damn thing before they got to him. *Him* being Constantine Jalier, French Algerian, a UN Security Council member.

Which explained how this guy was always one step ahead. He had the resources, law enforcement, access to what was going on when, especially with Interpol. He got to someone, or Kashir would still be alive.

Sam reached the top, braced his hand on the rock, and stared up at the terrace wall, then reached over his shoulder for the rubber-coated grappling hook—Max's handiwork—wishing he had his whip, but the distance was farther than its length.

Like Logan and Max, he swung the rope like a lariat and threw. The hook made a soft thump as it caught. He tugged and pulled, then climbed. His arms burned with pulling his own weight, and near the edge, he drew his rifle forward, then hoisted himself the last couple feet.

"I'm in," Sam whispered as he rolled over the edge, dropping to the ground.

Twisted banyan trees hung below the rim of the wall, with red banana trees crowding and creating a jungle cover as Sam moved deeper into the thicket. Several yards ahead, the bubble of a fountain and pool mixed with the squawk of annoyed birds like mutterings in the trees. Yet they didn't fly, content in their perches. The noise would cover any other sounds, but Sam didn't have to talk. He needed his hand for the throat mike to pick up a whisper, but his buddies knew the deal.

They fanned out, Max to his right, Logan to his left. Sam was forward of their positions. Point man.

Surprise was in their favor. Had to be. Not enough men for a nice, loud shock-and-awe assault. The grounds this side were a quarter acre, at least twenty yards from the terrace to the three-story house and enough room for four sets of furniture and a bar. Two floors were aboveground and the walls, shaped in a semicircle, were mostly glass windows and doors on the sea side to catch all the view the pricey land offered. The lowest was an underground garage, the only entrance from the road, according to Isarangura.

Sam pointed to his eyes, held up five fingers. *I see five guards, this level.* Then two fingers: two upper level. They were each armed with automatic rifles.

Logan advanced to the left and covered a short distance without sound. Sam went right, losing some cover to watch Max's back as he darted behind him to the garage to disable vehicles, then search for the diamond cutter. Sebastian was sitting in the chopper, waiting to airlift them out if need be, and watching the satellite imagery with infrared. The more info they received, the better.

Sam could pick off all four from his position and not be heard, the silencer would take care of that, but if a guy fell backwards, normal for impact, he'd hit the windows and they'd lose the surprise element. Hand-to-hand would have to be the way to go.

"Cameras at ten and two."

Logan acknowledged. "Standard pan." Left and right.

"Black them out."

On the rear patio, guards walked the perimeter of the patio beyond the windows toward the pool walk, one strolling close to their position and enjoying the sea breeze.

"I got him," Logan said. Sam heard Logan take out the guard, the grunt of strength barely audible. Logan lowered the body to the dirt and dragged him out of sight.

From his vantage point, Sam could see one guard forward of Logan's position, one directly in front of himself, one more at the right near the path to the lower garage. He waited till the man walked in the opposite direction, then used the spotlights and the shadows they created as he rushed to the side of the building and onto the patio. A guard was about ten yards from his position.

"Outlaw," Sebastian said in his ear. "I've got thermal all over the place. There's got to be at least ten, fifteen people in there."

A little more than he counted on, but doable.

"Several are forward your twenty. Looks like housed in separate rooms. Three hot spots on the upper level."

The buyers, Sam thought, then slid up under the camera and shot the lens. "Two o'clock camera out."

"Ten o'clock out," Logan said.

"Charges set," Max said. "I'm on the edge and going in."

Sam touched his throat mike. "Roger that. Two guards on the high walk and one more your twelve." Sam heard a grunt.

"Not anymore."

Two more to go this level.

The men acknowledged each other, yards apart down the long covered patio. Windows opened to the sea view, every third disguised as a door with a pull latch in the door frame. Shades were drawn over the glass, light filtering through and Sam tucked himself into the only darkened corner near the window. When the guard approached, Sam drew his knife slowly, as the guy went past his position, and Sam waited till after he spoke into the radio before he moved out of the shadows. His hand over his mouth, his knife into his kidneys, the guard went down without so much as an indrawn breath.

Sam searched him for keys, and took the radio before dragging the body into the bushes. Sam moved swiftly, ghosting the next guard and rolling him into the dark.

"Outlaw, nothing below but cars, there's an elevator this side," Max said. "Stupid shit didn't even put in stairs. I'm going to have to go west and find a new way in."

"I've got enough charges to blow the place off the map," Logan said.

"Save them. Narabi first, then we can do some damage. Room by room."

Logan cut the alarm wires, but with the guards patrolling, he didn't think they were on. That said Jalier was confident in his safety. Guess again, Sam thought, as he felt for alarm sensors, found magnetic and infrared beams housing, and disabled them. The guards would have tripped them. He tried the simple version and opened the door. Nothing. Too easy, he thought, going still. He eased the curtain to the side and looked in. He switched his goggles to infrared and saw the red grid lines marking the floor. Clever. He relayed to Logan and Max.

"Bet it's pressure alarmed, too," Max said. Logan advanced to the rear, to the land side of the property.

Sam circled the house, and on the side found a glass door half-open. He frowned at the steel slab in front of him, and backing to the side, he hit the only button on the wall. The steel slid back. He aimed into the empty cavern. "Got an elevator this side. I'm trying it."

"Jesus, Sam."

But it didn't move, merely opening on the opposite side. No chime, no numbers. He aimed into the room, his gaze bouncing to corners and doors.

It was completely open, sharp-angled furnishings and slick black floors. Another elevator was at the far end from him. Stainless-steel doors opened quietly and Max stepped out and signaled. Two flanking corridors. Max went left, Logan right.

Sam rode to the top and before the elevator stopped, Sebastian's transmission made him freeze.

"Outlaw, be advised. You are not alone. I say again, you are not alone. Two figures coming west across the grounds."

Did Isarangura jump the gun?

Twenty

Tashfin Rohki sipped coffee and paced the room. His patience was not infinite and he disliked being led by the nose for days, unable to trust his own judgment. And he wanted to end this and leave the country.

He listened to the woman bid, admiring her tenacity with the Pharaoh, but Tashfin was ready to call this a loss and leave. He put his hand in his jacket pocket, felt the CD, and pulled it out. He had the schematics to create a weapon himself. He didn't need to be here, but pulling out of the bidding after all this time, when the price had reached only a mere ten million, would have brought too much suspicion.

He went to the computer and slid the CD in the drive. He typed, opening the CD, then opened the file. It didn't appear and he tried again, frowning. He checked the properties of the file. Ten kegabyte. Enough for the title.

Then he realized, the CD was empty.

For the better part of a day, she crouched in the tree, hidden, watching till the men grew comfortable, lazy. They still patrolled the street beyond. But she'd seen them work. Put up more sensors, more charges. She'd been hidden since before sundown and her muscles were cramping. She'd seen them lift off in the chopper, suited up for war.

Noor no longer cared what Constantine did or his outcome. He and Zidane had discarded her when she'd done all they asked. Now it was her turn.

She spied the house across the water, a faint light in the darkness. She knew Jalier would be dying soon. It would be over, a failure. Noor planned to be the only winner.

"You can't give it to her."

"She has paid the price," Jalier said, not bothering to look at the man hovering nearby.

"Yeah, and she's not Russian mafia."

Jalier frowned between the man and the screen. "You are mistaken."

"I don't care. She's just a woman I met in the jungle. Bloody hell, this is blown."

The man started to leave and Constantine reached for the pistol on the coffee table. When he cocked it, the man froze and turned.

"Now that's not very sporting of you, Jalier," he said. "I got you information, the codes, that woman off the plane, and gave her to you. You have that stone because of me!"

"Yes, thank you, but your usefulness has worn out." He pulled the trigger.

Beecham's eyes widened. He looked down at the blood blooming on his belly, then sank first to his knees, then to his face.

Constantine was still moving, stepping over the body, and calling for Zidane to remove it. He hit the speaker on the wall. "Zidane, get them out of here, all of them."

Constantine went to his safe, pulling out the large wooden box and taking a long look at the cache of diamonds.

Zidane didn't respond. Constantine called to him again. No response.

Frowning, Jalier went to the intercom and pressed for the buyers. No one answered his call.

* * *

A floor below, Zidane hit the lock keypad. It sprang, swinging the door open. The buyer sat before the screen, turned and frowned. He rose and adjusted his jacket.

"You have lost the bid, time to depart."

The man walked nearer. "Where is the blind? The hood?"

"You won't need one." Zidane raised the gun and fired, then advanced before the man fell to the floor. He turned the computer toward himself and hit the keys, erasing the files, then popped out the CD. He pocketed it and left the room. The man was still moving and at the threshold, he fired again.

The room was acoustically sealed, and the silencer assured the kills remained undetected.

He went to the next.

Adam Kincade rushed the grounds, low and fast in the dark, to the area below the house.

Above him, a guard strolled the balcony deck. He'd given orders: no kills. Not that he wouldn't want to wipe them off the planet for beating a child, but they had to do this right or they'd incur more than an international incident. Kincade would go to jail for disobeying a direct order not to touch the diplomatic corps residence. Kids meant more than diplomacy, and Viva Fiori was the one who gave him the push. Clandestine shit, he thought, and signaled. The three-man team, himself included, was all he could spare and the ones he trusted to keep this under wraps. The only way to reach the guard was from the left-upper landing of the staircase. Out in the open. The house was on the hillside, its main portion no less than thirty feet off the ground. He pointed to his eyes, then held up two fingers. His teammate went to the right, climbing the hillside before they entered the house. His movements were slow, a sniper had to have patience.

Fifteen minutes later, he heard the whisper in his ear.

"I'm on him."

"Number three?"

"At the rear, one exit, one car. I'm ready to shut down the surveillance circuits."

They wouldn't cut them, just break the electrical connection. They couldn't be seen, no evidence of their arrival, or the USA or India would be in for some trouble.

"Wait till he gets to the edge of the balcony." The man moved back and forth, hot boxing a smoke and already reaching inside his jacket for another. Gonna get you killed, he thought. "Abort shoot till he lights up again."

They watched and waited, the house aglow with golden light from inside. They could hear nothing of the children and hoped at this hour they were sleeping. He looked back over his shoulder at his teammate, his equipment hidden somewhere in the grasses.

"I've got two: one on the balcony, one just inside, channel surfing."

"The third?"

"No visual."

"Alert, channel surfer is standing. In the kitchen getting coffee," his sniper said. "Get ready, he's coming back with two cups."

Kincade heard the countdown and rushed the stairs, took aim and fired. From the right his teammate fired. The two men sank slowly to the deck as the drugs instantly kicked in. The teammates climbed to the top, and up onto the deck.

They'd leave the darts in for a few minutes to make sure these guys were out for a while. Inside, the living room was empty, and silently they spread out, using only hand signals as they covered the house. They found the third asleep at a console, watching the monitors already gone black.

Adam fired into his chest.

"Number three out."

They searched the premises quickly, and couldn't find the children. "Jesus, what did they do with them?"

"They're here, they don't guard a house for nothing." Adam moved through the hall, opening closet and bathroom doors. Nothing. He stood still, thinking of the best place to hide a teenager and a little boy. He looked up, his gaze on the ceiling as he quickly searched again. Bingo. He found the attic opening inside a closet, the supplies on the shelves pushed aside, the edge of the wood scraped. He climbed, using his knife to pry the edge, a narrow staircase unfolded, and he climbed up, his rifle sweeping the room with light.

In the corner on a mattress was the girl, her body shielding her brother, and brandishing a piece of wood. Adam pulled off the hood and goggles.

He called the girl by name, then said, "USA."

She let out a breath and crumbled, then woke her brother and crawled with him across the floor. When the young boy put a death grip around his neck Adam knew going against orders was the right thing to do. Kincade hoped that when Wyatt and his team assaulted the house, they found the kid's father.

As quietly as they'd come, they took the only evidence, the tranq darts, and within moments, faded into the night with the children.

Max didn't have to force the door, it was already open. He eased up to the side of it, aiming in, then rolled around to the other side to get a complete view inside. It wasn't large—a bed, a sitting area, and a dead man slumped in a chair. He touched his throat mike. "Buyer ghosted."

"Here, too," Logan said, a moment later. "I count three dead so far." Logan entered the room and went to the computer, doing a search, and keyed up the schematics. "Plans are gone, erased."

Instantly they understood. Someone had betrayed Jalier. "He's still warm and bleeding."

"Outlaw, someone got to them first. And they're still inside."

Max met up with Logan and they tried the last door, and found it locked. Logan knelt and placed a charge on the lock. It hissed and smoked a little and the green light on the electronic lock popped. He scanned the small room; it was filled with tables and machinery, and the light on his rifle pointed out the video cameras and speakers. They eased in, covering the room in a breach circle. In the far corner was a cot and stretched out on it was a single figure, his eyes wide with fear. Max pulled off his goggles and leaned close. "Mr. Narabi?"

The man nodded, breathing hard.

"We're here to take you home."

The man went limp in the cot, tears in his eyes. Max cut his bond and removed the tape. Instantly the man asked for his children. "I don't know, sir. Let's get you out of here first. Stick close." Max moved to the door, Narabi behind him. "Drac to Outlaw, package secured."

Sam touched his throat. "Bug out."

Zidane went into the corridor, then heard movement and backtracked, tucking himself near the elevator. Three men left Narabi's room, the one sandwiched in between as they rushed him to an exit. Wyatt's people, he thought, and turned in the other direction. He lifted the radio to his mouth, gave orders not to shoot, then climbed the curving staircase.

He was too late.

The elevator door opened and Sam hung back, peering around the edge, sweeping left, then right. Empty.

Yet a good twenty feet beyond, a man sat on a sofa, his back to him. Jalier, he thought, so secure that he didn't bother to look his way. In front of him were three large screens, broken up into blocks. They were dormant, blank, yet there was a laptop and web camera in front of him.

"Zidane, where have you been? Take that away." He waved offhandedly at the body. Beecham, Sam realized, and squatted to check for a pulse and didn't find one. The man's presence said a lot and Sam assumed Beecham was the one who took Viva off the jet. He'd be the only one with that kind of access.

Sam advanced slowly, and over Jalier's shoulder, saw Viva

on the screen, looking lovely but a little ruffled. His gaze skimmed the room till he found the weapon. Under a high-ceiling dome of glass, it was like a rocket pointed skyward. On tripod legs, it had the look of a telescope with a flat silver platform on its back. Even from here, Sam could see the diamond in the channel. It was positioned to fire through the glass. Then Sam realized it was already powered up.

Aboard Night Watch, *AWACS*
35,000 feet above the Earth's surface

"Cougar to base, align with the l-87 satellite, now, now!"

The flight commander looked back at his radar operator.

She nodded. "Over Bangkok, Thailand, we have it, sir."

"Get ready for some vibration and God knows what else, people." He turned the craft into the path, the navigator giving him corrections in flight. They knew the instant they hit the beam. The jet shook. The Silent Fire vibrating the craft and sending all the instruments into a spin.

"We can only hold this for a moment," the navigator said.

"It's enough for the guys on the ground to stop it."

The beam hit the tail of the craft, knocking it off course and it started to pitch, the commander holding tight to the controls and keeping his gaze on the leveling. Yet when they passed through the beam, the vibration altered the tail rudder, and the monstrous jet started to tumble through the night, still in the path.

Cougar strained, his copilot pulling back. Suddenly, everything went still, then he slowed the jet, and hit the radio link to NMCC.

"Base to Cougar, what's your status?"

"We're still here, sir. All instruments back to normal." That was amazing, Cougar thought. "Did it help?"

"No, Colonel, it didn't."

They'd have to blow the satellite.

* * *

It was soundless, barely a hum, yet the laser heated up, glowing through the perfectly clear diamond. Sam moved swiftly forward and pressed the barrel to the back of Jalier's head. "Shut it down."

Jalier stiffened.

Sam nudged him with the barrel. "*Shut it down.*"

"You're too late."

Sam chambered a bullet. "Get up."

Jalier rose, his hands in the air, and as he faced Sam, he smiled. "You have chosen the wrong man, Wyatt." Jalier's gaze slid over the man's equipment, weapons. "You cannot touch me. I have diplomatic immunity."

"I don't care if you have the clap, shut it down!"

"Once it has power, it must finish the sequence."

"Like hell." Sam swung the rifle, firing at the tripod legs.

Viva watched it play out, saw the camera tip, and she got her first look at Constantine Jalier. He was handsome, dark hair with silver liberally at his forehead. Well dressed and a first-class bastard. Then she saw Sam try to reach the weapon.

"General. Do something!"

"We're trying, Miss Fiori."

"Blow the satellite!"

"We can't, it's ours."

Oh God. Viva could see only Sam, trying to hold his weapon when she knew he was feeling pain, sheer agony as it vibrated his skull. His nose immediately bled, blood rushing down into his mouth. He was on his knees and lunged toward the weapon now tilted on its side. It hit the polished stone and vibrated through the building.

She could do nothing but watch. Glass shattered as if punched, blasting outward. A second later, the ceiling of glass fell, showering him as he struggled to pull the diamond free.

She saw blood in his ears. "Help him!! He's dying!"

The machine collapsed, falling to its side, but Jalier was right. It didn't stop. The unseen beam ricocheted off the glossy stone and bounced back into the room. The effect was instant and angry. Sam's skull hurt, the back of his head vibrating murderously, his ears and throat tight with unimaginable pressure. He tried to keep standing. It was nearly impossible to command his muscles. Then glass exploded.

Sam's muscles collapsed, his chest feeling as if it would cave from the pressure. The sound was nothing more than a hum, the intensity of it magnified by the diamond, and he fell to his knees, his body pummeled with vibration. Worse than g-force training. He crawled toward the HSS, feeling his nose bleed as he dragged his body closer. He grabbed the weapon, his fist crushing the silver platform. It only distorted the soundwave, the force still powerful, and he gasped for air, blood dripping from his nose, and the pressure in his ears building. Christ.

Barely able to focus, he slid his hand along the channel and with his knife, pried the diamond. He pushed and it wouldn't budge and he slammed the machine onto the floor. Nothing. He tried again and the diamond dislodged and flew, hitting the floor and spinning.

Jalier rushed forward, diving for the stone like a greedy monger. He gripped it, smiling, then stood and pulled the plugs from his ears. "Wasn't that interesting?"

The sensations faded, yet Sam could still feel the weapon humming in his hands. He swung it forward, aiming like a rifle. At Jalier's head.

Jalier frowned at him, and staggered, reaching for the wall, for anything. Sam came to his knees, wanting to watch this fucker die slowly. Blood flowed from Jalier's nose, his ears. He choked as his lungs filled, yet it didn't stop him from lunging toward Sam. The diamond fell to the floor.

Sam pointed it close to his head. "This is for Riley, for Sri Lanka, for Guatemala, you asshole. And for Viva."

Jalier's eyes rolled to white, his tongue pushing out of his mouth without control. Blood pushed from the corners of his eyes, from his ears, and Sam backed off, lowering the weapon, and then dropped it when another man approached to swing his rifle forward, his footing uneven.

A figure emerged from the hall, staggering a bit, and Sam aimed. Rohki recognized the man just as Sam did. Sam took cover. Rohki darted behind a white stone column.

Jalier writhed on the floor between them.

"Time to face the music, Rohki." Sam wanted him bad.

Rohki's gaze shot from the machine to the stone on the floor a few feet from him. "We have all been betrayed."

"No honor amongst thieves, there's a first."

Rohki fired around the column. Sam returned it, his bullet chipping away at the stone.

"I have lots more for you."

Rohki stayed behind the column, trying to hear the man move, and failing, his gaze lowered to the floor, to Jalier bleeding from all orifices, and then to the stone. He needed it back, compensation for this failure. He chanced a look around the column, but gunfire sent him back. He fired blindly and a bullet struck his wrist, shattering the bone. He howled, the gun tumbling from his useless hand. He cradled his wound, pain flying up to his shoulder. He couldn't stay here, the man would hunt him. He glanced around, trying to see him in the reflection and couldn't. He reached carefully down to his spare gun under his pant leg. He checked the load, then mentally prepared himself. Many members of his organization were willing to die for their cause.

Tashfin wasn't one of them.

Sam was patient, his senses clearing slowly, his footing stronger. He moved right, and came around to Rohki's left just as he darted for cover.

Rhoki dove for the stone, hitting the floor. With his wounded arm, he reached out for the fat diamond, and fired with his left. There was no one there.

Rohki rolled and swung his aim.

"Wrong, again."

Sam shot twice, hitting him in the ribs, then the head. It wasn't pretty. An instant later, Sam caught movement to his left and swung the rifle.

The tall man, he realized, and he walked slowly forward, aiming a pistol at Jalier's head.

"Drop it," Sam said, shouldering the MP5 rifle.

"I have to finish the job." He held up a billfold, open to the ID. "I am Jai Zidane," he said. "Interpol." He fired at Jalier's head.

Sam didn't lower the rifle. "If you're Interpol, then what is Kashir Fokhouri doing on a slab?"

"I could not reach Kashir and he went to Beecham, believing he could trust him." Zidane glanced at Beecham's body. "He didn't know he couldn't."

"You killed the buyers."

"I had to make certain they were collected to get them all at once."

And throw off suspicion with the manner of the kills, Sam thought.

Zidane withdrew a handful of silver CDs.

"Here are the HSS plans. All data has been erased from the laptops, which are evidence of Interpol. We are done here."

Sam took them. "It would have helped to know you were in this deep."

"And risk my cover?" Zidane scoffed, then spoke into a radio. "Secure the perimeter, packages eliminated." A man replied in a language Sam didn't understand, and Zidane met his gaze. "Kincade has retrieved the children. They were in no real danger, Wyatt. My men were watching them." Zidane started to turn away, then said, "Noor, she knows your name, she will find your woman."

Sam paled and radioed Sebastian.

Noor's patience was over. The men were acting casual, relaxing their guard. She'd waited for this moment and eased from the tree, dropping to a crouch, then moving along the bushes, then to the house. The side door was unguarded, and she stepped around the charges she'd seen them set earlier.

Squatting, she worked the lock with a pick, uncaring of the alarm that sounded. Then a charge went off behind her. Shrapnel pummeled her back and she arched forward, smothering a moan of pain. Warm blood spilled down her spine, and the back of her head. She ignored it, forced the door open, and was inside, moving into the main portion of the house. She stilled at the entrance to the rear of the house, seeing the woman, her appearance changed. Noor cocked her head to the side, studying her from behind and thinking herself more beautiful.

Why did this woman have so many men willing to die for her?

Noor knew the moment the woman sensed her presence. She turned slowly and aimed a pistol.

"Somehow I knew you'd come," Viva said, inspecting the Thai woman from head to toe. Small and compact she was breathtakingly beautiful. Probably what got her close to men to cut off their balls.

"Give me the bracelet."

"You really think you can take it now?" Viva slipped out of her heels and moved to the left, circling the woman. The dart hunter, she thought. "Why do you want the bracelet so bad?"

"It is Thai."

"And you think I'm stealing it? I wasn't. I'd planned to turn it over to your king."

Noor scoffed and Viva lifted her aim. She didn't even realize that the woman had thrown till she felt the pain in her leg. The small, sharp knife was imbedded in her thigh and Viva buckled. Pain flared up her body, and it took Herculean strength not to take her eyes off Noor as she pulled out the little knife and threw it aside.

"You're really asking for a bullet in the brain, ya know."

"The taste of a kill is good, yes?" Noor threw again.

Viva rushed to the left. The blade sang past her into a painting on the wall. Then Noor bolted for her, throwing her body at Viva, and Viva fired. It missed and the pair tumbled to the floor. Noor straddled her chest, leaning over to grip Viva's hair and yank her head back. She put the blade to Viva's throat.

"The bracelet!"

"In the bedroom."

Viva tried moving her arms, pinned by the woman's knees and for a little thing, she weighed a lot. Then she felt her ankle, her foot, and Viva grabbed onto both, throwing her legs up and propelling herself forward. The motion sent Noor backwards and Viva clamped her legs around Noor's middle.

She squeezed, put all her strength into it, knowing if she didn't stop this twisted creature, she'd die tonight. Blood seeped from her wound as she pressed harder and heard Noor's breath labor. Harder still and Viva felt rib bones give under the pressure. One cracked, then another, and Noor screamed, pushed at her legs. The tortured sound brought more noise from outside.

Men rushed the door, slamming against it.

CIA doesn't know the codes to get in, she thought, refusing to let the woman go. Noor gasped for air, and Viva pressed till she had none left in her lungs and the woman faded into unconsciousness. Viva released her, kicking her away, noticing the blood on the woman's back as she jumped to her feet. She wasn't done. Noor regained consciousness in moments, and with both hands, Viva grabbed the woman by the shirt and dragged her to her feet. She could barely stand upright.

"I say never kick a woman when she's down." Viva breathed hard. "But in your case, I'll make an exception." With the last two words, she landed two sharp, quick punches to her face. Cartilage folded and blood poured.

Noor's eyes rolled, legs softening, and Viva released her. She fell, her head bouncing on the stone floor.

Viva exhaled, pushed her hair out of her face. "Bitch." She went for the gun, limping. Before she reached it, a shot fired behind her and she spun sharply. Her gaze went to

Noor, half-upright, an ugly hole in her head, and a knife in her hand.

A few feet beyond, Sam stood, his gun smoking. "Next time, disarm before you turn your back on them."

With a moan, she sank into the nearest chair. The team came in behind Sam as he rushed to her, sliding to his knees on the floor. He dragged her from the chair and into his arms, crushing her to him. Sam buried his face in her throat, breathing her in, the terror of seeing Noor with the knife poised at Viva's back flashing in his mind.

Too close, too close, he thought.

"I've got to stop meeting these crazy people," she muttered, her fingers digging into his back. The warmth and solid feel of him was more than good: it was glorious.

Sam drew back, holding her face and kissing her thoroughly. "You're crazy enough for both of us."

"Yeah, sure, like your life was really exciting before I came along."

He smiled, smoothed her hair off her face, wishing for the flame-red hue. "There's something I forgot to say before I left."

"Shoot first, ask questions later?"

He leaned in closer, his gaze locked with hers. "I love you, Viva."

She was so incredibly still for a moment, like a painting, frozen, and Sam knew he'd never forget that image, her eyes glossy, her hair wild. Then she opened her mouth. "Now that wasn't so hard, was it?"

He chuckled.

"I love you, too, cowboy. When you clear out the dead blowgun bitch, I've got plans for you."

Sam smiled against her mouth, laughing to himself as he fell back on his rear, the love of his life savaging his mouth and demanding more than eight seconds of his time.

Dr. Wan Gai was in his office, enjoying his morning orange tea when his new assistant knocked and entered. "Wait to be called, Nu."

"I cannot, sir. You have company."

Wan Gai looked up, midsip, then frowned. "Who?"

The young man gestured ineffectually, and a moment later, three men walked into his offices.

Royal Thai guards. "Welcome, welcome," he said, standing, then coming from behind the desk, put his hand out to shake.

The man in the center slapped a handcuff on his extended wrist. The other two turned him to finish securing him.

"What is the meaning of this? You have no authority over me to do this!"

"But I do."

Commander Anan Isarangura strolled into the office, his hands clasped behind his back. He glanced at the surroundings and made a sound of approval.

"You will not get away with this atrocity, Commander Isarangura."

"You are charged with trafficking humans, selling a human being for intention of murder."

"You have no proof."

His hands still clasped, Anan Isarangura peered at a piece of Thai sculpture on a wood pedestal before he said, "Your assistant Choan is more than willing to tell your story."

"My cousin will hear of this!"

Anan straightened and faced Wan Gai. They both knew Wan Gai spoke of the king, and Anan's smile showed his pleasure as he said, "He already has. Your cousin signed the arrest papers."

Wan Gai paled, his shoulders slumping. Anan waved his hand once, then joined them behind his back.

The guards escorted Wan Gai out of the museum, and as per the king's instructions, he was given no favor for his crimes.

"Wearing high heels twice in one week, this is a record for me," Viva said.

"I'll get you out of them soon enough," Sam whispered,

and she gave him a promising glance before a Thai court guard escorted her into the grand room.

She was stunned by the ornate beauty of the décor, but her attention went to the throne at the end of a long intimidating walk. The guard was a few steps ahead of her, and that the king of Thailand had requested her appearance left her in complete awe.

When the guard stopped, she did. He backed away to stand beside her, never giving his back to the king.

Viva remembered protocol, the curtsy, and knew she was one of the first who was not a dignitary to be granted an audience.

The king was in his seventies, his bearing speaking of his ancestry. Great posture, she thought. His garments looked military, adorned with precious stones and gold. He spoke softly, and the guard lightly grasped her elbow and ushered her closer.

"Miss Fiori," the king said, his voice resonant in the large room. She was formally introduced to his wife, and son, the next in line to the throne. The entire immediate family was spread out to the left and right of the king.

The prince moved near and Viva lifted her gaze. He smiled gently. "You have risked your life for our country's treasures, and for this we are eternally grateful."

She held out the velvet box. The prince took it, walking the steps to his father, and opened the box. The king of Thailand smiled brightly. The son backed away and His Highness gestured to the padded chair to his right.

Viva sat, hoping her slip didn't show.

"You would like to know of this bracelet."

"Yes, there is a legend?"

He nodded.

"Centuries ago, before society was fruitful, a Thai princess made a pilgrimage to the north. There she met a monk. As it is custom to gift monks, she gave him her most prized possession." The king waved a hand at the bracelet on the bed of velvet.

"How did the markings get on there?"

"The monk carved them, a sign of friendship with the princess. You know of the line of temples from Cambodia?"

She nodded, swallowing, so much in awe of his gentle spirit.

"The monk etched the markings." He waved and a servant brought him the bracelet. He turned it over in his hands several times. "In honor of the kindness between two worlds, the jewels of her eyes, the rubies of her soul, the Princess Noor shall be forever honored for her kindness."

"Simple."

"You thought it would be more, yes?"

"The way Dr. Wan Gai was after it I thought it would say something horrible."

He shook his head. "Wan Gai did you a great wrong. He believed that if this were discovered that it would, to the world, prove that Cambodia and Thailand were once one region and someone, perhaps officials of Cambodia, would try to lay claim to my country."

"But it's a relic."

"It is proof also that the cradle of civilization was here. Before the Chinese, before all, this is where the first society began."

Viva had her doubts, but kept her mouth shut. Carbon tests put the age of the bracelet in the BC's. But it was the beauty of the stones and their cut that said the Thai people were far more advanced than any archeologist gave them credit for.

"What can I do for you, Miss Fiori, to repay you for rescuing this treasure?"

She lifted her gaze, letting it skim over the royal family. "Some things don't have a price, Your Highness."

He nodded regally and she rose. She backed away, then, after a few feet, turned and left the throne room. Sam was there, smiling.

"Happy now?"

"Yes. But can we leave this country?"

His brows rose.

"As much as I like it, I think it's time to go home."

"You said you didn't have a home."

"Yeah, but you do."

Grinning, Sam slung his arms around her, kissed her temple, and they left the palace. "You sure you want to meet the family?"

"As long as they're not incarcerated."

"Nope, just the cows."

Viva laughed. "You're getting the hang of it."

Two weeks later
West Texas

"Viva!" Sam said. "Jesus, slow down."

"When did you get to be a wuss, Wyatt?" Viva dipped the chopper toward the big *X* in the middle of the field, Sam's version of a helo pad, then slowed to lower it. It touched down and she went through the routine of shutting down the engines. "That was a blast."

"That was heart failure. But you're a natural."

"It's all that personal attention." She leaned and kissed him.

"You just want another lesson."

"I want a lot of things right now, but I'm done flying for today." She glanced to the side, and Sam's senses were assaulted with memories and wanting to make more between the sheets.

"People will be arriving," he said when she kept kissing him. God, her mouth was amazing.

"Let 'em wait. Ever done it in the back of a chopper?"

"As a matter of fact—"

"Don't finish that sentence, cowboy, you'll regret it."

She climbed out. The blades were still moving as they crossed the pasture to his house. "I think I'll buy one."

Sam gave her a sideways glance. "Not a cheap toy."

"It's okay, I'm loaded."

Sam stopped short.

"I forgot to mention that?"

"Yeah."

"A girl has to have secrets."

"I can't wait." Sam laced his fingers with hers, and brought her hand to his mouth for a kiss. It was those little things that continued to shock and please Viva. He was rough on the outside, but a marshmallow deep down, and a real cowboy down to the core—cattle, horses, and even ranchhands.

"My father adored you," he said.

"My father was afraid of you. A good thing, considering."

"What other secrets do you have, Xaviera Fiori?"

His arm around her waist, she leaned into him. "Well, you already spoiled the sex-in-the-chopper thing."

Dust kicked up and they turned as a pair of big black SUVs pulled up to the front of the house. Men spilled from the trucks and she got bear hugs from Max, Logan, and Sebastian, then she met Riley. He was still bandaged up, his shoulder in a sling.

"I hear you avenged me a wee bit, Viva."

She adored his accent. "Not really, I saved my own ass."

Riley blinked.

"You'll get used to it," Sam said and called to Killian.

The man turned and Viva thought, *Whoa, he's a big one.* He smiled, then leaned down and kissed her cheek. "Welcome to the team, Viva."

She frowned at Sam. "You can't possibly want me to join Dragon One."

"Sure."

"And you call *me* crazy?" The last weeks hadn't clued them in that trouble simply *found* her?

"We wouldn't have come out of this if it wasn't for you," Max said. "The diamonds, the geology theory, the mafia thing, which was really cool. Language skills."

"You mean all that useless knowledge and odd jobs are finally coming in handy?"

"An asset around these guys," a female voice said, and Viva saw a woman walk around the rear of the car.

Viva's features pulled taught. "Jade?"

Alexa's eyes flew wide. "Oh, my God, Fiori?" They stared, rattling on like excited teenagers, Alexa showing off her wedding ring and the two hugging again.

Then suddenly Viva twisted to look at Sam. It wasn't a friendly look. "I thought you said her name was Alexa?"

"It is. Jade was a cover." Sam explained.

Viva looked back at Alexa. "CIA? How cool is that?"

Sam exchanged a confused look with Killian over their heads. "How do you know each other?"

Alexa cleared her throat. Viva met her gaze, arching a brow. "Your choice," Alexa said. "They know my past."

"We met at the Blue Dolphin in Spain."

Riley frowned. "Why is that familiar?"

"It's an exotic club."

Sam's gaze shot to Viva. She shrugged uneasily. "It was a job."

"As what?"

"Strippers."

"Holy shit," Logan said.

"Pole dancers," Alexa clarified. "Viva and I had a routine together." She looked at Killian. "I was on assignment, these particular weapons smugglers liked strippers."

"*Any* man likes strippers, honey," Killian said, bringing her close.

"Yeah, especially two women," Sebastian said.

Viva shook her head. "I never understood that attraction, except maybe more boobs."

"You got that right," Max added, chuckling.

They were all looking at her and Alexa oddly. Great.

"I don't want to hear about it." Killian said. "It's past."

"Well, I could show you the routine," Alexa said, and Killian grinned, then kissed her.

Viva cast a glance at Sam, looking worried. But Sam was staring at her, trying to imagine her doing that. "Apparently I've got a lot to learn about you." He smiled and Viva's fears fled.

"It was a lot of costumes and suggestion. I do the full Monty for only one man," she said, coming to him.

He pulled her a bit farther away from the group. "Lucky me."

"No, Sam, lucky me."

He kissed her wildly, uncaring of who watched, or how deeply he expressed himself, and Viva loved him all the more for it. She had a feeling the Sam she first met wasn't exactly known for showing his heart to anyone. Ever.

He brought her hand to his mouth, kissed it, then he leaned close to whisper in her ear, "Marry me."

Her gaze flicked from the ring on her finger to his face. Her mouth worked but nothing came out. He smiled widely. "Speechless, Red?" She just kept staring. "What do you say? Fifty, sixty years of driving me crazy?"

"Oh, yeah." Tears bloomed in her eyes.

"Don't cry, it kills me."

"So, again, it's all about you?"

He threw his head back and laughed, and knew the rest of his life would never be as entertaining as the day he set eyes on Xaviera Fiori.

His very own redheaded nightmare.

Author's Note

Writers gather elements for their work from everything surrounding them. While *Hit Hard* is a product of my imagination, there is some truth in it. I'd like to acknowledge the 2005 Lemelson–MIT Prize Winner, Woody Norris, the *real* inventor of hypersonic sound.

Mr. Norris is no stranger to seeing the possibilities where no one else had. In 1967, he invented a device that sent ultrasound through the skin and was the precursor to the sonogram. Later, he created a hands-free ear-mounted speaker/microphone device operating on the principle that sound travels through the bones in a person's head. While designed at the request of NASA as a replacement for the built-in microphones in astronaut's helmets, the commercial version is now a popular cell phone headset. Another invention by Norris is Flashback®, the first handheld recording and playback device that eliminated audiotape. It is solid state, no moving parts.

In the true American spirit, Mr. Norris is a self-educated, self-funded, and self-motivated inventor. At the time of this printing, he had 47 U.S. patents on his inventions. Web site: *www.woodynorris.com.*

Take a peek at "Love Potion #9"
by JoAnne Ross
in the sexy anthology
BAD BOYS SOUTHERN STYLE
available now from Brava!

The Swansea Inn had begun its life as an antebellum mansion belonging to a cotton broker. Three stories tall, created of the local gray Savannah brick that turned a dusky pink when bathed in the red glow of sunset, it overlooked the Polaski Monument in Monterey Square, which Roxi considered the prettiest of the city's twenty-four lush green squares.

She'd heard rumors that the inn had, for several decades prior to the War Between the States, been a house of prostitution, where wealthy planters and merchants had kept a bevy of women for their shared pleasure. There was even one bit of local lore that had General Sherman, after deciding not to torch the city, but to give it to President Lincoln as a Christmas present instead, a visit to the house to celebrate having concluded his devastating march across Georgia to the sea.

Like so many stories about the city, the tales were couched in mystery and wrapped in sensuality, and had been told and retold so many times it was impossible to know how much was true, and how much was the product of Savannahians' vivid imaginations.

She'd never been inside before, partly because she knew she'd never be able to afford the prices, but mostly because it was a private club. A place, yet more rumors persisted, of assignations. Even, she'd heard whispered, the occasional orgy.

She might have a liberal view of sex, but if Sloan Hawthorne had plans along those lines for tonight, he was going to be disappointed.

The moment the black car glided to a stop at the curve, the inn's glass door opened and a man came down the stone steps.

A sudden, white-hot sexual craving zigzagged through her like a bolt of lightning from a clear blue summer sky, sending every hormone in her body into red alert.

Roxi recognized him immediately. She'd Googled him yesterday after talking with Emma on the Internet, and while on all those websites she'd visited, he'd definitely appeared to be a hunk, up close and personal, he was downright lethal.

His hair was warm chestnut streaked with gold she suspected was a result of time spent beneath the California sun, rather than some trendy Beverly Hills salon. He was conservatively dressed in a crisp white shirt, muted gray striped tie and a dark suit, which looked Italian and probably cost more than her first car.

He opened the back passenger door. His eyes, which were as green as newly minted money, lit up with masculine appreciation as they swept over her.

"Wow. And here I thought the woman was fictional," he murmured.

"Excuse me?" Her body wasn't the only thing that had gone into sexual meltdown. Sexual images of she and Sloan Hawthorne writhed in her smoke-filled mind.

She told herself the only reason she was taking the hand he'd extended was that the car was low, her skirt tight, and her heels high.

Liar. Not only wasn't she sure she could stand on her own, she was actually desperate for his touch. Not just on her hand, but all the other tingling places on her body.

"I'm sorry." He shook his head. Sheepishly rubbed the

bridge of his nose. "I tend to talk to myself when I'm bewitched."

"I see." He wasn't just drop-dead gorgeous. He was cute. It also helped to know that she wasn't the only one who'd been momentarily mesmerized.

The butterflies settled, allowing Roxi to pick up a bit of her own scattered senses. "Does that happen often?" she asked.

"This is the first time." His gaze swept over her—from the top of her head down to her *Revved up and Red-y* toenails, then back up to her face again. "That is one helluva dress."

"Thank you." It was your basic black dinner dress. That is, if anything that was strapless and fit like a second skin could be called basic.

"Did you wear it to bring me to my knees?"

"Absolutely."

"Well, then." He flashed a grin that would've dropped a lesser woman to *her* knees. As it was, it had moisture pooling hotly between Roxi's thighs. "You'll be glad to know that it's working like a charm."

Like so many of the fine old homes in Savannah's historic district, the Inn had several steps originally designed to keep the dust and mud from the unpaved dirt streets outside the house.

Sloan put a hand on her back as they started walking up the five stone steps, hip to hip. Although the gesture seemed as natural to him as breathing, Roxi's own knees were feeling a bit wobbly as a doorman in a burgundy uniform with snazzy gold epaulets swept the door open for them.

Here's an advance look at
Susanna Carr's hilarious
EX, WHY, AND ME.
Available now from Brava . . .

It was difficult going all the way with a guy when you're required to wear a tiara, but Michelle Nelson managed it. Barely.

She just never thought it would occur in the middle of the night behind the pinsetters at Pins & Pints, Carbon Hill's bowling alley and the only source of entertainment one could have standing up.

Michelle shifted, her knees aching against the hard cold floor. The alley was closed, the lanes silent, but she was bumping up against ancient, oily machinery. The location hadn't been her first choice for her first time with her first love.

It didn't seem to hold the right ambiance for Ryan Slater, either. "Let's go back to my place," he suggested in a husky tone that made her skin tingle.

She glanced down at him, but the shadows made it difficult to read his expression. Michelle felt exposed as she straddled him, the weak overhead lights almost reaching her. Her evening dress from the J.C. Penney catalog bunched up against her thighs, the pink polyester rubbing her bare flushed skin.

"No," she whispered, her heart pounding in her ears. She pressed her hands against his shoulders, pulling at his T-shirt with desperate fingers. "I can't wait that long."

It had to be now. She was leaving for Europe in the morning. Her bags were packed, she'd said goodbye to her friends, but there was this one last thing to do.

It had taken her all summer to get Ryan Slater. She could have pursued another local guy in a lot less time, but she wanted Ryan and no one else would do. It had been that way ever since she could remember, at least twenty years. Unfortunately, all the prettier, bolder girls wanted him, too.

No matter what she had done in the past, it wasn't enough to compete for Ryan's attention. He never seemed to have noticed her. Not even when she'd worn the tiara and the Miss Horseradish sash for the past year. And God knows those were hard to miss.

He noticed her now. Had stared at her in awe. Or maybe he was staring at her tiara, which had a tendency to catch the light and blind people. That was probably it, but she couldn't do anything about it now. The crown was pinned and shellacked to her updo.

The glittery distraction would serve her well, Michelle decided as she glided the condom onto Ryan. She didn't want him to feel her hands fumble and shake. Rolling the latex down was not as easy as her best friend, Vanessa, had led her to believe.

The tip of Ryan's cock nudged against Michelle's flesh. The intimate contact made her feel hot. Tight. She grasped him at the base and lowered down.

Michelle jerked, startled, when Ryan clamped his fingers against her bare hips. "We'll take it slow," he said roughly, almost as if he said it through clenched teeth.

Her heart raced as he guided her. White heat crackled just under her skin when he gently filled her.

She closed her eyes, her breath hitching, as she relished every sensation. Michelle had been expecting pain. Nothing major, but something unpleasant. Nothing like the delicious heavy ache that flooded her muscles.

Michelle rocked against him, smiling as the pleasure heated her blood with a shower of sparks. She flexed her hips. *Ooh* . . . She swayed the other way. *Mmm* . . .

"Michelle, slow down," Ryan said hoarsely, his fingers tightening, sinking into her hips.

She wanted his hands elsewhere. Everywhere. Cupping her breasts. No, squeezing them. Pinching her nipples until she begged him to take them into his mouth.

She wanted him to thrust. Grind. Drive into her.

Maybe that wasn't possible in this position. But she didn't want to change sides. Here she felt alive. Bold. Free. She was wild. Sexy. Powerful.

She moved against Ryan, each move fierce and unchecked. Her world centered where they joined. He bucked against her, his moves shallow and hesitant.

Michelle countered with a deep roll of her hips, but his cock didn't stretch or fill her to the hilt. She frowned and wiggled.

"Not like that," Ryan said, his voice bouncing off the machines. He tensed. "Damn."

He lay motionless underneath her. No thrusting, no rocking. Nothing. *This was it?* Michelle thought. *You have got to be kidding me!*

She felt his cock softening, drooping—

Michelle froze. *Oh, no . . .*

—as it slipped out.

I killed it.

And now Sylvia Day's
ASK FOR IT
coming in August 2006
from Brava . . .

George looked easily over her head to scrutinize the scene. "I say. It appears Lord Westfield is heading this way."

"Are you quite certain, Mr. Stanton?"

"Yes, my lady. Westfield is staring directly at me as we speak."

Tension coiled in the pit of her stomach. Marcus had literally frozen in place when their eyes had first met, and the second glance had been even more disturbing. He was coming for her and she had no time to prepare. George looked down at her as she resumed fanning herself furiously.

Damn Marcus for coming tonight! Her first social event after three years of mourning and he unerringly sought her out within hours of her reemergence, as if he'd been impatiently waiting these last years for exactly this moment. She was well aware that had not been the case at all. While she had been crepe-clad and sequestered in mourning, Marcus had been firmly establishing his scandalous reputation in many a lady's bedroom.

After the callous way he'd broken her heart, Elizabeth would have discounted him regardless of the circumstances but tonight especially. Enjoyment of the festivities was not her aim. She had a man she was waiting for, a man she had arranged covertly to meet. Tonight she would dedicate herself to the memory of her husband. She would find justice for Hawthorne and see it served.

The crowd parted reluctantly before Marcus and then regrouped in his wake, the movements heralding his progress toward her. And then Westfield was there, directly before her. He smiled and her pulse raced. The temptation to retreat, to flee, was great, but the moment when she could reasonably have done so passed far too swiftly.

Squaring her shoulders, Elizabeth took a deep breath. The glass in her hand began to tremble and she quickly swallowed the entirety of its contents to avoid spilling it on her dress. She passed the empty vessel to George without looking. Marcus caught her hand before she could retrieve it.

Bowing low with a charming smile, his gaze never broke contact with hers. "Lady Hawthorne. Ravishing, as ever." His voice was rich and warm, reminding her of crushed velvet. "Would it be folly to hope you still have a dance available, and that you would be willing to dance it with me?"

Elizabeth's mind scrambled, attempting to discover a way to refuse. His wickedly virile energy, potent even across the room, was overwhelming in close proximity.

"I am not in attendance to dance, Lord Westfield. Ask any of the gentlemen around us."

"I've no wish to dance with them," he said dryly. "So their thoughts on the matter are of no consequence to me."

She began to object when she perceived the challenge in his eyes. He smiled with devilish amusement, visibly daring her to proceed, and Elizabeth paused. She would not give him the satisfaction of thinking she was afraid to dance with him. "You may claim this next set, Lord Westfield, if you insist."

He bowed gracefully, his gaze approving. He offered his arm and led her toward the dance floor. As the musicians plied their instruments and music rose in joyous swell through the room, the beautiful strains of the minuet began.

Marcus turned, held his hand out to her, and she placed her palm atop the back of his, grateful for the gloves that separated their skin. She appraised him for signs of change. The ballroom was ablaze with candles casting him in golden light and bringing to her attention the strength of his shoulder as it flexed.

He had always been an intensely physical man, engaging in a variety of sports and activities. Impossibly it appeared he had grown stronger, more formidable. Marcus was power personified and she marveled at her past naiveté in believing she could tame him. Thank God, she was no longer so foolish.

His one softness was his luxuriously rich brown hair. It shined like sable and was contained at the nape with a simple black ribbon. Even his emerald gaze was sharp, piercing with a fierce intelligence. He had a clever mind to which deceit was naught but a simple game, as she had learned at great cost to her heart and pride.

She had half expected to find the signs of dissipation so common to indulgent lifestyles and yet his handsome face bore no such witness. Instead he wore the sun-kissed appearance of a man who spent much of his time outdoors. His nose was straight and aquiline over lips that were full and sensuous. At the moment those lips were turned up on one side in a half smile that was at once boyish and alluring. He remained perfectly gorgeous from the top of his head to the soles of his feet. He was watching her studying him, fully aware that she could not help but admire his handsomeness. She lowered her eyes and stared resolutely at his jabot.

The scent that clung to him enveloped her senses. It was a wonderful manly scent of sandalwood, citrus, and Marcus's own unique essence. The flush of her skin seeped into her insides, clawing deliciously around her vitals, mingling with her apprehension.

Reading her thoughts, he tilted his head toward her. His voice, when it came, was low and husky. "Elizabeth. It is a long-awaited pleasure to be in your company again."

"The pleasure, Lord Westfield, is entirely yours."

"You once called me Marcus."

"It would no longer be appropriate for me to address you so informally, my lord."

His mouth tilted into a sinful grin. "I give you leave to be inappropriate with me at any time you choose. In fact, I have always relished your moments of inappropriateness."

"You have had a number of willing women who suited you just as well."

"Never, my love. You have always been separate and apart from every other female."

Elizabeth had met her share of scoundrels and rogues but always their slick confidence and overtly intimate manners left her unmoved. Marcus was so skilled at seducing women he managed the appearance of utter sincerity. She'd once believed every declaration of adoration and devotion that had fallen from his lips. Even now the way he looked at her with such fierce longing seemed so genuine she almost believed it.

He made her want to forget what kind of man he was—a heartless seducer. But her body would not let her forget. She felt feverish and faintly dizzy.